what he

never

knew

BOOK THREE

D1738657

what he

never

knew

BOOK THREE

KANDI STEINER

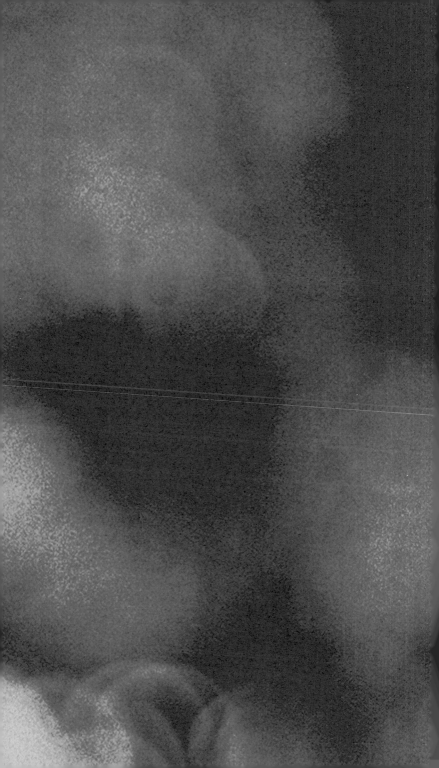

"WE DON'T MEAN
TO HURT EACH OTHER
BUT WE DO.
AND PERHAPS
NO MATTER HOW
RIGHT WE ARE FOR
EACH OTHER,
WE'LL ALWAYS BE A LITTLE
TOO WRONG."
BEAU TAPLIN

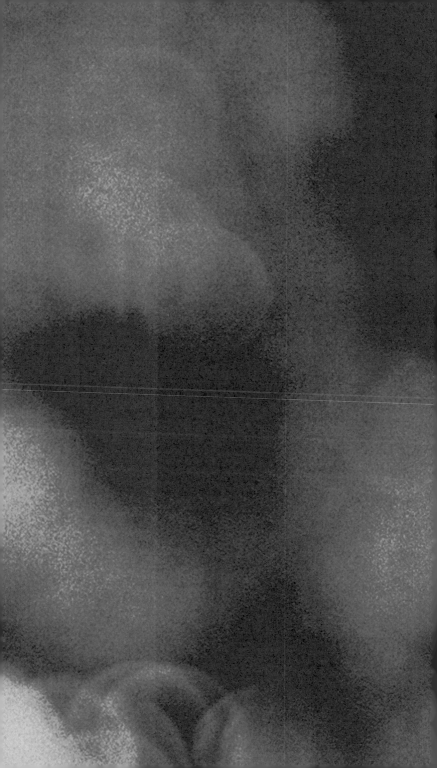

prologue

SARAH

I was the girl who cried wolf.

That was one story I never forgot from my childhood, the one that warned me against lying. *Don't cry wolf if there's not really a wolf,* my parents would say, *or when there is a wolf, no one will believe you.*

It seemed simple enough. And I'd held that story in the back of my mind ever since, weighing the possible consequences of lying. I never said I'd cleaned my room if I hadn't truly done it, nor did I say I was sick if I wasn't. That story had scared me honest. I'd learned from it.

Or so I thought.

Now, as the twenty-one-year-old version of me, I was sitting on the old, musky floor of my college dorm room in north Florida, tears staining my now-numb face, wondering if the lesson had been lost on me. Because they taught me what would happen if you lied, if you became known as a liar... but they left out what would happen if you were telling the truth.

It turned out, it didn't really matter.

No one would believe you either way.

I was the girl who cried wolf.

My wolf was not the kind that walked on four legs and hunted in a pack, nor was he the kind who mercifully killed his prey before devouring it. No, my wolf walked on two legs, dressed in the finest suits, and spoke with the elegance of a well-educated man. His hair was black with a touch of gray, though, and maybe that's why I saw him as a wolf. Maybe that's why the story I'd heard as a child was all I could think about while my wolf — disguised as my respected piano professor — bruised my wrists and spread my thighs in the same room where he'd taught me to play Beethoven's *Moonlight Sonata*.

I blinked, unwrapping my arms from where they'd held my knees and letting my legs flop out in front of me. For all intents and purposes, they were the same legs I'd had before. They looked the same, but they felt foreign to me, like someone else's legs. Surely, it couldn't have been my own that had been hitched up, spread wide for a man who assured me everything would be okay if I just cooperated.

I wished I could feel something — anger, sadness, resentment — anything. But it was as if I'd been submerged in the iciest, blackest depths of the Pacific Ocean, like my entire body had seized up, yet I was still breathing.

I was still alive.

And perhaps that was the worst part.

My phone buzzed with a text from my mom, asking when she should expect me home — *home* being our little two-bedroom apartment in Atlanta, Georgia. As far as she knew, the only notable event yesterday was my last final before winter break. As far as she knew, the only thing on my mind was getting home to her and her holiday cooking.

As far as she knew, her baby girl was still a virgin.

I blinked again, shooting back a text that I was loading up my car now, and I'd be pulling in a little after midnight.

Only a partial lie.

I *would* make it back to my mom's two-bedroom apartment outside of Atlanta a little after midnight, and I *was* loading up my car — with the very little I wanted to keep. For the most part, I was leaving everything behind. I wanted to light it all on fire, but settled for abandoning it in the hell hole that was my university.

Up until yesterday, it had been my home. Up until last night, it had been everything I'd wanted as a starry-eyed, music-loving girl who sacrificed going out with her friends in high school just to practice piano. Up until now, Bramlock University was everywhere I wanted to be.

Now, it was my prison.

And I knew one thing for sure — I was leaving for winter break tonight, and I was never, *ever* coming back.

As if that truth was the last bit of fuel inside me, I popped up off the floor and shot straight into my tiny bathroom. I shared it with my roommate and closest friend, Reneé — but she'd already finished her finals and headed home for break. I knew I'd miss her.

I also knew I'd never tell her why I wouldn't be back.

I ran the shower as hot as I could, so hot the steam fogged the mirror before I could undress. I didn't bother throwing my clothes in the laundry basket I already had piled high and ready to take care of when I got to Mom's. Instead, I tossed the ripped leggings in the trash. The skirt, tank top, and sweater quickly followed, and I didn't so much as give them a second look before I stepped into the piping hot shower.

3

I didn't pull away from the water, even though it burned. My dark, umber skin grew an angry red in protest, my nervous system warning me against injury, but I knew it'd survive.

If I could survive last night, I could survive anything.

I was the girl who cried wolf.

I'd waited to shower, because that's what they always told you. *Don't shower after being raped.* They give you a whistle at freshman orientation and a list of what to do if it ever happens to you, as if it's as simple as getting lice or the flu. *Here's how to remedy that rape, my child. Take this pamphlet.*

I laughed out loud at the audacity of it all, finally used to the water as it spilled down my bare back. That whistle they'd given me was buried somewhere in the bottom of my desk drawer. If I'd had it, would I have been able to get to it, to blow it loud enough that someone would have heard?

But I shook that thought away, because it wouldn't have mattered, anyway.

I did what was right.

I took all the proper steps.

I didn't shower and I went to the music director and I told her my story.

I showed her the bruises and relived every torturous moment while she pressed her lips together with a sympathetic bend in her brows, nodding as I replayed the assault.

And then, she grabbed my hand, squeezed it, and told me it was best to keep this between us.

This.

As if *this* was referring to something like a little white lie I was keeping from my roommate, or to something I'd walked in and witnessed her doing wrong. *Let's just keep*

4

this between us, Dr. Chores had said. *These are strong allegations, and you will have a lot of rough years ahead if you follow through with them. Go home tonight and think about what you're saying, and more importantly, about* who *you're saying it about."*

Because my wolf wasn't a wolf in the eyes of Bramlock University.

In their eyes, he was a god.

He was a piano legend, a blessing to our music program. *Thank God he'd wanted to retire in Florida,* they'd say, since that was where our university was. And how could it possibly be that such an accomplished man with so much respect could ever do something as horrendous as rape his student?

As the water started to run cold, I felt the soreness from my wolf between my legs. That's something else they don't tell you about in those stupid rape pamphlets. No one tells you that, when you're a virgin, rape doesn't just feel like an invasion. It feels like you're being ripped from the inside out, like your assaulter is splitting you in half. And I guess, in a way, he had. Half of who I used to be was still there, *somewhere*, but the other half?

I didn't even know who she'd become.

My eyes watered, the dream I'd have of giving myself to a man I loved one day shattered like a fragile tea cup thrown carelessly against a cement wall. I curled in on myself, as if I could shelter myself now, as if I could protect what damaged goods still remained.

As if anyone would want them, even if I could.

That soreness between my legs was enough to drive me insane, that constant reminder of who had been there. I didn't want to look, didn't want to touch, didn't want any more proof of what had happened. Instead, I deftly reached out a hand to shut off the spout. I pressed my back against the cold tile wall and slid down until I sat again, my knees against my chest, my hands in my wet, wild, and curly hair.

I didn't know what I expected.

All the *words* they say make it sound so easy. You get assaulted? You tell someone — and everything will be okay. But if there was one thing my father taught me before he died it was that actions speak louder than words. And the *actions* when it came to rape cases were loud and clear.

The victim was rarely believed. When she was, she rarely won in court. When she did, the attacker rarely got a sentence. When he did, he rarely served it all.

The truth was there *was* no winning — not when you'd been raped. Not when the first man to ever touch you did so without asking permission, without kissing you first, without telling you he loved you.

On that cold, wet, tile floor of my dorm room shower, I realized my home had been full of monsters all along. I'd just never seen them before. And now that I had, there was no going back.

I was the girl who cried wolf.

But I vowed to myself that I would not be the girl who let the wolf win.

⸻

REESE

My boots crunched the old, dirty snow with every step I took down Charlie's parents' driveway toward my car. My hands were shoved in my pockets, eyes on my feet, but my head was still inside that house.

My heart was still inside that house.

I'd long surrendered to the fact that I was a masochist. What other man in his right mind would keep contact with a woman and her family after she blatantly rejected him? Charlie had been my best friend's little sister when I was younger, but she'd always been something more. We both knew it. And when life had brought me back here — back to Pittsburgh and back to her — I thought we'd finally have our chance.

It didn't matter to me that she was married, not when I saw how miserable she was. But I was the stupid, selfish, cocky son-of-a-bitch who went after a married woman thinking there was no way she couldn't choose me.

It turned out, her husband wasn't going to let her go without a fight.

And fight we did, Cameron and I. For months, we fought for that woman's love, for her heart, and in the end, he won.

Right then and there, I should have let go.

I should have moved to a different city, or a different state altogether. I should have blocked them out of every facet of my life — starting with Charlie. But instead, I watched her from a distance at the school we both worked at, wishing she was mine, wishing there was someway to change her mind.

I would never act on it, of course, and I'd made that vow to both myself and to her. I loved her, and because I loved her, I respected her decision. If Cameron was who she wanted, if he was who made her happy, then that was all that mattered to me.

At least, it *was*... until I noticed Charlie's stomach rounding, growing, and heard those two words from her lips.

I'm pregnant.

My stomach sank at the memory, and it slid all the way down to the icy driveway when I added in the news I'd received today. Because as hard as the hit was when I found out she was pregnant, it never could have measured up to what I would feel when she told me the child wasn't mine.

Daisy wasn't mine.

Eighteen long months had passed since the day Charlie walked through my door and told me she was staying with Cameron, and all that time I had wondered if that child in her belly was ours. When Daisy was born, it was too much for me to bare. I bit down my pride and went to her husband and I *begged* him to let me be a part of the child's life — even if just as a distant "uncle."

And because Cameron is five times the man I am, he'd agreed.

All this time, I'd wondered. All this time, I'd thought *maybe...*

And today, Charlie had quieted my thoughts. She'd had a paternity test, and Daisy was Cameron's.

The door to my old car creaked when I opened it, and I ducked inside, ears ringing once the door was shut and I was alone in the too-silent vehicle. I shoved the key in the ignition, but didn't start the engine. Instead, my hands fell to my lap, and I stared at the steering wheel as if it were to blame for everything.

Then, I beat the shit out of it.

Screams ripped from my throat as I lashed out, fists flying, and only the sound of a knuckle cracking and the horn ringing out stopped me. I gripped the wheel with both hands, chest heaving as I tried to school my breaths. My eyes fluttered shut, and I loosened my grip, running one hand back through my long hair before I let out a heavy sigh.

That was it.

The last thing tying me to Charlie turned out not to be a tie at all. She wasn't mine, she hadn't been for a long time... maybe not ever. But it wasn't until that moment, until that final blow, that I really, truly believed it.

I'd still had hope.

I'd still thought there was a chance.

And underneath it all, I was trying to hide the pathetic fact that I wasn't anywhere near being over her or moving on.

A year and a half, and she was still all I thought about. A year and a half, and she was still all I wanted.

My phone dinged with another notification from the stupid dating app Charlie had convinced me to get on and I tore it from my pocket, deleting the app and all the messages that lived inside it with two taps of my finger.

I let my head drop back against the head rest, and my heart squeezed painfully inside my chest. I was surprised I could even feel that ache anymore, surprised it hadn't ebbed in any way as the months stretched and life marched on. I wondered if it was just a permanent part of me now, if there ever *was* a time I'd move on from Charlie Pierce.

The possibility that Daisy was mine had been my final tie to her. I didn't have an excuse to hold on any longer...

And yet, I couldn't imagine ever letting go.

FIVE MONTHS LATER

chapter one

SARAH

The Kinky Starfish.

My fingers rolled around the crystal hanging from my neck as I stared at the neon sign, the white script elegantly dancing around an artistic pink starfish. Uncle Randall was making jokes with the employee valeting his car, and he was still laughing when he slid up beside me, hand folding over my shoulder.

I flinched away, and my uncle's brows bent together before he dropped his hand back to his side.

"Well, this is the place," he said, eyes following mine up to the sign. We were both quiet for a long moment before he glanced at me again. "You know, you really don't have to do this. You don't need to work while you're here. Just, focus on the reason you came, and—"

"I have to work," I interrupted. "I need to continue saving and I'm also going to pay you rent."

"You're not paying us rent," Uncle Randall said, almost as a laugh. "That's absurd."

"But—"

"Look," he said, pulling me to the side so the other patrons of the restaurant could pass. His hands framed my arms, and I flinched again. "I know you have that same strong will as your mother, and I love that about both of you. But, please, Sarah — don't worry about paying us rent. If you want to work and save up money, *that* I understand. Put the money you would pay us toward your savings, instead." He smiled. "We are just tickled to have the time with our niece. We don't get to see you near as often as we'd like, and we're just happy to help you pursue this dream of yours."

I opened my mouth to argue, but Uncle Randall raised one thick, white, caterpillar eyebrow, as if he dared me to try to beat him on this. We both knew I'd lose in the end.

So, instead, I let out a heavy sigh and nodded.

"That's my girl," he said. "Now, let's go inside and I'll introduce you to everyone."

He trotted off in front of me, and I tucked my hands into the pockets of my coat before following.

In my eyes, Pennsylvania had always been a winter wonderland. Uncle Randall was my father's only brother, and he'd stayed here with their parents while my dad had gone south, attending university in Atlanta before entering the political circuit there. We'd visited Pennsylvania for nearly every Christmas, especially when my grandparents were alive, and I had memories of sledding with my dad and making hot cocoa with my mom. It was our getaway to a Christmas land, away from the southern heat and humidity.

But it was May, summer ready to bloom, and Pennsylvania was different in the spring. The air still held a cool crisp as the wind swept past me, but the evening air was warm, the sun stretching its way lazily across the sky. It wasn't a winter wonderland this time of year, but it would be my home for... well, I wasn't exactly sure how long. However long it took to get me where I needed to be, I supposed. I was just thankful to my aunt and uncle for agreeing to take me in.

And for getting me the connection to Reese Walker.

The past year had challenged me, tested me, changed me. As if the injury I'd suffered that hindered my piano playing wasn't enough, I'd been spread wide on the ground under the piano by the professor who was supposed to help me overcome my injury. He was supposed to help me get better, and instead, he'd taken the me that was partially broken and had completely shattered me.

And I wanted to give up.

I wanted to throw in the towel, quit, surrender. And that's what I'd done when I'd gone home for winter break. I told my mom I wasn't going back, and being that I was only a semester away from graduating, she didn't like that. She didn't understand. And when I'd shaved my head and completely changed my wardrobe?

Well, she'd gone from concerned to absolutely distraught.

My mother was a therapist, and though her specific focus was on failed marriage, she had always been locked into me as a growing child. She read my signs, my pleas for love and attention before I even understood them myself. So, shaving my head and quitting school a semester before graduation? She knew something was wrong.

Thankfully, my mom was a mom first and a therapist second.

I knew it killed her to let me be, to nod in understanding when I begged her to believe that I was okay, but that I needed time. I needed space. And when I was ready, I came to her, and I told her I wanted to study piano again.

In my own way.

I wouldn't go back to Bramlock, and whether she knew the reason why or not, my mom supported me. Instead, I thought of a man my dad had talked about often, one I'd followed online, one who I truly believed could help me overcome my injury.

Because as much as my wolf had stolen from me, I wouldn't let him steal my dream.

My injury was a repetitive strain injury, and it wasn't easy to overcome. I'd been on the very messy road to recovery before I left Bramlock, and once I'd acclimated to life back in Atlanta, I'd worked on it more, myself.

But on my own, I could only go so far.

I needed professional help if I wanted to make my dream come true, and I would do *anything* to make that happen.

I took my time as I followed behind my uncle, taking in the scenery of the busy downtown and the restaurant I would be working at while I stayed here. I knew him well enough now to know he'd be stopped several times on his way to wherever we were going. He was known by nearly everyone in Pittsburgh, it seemed, and definitely by everyone in Mount Lebanon — a small borough right outside the city. He was the headmaster at Westchester Prep, one of the top prep schools in the nation, and his reputation in the community was strong.

Still, when *I* was with him, he got a lot more curious glances than when it was just him and my aunt Betty.

If my aunt and uncle noticed the raised eyebrows and hushed whispers when I was with them, they faked that they were oblivious. But I was used to those kinds of stares.

I didn't fit in.

At least, not with them.

My aunt and uncle's skin was creamy white, their eyes a frosted blue, and though both of them now sported white hair, it was easy to see it used to be blonde. My uncle looked so much like my father, it often stopped me in my tracks. I saw the same kindness in my uncle's blue eyes that I always saw in my father's. And when he smiled, my heart would squeeze with the desire to see my father's smile again.

I would have given anything.

Yes, my aunt and uncle were always dressed to impress, never knowing who they might run into, and I'd yet to see my aunt without her pearls around her neck — even in her pajamas.

So, the question everyone wanted the answer to, then, was *why* were they walking with a young, freakishly tall, black female with baggy clothes and a bald head?

Maybe before, it wouldn't have been so jarring — when I wore clothes that were bright and cheery, pinks and yellows and oranges being the majority of my closet. Maybe, when my hair was curly and bouncy, framing my face in a wild, but feminine, bob that ended below my chin — maybe that would have been easier to swallow.

But the me who existed now? She didn't want attention. She didn't want to be seen as beautiful or tempting or in any way touchable. So, I'd painted the exterior to match the interior.

I was dark now.

Dark skin, dark clothes, dark eyes. No hair. No jewelry.

The only way I wanted to communicate with the world was through my music, and I didn't need to be sexy or cute to do that.

Still, the looks I got when I walked with my uncle were just like the ones I used to get when I *did* dress to impress — except they were harder, more curious, and harder to stomach. Maybe it was because even though my uncle had the same eyes my father had, I'd never felt like an outsider when I'd walked with *him*. When it was my dad, my mother and I, we were nothing more or less than a family unit. And we were the happiest when we were together.

I missed those times.

"Mr. Henderson!" the sweet, smiley young brunette greeted when we made it to the reservations desk. Her smile was half the size of her face, her cheeks rosy and round. "It's so nice to see you this evening. Shall I take you to your usual table, or would you like to try a new seat tonight?"

"Oh, the usual is perfect," my uncle replied, his smile just as big. "I have a special guest with me tonight, so please have a bottle of my favorite wine brought over as soon as possible."

"Will do, sir," she said. "Shall I take you back, then?"

"Oh, we can make it on our own. I want to stop by and say hi to a few people along the way." He winked at the hostess, and by the way she grinned in return, I imagined he probably never went straight to his table.

I followed my uncle as he made his way inside the restaurant, and my breath caught at the sight of the large, elegant chandelier that hung as the centerpiece of the room. Thousands of crystals sparkled as the chandelier slowly rotated, taking a new shape with every second. The rest of the restaurant was hidden in deep, romantic shadows, the walls a plush maroon and the floors a beautifully stained chestnut wood. The light from the chandelier danced along that wood, the beams changing shape before they'd disappear into the darkness. It was absolutely mesmerizing, and I found myself staring up at the diamonds that seemed to drip down from the top of the chandelier.

I followed every bead of it until I found the other object centered in the heart of the restaurant.

The piano.

My uncle paused when I stopped walking, looking over his shoulder at me with a smile. "Ah, I see it didn't take you long to find the main attraction, did it?"

"It's beautiful," I whispered, taking in the dark crown jewel mahogany, rich gold accents, and ivory keys. I didn't even have to get close to know that piano cost at least fifty-thousand dollars.

Uncle Randall nodded. "It is, indeed. Just wait until you hear it played."

My fingers itched to be the one playing it, though I couldn't imagine sitting in the center of this packed restaurant of people paying more for their meal than I would spend on a car payment. The Kinky Starfish wasn't just somewhere you went to eat — it was an all-night experience. There were four courses, spread out over the evening with the intent that you would eat slowly, enjoy great conversation with those at your table, and not just eat to get full — but to experience an unforgettable evening.

Your dinner was exquisite, your service the same, and the entertainment?

Well, it didn't get much better than the infamous Reese Walker.

"When does he start?" I asked, eyes still wandering over the design of the piano. I noted the way the chandelier lights played off the keys, creating the most dreamy and romantic atmosphere.

"He'll be here in about an hour, I'd imagine," my uncle said, checking his watch. "Come on, let me introduce you to a few people before we sit down."

My stomach flipped, excitement buzzing through me as we started walking again. I smiled and greeted the other patrons we passed as my uncle introduced me to everyone, but I couldn't take my eyes off the piano. I couldn't believe I would see Reese Walker play it in just one hour — and not online, but in real life.

And he'd agreed to work with me.

Me. The college dropout with a pipe dream about as possible as winning the lottery. I knew my uncle had connections, but when I asked him if it was possible, if I could take lessons with one of the most influential young pianists of my time, I figured there was absolutely no way. Reese Walker was a recluse, shut off from the music world once he left New York. Other than working with young students at Westchester and playing occasionally at The Kinky Starfish, he was out of commission.

How my uncle managed to rope a Juilliard graduate and piano legend into working with an absolute nobody was beyond me.

Then again, Reese Walker hadn't exactly made the most of his talent. He was more known for getting into trouble than he was for anything else in the music world. Maybe that was why I'd thought of him when I realized I needed help overcoming my injury — because I saw something in him that I felt in myself. His relationship with the piano was tumultuous, and his career had been anything but traditional.

But I'd watched videos of him playing online. I'd seen the magical way his hands moved over those keys, the way his body bent with the music, the way his soul seeped into every note like his flesh was transparent.

I didn't know why he wasn't still playing in New York, claiming his spot in Carnegie Hall like he should have as soon as he graduated with his masters. I didn't know why he was teaching at a prep school in *Pennsylvania* of all places. I also didn't know why he looked absolutely miserable in every video that had been posted of him in the last two years.

But honestly, I didn't care — as long as he could help me beat my injury and get my dream back on track. That's what I needed from Reese Walker. Nothing more.

I wasn't in Pennsylvania to make friends.

"Wine?" my uncle asked when we finally made it to the table.

I shook my head, unwrapping the light scarf around my neck and hanging it over the back of my chair. "I don't drink."

Uncle Randall smiled, but I noticed the tight edges of it. "Of course. I'm sorry, I shouldn't have assumed that just because you're twenty-one now that you'd drink."

"It's okay," I assured him. "I used to, when I first turned twenty-one." *And before.* "I just don't like to have my judgment impaired."

Uncle Randall smiled genuinely at that. "You are wise beyond your years, Sarah. And too smart for your own good."

I returned his smile, but my thoughts ran away with me as we both glanced over the menu. I wondered how he saw me now, if he missed the young lady I used to be. I would have bet money that he wasn't used to his sweet, bubbly niece being so short and direct. In fact, I'd thought both he and Aunt Betty were going to have to scrape their jaws off their front porch when I first arrived. I guess I should have warned them I'd changed a little since they'd seen me last summer — in the way of all my hair was gone now, and the dresses and skirts I used to live in had all been burnt — but I'd lost the desire to explain my actions or my appearance.

I was this way because I was this way, and that was really all there was to it.

"Thank you," I said, trying to make amends for not being the best guest in our little round of introductions. I'd barely said more than two words to the sweet man who was graciously letting me work back of house for him while I stayed with my uncle and studied with Reese. "For everything you've done for me. For letting me stay with you, for this job…"

Uncle Randall lit up again, bouncing a little in his chair as he filled his glass with red wine. "Oh, don't even mention it. As I said before, we're happy to have you."

A hush came over the room, and Uncle Randall's eyes went wide. He glanced over his shoulder, smiling with a tilt of his glass toward me when he turned back around.

"And now, it's time to meet your new teacher."

He turned back around, adjusting his chair for a better view as my eyes found the piano. And as soon as I did, the lights in the restaurant dimmed, the chandelier shining brighter, and the man everyone had come to see appeared.

Reese Walker emerged from the shadows as if he didn't exist if not in close proximity to a piano. He was so tall, his presence so commanding that it was hard to understand how no one had seen him before the light from that chandelier touched his skin. He'd walked the shadows of the room unseen, like a ghost in the night, and now he was the only thing anyone in the room could look at.

His long hair was pulled back into a hair tie just above his neck, his tuxedo black and tailored, his eyes like a forbidden mystery novel that somehow escaped a book burning as he glanced around the room. I didn't have to pull my eyes away from him to know everyone else was watching with the same rapt attention I gave him. It was impossible not to stare, not to wait with bated breath for him to speak. But he simply greeted the crowd with a small, modest bow before taking his seat at the piano.

And only then did he truly come to life.

A small, almost imperceptible smile touched his lips before it quickly disappeared, and his fingers hovered over the keys for what felt like the longest moment of my life.

Then, without an introduction or even a single word, he played.

To anyone in that room who had never studied piano, it likely just seemed like a talented man playing a beautiful song. I managed to tear my eyes away from Reese long enough to survey some of the faces, and they were smiling, eyes wide and glistening like children watching Christmas tree lights.

But when *I* looked at Reese?

When I watched his hands move, his chest inflate with every new breath, his eyes close on a rest before slowly opening as he began to play again?

I didn't see anything to smile about.

This was the power of Reese Walker.

He played like he was a man who'd lived three-hundred lifetimes of immeasurable joy and unbearable sorrow, like he'd seen so much despair that no words would ever do justice. Instead, he bent down and bled at that piano, shedding his skin and baring his soul for the entire room to see. Each note struck a chord in my heart, each crescendo sent a new rush of chills from my neck to my ankles. My eyes watched his hands, his furrowed brows, his flat lips — but I didn't see a man. I saw the song he played, the music he'd created, and it revealed so much more.

Reese was an entire universe, and the piano was a mere telescope we tried to see him through.

When he finished, he reached for the glass of water on the small table next to him while the room erupted in applause. I couldn't even hear it at first, not until I blinked for what felt like the first time in the fifteen minutes he had been playing.

"Are you okay, sweetheart?" My uncle asked, chuckling a little as he reached into his pocket for a handkerchief. He offered it to me. "You're crying."

I stared at the cloth between us, shaking my head and quickly swiping the tears from my face. I forced a smile. "I'm okay, it was just very moving."

Uncle Randall gave me a knowing smile, tucking his handkerchief away again. "That's how I feel when I hear you play."

I blushed, gaze falling to where my hands rested in my lap. I didn't know how to accept a compliment about my playing, especially not when I knew I was trying and failing at overcoming my injuries — both internal and external. The piano I'd used to find salvation in now scared me. It was hard, unfamiliar, intimidating.

And if I closed my eyes, I could still see the underbelly of the one at Bramlock — that smooth, dark surface that hid the strings and keys that brought music to life. It was all I could stare at with my wolf on top of me.

I couldn't find salvation in it that day, and I hadn't since.

The crowd quieted again as Reese cleared his throat, finally addressing the room with a smile so big I couldn't believe it belonged to the man I'd just heard play that piece. He tucked a fallen strand of hair back behind his ear and held out his hands. "Well, thank you for that very warm welcome."

The room applauded again, and this time I joined in, smiling at him from my little corner of the room.

His cheeks were red as he surveyed the crowd, and when his eyes swept over my section, they continued on without pause before snapping back to me.

Me.

At first, I assured myself I was imagining it. But the longer he looked, the less confident I became in that thought.

I stopped clapping as he watched me, feeling pinned to that booth by the weight of his gaze, but it wasn't the same stare I was used to — the one that said I didn't belong. It was one of wonder, of genuine curiosity — one that stole my next breath and held it captive in the space between us.

Just as quickly as that gaze had come to me, it was ripped away, and Reese was smiling again, quieting the crowd.

"My name is Reese Walker, resident pianist at The Kinky Starfish and local teacher at Westchester Prep. I'll be your entertainment this evening, though I'm not nearly as satisfying as the white chocolate truffle cake."

The room laughed, and I tilted my head in wonder. He was such a charming man, an entertainer, to be sure. It was fascinating how much the man speaking now contrasted with the one who had just played.

"That was an original piece called *The Darkest Dawn*," he continued, hands floating over the keys in a soft melody. "But I'd like to play some Beethoven for you now, if that's alright?"

Reese smiled at the light applause, and just like that, he slipped back into performance mode, and I slipped away into his universe.

And that's how the entire evening went.

Between small bites of my dinner that my uncle chided me for not eating more of, I sat enraptured by Reese Walker. He played everything from Beethoven to The Beatles and everything in-between. Some songs were played softer, meant to be heard only as background noise as the patrons conversed over their dinners. But other songs commanded the room's attention, and those were the ones I preferred.

He was simply magical to watch, and I was completely under his spell.

"Oh!" My uncle dabbed his mouth with his napkin before clapping his hands together. "Come on, he's taking his break. Let me introduce you."

"Oh, Uncle Randall, we can wait," I said, a slight panic in my voice as I watched Reese slip back into the shadows after announcing he would be back after a short break. "I'm sure he'd like some time to himself."

"Nonsense," my uncle insisted, already standing. "Reese is a friend, and I'm sure he's excited to meet his new student."

He was already four steps ahead of me by the time I had my napkin off my lap, and I had no choice but to take a gulp of water and follow.

I smoothed my hands over my dark, wintergreen slacks, forcing a steadying breath as my uncle grabbed Reese in a bear hug before he could get too far from the piano. I stood behind Uncle Randall as invisible as I could be for as long as he'd let me, watching Reese with my heart beating loud in my ears. But my time hiding in the corner was short lived, because my uncle wrapped one arm around me and pulled me between him and Reese, offering me up like a plate of cookies. It was a bit comical and a lot awkward, seeing as how I was a full three-inches taller than him.

I realized very quickly that I was *not* taller than Reese.

"Reese, this is my talented niece I was telling you about," my uncle beamed. "Your new student, Miss Sarah Henderson."

I wanted to shrink away the moment his eyes met mine.

They were two dark, endless wells that seemed to suck me into that universe I'd had a glimpse of when he played. There was color there, in those irises, but I couldn't make it out in the dim light of the restaurant. Instead, his eyes just felt like colorless hands that were rooting me to the spot where I stood. He held my gaze for a long pause, his head tilting just a fraction to the left before he extended an actual hand with more of a question in his eyes than a greeting.

"A pleasure to meet you, Miss Henderson."

"It's just Sarah," I said, and I was glad I got the words out before my hand slipped into his.

His grip was firm, palm smooth and warm, but all I could think of was the talent that rested in that hand, in those fingers that wrapped so easily around mine. They had played pieces I could only hope to play, had dazzled people from all over the world.

"Sarah was top of her class at Bramlock," my uncle said from beside me as Reese shook my hand. "Just wait until you hear her play. She's out of this world. And now, working with you?" He shook his head on a laugh. "I can't even imagine what will come out of this collaboration."

Reese hadn't taken his eyes off me, and I couldn't do anything but stare at the floor under our hands. When he finally dropped mine, I quickly tucked my arms around my middle, glancing up at him before dropping my gaze again.

"I'm not an easy pedagogue to work with, Miss Henderson. I hope you've come prepared to work hard and dig deep."

At that, I snapped my eyes to his, and didn't even attempt to hide my incredulity. He was speaking to me like I was eight years old, or like he was sixty, or like I was some cute little thing he was simply entertaining.

"Of course I've come prepared to work hard," I answered. "Do I not appear like a serious musician to you, Mr. Walker?"

"Now, I don't think that's—"

"I've only just met you," Reese interrupted my uncle. "You don't appear to be anything more than an acquaintance at this point in time."

His words were calculated, professional in manner but said with an undertone of challenge.

I narrowed my eyes, holding my head higher. "Well, I can guarantee I'll be the hardest-working student you've ever had. And I am thankful to you for agreeing to work with me."

Reese smirked at his tone being served right back to him. He turned to my uncle and clapped him on the shoulder. "I owe this man for many things, so I was happy to help." He paused. "Will you be joining us for the first lesson at my house, Randall?"

"At your house?"

The words flew out of my mouth before I could stop them, heart jolting from a steady beat to a chaotic one in a nanosecond. It hurt, it was pounding against my rib cage so hard, and I fought the urge to soothe it with a hand against my chest.

Reese may have been a piano prodigy, and one I was lucky to work with, but he was still a man. He was still a much older, much larger, much *stronger* human being than I was.

I didn't want to be alone in his house with him.

Reese lifted a brow. "Yes, my house. That's where all my private lessons are held. Is that okay?"

My throat was dry. "I just assumed we'd be at the school." Where my uncle is. Where other people are.

Where it's safe.

"Oh my," Uncle Randall said with a chuckle. "I'm sorry if I didn't make that clear, dear. School is out soon for the summer, and we try not to have any tutoring done, outside of our students, with the school equipment. If I made an exception for you, I'd have to make one for many other students who are eager to learn within those walls. But, rest assured, I've heard nothing but incredible praise about Reese's private lessons in his home."

"Will you come with me?" I squeaked out, the panic I was trying to hide more and more evident the more I spoke. "Just for the first lesson. Please."

Uncle Randall's brows tugged together, and he and Reese shared a look before he smiled, reaching for me. His hand folded over my shoulder, and in that moment, in his eyes, I saw my father.

I didn't flinch away.

"Of course," he assured me. "That would be okay, right, Reese?"

Reese nodded. "Absolutely. No problem at all." He watched me a moment, rolling his lips together. "You know, I wouldn't mind giving lessons at the school. If that would make you feel more comfortable."

"No, no," I assured him, embarrassment kicking in at my need for special treatment. "Whatever you already do, let's do that. You're already doing me a huge favor by agreeing to work with me when I'm sure you're very busy."

Reese chuckled. "I assure you, I'm far from busy — especially once school lets out. But, if you're okay with working at my home, it's where I'm most comfortable. I'll do everything I can to make sure you feel the same."

I stole a steadying breath at his words, oxygen finally making its way into my lungs.

He's not my wolf. He's not like him.

Breathe.

It was a little easier to do, now that I knew my uncle would be with us. I didn't know why the news of our lessons being at Reese's house took me by surprise, why it shocked me so. Even if we were at the school, I knew we'd have to be alone together. I knew I'd have to trust him as my teacher to respect me and my space.

I just didn't know how to do that, not now that that trust had been obliterated by the last man to have it.

"It was very nice to meet you," Reese said after a moment, a small crease between his brows as he watched me. "If you'll excuse me, I should get ready for my next set," he said, nodding toward the piano.

"Oh, of course, we didn't want to hold you up too long. We're really enjoying watching you play. My niece here," Uncle Randall said, chuckling a little as he leaned in closer to Reese. "She was *crying*, she was so moved by the first—"

I cleared my throat, neck so hot I could fry an egg on it as I grabbed my uncle's arm. "You heard him, Uncle Randall, he needs to get back to playing. Let's go to our table."

Reese smirked, his eyes watching me in that same curious way they had the first time he'd locked them on me from across the room.

And again, I wanted to shrink away.

"Thank you for the compliment," he said simply, and I fought against the urge to groan out loud in embarrassment. "I'll see you at school tomorrow, Mr. Henderson," he said to my uncle first, and then he glanced at me once more. "And you, Tuesday evening, I believe?"

"Mm-hmm," I managed.

Reese smiled again. "Have a good evening, Miss Henderson. Welcome to Pittsburgh."

And with one last nod to my uncle, the ghost weaved his way through the shadows and back to his home.

chapter Two

REESE

Two years.

It had been almost two years to the day since Charlie Pierce showed up at my house and told me she was staying with her husband, that our love couldn't be, that Cameron was her choice, and I was not.

Two years, and I still ached every time I thought of her.

Two years, and I still dreaded the fact that she was back to school today after having been gone the entire semester for maternity leave.

Two years, and I still wanted to run to her and pull her into my arms and beg her to be mine.

I was pathetic.

That was a fact I couldn't escape, and somewhere along the line I think I'd decided to embrace it. After three months had passed, and I was still a mess, I thought she would just be a little harder to get over than I imagined. After six months, I fell into despair. After the first year, I imagined I had to be getting close to a breakthrough.

But it had been two years. And at this point, I'd come to the conclusion that this was just how my life would be now.

I would always ache for the woman I could never have.

The school year was winding down, only a month left before classes would end and summer break would set me free from these walls for a few months. Spring was everywhere — in the green leaves growing on the trees, in the flowers blooming, the sun shining, the temperature rising. Everyone at Westchester was alive with the promise of warm weather and free time ahead, but I still felt like I was stuck in the middle of a grueling winter.

I'd managed to avoid Charlie all day, though I'd caught a glimpse of her in the hallway after lunch. I'd veered right then, going down a wing I didn't need to be in for any reason other than to *not* be in the same wing she was in. I thought I'd escape at least one day of her being here without having to interact, but of course, the universe couldn't give me that break.

"Reese!"

I heard her voice call from behind me as I made it to the metal doors that led to the teachers' parking lot. My hand hit the bar that released the lock, and I shoved it open, hoping I could fake that I didn't hear her.

"Reese, wait up!"

I groaned, pausing where my hand still held the door and forcing a slow breath before turning.

Charlie was the only one in the hallway, and she walked toward me with a little hop in her step, her long, curled brown hair bouncing. Her smile was wide, cheeks pink, eyes shining like I was the person she'd been waiting to see all day. She didn't hesitate when she made it to where I stood, but threw her slight arms around me.

I had no choice but to catch her, and I knew I always would.

"I've been looking for you all day," she said, pulling back with that same smile. "Where have you been hiding?"

This was what I hated about Charlie — she still cared about me. If our situation was under someone's microscope, they'd likely hate her because they thought the exact opposite. How could she talk to me the way she did, still want me around her, her family, if she really cared about me? Wouldn't she give me time to heal, wouldn't she leave me be?

But her hug, her smile, the way she looked at me — it was all genuine. It was who she'd always been. It was what I loved about her. She was the kindest woman, and her heart was too big for her own good. It had been hard on her, leaving me alone after what had transpired between us. She hated that she'd hurt me, and she wanted to make me better — even though it wasn't her job to.

She had left me alone.

It had been *me* who begged to come back into her life.

Of course, that was when I thought Daisy was mine. That was when I was desperately looking for anything to tie me to Charlie, to give me a chance to make her mine. Now that I knew that chance was nonexistent, that Daisy was Cameron's, that her life was moving on and I was stuck in place, I knew the truth.

I needed to let her go, and I needed her to leave me alone.

But I didn't know how to tell her that.

So, instead, I rubbed the back of my neck, trying to ignore the way my heart squeezed once she was out of my arms again. "Had some students come to me at lunch with questions. I was going to come find you once my after-school tutoring sessions were done."

"Clearly," she chided, eyeing where my hand still held the door.

I swallowed.

Charlie watched me a moment, and when her eyes softened with pity, I had to grind my teeth to keep from screaming at her to stop feeling sorry for me. She wouldn't even be able to deny it if she tried. We both knew it, anyone who saw her face when she was near me could see it. She felt sorry for me.

She wanted me to find love again, as if it was just so easy to do now that I couldn't have her.

That's the way it always went. The person who left had the most power, and the person left behind had the most despair. One would move on, the other would live in heartbreak until enough time had passed. And two years still hadn't been enough time for me to so much as open the damn door, let alone close it and move on.

"So, how are you feeling?" I asked, holding the door open for Charlie so we could both get out into the fresh spring air. The sun warmed my skin as we fell in step on our way to the parking lot.

"Oh, I'm okay. A little sad to have to leave little Daniel this morning, but he has his sister. And our day care is the best, I couldn't ask for better." She smiled. "I'll be back with them in a month for summer break. That's what gets me through."

I wondered why I'd even asked, like hearing her talk about her children with her husband would bring me any sort of relief. Then again, it was never about me when it came to Charlie. I only cared about her.

"Yes, you'll be back home soon."

We were quiet then, only our steps on the concrete and the distant sounds from the after-school practices filling the silence. I walked Charlie to her car first, opening the door to help her inside.

Tell her you need space.

Tell her you're happy for her, but you need to heal.

Tell her to stay away.

But I couldn't say any of those things, even when I knew I should. My heart was begging me to let her go and move on as much as it was threatening to abandon ship if I ever let her go.

Masochist — that's what I was.

"What about you?" she asked after a moment, that same flash of pity crossing her face. "How have you been? I haven't heard from you since Daisy's birthday party." Charlie paused, her voice lowering. "I miss you."

My head dropped back, eyes searching the sky like there was some sort of god who could deliver me from this misery. As much as I wished she'd never say shit like that to me, I couldn't deny the way my heart throbbed at the words, the way my chest fluttered with a hope that I was sure would kill me one day.

And somehow, I was thankful that she was oblivious to it, to the way her kindness killed me. If she was aware of it, she'd leave me alone. I'd get what was best for me — time and space to heal.

But I'd lose her in the process.

And that was the choice I never wanted to make.

"I'm doing great," I lied, smiling when I met her gaze again. "Picked up another night at The Kinky Starfish, and I've got a summer job lined up. Mr. Henderson's niece is in town and needs some help overcoming a repetitive strain injury." I shrugged. "Apparently she's pretty talented, so it should be fun."

"That does sound fun," Charlie beamed, like the fact that I had something even that small to get excited about somehow relieved her. "Have you met her yet?"

A flash of the dark, sad eyes I'd found across the restaurant last night hit me at her words, and I nodded. "Last night. She's... well, she's not what you'd expect when you think of Mr. Henderson's niece."

"Is that a good or bad thing?"

I considered her question. "Not bad. She's just... she's different than I imagined. But, we didn't talk much. We meet for our first lesson tomorrow night."

Charlie smiled. "Well, you'll have to keep me posted with how it goes. Oh! Also, my parents are having dinner this Saturday and wanted to invite you, if you're free? It'd be all of us."

All of us.

That was her nice way of saying Cameron would be there, and her children, too.

I cleared my throat. "I work that night, but thank you for the invite."

She nodded, her smile sad again. "Okay. Well, have a good evening, Reese," she said, sliding into her car.

"Goodnight, Charlie." I shut the door behind her, knocking on the top of her car before crossing the parking lot to my own.

I dropped my keys on the table next to the front door later that evening, kicking off my chukkas before crossing the living room to the kitchen. It was just as quiet as always as I placed the paper bag in my arms on the counter, opening the sliding glass door to let the fresh air and last bit of sunlight in.

My home was modest, a two-bedroom house not too far from school with a yard and garage. My neighborhood was nice, neighbors only slightly annoying, and though it wasn't anything special, I'd made it homey.

Correction: my ex, Blake, had made it homey.

I met Blake in New York City shortly after I graduated from Juilliard, and she'd been there in one of the most difficult times of my life. But, we'd always been casual, never more than friends who occasionally hooked up. When she showed up on my doorstep a few months after I'd left New York and come to Mount Lebanon, I'd been shocked.

When she told me she loved me and wanted to be with me, I'd nearly shit myself.

It was the worst possible timing, especially since I was still tied up with a married woman at the time. And of course, Blake found out, and she asked me to choose between her and Charlie.

We both knew the answer even before she asked it.

This was my curse — hurting anyone who ever dared to love me. Even when I didn't mean to, I still did. I was better off alone, and I knew that now.

Still, Blake had made my little house into a home in her short time staying with me, and I couldn't walk through the modestly decorated living room or see the paintings hanging on the walls without thinking of her.

I thumbed over to my favorite playlist on my phone, turning on my Bluetooth speaker near the sink before digging in the bag on the counter for my dinner: beer and cigarettes.

At thirty-seven years old, I should have known how to take better care of myself. Maybe part of it was that I just didn't give a fuck. I wanted a buzz, and a nicotine high, and to think about anything other than Charlie.

Popping the first beer open, I stepped outside onto my small back patio and lit up a cigarette. The smoke filtered up into the purple sky, the sun slowly making its descent in the west as I propped my feet up and kicked back. I listened to the bugs chirping to life, the birds singing their good evenings, the cars passing by on the street out front. They were the quiet sounds of suburbia, and they let my thoughts drift. For the first time in as long as I could remember, Charlie wasn't the first one they drifted to.

Sarah Henderson.

I let out a long exhale of smoke as her face settled in my mind. She was just a girl, and yet she wore her scars on her sleeve like a woman who'd been through as much hell in her life as I had. Before I'd even known who she was, she'd captured my eye from across the restaurant. And it wasn't necessarily because she was beautiful — although, she very much was — or because she stood out in the crowd she sat among.

It was because she was haunted.

I knew the shapes of the demons in her eyes, the weight on her shoulders, though she held them back and straight. I saw the way my music moved her — the same way it moved me — and I knew from that alone that she'd been cursed by her creativity, by her inability to see the world like a normal, well-functioning human would.

It was the same curse I bared.

There were people who lived, people who watched movies or listened to music or read books. But then, there were the people who created them, who wrote them, who brought them to life. *Those* were the poor, unfortunate suckers who had so much going on in their minds that they *had* to find a way to release it, to breathe life into it, to touch it and feel that it's real.

Sarah was one of those people, and she was asking me to help her.

The first drink of beer was cold and refreshing, and I sucked down nearly half the can. The more I sat there and thought about my new student, the more I wanted to play.

I tapped out my cigarette in the ashtray, swinging back inside to trade my empty beer for a new one before crossing the house to my piano room. It was a room meant to be a study, or perhaps a dining room, but it held only a casual seating area and the most important material object in my life.

My baby grand.

A photo of my parents and my baby sister stared back at me as I sat, flipping the wood panel up and revealing the ivory keys. Their smiles made my heart warm as much as they made it ache. Their lives were stolen too soon, my sister too young, my parents too in love with too much still left to do.

But the man who shot them didn't see them the way I did.

I shook those thoughts away, my hands moving over the keys on autopilot as I thought of Sarah, of what working with her would be like.

It was the most money I'd ever been offered to teach, and I knew it spoke both of how Mr. Henderson felt about me and how important this was to him and his family. I didn't know her story yet, but from what he'd told me, she'd been through something outside of her injury that had her family worried sick. I wondered if that was why she'd shaved her head, if it was her acting out more than a fashion choice.

Somehow, it didn't strike me that way.

She didn't seem like the kind of girl who would pull a stunt just to get attention. She seemed pure, genuine, and like she had a plan for everything. After all, it was *her* who had moved halfway across the country to study with me, because she felt like I could help her.

I didn't know what I was walking into with her, but for some reason, I was excited for it. Sarah would also be the oldest student I'd had since leaving New York City, and I knew she'd be a completely different challenge than the young kids I worked with daily at Westchester.

She was a walking contrast, it seemed to me, and I closed my eyes as my hands moved over the piano keys, remembering her. She wore oversized, baggy clothes that covered her neck to ankle, hiding whatever curves or lean muscles were beneath. It was unlike any other girl dressed at her age — at least, any who I'd seen. And she sported a shaved head, as if she wanted to disappear, and yet she achieved the exact opposite of what she desired. Her skin, rich and dark, like a night sky peppered with freckles instead of stars, was impossible not to notice. Her eyes were bright golden hues, wide in nature and tilted at the edges, like those of a panther. Her lips were plump and round, bowed at the top, and she carried her tall figure in a way that screamed she was afraid of nothing.

The way she dressed, the hairstyle she chose — they told me she wanted to be hidden. She didn't want to be seen.

But by her very nature, she was impossible to ignore.

Everything about her seemed to be a warning — dark clothes, eyes that searched the room like she was looking for a reason to bolt, arms that crossed over her chest like a shield.

I closed my eyes, moving with the music my hands created. I'd never played anything like it before, and it didn't sound great, but it didn't sound particularly awful, either. The notes clashed together in an unfamiliar way, my hands stumbling over themselves as they tried to find a melody, a rhythm. It was always my favorite part of birthing a new song, of bringing music to life that had never existed before. Nothing was perfect the first time it came out, but it would grow, and change, and one day, stand on its own.

I didn't know what to make of the music I made that evening, a half-empty beer can the only audience in the room. The song was pained. It was real. It was raw... and new. Fresh, like nothing I'd played before.

And all the while I played it, I thought of my new student.

That should have been my first warning.

chapter Three

REESE

It'd been a shit day.

There just were no other words to describe how I felt when I stepped out of my shower Tuesday evening, thirty minutes before my first lesson with my new student.

I was no stranger to anxiety, but I'd had the worst kind last night — the kind that keeps you up and then invades your dreams when you do finally manage to fall asleep. I'd had nightmares of Charlie all night long, and then I'd had to see her bouncing around school all day just as happy as can be.

And I *wanted* her happiness. I did. But it would have been so much easier to see her happy if I could say I was happy, too.

I tried to let those selfish, negative thoughts wash away in the shower, but I still felt them clinging to me as I dressed and tidied up my home. It was just the first lesson, we wouldn't do much more than get to know each other and discuss her goals, but the first lesson was always the most important to me because it was when I got to see what our challenges would be.

I'd helped students through RIS injuries when I tutored at Juilliard, but it had been so long since I'd worked with a mature student. At Westchester, the oldest student I had was twelve. They were all early in their studies, finding their styles and learning the fundamental elements of playing. In all honesty, it was easier to work with a child who was at the beginning of their practice than it was to teach a student who had already been taught by others. Not only was my teaching style sure to be different from what Sarah had previously had, but coming off an injury, it wouldn't be easy.

She was going to get frustrated. She was probably going to hate me, because I demanded excellence from all my students. She was probably going to want to murder me by the time we were finished working together.

But I was okay with all of that, as long as I could help her achieve her goals.

And, in all honesty, she studied at Bramlock — so I knew she was accustomed to a tough curriculum. I also knew she was here of her own accord, because she wanted to be here, she wanted to work, to overcome her injury.

She could have given up. Most people probably would have. But she was here, and ready to work.

That spoke volumes.

I lit a few candles in the piano room and put out a pitcher of water with a glass for each of us. At seven on the dot, there was a timid knock at my door.

A jolt of nerves hit me, but my feet moved with confidence across the house. When I opened the door, Sarah Henderson stared back at me like a feral cat in a newfound shelter — wild, but subdued, her eyes wide, shoulders back. She wore a long, flowy, black dress that covered her from her neck to her ankles, and a light jean jacket shielded her shoulders and arms from view, too. There wasn't a stitch of makeup on her face, but her eyes burned bright, like they were the only accessory she needed.

"Evening, Reese!" Mr. Henderson called from where he was climbing out of the car. He waddled up to the door, standing beside Sarah with a wide grin. "Betty sent me with these."

He held a Tupperware container in his hand, and I didn't have to look to know it was her famous baklava. That woman's baking was revered in Mount Lebanon, and my mouth watered at the sight.

"She's too good to me," I said, taking the container from him as I held the door open wider. "Please, come in."

Sarah slipped past me first, tucking into the corner of the foyer as I shut the door again behind her uncle. For a moment, we all just stood there in that tiny space, and maybe it was the terrible day I'd had, but for some reason, I smiled at having Sarah in my home. She was a burst of color in an otherwise dark place, and I liked the energy she carried with her.

She, on the other hand, looked like she wanted to crawl out of her skin.

I led the way into the kitchen first, pouring us each a glass of water.

"I have some business to attend to," Randall said when I handed him his. "Do you mind if I set up in your living room?"

He tapped the laptop peeking out from his messenger bag, and I nodded.

"Of course. Let me know if you need anything."

"Oh, I'll be fine. You focus on your new star student here," he said with a proud grin and toward his niece. Her eyes were still shifty as they surveyed her new space, but she returned his smile. "I'll just be in the next room, if you need me. Okay?"

He said the words slowly, purposefully, like he knew Sarah was scared. I could sense it, too — though I wasn't sure why. Maybe she was just nervous, or maybe she didn't do well with being in unfamiliar places. Regardless, when Randall excused himself into the other room, I watched Sarah for a long moment, wondering what she was thinking.

"How are you?" I asked first.

She looked around without moving her neck, as if she was afraid I'd yell at her for taking in the space I lived in.

"I'm well," she answered, and she glanced toward the living room where her uncle had just set up camp. She stood on the opposite side of the island, hands folded over the granite, everything about her screaming discomfort. "How are you?"

I smiled. "I'm alright."

She took a sip of the water I'd slid across the counter to her, and I couldn't help but take a moment to digest her. She was quiet, but in a way only a fire can be. Because though she seemed to only crackle softly, she had the power to burn, to bring light and warmth to a room, or to bring an entire building to the ground.

"There's no need to be nervous," I said, taking a seat on one of the barstools.

Sarah's eyes widened then, her little mouth popping open in a soft O. "I'm not nervous," she insisted, smoothing her hands down her dress before folding them on the counter again.

I lifted a brow.

She let out a low breath, shaking her head with her eyes falling to her hands. "Okay, I'm a little nervous. I admit, I haven't worked with a teacher since..." She swallowed. "It's just been a while, and with the injury... and then of course, knowing who you are..."

"Knowing who I am?" I questioned.

Her eyes doubled in size. "Uh... well, yes. I mean... of course I've seen videos of you play... online and everything."

"Videos?"

"On YouTube..." Sarah lifted a brow at my confusion. "You really don't know?"

I shrugged. Of course, I'd heard of the videos being posted. My students loved to tease me about being their "famous" music teacher. But I was thirty-seven years old and about as far removed from social media as a person could be. I didn't tweet, or have a Facebook, or Instagram, or whatever the hell else there was.

"I don't put them up," I finally offered. "It's just the people who tape me at the restaurant, mostly."

"You have like... hundreds of thousands of views on those videos, Reese," Sarah said. Then, she cleared her throat. "Mr. Walker."

"No, it's okay, call me Reese," I assured her. "And videos aside, there's no need to be nervous. This," I said, motioning between us. "Us working together? It's about you. I know every student is different, and I'm hoping to take this opportunity of our first lesson tonight to get to know a little about you."

Sarah nodded, brows narrowing in a confident focus.

"But," I said, taking a sip of water before continuing. "I want to be clear about one very important thing. I demand excellence from my students, Miss Henderson. Working with me will likely not be your favorite thing in the world. I won't take it easy on you, and I won't dance around something just to save your feelings. Piano isn't easy, it isn't for everyone, and I won't be too shy to tell you if I think you fall into that category."

Her eyes softened at that, like she was afraid she actually would.

I could tell just by the way she carried herself that it wasn't possible.

I'd always felt like I had an eye for phonies, for people who wanted to play piano for all the wrong reasons. There was a difference between someone wanting to be the center of attention or have a party trick to pull out when someone has a house piano, and someone who genuinely loved music, who had to play it to breathe, to exist.

Sarah was the latter.

"I want to hear more about your injury first," I said. "Then, I want to know what your goals are — short and long term. Finally, I'll have you play a piece for me, and then we can discuss how I can help."

"Okay," Sarah said, letting out a long breath. She finally took a seat at the barstool across from me, and she splayed her long, thin fingers out on the counter before tucking her hands in her lap. "I was in my last year at Bramlock. I was supposed to be graduating this month, actually," she said. "But..."

"The injury," I finished for her.

Her eyes clouded over then, and she sniffed, taking a quick sip of water. "Yeah. The injury."

"Tell me more about that."

She swallowed. "It was last summer when it first happened. I was taking summer classes, and there was a performance exam coming up. My professor..." She paused, taking a sip of water again before continuing. "He was riding me really hard. And I don't blame him," she said quickly, her eyes snapping up to mine before they fell to the counter again. "It wasn't his fault I took it all so seriously and played nearly every hour of every day for that whole week."

I could already feel where the story was going before she finished, and though I applauded her for not placing blame on her professor, something told me he *did* play a big part in it. Any experienced teacher would have seen the signs, the duress, long before the injury occurred.

But at a university, when there are hundreds of students to look after, it's harder to do.

"I knew I needed to rest before the exam," she continued. "So, I gave myself the weekend off before the performance on Monday. I knew my wrists had been hurting, my hands, but... I didn't realize *how* badly I'd been pushing. And when I stopped playing..."

"Everything seized up."

She nodded, eyes glossing over. "Like an old car engine." She extended her hands out toward me. "My wrists swelled up like balloons, I couldn't even hold a pen."

Sarah let her hands fall to the counter again, staring at them like they were someone else's, like they'd betrayed her the way an ex-boyfriend might have. She started picking at her nails for a second before she pulled them back into her lap. Her eyes had changed, had darkened with her story. And we both knew there were no words I could say to take back what happened to her.

I let her sit in silence for a moment, refilling her glass and waiting.

"So," she finally said. "I went to the doctor, obviously. Essentially, I had completely shredded the primary muscles I needed to play and then fucked up my secondary muscles, too." Her hand flew to her mouth. "Oh, I'm so sorry."

I smirked. "It's okay. Trust me, my vocabulary is at least thirty-five percent curse words."

"Fifty percent," Randall called from the other room.

We all laughed, and Sarah seemed a bit relieved at that, folding her hand back in her lap.

"Anyway," she said. "I couldn't play all fall semester. I was falling behind, and I knew I was about to be faced with more school time if I didn't figure it out. But there were so many steps before I could even *play* again." She counted off on her fingers. "Nerve testing, deep tissue therapy, all these trips to the doctor... it was terrifying. My professor said he could help me, he could keep me on my trajectory to get where I wanted to be if I worked with him..."

Her eyes grew even darker at that, her face stone. I didn't like the way she spoke about her piano professor, because I knew without her having to say it that she didn't trust him and he didn't favor her. Not that a student *needed* to be favored to be successful, but if all you ever had was someone riding your ass, it was hard to ever feel like anything but a burden and a failure.

And that's why she'd pushed herself to injury.

"But, we just didn't mesh well. And in the end, I left Bramlock for winter break and I never went back." She sat up straighter. "I've been working on my own," she explained. "And I'm finally playing again, but... I'm rusty. And I'm far from where I need to be at this point... to get to where I want to be."

"And where is that?"

She let out a long breath, and with the most confidence she'd had all evening, with her eyes locked on mine and her back straight, she said the last thing I expected.

"Carnegie Hall."

It took every ounce of muscle control I had not to let my eyebrows shoot up into my hairline or my mouth flop open on the kitchen island. Instead, I took a drink of water, letting her words sink in.

"So, you want to be a concert pianist?"

Sarah nodded. "I do. But, I want Carnegie. I want a solo. I want..." She smiled for the first time all evening, hope shooting out of her eyes like visible stars. "I want to be on the Ronald O. Perelman Stage. I want to be one of the greats. I want to be at the top of the entire city's list when they think of who they want playing their piano for an upcoming concert."

Right then and there, I wanted to reach over and pet her hand like she was a young girl who didn't understand what she was asking. But I knew better, because though Sarah *was* young, I knew just from hearing all she'd endured that she wasn't stupid. She knew what she was asking. She knew the odds.

And still, she was here.

I stood without another word, draining the last of the water in my glass and wishing it was beer as I considered everything she'd said. It was far from what I expected to walk into, and far from what I felt I could achieve as a piano teacher. Still, I held my hand out toward the room that housed my baby grand piano, quieting my pessimistic thoughts as I looked down at the hopeful girl seated at my kitchen island.

"I think it's time I heard you play, Miss Henderson."

SARAH

He doesn't think I can do it.

I knew it before I even sat down at his baby grand piano, feeling the keys under my fingers as I warmed up with his eyes on me. He'd listened to every word I'd said in that kitchen, and he hadn't *said* anything that should have made me feel like he didn't have faith in me.

He didn't have to.

It was all in the way he watched me, in the way he didn't smile, didn't nod or assure me in any way that what I wanted was achievable.

But he wasn't the first one who didn't believe in me.

And he wouldn't be the first one I proved wrong.

A candle burned in the corner of the room with a warm vanilla scent as I got familiar with the piano, my wrists and fingers warming up with each note. My stomach churned a little as I played, just like it had when I sat down at a piano ever since that last night at Bramlock. I used to feel the cool keys under my skin and get a tingle of joy, one that flowed from my neck to my toes. I used to smile, and instantly feel in my zone, in my element.

Now, I thought of what the bottom of the piano looked like from the floor, what the weight of an unwanted man between my legs felt like. I thought of my injury, felt every stiff, sore muscle that surrounded my wrist bones like hot barbed wire cutting me over and over again.

I didn't just have to work on technique with Reese. I had to learn to love the piano again, to not be afraid of it, to not associate it with that night.

Perhaps that would be my biggest challenge.

Reese stood in the corner, giving me space, but his eyes watched me like no eyes had ever watched me before. I opened my mouth, but the words I wanted to say stuck in my throat. I wanted to tell him that I knew I was rusty, that I knew I needed work. I wanted to tell him that I was one of the top students in my class at Bramlock, and that I had potential. I wanted to tell him that I *could* do this — with his help.

But instead, I decided to let my hands to the talking.

Once I was warm, I stopped playing and stretched my wrists out in front of me, rolling them a few times before wiggling my fingers. I closed my eyes, cracking my neck once on each side, and I let out a long, smooth breath.

When I opened my eyes again, I wasn't with Reese.

I was alone, in the house I grew up in with both parents. I was at the piano my mom bought for me on my tenth birthday, the one I'd lost entire afternoons with, the one that still sat in our little apartment in Atlanta. My father was there, too — standing in the corner instead of Reese — and he smiled at me with shining eyes, the same way he had when he was alive.

My heart beat grew steadier, my rib cage loosened its grip on my heart.

And then, I played.

I chose *River Flows in You* by Yiruma, or should I say, it chose me. I hadn't planned a piece to play, but it was the first one that came to me, and I felt those beginning notes like a long walk home on a sunny day. It was a more modern song than what I typically played, but one that I felt so deeply every time I brought it to life. And with every new chord, with every second of the melody, I felt myself slip away, into that piano, into the music.

There was a sort of sad hope weaved throughout the song, with prominent rests that seemed to impress that hope into your soul, and it spread over me like the warmest blanket.

It was a short piece, but it showed my strengths, the arpeggios and rests so beautifully connected that I could display my emotion along with my talent. My nerves still fired to life with each stretch of my hands, the recovering muscles reminding me how fragile the human body really was. I used that painful reminder as fuel, letting it flow through me and into the song.

When I played the last notes, I held the keys down, eyes still closed. I didn't want to open them yet, to see if Reese was emoting with me, to see if he believed me yet.

And I didn't have to.

I felt the heat of his body take the space next to me on the bench, and I withdrew my hands from where they'd held the final notes, folding them in my lap before finally creaking my eyes open. He was close... too close. I stared at his thigh, just inches from mine, and I prayed he wouldn't touch me.

Please don't be like him. Please don't be like him.

I stared at the black and ivory keys, and Reese stared at me.

"I see you," he said, his voice low, almost so low I couldn't be sure I'd heard him right.

I turned, eyes cast up at him as he furrowed his brows. He searched my gaze like I was a puzzle with all the right pieces shoved in all the wrong places, and I'd never felt more pegged down in my entire life.

For a moment, he just watched me, concern etched in his expression. When he finally spoke, his voice was louder, deeper, commanding all my attention.

"Even when you are the most talented pianist at your school, or perhaps in your area of the country, or in the entire country as a whole," he said, pausing a moment. "And even when you know all the right people, in all the right places..." Reese rolled his lips together, a slight shake to his head. "Being invited to play at Carnegie Hall is still a pipe dream. And being a concert pianist in one of the largest, most artistically competitive cities in the world isn't an easy job. It's going to be incredibly difficult, every step of the way, and the truth is... you may never make it."

I scowled, chest tightening again.

"Look, I've gone my entire life having people like you tell me what I can and can't achieve, and I'm not subscribing to this channel anymore." I sat up taller, eyes fixed on his. "I can do this. With your help, I can likely do it better, and faster, but make no mistake, whether I have you in my corner or not, I *will* play at Carnegie." I swallowed. "And I will be a concert pianist in New York City."

There was a twitch of a smile at the corner of his lips as he lifted one brow. "If you would have let me finish," he said, searching my gaze. "I was going to say that though it may be difficult, I'm ready to put in the work if you are."

"Oh." I blinked, heat spreading over my cheeks and down my neck. "Well... in that case, yes. I'm ready to put in the work, Mr. Walker."

He kept his eyes on mine for a long moment, almost as if he was looking for a sign of breakage. Then, he simply nodded, closing the lid on the piano keys and standing.

"Let's outline this lesson plan, then," he said, already making his way back to the kitchen before I could stand to join him.

He paused in the open doorway, glancing back at me with a curious look. His hair was pulled back in a low bun, a few strands framing his face, and I traced the hard edges of his jaw and nose as he stared back at me.

"For the record," he finally said. "I am in your corner."

With that, he left the room, and once I was alone in it, I took the first breath that didn't burn since I'd walked through his front door.

"He's just very... *moody*," I said around a mouthful of carrot the next evening, already dipping my next one in hummus. "Like, he stares at me a lot without saying anything. And he smiles, but it's not like a *real* smile. It's subdued."

Mom chuckled, her soft voice soothing me through the phone. "Well, maybe he's just a quiet man. Or maybe he's been through hell in his life. I'm sure you'll get to know him more as you practice together, and he'll open up."

I chomped on another carrot. "Maybe," I mumbled. "But, it's kind of intimidating."

"Nothing intimidates my girl."

"Say that to Captain Moody Face." I swallowed the bite, waving what was left of my carrot around as I spoke. "I swear, it doesn't make sense how he doesn't have the thickest wrinkles in the middle of his forehead. He's always scowling, especially when he plays."

Mom laughed again. "What did he say when *you* played?"

I ate the last of my carrot, setting my plate on my bedside table and leaning back against the mountain of pillows on my bed. Aunt Betty loved pillows, I'd learned, and the room she'd set me up in had at least a dozen if you combined the bed and the chairs.

"He said he *sees* me," I said softly, letting those words settle over me once more. "And then, he reminded me how impossible what I want is. But... he also said he was in my corner." I huffed. "Do you see what I mean? Captain Confusing."

"Is it Captain Moody Face or Captain Confusing?"

"Both."

Mom chuffed. "It sounds to me like he sees the potential in you, but he is also a realist. And there's nothing wrong with that. You've always loved to prove people wrong," she reminded me. "So, just think of it as another chance to do something you're passionate about."

I wrapped my hand around the crystal that hung from my neck with a sigh. It was the crystal my mother had given me on my sixteenth birthday, one I'd worn as a necklace ever since.

My sixteenth birthday was my first without my father.

There were very few nights that I could remember clearly from when I was in high school, most of them blurring together in a mix of piano recitals and evenings spent reading classical romance novels or playing Scrabble with Mom. I'd always been a home body, preferring to spend time with her, my close friends, or just with myself.

But the night my mom had to wake me up and tell me my father was gone was a night I'd never forget.

You don't prepare for the death of a parent, not that young, maybe not ever. It didn't make sense to me, that he could be there for dinner, go out to a fundraiser event for work, and never make it home. The more I searched for answers, the more hurt I was, because answers never came.

There *were* no answers for why the young boy, only a few years older than me, shot my father in the process of robbing a convenience store.

That was the first catalyst in my life, the first *thing* that happened that really changed me. My life was different before he was gone, and the person I became after he'd passed was one I never knew before. The same was true for Mom, who threw herself into work to cope with the pain. She booked evening sessions with clients, something she swore she'd never do, and even started doing video chat sessions that kept her working until after I went to bed. Our evenings that were once filled with family dinner and games turned into me doing homework, playing piano, or reading while she worked.

I was never mad at her for that.

She had to grieve the best way she knew how, and she was always there for me when I needed her. It didn't bother me that she wanted to stay busy. If anything, I understood — I just threw myself into piano instead of work.

That fluorite crystal that hung from my neck was meant to bring me peace in anxious times, its swirls of blue and purple meant to keep me grounded and focused. It was to remind me that not all answers can be seen, but that everything happens for a reason — a reminder to trust in myself and life's journey.

At twenty-one, I no longer saw it as an accessory, but as an extension of myself — like an extra, essential limb.

"You always know how to take something I'm so uneasy about and make me feel silly for ever worrying in the first place," I mused. "Wouldn't have anything to do with why you're a therapist, would it?"

"I don't want to make you feel silly," Mom said. "And, believe it or not, I try not to therapy you too much. You're my daughter, after all. I just want to be Mom to you."

I smiled.

"But, I'm glad I can help ease the anxiety," she continued. "You are the most incredible pianist I know, *mwen chouchou,* and I believe this Mr. Walker wants to help you."

I smiled at the endearment in my mother's native tongue. I'd never learned the Haitian Creole language, but I loved to hear her speak it. Sometimes, I would close my eyes and try to picture her as a young girl on the island, working with her parents on the farm, her own mother using that same nickname she used for me. *My pet.*

"That reminds me, I think Uncle Randall is giving everyone a minor heart attack by introducing me as his niece," I said. "They are very confused by our... *differences.*"

She let out an understanding sigh. "I can only imagine. I remember when your father first introduced me to his family as his girlfriend." She chuckled. "If you think they look at *you* with a confused look, imagine how it was for me. For *him.*"

I chuffed, trying to picture that beginning time for my parents. I knew they were both brave to be in an interracial relationship, especially when my father was in the political circuit in small-town Georgia. But, they never hid, never made excuses. Their love spoke for the both of them, and it was so loud, it was impossible for anyone to refute.

"Ah, but you know what?" Mom said after a moment. "Your differences are what make you so beautiful."

"They also make me stand out like a fish trying to blend in with the birds."

"I had a dream about a flying fish once," she said. "Perhaps it was a vision of you."

I smiled, heart squeezing in my chest as I reclined more, hand still wrapped around my crystal. "I miss you, *Manman*."

"And I miss you. We'll be together again, soon. For now, focus on this dream of yours. I have no doubt that, like the fish in my dreams, you will soar."

My heart ached a little at her words, because I heard what she *didn't* say, too. She missed me, but she knew something had happened to me at Bramlock. She knew I needed this time with Reese not just to study and overcome my injury, but to heal, to find my love for music again. My mother was a therapist, and I knew just as well as she did that her daughter dropping out of college a semester before graduating, moving home, changing her entire wardrobe and shaving her head didn't just happen without cause.

There was a reason. And she knew it.

It had to hurt her, to see her daughter hurting, struggling, and not be able to help. She was doing everything she could within the realm of what I'd asked of her. That was what I loved about her most — she respected me, and my wish for her to let me deal with it on my own. I assured her I would tell her more one day, when I was ready. And thankfully, she hadn't pressed.

She was my supporter, even when I couldn't give her all the answers. My warrior. My one and only teammate.

I stayed in bed once we ended our call, eyes on the ceiling and fingers dancing over my crystal. I wanted to believe my mom when she said everything would be okay, that I would achieve what I set out to when I came to Mount Lebanon, but inside, I heard my own voice questioning every aspect of it.

Could I really overcome my injuries and play the way I used to? No, play *better*? Could I get to Carnegie Hall without the normal trajectory most people take to get there? Could I hold myself to Reese's standards, or were all his warnings about how impossible this all was a glimpse into my future?

I didn't have the answers for any of it, and being in a new town with a part of my family I usually only visited at holidays, I didn't have any comfort, either. Nothing was familiar. Nothing felt like *mine*.

The bed I slept in was Aunt Betty's guest bed. The clothes I wore were the ones I begged my mom to take me to get after I got home from Christmas break, when I was determined to hide away, to not be seen. My hair that I once loved and spent hours grooming was now gone. I was in a town where I was the new girl, but not even in a way where anyone cared. I was just passing through, a guest, and to top it all off, I was a guest who didn't fit in.

My wolf told me I would never make it without him. He wanted me to believe I had to give up my mind, body, and soul if I wanted even a chance at sitting on that piano bench in New York City. *I* told myself when I left Bramlock that I didn't believe that. I told myself I could do this without him.

Now, I wasn't so sure.

I sighed just as a soft knock rapped on my door, and Aunt Betty creaked it open a few inches, making sure I was decent before she let herself all the way in.

"Dinner's almost ready," she said, a sweet, genuine smile on her face as she folded her hands in front of her. It was odd how much of my uncle I saw when I looked at her. It was as if spending years of their lives together had combined them slightly, like they were one person cloned instead of two individuals. "Was that your mom on the phone?"

I nodded. "Yeah, we were just catching up a little. I told her about my first lesson with Mr. Walker."

"Ah," Aunt Betty said, crossing the room until she sat at the foot of the bed. "And how was that first lesson?"

"It was... interesting."

She smiled at that, as if she knew that answer was coming before I gave it to her. "Well, Reese Walker is *interesting*, isn't he?" She sighed. "That boy has been through a lot, what with everything that happened to his family. And then there's..." She paused, fingers floating up to her lips like she wanted to physically stop her next sentence. "Well, he's just had to endure a lot of heartache in his life. Poor man. But he sure does seem to throw all of that hurt into his music, doesn't he?"

I sat up, leaning my back against the wall of pillows. "What happened with his family?"

My aunt's brows bent together then. "I'm not sure that's my story to tell, but I bet he will talk to you about it. When he's ready to."

I nodded, both of us falling quiet as I thought back through the videos I'd watched of Reese. They were mostly recent ones at The Kinky Starfish, and none of them really offered much detail about the man playing. I was sure I could get online and do some searching for his family, but the thought of invading his privacy like that made my stomach knot.

I knew what it was like to be invaded, and I never wanted to impress that feeling upon anyone else.

"Sarah?"

I blinked, snapping back to the moment. "Hmm?"

Aunt Betty's eyes softened, her hand reaching out to touch my arm. Even though I saw it coming, I still flinched involuntarily, and that made my aunt frown more. "I just want you to know that your uncle and I are so happy to have you here, and we love you very much," she said. "I know it must be hard being away from your mom, and from your school... and I just wanted to say if there's anything I can do to help you get acclimated here, don't hesitate to tell me."

The way she spoke, I wondered if she'd overheard my conversation with my mom on the phone. Did she hear me expressing how I felt in their home, in their town?

It hit me then that out of place was the last thing I should be feeling when my family had reached such a gracious, welcoming hand out to me.

"I know," I said, squeezing her hand where it rested over my arm. "Thank you so much, Aunt Betty. I couldn't do this without you and Uncle Randall helping me."

"Oh, posh," she said, standing. "You could. You're the most determined young woman I've ever known. I would be scared, if I were Reese Walker." She winked. "He's certainly not prepared for Sarah Henderson."

I chuckled.

"Anyway, wash up and come to the dining room. I made the most *fantastic* vegan spread." She smirked. "Much to your uncle's disdain."

"You didn't have to do that," I offered with a cringe. "I could have cooked my own."

"Don't be silly. Your uncle and I could both stand to eat a little better, anyway. Lord knows we've had enough dairy and meat to last a lifetime."

I smiled. "Thank you, Aunt Betty. For everything."

She just winked again, closing the door behind her when she'd gone.

I peeled myself out of bed and into the guest bath, washing my hands and splashing some cool water on my face. When I looked in the mirror, dabbing the water off with a towel, my eyes skated over the young woman staring back at me — the smooth head, the dark skin, blotted with freckles and completely free of makeup, the high cheek bones and thick lips.

She somehow felt years older than the girl who had stared back at me in December.

I wondered if I'd ever see that girl again.

chapter four

SARAH

I went back to Reese Walker's house the following evening, and this time, I was alone.

I thought my hands couldn't shake more than they did when I stood on his porch, waiting for him to open the door after I knocked. I thought I couldn't get any more nervous than I already was to be alone with him — a man. An *older* man. An older man who could easily overpower me, if he wanted to. And I thought my stomach couldn't wind up any tighter than it already had as I drove across town to his place.

But when he opened the door, every sensation doubled.

Everything about Reese's presence was large — his stature, his muscles, his energy. His hair was swept back in a loose, knotted-like bun, a few strands falling behind his ears, and he was dressed like he'd just gotten home from school — khaki pants, hunter green button-up, the sleeves bunched at his elbows. He smiled, stepping aside to let me through the door, but all I could do was stare at the space with my feet glued to his porch.

He's not my wolf.

I tried to soothe my racing heart, tried to assure my labored lungs that there was nothing to be afraid of. But how could I be sure? I wanted to trust Reese, to trust *anyone*, but the truth was nothing had been earned yet.

And I'd learned my lesson about giving trust to someone just because of the position they held.

Reese cleared his throat. "It's safe, I promise. Cleared out the boogie men right before you got here."

I sighed at that, shaking my head at myself as I scooted past Reese and into his foyer. He shut only the glass door behind us, leaving the big door open so the evening sun could stream through the living room. I adjusted my messenger bag on my shoulder, offering him a timid smile.

"Sorry," I said. "I get a little nervous in new environments."

It wasn't the whole truth, but it wasn't necessarily a lie, either.

"Hey, no need to apologize. I think it's smart of you to be wary of your surroundings. But, hopefully, I can make you feel comfortable the more we work together." He slid his hands in his pockets. "Would you like something to drink before we get started?"

"Water would be nice." My throat was still dry, hands clammy.

"You got it. I'll meet you in there," he said, pointing to the piano room. Then, he turned, leaving me alone in the foyer.

I took my time making my way into the room where his piano was, surveying the paintings on his walls and the lack of any personal photos. There was only one that I'd noticed, and I'd seen it two nights before during our first lesson — a photo of an older couple and a beautiful young lady that sat perched on top of his piano. Judging by the man's strong jaw, by the smile of the woman to his left, and by the eyes of the young girl that stood in front of them, I could only guess that it was his family.

My aunt's words from the night before had me staring at that photo a little longer this time.

I wondered what happened to them. I wondered if he'd ever tell me. The urge to search online to find out hit me again, but I subdued it, reminding myself that Reese Walker was a human just like the rest of us. I wouldn't want anyone digging up information on my father when I could be the one to tell them myself.

It was unnerving, how much of our past could be exposed by a quick Google search.

I sat my messenger bag on the piano bench, trailing one finger along the wood before I crossed the room to the set of bookshelves by the window. They were small, only about twenty books or so filling them, and I eyed the spines with my hands folded behind me.

Agatha Christie.

Edgar Allen Poe.

Lee Child.

John Grisham.

Stephen King.

It was like a gathering of mystery and thriller, of horror and suspense. The bookshelves in my room in Atlanta were much different — brighter, lined with romance and poetry and fantasy. Of course, I hadn't been able to read a single book since I left Bramlock. I tried, but every time I opened a story and started reading, I found myself rolling my eyes.

How could romance be real?

How could it be that someone could care about you enough to put you ahead of everything else in their life? How could it be that someone could touch you, kiss you, *love* you if you were like me — damaged, used.

Fucked up.

I once believed I'd find my prince, my one and only soulmate who would make all the pieces of my life fall perfectly in place. Now, the only love I believed in was the love I felt for the piano.

And even that relationship was strained now.

"Do you like to read?" Reese asked, his voice startling me a bit as he handed me a full glass of water.

I took a tentative sip, embarrassed by the way I jumped when he spoke. "I used to."

"Used to?" He cocked a brow. "I've never heard of someone falling out of love with reading."

I shrugged. "Well, let's just say I outgrew it."

Reese was quiet a moment, and my eyes stayed on the books as his assessed me.

"What did you used to read?"

"Romance, mostly. Some fantasy. Poetry."

He nodded. Then, he reached forward for one of the books on the top shelf — one with a large mouth on it, a broken-toothed smile.

"Read this," he said, offering it to me.

I took the book from his hand, one brow lifting as I read the title. "*Fight Club*? As in, the movie with Brad Pitt?"

Reese scoffed. "Come on, now. As a fellow bookworm, I know you don't believe the movie is ever as good as the book. Have you seen the movie?"

"No."

"Even better. Just, trust me on this," he said. "Maybe you fell out of love with romance books and fantasy books because you want something a little more real, a little less perfect, a little more messy. I think you'll like this." He thumped the hardback in my hands with his knuckle. "Plus, Palahniuk is a phenomenal writer. He'll make you think."

I smoothed my hand over the cover, and for some reason, a gentle ease came over me. I knew how precious all of my books were, and I couldn't imagine offering one up to a practical stranger. It was a special gift to have a book purchased for you, but to have one lent to you, to have someone trust you to take care of a piece of art so precious to them?

That was rare.

"Thank you," I said, turning back toward the piano. I slipped the book in my messenger bag, placing my glass of water on the coaster on top of the piano before I met Reese's eyes again. "And thank you again for letting my uncle accompany me the other day. I'm sure that was a little out of the ordinary."

"It didn't bother me at all," Reese said quickly. "Invite him any time."

I smiled. "Thank you."

My eyes slipped to the piano, to where the wood panel covered the keys. I let my gaze wander over the rich wood, the smooth edges — and with every second that passed, I felt my heart picking up speed.

"I have a piece I'd like you to play today," Reese said after a long moment, stepping up on the other side of the piano. He flipped the cover off the keys, opening a book of music that had been sitting in the holder to a bookmarked page. Once it was in place, he crossed the room to the far corner by the bookshelves, leaning against the wall. "No rush.

Warm up, take your time, but I want you to take a stab at that."

I nodded, setting my messenger bag to the side as I took a seat at the bench. The nerves that had subsided a bit as we talked books were back in full force when I was seated, my fingers resting gently over the keys as I digested the piece of music in front of me. It was a feeling I still wasn't familiar with, almost a sense of dread as I warmed up my wrists. I used to sit down at a piano with eager anticipation, with excitement, with joy.

Between my injury and what happened at Bramlock, I wasn't sure I'd ever feel that again.

Now, my relationship with the piano was one I had to work at. It was a love I had to wake up every day and choose, over and over again. Sometimes, I wondered why I did at all, why I hadn't turned my back on piano the way I had on my romance books.

But I knew the answer, even if I couldn't admit it out loud.

The truth was, music *was* my life, my heart, my soul. Without it, I couldn't breathe. Without it, I couldn't survive. So, choosing the piano, choosing to fight for us even when it seemed hopeless? Well, it was my way of saying I still wanted to be here. I wanted to survive.

And I would.

When I was warm, I played the piece Reese had set up on the piano, stumbling through the first part of it until I got my bearings. It was a quick and bubbly piece, cheery and jubilant. It reminded me of a song I'd selected for my spring recital my sophomore year of high school, a Chopin piece that was one of my father's favorites.

I tried to latch onto that feeling, to the memory of my father, of my youth, but it slipped away as soon as it had come. I finished the song without fanfare, and then I pulled my hands to my lap, a long sigh leaving my lips.

Reese cleared his throat from the corner, kicking off the wall and making his way across the room. He stopped when he was a few feet from the piano, that little crease between his brows reappearing as he stared at the keys with me, like he wasn't sure what to say. After a long pause, he settled on, "How did you feel?"

I swallowed. "Detached."

He nodded, hands slipping into his pockets as he worried his bottom lip. After a long moment, he rounded the piano, tapping the bench with his eyes on me. "Mind if I sit?"

I slid over to the right, making room for him to sit next to me. My heart kicked up a notch again at the heat of him filling the empty space, and I swallowed, smoothing my damp palms over my dark jeans.

Reese flipped back a few pages in the book, back to the beginning of the piece, and began playing. He played softly, like background music, and once he flipped to the second page, he spoke again.

"How long have you been afraid of the piano?"

He didn't take his eyes off the sheet music and the keys, but I felt like he'd just pinned me with a heavy, accusatory stare.

"I'm not afraid of the piano," I argued.

Reese glanced at me with a cocked brow. "You look at it like you are. You touch it like you are." He shrugged, fingers floating over the keys as he played. "Even in our first lesson, it seemed like you would rather submit yourself to a

71

hundred paper cuts than play. And that doesn't make sense for someone who wants to make a career out of piano."

I sighed, hating the truth in his words — hating the fact that he *saw* my fear even more than the fact that it was there at all.

"It's not that I'm scared of it," I tried to explain, watching his hands so I didn't have to meet his eyes. "But, it feels... foreign. Sometimes. Like, someone who used to be my best friend, but now is so different, I hardly recognize them. And everything that used to come easy, doesn't." I shook my head. "Nothing comes easy anymore."

Reese nodded in understanding, finishing the piece before he let his hands hit his thighs. He turned, eyes flicking between mine. "It won't be like that forever."

"How can you be so sure?"

He cracked his neck, debating his next words. "Well, for one, because you won't give up on it. If you were going to give up, you would have already. And, for two, because this is a completely normal reaction to an RIS injury. Your body has failed you, betrayed you, and you don't know how to respond to it. It makes you feel out of control, and no one likes that." He smiled softly. "But, it will get better. We have work to do, but we'll get there. If you trust me to help you, that is."

Trust.

I hated that word.

I hated the sick wave that rolled through me at the sound of it.

"Take this home with you," he said, reaching for the book propped on the piano. He shut it, handing it to me. "Try this piece a few times over the weekend. I don't want you to get mad at it, though. I want you to really take it apart, try to understand it — why it was born, the emotions behind it, what your audience should feel as you play it. We'll try it again next week and see how you feel about it then."

I nodded, taking the book from his hands. "What if I still suck?"

He chuckled. "You don't suck now, so don't worry about that. Just, try to open yourself to the music, instead of just *playing* it. You can read the notes. You can execute the music. But, try to take it a step further. Try to connect with it, like a human instead of a song."

I had to fight back the urge to laugh at that. If he only knew the only human relationship I'd been able to keep intact was with my mother, he'd have chosen a different analogy.

"Honestly, I think I can connect with it easier if I think of it as music. I'm not the best with humans."

Reese laughed again as he stood, knocking his knuckles on the piano. "That makes two of us, kid."

Kid.

I should have hated that, too.

But for some reason, it left me warm.

REESE

Saturday nights were like a concert at The Kinky Starfish.

With the weather warming up, guests were alive with the promise of summer, and I tapered my playlist to match the mood. Unlike in the blistering cold of winter, guests now would occasionally get out of their seats and dance on the small floor beside me, bringing my music to life with their movements. I smiled and bounced along to the melody of Mozart's *Sonata 17,* nodding to a young girl hopping around on the dance floor before scanning the room. All the faces were bright with laughter around the restaurant.

It was almost enough to make even my poor, cold soul thaw a little.

Until I saw table thirty-two.

It took every ounce of brainpower I had to keep playing, to not miss a note when I realized who occupied that back corner booth. Of course, it was Charlie's eyes that captured mine first, and she gave a smiley twiddle of her fingers when she realized I'd finally seen her. My smile was tight in return, and when I glanced at Cameron — her husband — his eyes were hard on me in warning.

And he held their youngest child in his lap.

I sniffed, tearing my eyes away and playing the last of the song with more gusto than was necessary. I took artistic liberties, plucking away at the keys with a fierce determination to finish the song and get the fuck off that floor for my break.

They were supposed to be having dinner at home. I wasn't supposed to have to deal with Charlie until Monday, until we were back at school, in the space we shared.

It felt like I'd never truly escape her, not even for a weekend.

When I finished the piece, I stood with a quick bow and brief announcement that I'd be back in twenty. The young girl on the dance floor pouted before her mother steered her back to the table, and I was set on making a beeline for the back kitchen door where a cigarette had my name on it.

But I didn't make it two steps before I was stopped.

"Reese Walker," a smooth, familiar voice said as a warm hand grazed my arm. "Well, well. Fancy meeting you here."

Jennifer Stinson smiled back at me, in almost the same way she had the first night we'd met. That had been in my first couple of months back in Mount Lebanon, and she'd asked for a dance at Charlie's parents' annual fundraiser. Of course, Charlie had been all I could see that night.

Not that much had really changed.

Jennifer still had the same, sultry blue eyes and thick lips — the bottom one with an indent that I was sure drove every man she talked to absolutely insane — and her long, curly blonde hair waterfalled down her back as she stepped closer. Her perfume was tangy and sweet, like a citrusy fruit, and I wished I could be a normal man for once. I wished I could be the man I was *before* I came back to Mount Lebanon, before my family died, before everything inside of me capable of love or lust was completely obliterated by Hurricane Charlie.

But I felt nothing.

"Nice to see you again, Jennifer. It's been a long time."

"Indeed, it has," she said, her eyes crawling their way back up to my face. "I know you're working now, but are you free later this week? I'd love to grab a drink, catch up."

I swallowed down the sticky knot in my throat, the same one that emerged any time I thought of a situation even remotely close to a date. "I'm pretty busy with school and evening lessons right now," I tried. "But maybe once the semester finishes."

"I'm going to hold you to that," she said, not fazed in the slightest by my dodge. She held out her hand, red lips curling into a smile. "Phone?"

I cleared my throat, so desperate for a cigarette now that I shoved my phone into her hand. She typed out her number, saved it, and handed it back to me.

"Talk to you soon, Reese Walker."

With that, she winked, slowly and purposefully swinging her hips as she made her way back to her table.

I just blew out a long breath, picking up my pace toward the kitchen. And I was almost there, almost through that swinging door when my path was blocked again.

By the one person I was trying to avoid.

"Hey, you," Charlie beamed, her cheeks pink like she'd just been walking in the snow when it was nearly eighty degrees outside. She held a smiling Daisy on her hip, and my heart squeezed painfully in my chest at the sight of them together.

At the sight of what could have been mine.

"I know you're on break, but I just wanted to bring Daisy over. She's been trying to wiggle out of my lap all evening to come say hi to you."

Charlie grinned down at Daisy, who was holding out two chubby hands toward me. And I loved that kid, I did — but now when I looked at her, I saw Cameron's eyes instead of my own. I saw the child who brought the woman I loved so much joy, and me so much pain, and I felt like shit that I couldn't be happy to see her.

It was my own fault, as much as I wanted to blame Charlie for the pain I felt in my chest while looking at her daughter. I had been the one to go to Cameron, to ask to be a part of their life after everything that had happened. Maybe, back then, I thought it would be easier. Maybe I thought the pain of being around them was better than being without them entirely.

But the biggest driving motivator was that I thought that little girl was mine. And now that I knew she wasn't, it killed me to see her.

"Hey there, pretty girl," I said, letting Daisy take my thick finger in her hand. I couldn't help but smile then, and she rattled off something that sounded almost like my name as my eyes floated back to her mother. "I thought you guys had family dinner at the house tonight."

Charlie smiled. "Yeah, so did I. But when I told them you were working and couldn't make it, Dad booked a reservation here. They miss you," she said, and then her smile slipped a little. "We all do."

Daisy freed my finger, and I tucked my hands in the pockets of my slacks, clearing my throat with my eyes on the kitchen door behind Charlie. If I didn't get a fucking cigarette in my mouth within the next two minutes, I was going to flip tables.

"I'll come over and say hello after my set," I said. "But, I just have a short break now, so, if you'll excuse me."

I nodded toward the door, and Charlie looked over her shoulder before moving out of the way. "Oh, of course. I'm sorry. I should have waited."

"It's alright. I'll talk to you in a little bit, okay?"

I didn't hold my smile or wait for her to respond before I shoved through the kitchen door, weaving my way through the mess of chefs and bussers on my way to the back. One of the sous chefs, Ronaldo, tossed me his pack of cigarettes and lighter as I passed, already well accustomed to my break times. And as soon as the warm, spring air hit my face, I lit one up, letting out a long sigh of relief after the first inhale of nicotine.

I closed my eyes, letting the cigarette dangle between my lips before puffing on it again. Each new inhale calmed my breathing, but my chest was still tight, Charlie's eyes still fresh in my mind. I tried to focus on the warm night air, on the high of the nicotine, on literally anything else.

It was like trying not to smell the delicious scent of the gourmet food wafting out from the kitchen.

There was a sinking feeling in my gut as I stood there, inhaling another pull of nicotine. I knew the time was coming when I'd have to confront Charlie, when I'd have to tell her that being around her, around her family, wasn't good for me anymore.

But how could I do that?

How could I tell her parents, the closest thing I had to family in this world, now that my own family was gone, that I couldn't be around them? How could I explain to her father, her mother, or even worse — to her brother, my childhood best friend? It didn't matter that we didn't talk all the time anymore, that our relationship had changed with the distance and time.

They had all been there for me, ever since I could remember.

And I didn't know how to say goodbye, even if it was the "healthy" thing to do.

"Do you have to do that here?"

A cloud of smoke left my lips as I opened my eyes again, and when they adjusted to the night, I had to blink several times to be sure I was actually seeing what I thought I was.

Sarah Henderson was seated on a yoga mat a few feet to the left of me, her legs folded, palms on her thighs and back straight like she was meditating. Her shoes were abandoned at the edge of the mat, pants rolled to her ankles.

It was the strangest thing I'd ever seen behind that restaurant, and that was saying something.

"Do you have to do *that* here," I challenged.

Sarah scoffed, shaking her head before she pulled in a long, steady breath and straightened her back again. Her eyes were closed, and one hand floated up to cup the crystal necklace around her neck. "I think we can both agree that what I'm doing is the healthier of the two."

"Maybe," I conceded, taking another puff of my cigarette. "But, judging by the other cigarette butts and other disgusting things littering the ground, I think we can both agree that mine is the more *normal* of the two in this space."

Sarah's eyes shot open, and as if she just noticed them, her lip curled, eyes scanning the abandoned cigarettes on the concrete around us. She let out a long breath, closing her eyes again and pulling her shoulders down and back. "Well, I needed to mediate. Sometimes I get off kilter around big groups of people. I just wanted to get centered." She held up one finger. "And before you say anything, I know work isn't the best place for that. But it's been a stressful day and I needed a minute." She paused. "And this might not be the most appropriate spot to clear my mind, but I have a feeling our boss wouldn't be too keen with me rolling out a mat next to the piano."

"Hey, I'm not the one judging," I said, cigarette between my teeth again as I held my hands up. "That was you."

"I wasn't judging," she defended, brows furrowed as she glanced at me. She shifted, her back slouching a bit before she straightened again. "I'm just saying, that's not the best thing for you."

"Trust me," I said on a laugh. "I've never been one to gravitate toward the things that were *best for me* in my life."

We were both silent then, and Sarah stretched her hands out in front of her, rolling her wrists with a grimace.

"How are your wrists feeling?" I asked, extinguishing the last of my cigarette on the concrete before tucking it in my pocket. The least I could do was not add to the butts around her.

"A little sore, but not too bad," she answered. "I've been working on that piece you assigned me Thursday night."

I nodded. "You're not pushing too hard, though, right?"

"About four hours a day right now," she said. "I could do more, but I'm trying to ease into it."

"Good," I said. "Slow and steady will win this race. I don't want you injured again before we can even work on your technique."

I watched her for a long while, content with the silence as I thought over our week together. We'd only had two lessons, but we'd kick it up to four times a week once school ended. I knew just from our first hours together that Sarah thought I didn't believe in her. She thought I doubted her abilities, her drive, her talent.

But it couldn't be further from the truth.

I saw the natural talent she possessed, the emotion she brought to the piano when she played, the technique she'd been fine tuning her entire life. Yes, her injury had set her back, and we had work to do — but it wasn't her technique that worried me most.

It was everything she held inside, everything she wouldn't release at the piano when she had the chance to.

In our first lesson, she chose such a short and simple piece, one that could showcase her talent easily without her having to dig too deep. I didn't judge her for it, most students tended to choose a piece they were familiar with, one they could play well, when I asked them to play for me at our first lesson.

But when we worked together Thursday night, when I asked her to play a piece of *my* choosing, that's when I realized the tensions she brought with her. Every muscle was wrapped tight as she played, her face devoid of emotion, though the piece was cheerful, energetic, joyful. Sarah played like she wanted to be background music, not the center of everyone's attention — like she wanted to slip away, hide behind the music rather than pour herself into it.

And later in that lesson, when I'd had her play a more dramatic, melancholy piece, she'd hidden away even more. She didn't take the pain I knew she felt and use it — she ran from it.

That would be our biggest hurdle.

"What do you think so far?" I asked when I spotted *Fight Club* sticking out of her bag next to her mat. The bookmark was about a third of the way in.

She eyed me curiously for a second before she followed my gaze, and she smiled. "Honestly, I'm just happy I got past the first chapter. I thought for sure it'd go into my *did not finish* pile, along with every other book I've tried to read this year."

"So, you like it so far?"

She shrugged. "I think so. He's got a dark sense of humor, and I love the subtle hints of minimalism. Crazy to think about how much we think we need that we really don't."

I nodded, impressed that she'd already picked up on that. "You meditate, eat plant-based food, and know the definition of minimalism. Are you sure you're only twenty-one? Because you take better care of yourself than I ever did at that age."

Sarah chuckled. "Not hard to do, judging by all the cereal at your place."

"Touché."

We fell silent then, and she slipped back into her calculated breathing while I fought the urge to light up another cigarette. I needed to get back inside, but as I watched her on her mat, I couldn't shake our last lesson — the way she'd looked at my piano, like she was about to fight it instead of play it. I'd never battled an injury like hers, but I *had* experienced the same shift in relationship with the piano. It was the most unnerving thing, to have an instrument that was supposed to be your closest friend, your easiest confidant, shift into a monster before your very eyes.

The road to rekindling that relationship was long and dusty and rough, and I wished she didn't have to travel it. But she did, and I needed her to understand what the journey would require of her.

"What are you doing tonight?" I asked when she started rolling up her mat.

Sarah stilled, her hands clamped over the rolled-up mat as she flicked her eyes to mine. "I..." She opened her mouth, shut it again, and then cleared her throat. "I mean, I work until ten."

"And after?"

She shrugged. "I'm new to town and I live with my aunt and uncle," she answered with a subdued smile. "I don't exactly have big plans."

I fought the urge to smile. "Good. I want to take you somewhere."

Sarah's eyes widened. "You do?"

"It'll be part of our lesson," I explained, checking the time on my watch. I was already a few minutes over my break, and not that I was being watched that closely, but I knew the sooner I finished my set list, the sooner I could get out of there. "Meet me here when you're done."

"Wait," she said, standing with the mat under her arm. "Where are we going?"

"I'd like to just take you there, if that's okay. Trust me. It'll make sense when we get there."

"Okay," she answered softly, but there was a hint of panic behind her wide eyes — one that made me instantly aware of how aggressive I'd been.

"Are you comfortable with that?" I asked her. "With going somewhere with me? It's a public place, and I won't keep you out too late. I promise."

She breathed a little easier then, nodding. "Yeah. Sorry, I just..." But she didn't finish her sentence. Her words faded, and she closed her eyes, smiling when they opened again. "Just know I'm bringing my pepper spray. And I'm not afraid to use it."

I pushed off the wall on a laugh, swinging the door open as the chatter from the kitchen filled the space around us. "Deal. And just so *you* know, I'm bringing my pepper spray, too."

Sarah chuckled.

"My time's up. I'll leave you to your good habit and take my bad one back inside with me."

She flushed then, and like she still had hair on her head to brush away, one hand slid behind her ear as her eyes fell to her mat. "Sorry I ragged on you."

I chuckled. "Honestly, I needed it. It's been a while since someone has called me on my shit." I knocked my knuckles once on the door, offering one last smile. "See you in a bit."

"See you," she squeaked.

My smile slipped the farther I walked into the kitchen, the temporary relief I'd found from the nicotine and my conversation with Sarah disappearing altogether once the door shut behind me. I handed Ronaldo his pack and lighter with dread settling back in my stomach.

Just a couple more hours, I told myself as I swung through the kitchen door and back into the restaurant.

My eyes involuntarily drifted to table thirty-two, and Charlie's parents waved back at me excitedly as I forced another smile, remembering what I'd run outside to escape in the first place. Cameron was smiling at something Charlie had said, and he leaned in to kiss her cheek, sending my stomach churning. I wondered if he knew I was watching, if that was the reason he'd done it.

But that wasn't Cameron.

If I knew anything about him, it was that he was twice the man I was. And truthfully, he probably didn't even care that I still existed. He'd won, after all. He had the girl. The family.

He had everything I wanted.

Just a couple more hours, I repeated.

Why did it feel like a lifetime?

chapter five

SARAH

M y father grew up in Mount Lebanon.

We'd made the trip north for nearly every Christmas when I was younger, but we'd mostly stayed at my grandparents' house or at Uncle Randall's. Exploring the city wasn't at the top of our list, especially since my father's side of the family was all the family we really had. My mom had fled from Haiti, and her parents had passed away only a few years after she'd left, so when we were fortunate enough to visit my father's family, we cherished the time.

Maybe that's why my face was pressed against the glass of the rickety old car that slowly pushed us up the side of Mount Washington, the city lights spanning out and growing wider the higher we got. The Duquesne Incline was one of the top tourist attractions in Pittsburgh, and yet I'd never had the experience.

Until tonight.

I wondered if my dad had ever sat there, in that same spot, looking out that same window. I wondered if he brought my mom there, or if my grandparents took him and my uncle when they were kids. I wondered how many generations of my family had existed in the same space I now resided in.

Somehow, I felt them all there with me.

My hands were in the pockets of my light jacket, one wrapped around the pepper spray I'd brought with me. I was pretty sure Reese thought I was joking about it earlier, but I'd been as serious as a car accident. Being alone with him in his house was one thing, but going to a non-disclosed place with him at night was another. I liked Reese. I liked the way he talked to me, the way he played piano, the way he seemed to see what others didn't.

But that didn't mean I fully trusted him.

He was still a man. And I was on my guard.

Reese sat quietly in the far corner, the two of us the only ones in the small cable car. It ran until half past midnight, which gave us just a little over an hour before we'd have to make the trip back down. I didn't know why we were here, or how any of this could possibly be tied to our piano lessons. But, I knew he wouldn't have asked me to come if it wasn't important — especially on a Saturday night. A man who looked like him, who played the way he just played in front of a restaurant packed with people? I was one-hundred-percent positive he had better offers on how to spend his evening.

But he wanted to take me here.

When the car clicked to a stop at the top, I followed Reese through the small museum and out to the viewing deck. We passed a couple who was waiting for our car to go back down, and we exchanged pleasantries as we switched places. Once they were gone, it was just the two of us again.

The viewing deck was just a long railing over the edge of the mountain, a few binoculars set up for viewing, though there was the buzz of music and conversation floating on the breeze from the little restaurants that surrounded the museum. I relaxed a little at the realization that even though we were the only two on the deck, there were other people close by.

If I needed to scream for help, someone would hear me.

I cringed at the thought, at the fact that my brain automatically went there now. Before, I would have gone anywhere with just about anyone. I was openly trusting — perhaps too much so. That was probably why it never occurred to me to be worried when my professor wanted me to do my final exam after hours, why I didn't feel uneasy at it being just the two of us at his piano that night.

I wasn't aware of the fact that I needed to be afraid, not until it was too late.

Reese slid up to the railing, balancing his elbows on the metal as a long breath left his lips, his gaze on the city. He seemed to be just as lost in his own thoughts as I was in my own.

The air around us shifted, a heavier presence settling in as I took my place a few feet next to him, my stance mirroring his. My eyes drifted to him, and it was like pain radiated off him the way heat comes from a fire. Each time the breeze blew his long hair back, I caught another whiff of it. Every edge of him was hard — his jaw, the line of his nose, the crease between his brow.

And still, somehow, he seemed soft in that moment.

I tore my eyes away from him and let them sweep over the city below us.

The lights twinkled in the distance, and I scanned the points of interest I could make out — the stadium where the Steelers played, the point where the Allegheny and Monongahela rivers met, the Fort Pitt Bridge. Below us, it was easy to see the city was alive, cars and boats weaving in and out of each other, but on top of Mount Washington, it was like we were in a bubble — like we were watching from a completely different planet.

"I used to come here all the time with my family," Reese said after a moment. He didn't look at me, his gaze still fixed on the city sweeping out in front of us. "It's crazy how no matter how old I get, the view still takes my breath away."

I smiled a little at that. "It's beautiful."

Reese nodded, a comfortable silence falling over both of us before he spoke again. "You're probably wondering why I brought you here."

"I'm a little curious," I confessed. "But, if I'm being honest, I'm just glad to be out of the house."

"Do you have any friends here?"

I shrugged. "I knew a few people when I was younger, kids I used to play with when we'd come visit at holidays. But none of them still live here. They're all in college."

I swallowed at that, my stomach twisting uncomfortably. *I* should have been away at college, too. I should have been graduating, with my sights set on higher education in New York.

I should have been so many things that I wasn't, and I tried to pretend like that didn't bother me.

"It must be hard," Reese said, glancing at me over his right shoulder. "Being away from your family and friends."

I didn't return his gaze. "I don't really have friends to miss back home," I said, voice low. The unanswered texts and calls from Reneé weighed heavy in the phone I'd tucked in my back pocket, and they all begged to differ. "I miss my mom, though. She's more like my best friend than my parent."

I paused, sadness creeping in as a warm breeze blew up from the mountain. I shook it off as quickly as it had come, letting it float away with the wind.

"But, I'm here for a purpose," I continued. "I want to be here. I have my eyes on the prize, and I know this is just a step on the ladder that will take me there."

It sounded so cliché, the way I spoke about my dream. I didn't know how to explain how badly I wanted it, how badly I *needed* to be in New York City, to play at Carnegie, to do everything I said I'd do before my wolf had changed my entire life. How could I convey that feeling, that physical *need* to excel despite what had happened to me? It wasn't just to prove my wolf wrong, or to rise up against the odds... it was to have purpose, to have something that made me feel alive again.

I was so tired of just feeling like a walking corpse, waiting to die.

Reese nodded, like he really understood as he pulled his gaze back to the city again. "Well, that's part of why I brought you up here."

It was my turn to look at him, though he kept his eyes cast toward the skyline. He was quiet for a long moment before he spoke again, as if he wasn't certain what to say now that he had my attention.

"As beautiful as this view is," he finally said. "This is a painful place for me to be."

He swallowed, the motion visible in the constriction of his throat.

"If I were a pragmatic, normal human being, I wouldn't ever come here. Ever. Because every time I do, it hurts. I mean, there is this *physical* pain in the center of my chest standing up here," he said, hand splaying over his chest to illustrate. "Like someone has their fist inside my rib cage, fingers wrapped around my heart in a vise grip."

I frowned. "Why would you come here, then?"

"Because," he answered, his hand slowly falling back to the railing. I thought that was the only explanation he was going to give, but after a long pause, he continued. "I'm *not* a normal, pragmatic human being. And neither are you." He glanced at me briefly before gazing at the city again. "We're artists. We're musicians. We're..." He sighed, shaking his head. "We're not destined to run from our misery, we're destined to bathe in it — and to somehow find a way to make it beautiful."

I leaned a hip on the railing, shifting until my entire body faced him, but I didn't know what to say. That heavy presence I'd felt when we first made it up to the incline radiated tenfold, and my heart kicked up a notch, as if it were preparing to fight or fly.

But I didn't know who or what I'd be flying from.

"I brought you here because you need to understand," he said, and he shifted until he faced me, too.

When his dark eyes locked on mine, my heart stopped altogether before thumping back to life in a quick gallop to catch up on the beats it had missed.

"In order to play the way you want to play," he said. "In order to make the dreams you speak of a reality, you're going to have to go to painful places — to the places you never want to go again." Reese swallowed. "You're going to have to look in the mirror at the worst parts of yourself, and at your past, and you're going to have to get comfortable with the scars you see. No, more than that," he clarified with a shake of his head. "You're going to have to get to *know* each scar like it's a permanent piece of every song you will ever play. Do you understand?"

For the first time since the night I left Bramlock, tears welled in my eyes — but I didn't know why. It was as if that pain that radiated off Reese had penetrated me, and that vise grip he felt had transferred to my own heart.

My wolf's eyes flashed in my mind like a bolt of white hot lightning.

"I... I don't have any of that," I whispered, mentally shaking him away. "My life has been pretty boring, I don't really have scars to—"

"I don't believe that," Reese interrupted, voice firm. "And you don't either."

My mouth zipped shut at that, and I tried to stand taller, but somehow felt rooted so deep I couldn't even gain an inch of height.

"Watching you play this week, I already know some areas we are going to have to target to help you overcome this injury and get to where you want to be." Reese leaned one elbow on the railing, holding out his fingers and counting them off with his other hand. "Tension. Technique. Inflection." He paused. "You know all those things, too. Those are the easy lessons, the ones you can go home and practice and see a gradual improvement in each week."

Reese faced me, the warmth of his breath mixing with the night air that brushed my nose. There was a bright moon above us, and it cast his face in a haunting mix of glow and shadows, light and dark.

"But, do you know what you need to overcome more than anything?" he asked.

I shook my head.

"Vulnerability."

That word hit me like an anvil, so much so that my shoulders sagged and my knees buckled from the pressure. Every part of my body reacted to the possibility that I might feel what Reese was saying, that I might open up that box that hid everything painful in my life, the one I'd worked so hard to put a lid on and shove away in a figurative attic. Those monsters stirred from inside that box, their growls rumbling through me, and I felt myself gearing up to fight them back into that box should they even think about escaping.

Reese must have sensed my unease, because he stepped a little closer, lowering his voice and his gaze to meet mine. "You sit at that piano, and I don't know who you are or what you've been through." He held up his hands. "And I don't *care* to know, because you don't make me curious enough to *want* to know. You play it like an instrument instead of like an extension of yourself," he explained. "And *that's* what is holding you back from where you need to be. From where you *want* to be."

I swallowed, finally garnering enough strength to straighten my spine. "But, I've played my entire life. I was the top of my class. I have the technique, I play with emotion," I argued. "I once made my entire class cry with an original piece. I—"

"You *were*. You *once did*. Both past tense," Reese said. "I don't doubt that you moved your classmates with the way you played, because you don't play like the twenty-one year old girl you are." He rolled his lips together, debating his next words. "You play like a woman twice my age, Sarah, but like a woman trying to hide instead of trying to share her experiences with the audience. And *that's* what they want from you — they want to feel your pain so they know their own is valid. Just like any kind of art, any kind of expression..." He shrugged. "We are all just humans who want to feel like we're not alone, even when we are."

My eyes welled more with that, and I hated that my emotion was threatening to leak out without permission. I sniffed it back, nodding in understanding as I digested his words. I was more terrified in that moment than I had been the first time I'd been inside his house alone with him, or than I had been with my hand wrapped around my pepper spray on the way up here. Because although he was telling me I was hiding, what he didn't realize was that he also told me that he saw me, anyway.

And that scared the hell out of me.

"I'm just telling you now," he said after a moment, his eyes still fixed on mine. "If you want to work with me, you're going to have to be willing to sit down at that piano and bleed." He pointed to the empty space next to us, as if the piano were right there, waiting for my decision. "Are you ready to do that?"

My heart squeezed painfully, begging me to say *no*.

"Yes," I whispered.

"Are you?"

I cleared my throat, nodding more emphatically as I quieted my pleading heart. "Yes, I'm ready. I want to do this. I..." I shook my head. "There is no other option for me, Mr. Walker. The piano is my life, it *is* an extension of me... even if I have lost a little of that connection." I hated the truth behind that, my chest tightening with the admission. "I know I have to work, and I'm ready to do whatever it takes to make my dream a reality. Even if it is outrageous. Even if every odd is stacked up against me like a brick wall." I blew out a long breath that seemed to unwind every ounce of tension around my ribcage. "Whatever it takes, I'm in."

It wasn't just for my father, who died before he could see me on that stage in New York City. And it wasn't just for my mother, who had worked harder than anyone I knew to put me through school, only to watch me drop out a semester before graduation. I owed it to both of them, to my entire family — but more than anything, this was for me.

If I didn't have the piano, I didn't have anything at all.

And I wasn't ready to die.

Reese watched me closely, his eyes flicking back and forth between mine like he was searching for any hint of doubt in that statement. Seemingly happy with not finding any, he nodded. "Good."

Once his gaze was off me and back on the city, I let out another breath, releasing even more tension, as impossible as that seemed. We were both quiet, shifting until we faced the railing again, and I let my thoughts run wild with everything he'd just said as the silence stretched between us.

"Reese?" I asked after a long while.

"Mmm?"

I swallowed. "You said this is a painful place for you to be... why?"

Reese let out a long breath through his nose, like he suspected the question was coming and was almost disappointed that it actually did.

"I was in love with a married woman," he answered nonchalantly, like he'd just said it was a nice night out. Then, he sort of laughed. "I still *am*. And this place reminds me of her, along with about a dozen other things that hurt."

A thick, sticky knot formed in my throat and I couldn't swallow it down as I stared at Reese. Maybe it was his hurt still permeating off of him and into me, but there was an icky twist of my stomach when he said he still loved her.

"I'm so sorry, Reese."

He shrugged. "Don't be. I'm the idiot who didn't leave her alone when I should have. She was married, but she wasn't happy. I thought I could save her," he said, voice low. "I thought I could make her happier."

I finally found the will to swallow. "She's lucky, to be loved like that."

Reese's brows pulled inward, and he shook his head. "God, I'm sorry I told you all of that. I shouldn't have... I brought you here to illustrate a point, not to vent about my own stupid shit."

"It's okay, really," I assured him hurriedly. "I... I know I'm just your student, but I appreciate you sharing with me." I swallowed when his eyes found mine. "Maybe it will help me share, too. Eventually."

Reese nodded, but I could see it in his eyes that he was disappointed in himself, or maybe in the fact that he was still hurt by this woman who didn't return his love. "Thanks for listening."

"Thanks for bringing me here."

He nodded again, this time pushing back from the railing. "We should go. It's late."

My heart sank at that, but I knew without even looking at my phone that the last three buzzes were likely my uncle checking in on me. I hadn't come to Pennsylvania looking for friends, but I'd have been lying if I said I didn't wish I could say at the top of that mountain with Reese a little while longer.

Questions raced through my mind like hamsters on a squeaky wheel as we made our way back down the mountain in the cable car. Reese was quiet, lost in his own thoughts as he gazed out the window, and I watched him in a whole new way. I wanted to know more about him, about the family my aunt had mentioned — the photograph on top of his piano — and more than I cared to admit, about the married woman he loved.

Did she live here? Did he still see her?

And why did I feel so invested in the way he felt about her?

It was almost like a pinch of jealousy that jabbed at my stomach as I watched him, like I was envious of a woman who could bend Reese Walker so out of shape like that. It was ridiculous, I knew, because he was my teacher. He was nearly twice my age. He was a man, and I was a girl, and he was there to help me surpass my injury and fine tune my technique. That was where we existed, in that small realm.

But when he looked at me, his eyes dark and sad and searching for *something*, those lines blurred. And I didn't look away. I didn't run from the heat his gaze brought inside that tiny cable car. If anything, in that moment, I realized I *wanted* him to find whatever it was he was looking for. I wanted him to find it when he looked at me.

And somehow, though I couldn't digest it fully, I knew that was a very, *very* dangerous thing to desire.

chapter six

REESE

"Killin' 'em out there tonight, Walker," Ronaldo said the following Wednesday as I passed him in the kitchen, tossing me his pack of cigarettes and lighter. His hair was longer than mine, weaved into small braids and pulled into a thick wrap at the base of his neck. He had to finagle two hairnets together to get all of it tamed enough for the kitchen, and he flashed me a cocky grin as he adjusted it. "I can smell the panties from back here."

I laughed, pausing to pull a cigarette from the pack before handing it back to him. I tucked the one I'd taken behind my ear with a shrug. "Ladies love Chopin," I explained. "It's just science."

The pan Ronaldo was tossing around went up in flames, and he tossed faster, shaking his head with a smirk. "How the hell are you still single, bro? Literally every single woman in that room would pay good money to be the one on your arm," he said, nodding toward the dining area. "Including the married ones."

That comment struck a nerve, but I smiled in spite of it, shoulders lifting again. "Ah, they *think* they want to be the girl on my arm, until they realize how fucked up I am."

"We're all fucked up," Ronaldo said, face screwing up like that was an obvious statement and not at all a reason to stay away from someone. "At least you have panty-melting piano skills and the jaw of a Greek god to combat the crazy."

"Are you hitting on me, Ronaldo?"

He held up his finger and puckered his lips, making a clicking noise with his mouth. "You wish, honey."

I just laughed, plucking the cigarette from behind my ear and holding it to him in a thanks. "I'll try to ease my bruised ego with nicotine."

"Here, take another for your broken heart."

He tossed me a second cigarette, and I was still chuckling when I shoved my way through the back kitchen door. I lit the cigarette as soon as the evening air touched my skin, letting out an exhale of relief like I always did after the first drag. It was slammed inside, which was unusual for a Wednesday night, but with summer sneaking up on us, everyone in the area was eager to be out and about. After a long winter of mostly staying in and retreating from the cold, Pennsylvania always came to life with the warm weather.

Of course, it being busy in the restaurant didn't really affect me. I'd play whether there was one person or one hundred. Still, the energy buzzed me to life inside, and exhausted me once the night was over. No matter how tired I was after work, I still had *more* work to do. Not only were we in final preparations for the end-of-the-year concert at Westchester, but I had another lesson with Sarah tomorrow, and I needed to prepare.

I sucked in another breath of nicotine and tobacco, finding comfort in the familiar taste as I thought about her, about the Incline. I'd taken her there to prove a point, to try to show her the kind of vulnerability she needed at the piano. I expected it to be emotional, and I expected it to be hard on both of us.

I *didn't* expect to tell her about Charlie.

I also didn't expect her to listen.

She was the first one I'd told, though I knew the entire staff at Westchester and half the town of Mount Lebanon had their suspicions. There were rumors about what had happened between me and Charlie, between Charlie and her husband. But rumors were just that — rumors. Hearsay. No one knew the truth.

Well, except now, Sarah did.

What surprised me most wasn't necessarily that I told her, or that she'd listened. It was that she didn't look at me with pity once I'd let the words slip out. If anything, it almost seemed like she respected me, which I couldn't quite place.

Regardless, I'd gotten my point across. I'd shown her vulnerability, and explained that she'd have to do the same if she was to get where she wanted to be.

And I'd be lying if I said finally talking to someone about Charlie didn't bring me a relief I didn't know existed.

Smoke left my lips as I shook my head, that relief a joke compared to what tension still existed. Even *thinking* about Charlie made my chest tight, and that just made me feel pathetic. To make matters worse, she'd been assigned to work on the end-of-the-year concert with me again. She'd been blowing up my phone all week, trying to get together to discuss some details, but I'd been avoiding her.

I couldn't wait until school was over, until I didn't have to see her every day in the halls of Westchester.

Summer break couldn't come soon enough.

I leaned against the brick wall of the building, crossing my right leg over the left as I took another drag of my cigarette. I lazily scanned the employee parking lot, not really seeing anything, just existing, relaxing, taking a break. But when I noticed a familiar face, I did a double take.

Sarah wasn't supposed to be here, Wednesday being her night off, and yet there she was, not even a full fifty-feet away. She was barefoot on her yoga mat again, wearing her work uniform, but she wasn't meditating this time.

And she wasn't alone.

One of the bus boys at The Kinky Starfish had his apron slung casually over his shoulders, his arms folded over his chest as he said something that made Sarah laugh. My chest pinched at the sight of her cheeks flushing, the same way they had the first night she'd met me.

Sarah's stance mirrored his, her arms crossed in the same manner, and the way she shifted her weight side to side told me she was nervous.

I realized the longer I stared, the more I should have looked away. They were having a conversation, one I wasn't a part of. But I found I couldn't look anywhere else now that I'd seen her.

I recognized the kid the longer I watched them. It was Danny Caruso, the owner's son. I didn't know much about him, but from what I did know, he was a good kid. He treated his mom like gold and was a hard worker around the restaurant. He went to college and still managed to pick up extra shifts when people called out. I didn't really know him, but he'd always been nice to me.

I couldn't place my annoyance with the way he was staring at Sarah.

He waved goodbye to her after a few minutes more, and I lit up the second cigarette as I watched him walk away, making sure Sarah was safe. I had no reason not to trust Danny, but Sarah was young, and new to town. I didn't want him taking advantage of that like most guys his age would.

Like I would have when I was that young.

Sarah bent to pull on her shoes once Danny was gone, rolling up her yoga mat with a smile that stretched from ear to ear when she stood again. It was almost as if she was laughing at an inside joke she had with herself, or maybe it was something Danny had said, something she was replaying.

Whatever the case, that smile slipped when she saw me.

I took a drag from the cigarette hanging between my lips as she made her way toward me, mat under her arm. She stopped when there were a few feet between us, and I glanced over her shoulder, watching Danny pull out of the parking lot.

"Hey," she said on a breath.

"I thought you were off tonight."

Her smile slipped even farther, brows tugging together. "I was... they called me in."

I nodded, taking another drag. "You know Danny?"

Confusion washed over Sarah's face before she followed my gaze to where she and Danny had been standing. "Uh... yeah, kind of. I mean, we work together." She paused, facing me again. "Obviously."

"What were you guys talking about?"

The question left my mouth before I had the common sense to stop it, and once it was out in the air, I couldn't take it back. I aimed for nonchalance, leaning against the brick wall and flicking the cherry off my cigarette. It was just an easy question. I was just making conversation.

Sarah lifted a brow. "He asked me on a date."

I sniffed, bracing the sole of one shoe on the wall behind me. "He's a good kid."

She watched the smoke floating between us for a moment, adjusting the mat under her arm before her eyes found mine again. "He is."

"So, when are you going?"

"I'm not."

I frowned. "What do you mean?"

"I'm not," she said again with a shrug. Her dangly earrings moved with the gesture, and I realized I'd never seen her wear them before. She was always so natural — no makeup, no accessories — but tonight, she wore two long, flowy, sparkly earrings. "I told him no."

"Why?"

Oh my God, stop fucking talking.

Sarah shook her head, face twisted up like she was as uncomfortable as I was. I didn't know why I was being weird. I was her teacher, but if anyone had seen us in that moment, they'd have thought I was a protective older brother. I didn't have any right to be so invested in her safety, and judging by the look on her face, she felt the same.

"I don't know," she finally said. "Because I don't want to."

I waited for her to explain more. *Did she already have a boyfriend? Was Danny not her type? Did he creep her out?*

My jaw ticked.

Did he make an unwanted move on her?

Frustration seeped through me as I reminded myself, yet again, that I didn't have a right to ask any of those questions. I sucked on my cigarette, instead.

"Are you okay?" Sarah asked, searching my face. "You seem... irritable."

Great. And now I was creeping her out.

I blew out a breath, snuffing what was left on my cigarette and tucking the bud in my pocket to throw away inside. "Sorry," I said. "Just been a weird week. I should get back inside. I'll see you tomorrow night?"

Sarah frowned. "Yeah, see you tomorrow."

I gave her one last curt nod before ducking back inside, tossing Ronaldo his lighter and making a beeline for the piano. I needed to play, needed to work my muscles in a way that felt familiar and safe. I felt like an animal, triggered by the need to protect a girl who I knew without a *doubt* did not need my protection.

Maybe it was that I'd opened up to her, that I'd let her in. Maybe that vulnerability had caused me to feel some sort of unnecessary connection, some strange need to ensure she was okay. Either way, judging by the smile she had when Danny left, she was just fine.

I didn't have an explanation for my sudden awareness of her, or my bizarre behavior. All I knew was that by the time she showed up to my house for our next lesson tomorrow night, I needed to box away whatever the hell that just was and be professional.

As I sat down at the piano, hands moving on autopilot over the keys, I repeated that sentiment over and over until I slipped away into the music, into the night, into another dimension.

I needed to get out of my head.

And that's exactly what I'd do.

SARAH

"Relax."

Reese's voice was soft, gentle, mixing with the notes I played on his piano. He didn't yell and there wasn't an ounce of attitude laced under his request.

Still, I had to force a stiff inhale to keep from screaming at him.

I played *Sentiment* by Robert Gafforelli, each note strong and romantic, dripping with emotion. My wrists felt good that day, and I was doing everything I could to lay myself bare at his piano. That's what he had requested I do that night he took me up the Incline, and that's what I had promised him.

It had been nearly two weeks since that night, and every lesson with him, every night I went home to practice on my own, I felt myself getting stronger. Still, he watched me each lesson with a quirk in his brow that unnerved me, like he was disappointed, like there was something missing.

It was maddening.

I saw him every Tuesday, and Thursday night for lessons, and starting next week after school let out, we'd add Sunday and Monday, too. When we weren't at his house, at his piano, I saw him mesmerizing the crowd at The Kinky Starfish.

It seemed every facet of my life was tied up in Reese Walker in some way.

When we were on top of that mountain, I'd seen a side of Reese I knew for a fact he didn't show anyone. And ever since then, that version of him had been put under lock and key again. The first couple of lessons we'd had after that felt heavier, like by asking me to be vulnerable, he'd agreed to do the same. But just as quickly as that wall had come down, it was up again, and we were back to only talking about piano and music and tension and technique.

We didn't talk about the Incline, or that night, or the woman he loved who was married to someone else.

And even though that was normal, and that was what our relationship as teacher and student should have been, I couldn't get the *other* version of Reese out of my mind.

There were so many layers to him, so many sad, broken, busted-up pieces that made the man who sat down at that piano every night and left the residents of Pittsburgh speechless with his musical ability.

I'd only gotten a glimpse, but it was enough to make me crave more.

"Relax, Sarah," he said again, this time a little firmer as I moved with the music.

I blew out a breath, closing my eyes and focusing on the notes I brought to life. I felt the keys under my hands, the pedal under my foot, the music in my soul. That song was meant to be played with emotion, and I felt it — I truly did.

Until Reese told me to relax again.

I huffed, tossing my hands up in the air as the song came to an ugly end, the notes dying all at once as soon as my hands were off the keys.

"Damn it, I *am* relaxed!" My chest heaved as I found Reese standing in the corner of the room. He was leaning against the wall, in the shadows, like he wanted to disappear and leave me alone with the piano.

Except he kept interrupting me.

He just watched me as I tried to steady my breathing,

not affected in the least by my outburst. "Clearly," he finally said, kicking one foot off the wall behind him. He crossed the room until he stood next to the piano, and he pointed one finger down at the keys I'd abandoned. "Try again."

"I think I need a break."

"Just... try again, Sarah," he said, voice softer. "Please."

His eyes were patient, but tired — like my own. Still, even with what seemed like the weight of an entire lifetime resting in that expression he wore, he was handsome. Tragically so. And though I'd noticed the beauty in his music, in his playing ability, that was the first time I noticed the beauty in *him*.

For a moment, I wondered what he had looked like when he was my age, before life had creased the skin around his eyes. He was still dressed in the teacher get up I assumed he wore the entire day at Westchester — khaki slacks, dark brown chukkas, a navy blue button-up with the sleeves shoved up to his elbows, the top two buttons unfastened, tie hung haphazardly on the chair in the corner of the room. His long hair was pulled back in a loose bun at his neck, just the slightest bit of stubble peppering his strong jaw.

I wondered how many young middle school girls had his name sprawled across their notebooks, outlined with little hearts.

I sighed the longer he looked at me, finally rolling my shoulders a few times before my hands hovered over the keys again. I closed my eyes, steadied my breath, and began to play.

I hadn't made it twenty seconds in before Reese spoke.

"I can feel your tension from here."

"I'm not tense," I almost sang, forcing a smile as I

continued to play. I opened my eyes and glanced up at where he stood as my fingers still moved over the keys. "I'm relaxed, and if you'd stop talking, you'd be able to see the emotion in my playing, too."

"Not with every part of you wound up like that, I won't."

He moved until he stood behind me, and I frowned, still playing but with a bit of nerves now that he was out of sight. I still felt the heat of his body radiating off him and warming my back as I closed my eyes again. The song was sad and slow, and I found myself considering what the composer felt when he created it, when these notes were sewn together and a new piece of music was born.

"The technique is there," Reese said from behind me while I continued playing. "And I see you closing your eyes, see the way your face twists with each note, like you feel it, like you've lived it."

He paused, and I nearly missed a note when his hands found my shoulders, light and easy, without any pressure or demand.

"Relax," Reese said.

Relax, I heard another voice say in the back of my mind. It was a darker voice.

The voice of my wolf.

I flinched away involuntarily, the notes crashing together chaotically before I picked the song up again.

"Sorry," I murmured, my next breath burning on the inhale. I could still feel the heat of his hands, even though they were gone now, back at his sides.

Reese was quiet a moment before he cleared his throat. "No, no, I'm sorry. I should have warned you. I, uh... I just want to illustrate something. Is that okay?"

I nodded, though my heart was galloping like a wild

stallion in my chest. I focused on the music, on not missing another note as his hands came down to rest on my shoulders again.

The instinct to pull away again was strong, but the warmth of his hands, of his care, permeated through that instinct the longer he held the touch. It was gentle, easy, and light — like he was ready to pull away again if I said the word.

He's not your wolf. He won't hurt you.

"Like I was saying," he continued when I didn't pull away. "The technique is there. But, with your shoulders tied up to your ears like this, I don't believe it. And I don't *feel* what you want me to feel."

Gently, he pressed his palms down on my shoulders, his thumbs pressing into the muscles that framed my spine, and I let him guide me until my shoulders were back and relaxed. I somehow felt the weight of his hands everywhere in that moment, like he'd slid them down over my collarbone and ran them the length of my back at once. Without him even instructing me, a long, breathy exhale left my chest, and every muscle relaxed.

"See?" he said, a tone of satisfaction in his voice like he'd made his point.

I couldn't register much at the moment, other than the fact that someone was touching me, and I was okay with it.

"Stop playing for a moment," he said, removing his hands.

Chills broke over every inch of my skin at the loss of heat, but I did as he asked, straightening as he took a seat next to me on the bench. And just as quickly as that heat had been stolen, it was back again, his leg just barely grazing mine under the piano. My stallion heart picked up speed again as I stared at that point of contact, nearly racing out of my chest completely before I finally scooted over a few inches, putting space between us.

"Okay, place your hands on the keys like you're about to play," Reese instructed, oblivious to my inner freakout.

I did as he said, pulling my focus back to the lesson.

"Now, relax your elbows, like you would if you were resting and not playing."

I looked down, surprised to see that I was holding my elbows out from my side. When I relaxed, they dropped in, and my shoulders fell with them.

My eyes widened.

"Press your hands on top of this piano," Reese said, demonstrating with his own massive paws sprawled out on the wood.

His knuckles were white from pressing down, and I copied him, pressing my own hands on the wood.

"Now, release."

When I did, I felt the ease of tension up to my shoulders again. "Wow," I breathed.

Reese nodded, hands falling back to his lap. "You're always going to be battling sore muscles if you don't learn to relax while you play. If it's not your wrists, it'll be your shoulders. If it's not your shoulders, it'll be your fingers. Have you ever experienced pain in your right pinky?"

I gaped at him. "Oh my God, all the time, actually."

He nodded again. "You curl it when it's inactive instead of letting it rest, and that's putting too much tension on the muscles keeping it wrapped up like that. It's like gripping a pencil too tight and writing a two-thousand-word essay."

I stretched my hands out in front of me, feeling the

stiffness as if I really had been gripping a pencil too tightly.

"We can work on that next," Reese said. "I have some finger exercises, some ways to practice relaxing the muscles you're not using. But for now, I want you to try that song again, and this time, check in on all of those areas I just pointed out. As you play, *actively* relax your shoulders, your elbows, your wrists. Let them flow *with* you, with the music." He raised both brows. "Okay?"

He was so close, sitting there on that bench beside me, that I noticed the gold flecks in his otherwise emerald eyes. They'd always seemed so dark to me, like they were brown or almost black. But there they were just a few inches from view now, green and gold and everything I never saw before.

I nodded. "Okay."

Reese stood, making his way back to the corner, and I felt the loss of his heat like taking a jacket off in the middle of a blizzard. A shiver ran through me, but I ignored it, resting my hands on the keys a moment and mentally touching all the places he'd just pointed out before I began to play.

"Good," Reese said when I was almost to the chorus. I glanced over to see him nodding, his thumb and forefinger framing his chin as he listened. "Much better."

There was a knock at the door, and Reese's eyes darted to it the same as mine. We both glanced at each other, Reese's brows tugged inward before he pushed off the wall.

"Keep going," he said, disappearing into the foyer.

I did as he said, mentally checking my shoulders and elbows before ascending into the next verse, but I craned my neck to get a better look when I heard a woman's voice at the door. I couldn't stretch back far enough to see who was there without my hands coming off the piano, but I could see

Reese, and his hand was gripping the back of his neck like it was the only thing keeping him grounded at that moment.

He stepped back, and I got a flash of a purse swinging through the door before I ripped my gaze away and pretended I hadn't taken my eyes off the piano. Reese stepped back into the room, and right behind him was a petite little brunette who had to be around his age. She was slight, like a bird, her skin a creamy porcelain white and eyes wide like saucers. Her bright smile doubled when she saw me, and she clasped her hands together, watching like I was what she'd come for.

My eyes found Reese, and he held my gaze for a short moment before clearing his throat and dropping his eyes to the piano.

I watched him a moment longer before offering the woman a tight smile, then I pulled my attention back to the piano, and focused on relaxing as I finished the song. When the last note played, I chanced another look in Reese's direction.

And he was smiling.

I did it.

"Beautiful," the woman said before Reese could speak, and I pulled my hands away from the keys, smiling at her again. She clapped softly, lifting her steepled fingers to her lips when she was done. Her eyes were wide with adoration. "That was just... stunning. So moving. So slow and sweet and romantic. You're quite good, Miss Henderson."

She knows me?

I folded my hands in my lap, noting Reese's furrowed brows as he glanced between me and our new guest. "Thank you."

"That was much better," Reese finally said. "*Much*

better, Sarah."

I couldn't help the way my smile spread at his words, at his affirmation. I could feel his pride like it was swelling in my own chest.

"Thank you," I said again, cheeks warming.

The corner of his mouth quirked up, but it fell quickly, his eyes flashing to our guest before he cleared his throat again. "Sarah," he said, gesturing to the woman. "This is Charlie Pierce. She's a teacher at Westchester, and a long-time friend."

His lips flattened with the end of that sentence, like the word *friend* tasted bitter on his tongue. And when my eyes snapped back to the woman, to Charlie Pierce, to the soft, sweet eyes and shining smile — everything clicked into place.

It's her.

There was no other explanation for Reese's sudden tension, for how he looked like he wanted to crawl out of his skin all of a sudden. He wasn't introducing me to Charlie the way he would an *actual* friend. The introduction was laced with a sense of foreboding, and when he glanced at me again, the plea in his eyes was all I needed to put the puzzle pieces together.

I stood, smoothing my hands over my long, burgundy skirt before extending one toward Charlie. "Nice to meet you, Mrs. Pierce."

"And *you*, Miss Henderson," she said, shaking my hand firmly. "Your uncle is a good friend of mine, too, and he loves to brag about you. Of course, in the photo he showed me of you earlier this week, you were maybe fifteen." She assessed my appearance with a genuine smile, and I hated that I couldn't find an ounce of malice in the stare. For some reason, I wanted to hate her — but she wasn't giving me a single reason to. "You have certainly grown into a beautiful young lady."

The smile on my lips felt foreign and weak. "Thank you. Let me guess, the picture... was it the one of me in the pink dress?"

Charlie dropped my hand and smiled. "I take it he's not the only one who loves that photo, huh?"

"My whole family has that one framed," I replied with a roll of my eyes. "Probably because it's the only time they've managed to wrangle me into anything pink since I was seven."

Charlie chuckled at that, and I didn't miss the amused smirk on Reese's face in my peripheral. I shifted on my toes, folding my hands behind my back as both mine and Charlie's eyes drifted to him.

He shifted his weight uneasily, like he'd missed a cue. "Uh, Charlie was just stopping by to discuss the end-of-the-year concert we have next week," he explained.

"Because *someone* has been dodging my calls," she teased him, nudging him with an elbow. In her eyes, you would have thought they truly were close friends, like she could tease him like that without a single thing being weird or feeling off.

His eyes told a different story.

"We've worked together on it the last few years," Reese explained. "And when Charlie heard you playing from the foyer... well, she had a great idea."

I lifted one brow, first at him and then at Charlie, who was practically bursting as she waited for him to continue. When he didn't speak fast enough, she spoke for him.

"We'd like you to open the concert this year."

I blanched. "*Me?* Isn't it for current students?"

"It is," Charlie affirmed. "But, you're the headmaster's niece, and part of the family. It'd be such a treat, the parents would love it, your uncle would be so excited to show you off, and I know the kids would love to see someone so talented play." She bounced a little, hands wrapped around the purse still hanging from her arm. "What do you think?"

I glanced at Reese, and he offered a tight smile. "It would be a good chance to practice in a performance atmosphere."

His words were solid enough, but I didn't miss the pained crease between his brows at the near proximity of Charlie. It was like he was holding his breath or breathing in straight smoke, and he wasn't going to have another clean breath until she was out of his house.

Suddenly, that became my only mission.

"I think it sounds like a great idea," I said, more to Reese than to Charlie.

"Wonderful!" she said, smile doubling at me before she turned back to Reese. "Well, again, sorry I interrupted your lesson. I just wanted to go over those last details since I won't be back in the office until Monday."

"It's no problem at all. Here, let me walk you out." Reese extended one arm toward the door, the opposite hand hovering close to Charlie's lower back. He didn't touch her, though, and I wondered if he was afraid it'd burn if he did.

I stood rooted to the spot as Charlie said her goodbyes at the door, and when Reese rounded back into the room, he stopped at the door frame, leaning against it with his hands sliding into the pockets of his slacks. His eyes searched mine, but he didn't say a word.

"That was her, wasn't it?"

The only indication that he'd heard me was the slight bob of his Adam's apple, and the barely visible crease between his brows.

My heart broke staring at him in that moment, seeing the pain that still crippled him when she was near.

"You *work* with her?" I asked after a long pause. "You see her every day, and you talk to each other... and... are you *friends*?"

Reese blew out a long breath, pushing off from the wall and crossing to where I stood. At first, I thought he was going to run right into me, blow me over like a stick in the wind, but he swept past, sitting at the piano behind where I stood.

"It's complicated," he said, hands already floating over the keys. It was like he needed to touch the piano in that moment, to let his hands do something familiar and comfortable now that he'd been shaken by Charlie's unannounced visit.

"I'd say."

I took a seat next to him, listening as he played, watching his face and wondering what the hell was going on in that dark, guarded mind of his.

"We were friends as kids, but there was always something more... we both knew it," he said, eyes on his hands. "When I left for New York, for Juilliard, she asked me to kiss her. And I didn't." He swallowed, like that was the biggest mistake of his life. "And when I came back, she was married."

He shook his head, hands picking up speed where they played.

"She wasn't happy, not when I first came back. I hated it, hated seeing her so miserable, seeing her husband so unaffected by her visible pain. But, of course, once I showed up? Her husband *woke* up. He fought for her," Reese said, hands pausing over the keys. They kicked back to life with his next words. "And he won."

I swallowed, watching his fingers flick over the keys, bringing a familiar melody to life. It was the one he'd played the first night I'd met him at The Kinky Starfish.

What had he said it was called again? *The Darkest Dawn?*

"But," Reese continued after a moment. "I'm still close with her entire family. Her parents are like the *only* family I still have, if I'm being honest."

My eyes floated up to the one and only framed photo in the room we sat in, the family that stared back at Reese as he played. The man in the photo looked like Reese in ten years, and the woman standing next to him shared Reese's smile. The girl in the photo, the one standing next to Reese, had his eyes.

And though I didn't have details, I now had confirmation of what I'd always wondered.

They were gone.

His family was gone, just like my father.

"And yes," he said, still playing that soft, sad melody. "We work together. So, I see her a lot. I see them *all* a lot."

"All?"

He nodded, a sickening expression sweeping over his face. "Her. Her parents. Her husband," he explained, pausing again before he dropped another bomb. "Her kids."

"*Kids*?"

At that, he stopped playing, running his hands back through his hair with a huff. "Alright, that's enough for today. We can pick up on this next week."

Reese stood without another word and blew out of the

room, leaving me alone on the bench. My eyes scanned the photo of the family on top of the piano, and I took a steadying breath before standing to follow.

He was in the kitchen, downing a glass of cold water as I slid onto one of the barstools. He wouldn't meet my gaze, just stared at his hands splayed on the granite between us, and I knew in that moment he felt ashamed. Something told me he didn't open up like this to anyone, that maybe I was the first one he'd talked to about Charlie.

And I heard him in my head, asking me to be vulnerable, to sit down at his piano and bleed.

I knew I wouldn't be able to if I didn't start opening up, too.

"I've never been in love," I whispered.

Reese looked at me then, the crease between his brows softening. "Never?"

I shook my head.

He stared at me for a long moment, like he wasn't sure what to say. But the longer he looked, the more his shoulders relaxed. I hoped the change in subject was a welcome relief.

"I honestly find that incredibly hard to believe," he said, standing straighter as he watched me.

I wrapped my hand around the crystal hanging from my neck with a shrug. "Yeah, well, the piano was the only boyfriend I ever really had time for. I prioritized it over everything, including any social outing that might have somehow landed me in a romantic relationship. The only boyfriends I ever had were the dukes and kings and princes in my favorite books."

Reese smirked. "That's what makes you different, you know that right?"

"What, the fact that I tanked my social life so I could

focus on piano? And still do?"

"Exactly that. I mean, look at me. I have the talent. I was born with it, as unfair as that is. It just always came naturally to me. And I *love* playing, I think that's obvious." He shrugged. "But, I wouldn't make the sacrifices to get anywhere with it. There's a reason I have my masters from Juilliard and I'm a teacher at a prep school in Pennsylvania, playing at The Kinky Starfish for extra cash."

"You didn't want it," I assessed.

And he agreed. "I didn't want it. Not bad enough to do what it takes, anyway. For me, just being able to play piano and make enough to pay my bills has always been enough. Past that?" He shook his head. "I didn't have the drive you do. And that's what makes you different. It's what will make you successful."

I smiled, crossing my arms over my chest as my eyes fell to the granite, a blush spreading on my cheeks. "Thank you."

It was strange, hearing such a genuine compliment from my teacher. The first few teachers I worked with were harsh, showing their love in the way they yelled at me or demanded more from my playing. And I accepted that, because I just assumed that's how it worked. The same was true when I went to Bramlock, when I started working with the professor who would ultimately drive me to injury.

I swallowed, his face clear in my mind as that box I'd shoved him in creaked open.

"So," Reese said, pulling me back to the moment. "Is that why you said no to Danny when he asked you out?"

My chest tightened, thoughts still caught back on a warm night in December in north Florida. I shook them away, clamping my figurative hands on the lid of the box threatening to open and spill out all over the counter between us. I considered for the briefest moment being honest in my response to Reese's question about Danny, considered telling him the truth. But I didn't know where to even start. I didn't know how to tell Reese — or anyone — what had happened to me.

And there was no point in telling anyone, anyway.

I'd learned that lesson.

"I can't really say yes to anyone right now," I said, voice soft and low. "Right now, it's just about the piano for me."

And I can't stomach the thought of anyone else touching me because the only one who ever has didn't ask me before he did.

I felt Reese's eyes on me, and I knew he wanted to ask more questions. I knew he saw the same pain in me that I saw in him. And maybe that was the only reason we saw it at all — because we lived it. You had to understand what that felt like to be able to recognize it, like there was an exclusive club for the eternally heartbroken.

"You did good today," he said after a moment. "We're making progress already, and it's only been a few weeks. So, just know your dedication is paying off."

I smiled, making a noise with my next breath before popping off the barstool and looking at Reese. "Awesome. Looks like I have a prayer of saving my long-term relationship with my piano boyfriend, after all."

Reese chuckled at that, and we slipped back into easy conversation as we went over my homework until we saw each other for our next lesson. He walked me to the door, the same way he had with Charlie, and I climbed into my car with my chest still tight.

I stared at the wheel with the key in the ignition but not

turned for what felt like a lifetime, Charlie's eyes in my mind just as much as my professor's.

Reese and I shared a similar pain, but there was a difference — because he didn't run from his.

I'd fled Bramlock the morning after my professor assaulted me, too much of a coward to even tell my roommate that I wasn't coming back. And here was Reese, living day in and day out with the woman he loved, the woman who didn't love him in return, prancing around him and reminding him of everything he had lost.

They worked together.

He was a part of their *family*.

Reese thought *I* was the dedicated one, the strong one, the driven one. I may have given up what was necessary to chase my dream, but it was *him* who was strong. It was him who was dedicated.

He loved that woman so much that he put himself through a daily self-flagellation just to keep her in his life.

I didn't know how to feel about that. I didn't know if I was even allowed to feel anything at all.

But as I turned the key and backed out of his driveway, it was the only thing on my mind.

chapter seven

REESE

The following week, Sarah stood beside me backstage at the end-of-the-year concert with wide eyes and hands wringing together like she wanted to squeeze the sweat out of them.

"You're going to be fine," I assured her, straightening one of my students' ties. He smiled up at me when I was done, scampering off to join his friends as I stood again. "And once you hear these kids play, you'll understand why you shouldn't be nervous at all. They're still learning basics."

"I'm not nervous," she finally said.

I cocked a brow. "Those three words are the most you've said since you got here."

Sarah smiled, letting her shoulders relax a little. "I'm just excited. It reminds me of my recitals when I was younger. I mean, we did shows at Bramlock, but I couldn't ever get excited about those, because they were always for a grade. You know?" She shrugged. "Today, I just get to play for me."

"You get to play for you," I agreed with a nod. "You know, it's been so long since I was in school, I almost forgot that pressure. Of course, for *me*, it wasn't bad — mostly because I didn't give a shit about anything."

Sarah smirked.

"But, for *you*? For someone who cares and wants to excel?" I shook my head. "I can't even imagine that kind of pressure. And your uncle told me your professor at Bramlock was Wolfgang Edison. He's a legend, an absolute legend. I mean, his parents even named him *Wolfgang*," I added with a laugh. "He was literally born to play. I'm sure that was a lot of added pressure, being taught by him."

I glanced over at Sarah, and when I did, my smile slid from my face like a runny egg. Her wide, cat-like eyes were doubled in size now, like she'd seen a ghost, and her face was pale and long. She didn't respond to my assessment, and my stomach sank with the realization that I'd said something wrong, said something to make her nervous when she'd been only excited.

"Sarah?" I reached for her, but she cleared her throat and moved away from the touch. I still had that hand extended toward her when someone else's hand clapped me on the shoulder.

"Ah, another year come to an end," Mr. Henderson said, sidling up beside me. "You know, this concert has only gotten better since you've been with us, Reese. I was just talking to some parents out on the floor, and they all agree."

Sarah was staring at the piano on the stage — the one waiting for her — like it was a bomb she knew would detonate at any moment. She wouldn't look at me, and my stomach sank further as I tore my gaze from her, forcing a smile at her uncle, instead.

Way to fucking go, Reese.

"I'm just thankful to be here," I said, sliding my hands in the pockets of my slacks.

"Ah, we're lucky to have you," Mr. Henderson said. He always looked like he'd just indulged in a glass of wine, his cheeks high and rosy, smile a little too wide as he turned his gaze to his niece. "And we're *extra* lucky to have *you*, Sarah. It's been so long since I've watched you perform..." He shook his head. "How old were you last time? Fifteen?"

Sarah blinked, but otherwise, didn't acknowledge her uncle's question.

I cleared my throat, leaning toward Mr. Henderson. "She's a little nervous. Why don't we give her some space to get ready, I wanted to go over the program with you one last time, anyway."

He winked conspiratorially, offering one last *break a leg* to his niece before we made our way farther backstage. I glanced over my shoulder at Sarah, hoping she was relieved to have us gone, but she didn't move an inch.

She was still staring at that piano.

I should have been focusing on what Mr. Henderson was saying as we roamed around backstage, should have had my attention fixed on Charlie as she trotted over to us with last-minute changes. But all the while, I listened to them and spoke to them with my mind on an earlier conversation.

I ran through everything I'd said to Sarah, wondering where I'd gone wrong. I wondered if just talking about Bramlock made her uncomfortable, if it reminded her of her injury. Or maybe she missed her professor. I knew *I* would have seen me as a downgrade from Wolfgang Edison, but it had been Sarah who'd asked her uncle if he could get her lessons with me. She'd been the one to ask for me by name.

Still, something I'd said had rattled her. And I felt the weight of that guilt as her uncle introduced her on stage, bringing the concert to a start. It was too late to do anything about it now. All I could do was hope I hadn't messed her up too bad, hadn't shaken her confidence so much that it'd show in her playing. It didn't stop me from feeling like an ass as I tucked myself behind the stage right curtains, watching the light and shadows play on her face as she took her seat on the bench.

The room applauded politely, and Sarah smiled briefly at them before tilting her head to each side and stretching her wrists out in front of her. She rolled them twice, and when she dropped them to the piano, her eyes caught mine for the briefest second.

That second felt like a lifetime.

I didn't believe in a god, but if there was one, I was sure he'd touched the hand of time then, holding it still, stretching one second until it felt like hours. I'd also have sworn he'd unveiled my student in that slow stretch of time, that he'd helped her remove a mask I didn't even realize she was wearing — perhaps, no one did.

Sarah Henderson may have been my student, and she may have been my boss's niece, and she may have been sixteen years younger than me. None of that changed the fact that she was irrefutably the most beautiful entity to ever grace that stage.

Her long lashes graced her high cheeks as she blinked, eyes watching me from where I stood backstage. Those eyes were dark and deep, like an endless pool of emotion that had yet to be locked down with a word to describe it. Her full lips parted in a breath, her shoulders pulling away from her ears as she relaxed, and I found myself taking a breath with her. As usual, she was dressed modestly, covered from collarbone to ankle in the flowy dress she wore. But for the first time since I'd known her, she wasn't wearing black or burgundy or navy blue. This dress wasn't dark at all. It was bright, cheery, a mustard-yellow that painted her like a sun. The contrast of color made it hard not to appreciate the unique umber shade of her skin, the dark freckles that speckled her cheeks — and the crystal that hung from her neck sparkled in the light like a tiny chandelier.

Why was it that I hadn't seen her, not really, not until that exact moment?

All of that hit me in the one split second she held my gaze, and then, the hand of time kicked back in gear, and her eyes descended to the piano. In the next breath, her hands began to move, and I slipped away with her to another planet.

I'd listened to Sarah play in my home for the last month. I'd watched her sit there at my piano, her brows furrowed and delicate fingers stretching out over the ivory keys I'd played on for years. But in all those times, I'd never seen her *play*. We'd been practicing, working on technique, focusing on tension, tackling the hurdle of emoting while working.

That wasn't how she played on that stage.

For the first time, I *felt* the song Sarah was playing. We hadn't discussed which one she would choose, but as she played through the slow, melancholy notes of Liszt's *Hungarian Rhapsody*, I felt all the things that made me human slip away like she'd stripped me bare — along with the rest of that audience. Her body moved in time with the rests, her eyes closing in the most powerful moments before shooting open as her fingers moved quickly over the keys.

The song started with these long, dramatic and deep notes with purposeful rests, but as the song stretched, so did her fingers, picking up tempo and flying over the keys in what seemed like an impossible feat if you were anyone who hadn't been studying piano your entire life. I knew the kind of concentration it took to accomplish the musicality of the piece she was playing, and somehow, she made it seem effortless, like her hands were moving of their own accord and she was just the body that hosted them.

She was spectacular.

Time shrank away with her on that stage, and before I could grasp what we'd seen, what we'd heard, Sarah was standing and the crowd was cheering in a deafening roar. Her uncle screamed from beside me, his pinkies shoved in his mouth as he whistled around them, tears glossing his eyes.

I scanned the audience and found he wasn't the only one moved to tears.

The entire room was on their feet, many of the parents blotting wetness from the corners of their eyes. I knew Sarah had moved them, and perhaps they were even envisioning their own children being able to play like her one day. I wondered if they'd ask me, if they'd inquire if their kids stood a chance to do what she'd just done.

And I wondered if I'd have the heart to tell them there wasn't a chance in hell.

We may have only been working together for a month, but it was long enough for me to know that no one worked as hard as Sarah Henderson. She would make it not just because of her talent, but because of the sheer drive she had to get to where she wanted to be.

Sarah was an unstoppable force, like a Category 5 hurricane, and we'd all just been wrecked by her power.

When she finally made her way backstage, the crowd still cheering, her uncle wrapped her up in a bear hug while talking a thousand miles a minute. It was actually quite comical to watch, since she was taller than him. I just stood to the side, letting them have their family moment before Mr. Henderson scurried back out to the stage to introduce the first group of students.

It was just me and Sarah, then.

She worried her bottom lip as her eyes found mine, one hand floating up to clasp her crystal necklace like she'd find the thoughts in my head if she rubbed it hard enough. "Well?"

I laughed. "*Well?*" I tucked my hands in my pockets and took a step toward her, shaking my head. My voice was low, meant for only her to hear when I spoke again. "You were sensational, Sarah."

Her cheeks flamed, that bottom lip slipping from between her teeth as she smiled. She let out a long, exaggerated breath, like she'd genuinely been worried. That just made me laugh harder.

"I *felt* it, Reese. For the first time since..." She paused, swallowing. "Since my injury, I sat down at that piano and wasn't afraid of it. I was ready — ready to bleed, to be vulnerable, to trust the keys again."

I nodded, because I knew that feeling — that sensation of coming *home* again. It wasn't the piano that ever changed, or ever left. It was the human who played it that shifted over time. And sometimes, that made it hard to ever come back together, to ever find that same relationship.

Sarah had found hers again, even if it was different than before. And I knew more than anyone what it felt like to find that joy again when everything seemed hopeless.

"I know," I said, smiling at her bouncing joy. "I felt it, your reconnection."

"Thank you," she breathed, then her brows tugged together. "That was it, wasn't it? A sort of... homecoming."

I smiled wider then. "I think so."

Her eyes were bright and shining, and she bit her bottom lip against a giant smile before shaking her head, like she was afraid to feel joy over how she'd just played, like she was afraid it wasn't real.

I knew that feeling, too.

"Any notes?" she asked, a sort of cringe on her face now.

"A few, but we can go over them on Monday. Tonight, be proud of how you played. It was truly magical to watch."

Sarah narrowed her eyes, like she still didn't believe I'd enjoyed her performance. I held my steady, confident gaze as her eyes searched mine.

Then, before I could register what I was doing, I pulled my hands from my pockets and opened my arms.

Sarah swallowed, and for the longest time, she just stared at me — like I was a stranger offering her poisoned candy instead of her teacher offering her a hug after a performance. My chest tightened, and I wondered if I'd crossed a line, if I'd assumed it was an appropriate celebration when it wasn't.

But I *wanted* to hug her. It didn't feel wrong to me.

I was just about to drop my arms and apologize when she took a tentative step forward.

Her hands lifted, wrapping around my upper back in a light, awkward graze. I wrapped my own arms around her, and then, with a gentle laugh, her long, slender body relaxed in my arms. Her hands slid up, draping around my neck, and she squeezed me tight, a relieved sigh leaving her lips.

"Thank you, Reese," she whispered, and it wasn't until she spoke those words that I realized how close we were, that

I felt her presence like a weighted anvil pressing down on me from every angle. "Thank you."

My hands were on her lower back, and I swallowed as my fingertips brushed the small sliver of skin exposed by the back of her dress. It was the most skin she'd ever shown, and I hadn't even noticed it until that exact moment that our skin connected. I swallowed, hands splaying over the bare space, reveling in the smoothness of it.

Sarah stiffened in my arms, and her reaction snapped me back to reality.

I pulled my hands away, clearing my throat as we both stepped back from the hug, Sarah's arms immediately crossing over her chest once they were no longer around my neck. Her eyes flicked between mine before falling to the ground between us, another blush shading her cheeks.

"I haven't felt that good playing in a long time," she said. "I think we're making progress."

"We are," I assured her. "*You* are. And now that school is out, we'll have more time to work on the areas you're struggling with. Which, if I'm being honest, aren't that big."

"If I want to play at Carnegie, they are. You and I both know it."

I sobered at that, because as beautiful as her performance had been, Carnegie Hall was a whole other ball game.

"We'll work on it. Like I said, we have more time now that school is out."

Sarah's eyes floated somewhere behind me then. "Are you going to miss it?"

I followed her gaze, a knot the size of a rubber band ball forming in my throat at the sight of Charlie. She had her hands clasped together near her smiling lips as she watched the performers on stage. Even being a mother of two now, she was still so slight, so small, like the birds she loved so much. A familiar pain zipped through my chest, but somehow, it didn't hurt the way it had even four weeks ago.

When I turned back to Sarah, I tried not to question why.

"Not at all," I answered.

And it was the truth.

⸻

I'd never been much for routines.

When I was studying in New York, I'd often skip classes to wander aimlessly around the city, convinced that watching the people who lived there and taking in that concrete jungle for all that it was would have more of an impact on my piano playing than listening to some stuffy professor would. And after, though I had a steady job, I never filled my time *outside* of work in the same way. Every day was different. To me, routines were synonymous with comfort and complacency, and those two C words were the death of artists.

Of course, after the actual death of my family, everything changed.

I slipped into a routine in Mount Lebanon because I had no other choice. If I didn't get a grip on something in my life, I was going to float out into space and never come back to Earth. I believed that as much as I believed there was no religious entity that could save a shitty soul like mine. And so, Westchester became my routine. And it wasn't until last summer that I realized without it, I found myself slipping into old bad habits.

Like drinking before noon and well into the night, or sleeping until most people were eating lunch.

But this summer was different.

This summer, I had Sarah Henderson.

After the recital, we fell into a routine, and I found myself depending on it just as much as I did the one I had during the school year. Every Monday, Tuesday, Thursday, and Sunday I was with Sarah. Every Wednesday, Friday, and Saturday, I was at The Kinky Starfish. If I wasn't playing piano, I was teaching it. And if I wasn't with Sarah or at work, I was *preparing* for the next time I would be.

My time was filled with purpose, and that's exactly what I needed.

Not seeing Charlie was the icing on that routine cake. It wasn't that I didn't love her, that I didn't want her to be happy, or that I didn't want to spend time with her family. But something over the past few months had helped me realize that I was far from healed, far from moving on from what had happened between us.

As much as I wanted to be her friend, I wasn't *ready* to be her friend. That was just all there was to it.

Still, I wasn't exactly ready to *get out there* and start dating, either. Jennifer Stinson was no stranger to my text messages, making sure I remembered that I'd promised her an evening together once school was out. But I'd tried dating in the aftermath of Charlie, and all it'd done was enhance my depression and make me want to throw my phone into a dumpster and set it on fire.

Filling my summer with piano was much more appealing.

So, I kept pushing off the date, telling Jennifer I was wrapped up, but that we'd make it happen. Eventually.

Non-commitment suited me well.

And as for my time with Sarah, it was becoming more and more specialized. We'd still work on technique and tension, on scales — though those were becoming almost obsolete as I gave Sarah more challenging pieces to play. The truth of the matter was that we'd reached a point where it was less about what I could teach her, technically, and more about what she still needed to learn musically.

It was becoming a matter of *sensational* versus *Carnegie Hall phenomenal.*

And it was almost impossible to explain the difference until she got there on her own.

"Ugh!" she screamed one afternoon, tossing her hands up in the air before her elbows landed hard on the keys, her face burying between her hands. "I suck. I suck, I suck, I suck."

I chuckled, taking a seat next to her at the piano. "You do not suck."

It was a beautiful day outside, the sun shining and a cool breeze cutting through the heat that big star in the sky brought. We had all the windows open, the fresh air sweeping in, but it did nothing to calm Sarah in that frustrating moment.

I'd been there.

She removed her elbows with a pouty lip as I started to play the piece we were working on, one that challenged her reach. "We only have ten fingers to play with," I said as I played, Sarah's eyes on my hands. "You know the scales. You know how to get to the notes that need to be played, but sometimes, that knowledge works against you. Sometimes, you have to play a little unconventionally to achieve what you desire."

Her little mouth popped open as my fingers moved across the keys like ice skaters on speed, hands hopping over one another in a way that would have made any piano pedagogue cringe.

"The *way* I'm playing right now is wrong," I said, foot tapping on the pedal below us as my fingers stretched and curled. "But no one sitting out in that audience gives a fuck about technique. They care about the music, what they're hearing, and what they're *feeling*." I nodded toward her. "Close your eyes."

She did, inhaling a long breath through her nose as she relaxed.

"Listen," I commanded.

I worked through the piece, taking artistic liberties in my favorite sections, and when Sarah opened her eyes again, they were wide with wonder. She watched my hands to the finish, and kept her gaze on them even after I'd pulled them back into my lap.

"You're a freak," she whispered.

I barked out a laugh. "Wow. No need to abuse the teacher, Miss Henderson."

She rolled her eyes.

"The difference between what you just did and what I just did has nothing to do with me being a freak," I said, still smiling. "It has everything to do with me playing the piano, versus the piano playing *me*."

Sarah frowned, eyeing the musical beast we sat at like it had offended her. I tapped her temple, and she looked back at me.

"You know how to play," I said. "You know the music, the scales, the keys, the notes. You have all of that knowledge, but you don't trust it. You think about it *every* time you sit down to play instead of trusting that your fingers will catch up to your mind if you just let it run free." I shrugged. "Who *cares* if the way you play isn't technically correct, if it leaves the audience stunned and begging for more?"

She nodded, but her brows were still furrowed, and I could see the doubt lining every crease of her skin.

"Look," I said, turning more toward her. My left knee touched her thigh with the motion, and her eyes flicked down before she looked at me again. "Certain trees yield certain types of fruit, right? No matter what you do, an apple tree is never going to give you lemons."

She nodded.

"Well, that's how it is with the piano. It will never help, nor hurt you. It will give you exactly what it has always given you, time and time again. It doesn't change." I leaned down a bit, capturing her gaze. "But *you* do. You learn and grow, and become better. In the same breath, though, I'll point out that you are also a product of what has happened to you on the specific day you sit down to play, as we all are. If you approach the piano impatiently or impetuously, it's going to show. But, if you come intelligently, patiently, and with an open mind, an open approach to how you play?" I shrugged. "Well, you might just be lucky enough to be called a freak by one of your students one day."

Sarah closed her eyes on a snort-laugh, shaking her head. I chuckled, too — but that noise died in my throat when she opened her eyes again.

Her gaze lingered on mine, both of our smiles slipping away as an unfamiliar weight pressed on us. She'd never looked at me like that before, though I couldn't place what was different about it. All I knew in that moment was that I couldn't look away.

She glanced at my lips, and in the first time in two years, a line of heat scorched a path from the back of my neck all the way down my spine. Warnings flashed in bright, hot neon somewhere in my mind, but they were muted, the present moment too loud to hear anything else.

Sarah's lips parted, her next breath touching my own, and it was like that whisper of air broke the spell I'd been under.

I swallowed, breaking all contact as I stood and crossed the room.

"Work on this piece tonight, and we'll try it again tomorrow," I said, pretending to look through the folder that held my lesson plans. My heart was thundering under my ribcage so loud it might as well have been the percussion line in a high school band.

Sarah didn't move at first, and when she finally did, it was like she was in a daze as she slowly gathered her things and packed them away in her messenger bag.

She slung it over her shoulder, and I turned, smiling at her like everything was fine. "See you tomorrow?"

"See you tomorrow," she said, returning my smile, but I felt the uncertainty of it as she turned and let herself out.

As soon as she was gone, I dropped the folder on top of the piano with a *slap*, taking a seat on the bench with my hands running back through my hair.

What the actual hell, Reese?

It made sense for Sarah to look at me like that, to *think* that she maybe wanted to know what it felt like for her teacher to kiss her. It was normal. She was a young girl, we were spending nearly every day with one another, and we both had to be vulnerable to work together. It was the nature of the agreement we'd entered into.

But it was *my* responsibility not to let it go past that.

Maybe she had a crush. I involuntarily smiled at that, and then shook my head so hard I nearly broke my neck to reprimand myself.

No.

I said that one word as loud as I could out loud, then repeated it mentally as my hands moved to the keys, playing nothing and something all at once. It was similar to the song I'd played after the first time I'd met Sarah, but something in it had shifted, revealing a more dramatic, emotional element beneath the notes than I'd originally played.

I let myself get lost in that melody, in that piece of music being brought to life by my hands. And all the while, I reminded myself where our boundaries existed.

Maybe she had a crush. Maybe she wanted to kiss me.

Maybe I wanted to kiss her.

I let out an audible growl, playing with more gusto as I shook my head again.

No, Reese.

I thought of Charlie, of her and Cameron, of the way I'd given my heart to her even though I knew hers wasn't for the taking. Sarah was off limits to me in the same manner. She was my student, and she trusted me to be her teacher — nothing more. I wouldn't take advantage of the vulnerable place I had her in, in the time she was forced to spend with me.

I wouldn't mistake that vulnerability for actual feelings, because I'd learned that lesson once before.

And once was all it took.

A crush was one-sided, as long as I didn't entertain it. And *that's* what I had to remind myself.

It was in my hands, our relationship. I had to draw the lines, trace them with a permanent marker, and constantly be the one to point them out. It didn't matter that I wanted to kiss her, too. It didn't matter that every day made it more and more impossible to look at her and see a girl, a student, instead of the captivating young woman and artist she was.

I existed in her life to help her reach her goals in piano, and that's what I would do. It was my job. It was my responsibility — both to her and to myself.

I liked our routine. I liked being her teacher, and I liked that she trusted me to teach her. *That* was what mattered most. That was what I would do anything to protect.

And I sealed that sentiment with the last notes of a song she was creating inside me.

One she'd never know about.

chapter eight

SARAH

I tried to let go, tried to focus on my breathing and nothing else as I followed the guidance of Deepak Chopra. His voice was calming, smooth and steady as it floated through my Bluetooth speaker. He asked me to set an intention, to repeat that intention when other thoughts made their way into my meditation. My mom sat on her mat in Atlanta, meditating with me over a video chat, and I even tried to channel *her* focus in an attempt to keep my own.

But for twenty-two minutes, instead of clearing my mind and re-centering my spirit, all I did was think about Reese Walker.

It was the first day in a full month that I hadn't seen him. If I wasn't sitting in his home, at his piano, I was watching him play as I bussed tables at The Kinky Starfish. But, today was Wednesday, which meant no lessons. And I had the night off from work, too.

I had no idea what to do with myself.

Though it was still technically spring, summer seemed to be in full bloom in Pennsylvania now that school was out, and I often played at Uncle Randall's piano with the curtains drawn so I could watch all the life happening outside the window. There were mothers pushing their newborns in strollers, laughing as they caught up on the latest gossip. There were kids riding their bikes up and down the street, dogs chasing their wheels, cars slowly passing by with camping gear strapped to the top. The weather was hot, the days were long, and everyone, it seemed, was happy.

Myself included.

Maybe it *was* just the long, warm, spring-almost-summer days that had lifted my mood, or maybe it was that I felt my wrists getting stronger, my hands stretching farther, my playing ability shifting into something it had never been before. Maybe it was that music was alive again for me, that it was speaking to me instead of lying there like some heavy, dead thing any time I tried to find comfort in it.

I was finally sitting down at the piano and finding joy again instead of fear. I was finding comfort instead of anxiety. I was feeling like I was home instead of just wandering this Earth aimlessly.

Something inside me had shifted since working with Reese Walker.

And maybe *that* was the real reason for my happiness.

I shook him out of my head with an exasperated huff near the end of our guided mediation, anxious to get through the last few minutes so I could talk to my mom.

Happiness shouldn't have made me feel so uncomfortable, but it was such a foreign feeling now, one I never thought I'd get back.

I found that happiness scared me more than numbness did.

So, I spent the entire mediation trying to figure out *why* that was. If my mother knew what had happened at Bramlock,

I imagined she'd peg it down as something near the lines of Stockholm syndrome. I was abused by my piano teacher, and since I hadn't worked through the tragic ramifications of that, my stupid female brain was latching onto my *new* piano teacher as a safety net.

But it felt like more than that.

But it *couldn't* feel like more than that.

The meditation closed with a soft *ding* and a salutation from Deepak, and as soon as the closing words left his lips, I closed the app and let my legs flop out in front of me with a sigh.

Mom chuckled from her mat in Atlanta, opening one eye and then the other. "I take it you had a hard time clearing your mind today, *mwen chouchou?*"

"Can you ever be unhappy about being happy?"

Mom frowned a bit at that, stretching her arms over head before exhaling them back down to her sides. "That's a very interesting question," she assessed, and I watched her therapist brain kick into gear as she chewed the inside of her cheek. "It's possible that, in an effort to *be* happy, you're making yourself even more unhappy. As in, you could be focusing so much on trying to be what everyone else is, what everyone else wants you to be, that you just do more damage than good."

I shook my head. "It's not like that. I just..." I sighed, eyes floating up to the ceiling as I tried to explain it. "I feel good here, *Manman*. All I'm doing is working, practicing with Reese, and playing on my own. But, it's like in the past couple of months, everything has changed. My attitude. My skill level. My outlook on the future."

My inability to be turned on... until recently.

I left that one out, mostly because the surprise of it had shocked me into a daze when it'd hit me. I could still close my eyes and see it — that long, suspended moment where I sat on Reese's piano bench, staring at his lips.

Wishing I could taste them with my own.

It was the first time I'd felt anything even remotely close to desire since the night I'd had my innocence ripped from me like it was nothing. And of course, I'd felt it for the absolute last person in the world I was supposed to.

The left corner of Mom's mouth inched up, a light sparking in her eyes — eyes so much like my own. "It's a rebirth," she said.

I frowned, digesting the word.

"Sarah, when you came home from school in December, you were not the young lady who had left for school in the fall," Mom explained, rolling her shoulders back and down as she considered her words. "And I don't know what happened. I don't know why you came home with the decision that you were never going back, or why you threw out every bright color you'd ever owned in exchange for darkness, or why you wanted to shed weight — so much so that you even shaved your head." She swallowed at that, but her face wasn't one of disappointment — only one of understanding. "What I *do* know is that just as the trees shed their leaves and went dormant for the winter, so did my daughter."

My heart ached at that, at the suffering I knew I'd put my mother through when I'd quit school. I couldn't tell her why, not without upsetting her over something neither one of us could change. That was just the way the world was set up.

Justice didn't favor rape victims. And there was no changing that narrative.

Still, I hadn't given her any kind of explanation for why I'd dropped out, shaved my head and donated nearly all of my clothes before shopping for an entirely new wardrobe. I didn't know how to explain to her that I didn't want to be seen, that I only wanted to exist at my piano, that I only needed to be alone with what music I could still wrangle out of my bruised and bloody heart.

In the process, I'd broken hers, too.

"When you told me you wanted to stay with your uncle and study with this Reese Walker, part of me was worried. Part of me wondered if you'd lose yourself further, if you'd slip away from me even more than you already had." Though her words were sad, she smiled, her hands floating to heart center as she pressed her palms together. "But, you have soared, my love. Your smile, it's brighter than I've seen it in months. Your eyes, they are wide again with possibilities." She tilted her fingertips toward me. "You have been reborn, *mwen chouchou*. And like a baby fawn, you're trying to learn to walk on very unstable legs. Take your time. Be patient. And know that it's okay to smile, to be happy." She chuckled. "Even when you're falling down."

Something stirred low in my belly when I thought about it, when I realized all Reese had done for me without even knowing. He didn't know how broken I was the first day I stepped into his house, or how much I doubted my own self before he even heard me play, before he told me how hard the road ahead would be.

But just like he promised that first day, he was in my corner.

And in my corner he had stayed.

Every day, I strived to see that little spark of pride in

142

his eyes, that quirk at the corner of his mouth when I did something impressive, something he'd taught me. Earning a *good job, Sarah* from him was my new favorite pastime, and it'd fueled me with purpose.

Purpose.

That was what I'd been missing before.

"Now," Mom said after a moment. "Tell me who the boy is."

My eyes shot open, heart picking up speed under my ribcage like a locomotive. "What?"

Mom smirked. "It's not just music making you feel uncomfortably happy," she mused. "Who's the guy?"

I tried shaking my head, but my cheeks warmed, betraying my verbal insistence that there was no guy.

Mom just quirked one brow.

I sighed. "I mean... I guess, there kind of *is* a guy, but... we can't... he's kind of unavailable."

"Does he have a girlfriend?"

"No," I answered, picking my nails. "But, he's just..."

My voice faded, because I had no idea how to even allude to the fact that the one and only male who could possibly be having an effect on my happiness was my piano teacher.

Mom smiled knowingly, rolling off her mat before carefully folding it up. "There are some situations when mothers aren't the best source of advice," she said. "Maybe you should call your roommate from Bramlock. I know she'd love to hear from you."

My stomach twisted, months of unanswered texts throbbing at me like they were alive in my phone. When I'd left Bramlock, I'd left everything and every*one* behind — including my roommate and closest friend, Reneé. I'd stopped posting on social, deleted my accounts altogether after a month, and I knew my mom's heart wasn't the only one I broke over the winter.

Reneé was my friend, and I'd blown her off. I'd blown *everyone* off. But, at the time, it felt like the only thing I could do. It felt like survival.

Fight or flight. And I flew.

"I don't know if I'm ready for that..." I whispered.

Mom's brows furrowed, but she offered a knowing smile. "Okay. Well, I'm here if and when you do decide you want to talk about it. Until then, try to meditate on it." She gave me a pointed look. "*Actually* meditate, not overthink."

I laughed.

"I think it will help."

"I think you're right," I agreed, hand floating up to my crystal. I rubbed the smooth sides of it, thoughts still whirling. "I had a dream about Dad the other night."

A familiar shade of sadness passed over my mom's face, one that mine favored more and more the older I got. "Oh?"

I nodded. "I wish he could see what I've been working on, that he could hear how I play now." I paused. "I wonder if he'd be proud of me."

"He *is* proud of you," Mom assured me, a soft smile touching her lips. "And he does hear you. He's with us, even when we feel alone."

I nodded, but my heart ached with the yearning to have him *actually* here with us instead of metaphorically. I didn't have the heart to tell my mother it wasn't the same, but then again, I believed she already knew.

"I miss him," I whispered, still rubbing the crystal.

"I miss him, too."

A heaviness settled over us, but it was interrupted as Uncle Randall swung through my bedroom door with barely a knock to announce he was coming in. He smiled at me, and that smile doubled when he saw Mom's face on my computer screen.

"Farah! What a lovely surprise. How are you, my dear?"

Mom smiled, but the edges of it were tight after what we'd been discussing. I wondered if seeing Uncle Randall was as hard for her as it was for me sometimes. He had the same eyes my father had, and the same too-wide smile.

"I'm very well, Randall. How are you?"

"Ah, can't complain," he said, rubbing his belly. "Especially after eating three of your sister-in-law's lemon poppyseed cupcakes." He turned to me then. "Don't worry, I left the vegan ones for you."

"I'm sure that was so hard for you."

He chuckled. "Very tempting, I assure you."

Uncle Randall chatted with my mom for a bit as I thought over all she'd said, wondering if her assessment of me having some sort of rebirth could be true. I *did* feel different, and I did feel more alive than I had since December. Still, it felt like there was this part of me that would always lay dormant, like there was a section of my heart and soul that I would never be able to bring back to life, no matter how I tried.

When Mom ended the call, Uncle Randall hung his hands on his hips, watching me fold up my yoga mat. "So, how have your lessons been going?"

"They've been going really well, actually," I said as I stood, tucking my mat away behind the post of my bed. "I think we've really hit a stride."

"It seems that way. You know, you're smiling a lot more than you were when you first got here."

His words manifested a smile in real time. "I've noticed that, too."

"Have you noticed that Reese has *also* been smiling more?" my uncle asked. "I know you didn't know much about him when you came here, but, he's been through a lot. It's nice to see him not as... *moody*." He shook his head. "I swear, that man has a knack for bringing down everyone's cheer when he walks into the teachers' lounge. It's like his gray cloud rains on anyone he gets around."

I laughed, but couldn't ignore the sting in my chest as I imagined a literal cloud pouring down constant icy rain on Reese. It might as well have been the truth, for what he'd been through. I didn't know the details about his family, but I knew they were gone. Add in the fact that he still had to see the woman he loved, the woman who *didn't* love him in return, on a daily basis?

I didn't know how he was still standing.

Realization trickled down my spine like water from a leaky faucet.

Maybe part of my discomfort with my newfound happiness came from it feeling so one-sided.

Reese had helped bring me to life, had given me a new purpose, new goals to chase and new recognition when I achieved them. He'd transformed the piano for me, helping me tap into feelings I'd been trying to subdue, to run away from. And in the process, I'd found joy again in the one thing that had always mattered most to me.

My relationship with the piano was on the mend. And it was all thanks to him.

I wanted to do something for him, too.

A flash of us sitting together at his piano sparked in my mind again, and heat rose on my cheeks as I remembered the way the air had grown thicker, the way I'd felt when I realized how close his lips were, how easy it would have been to touch them with my own.

I almost rolled my eyes, knowing it was a childish thing to desire. It was all too cliché that the first male I fantasized about in months and months of my libido being deceased was my ridiculously attractive and irreversibly broken piano teacher. We were spending all our time together, putting ourselves in vulnerable situations, opening up to each other so we could take that vulnerability and transfer it to our music.

I didn't *actually* want to kiss him, I convinced myself. But, maybe I *did* want to repay him somehow, to help him find a new happiness the same way he'd helped me.

And as my uncle dragged me to the kitchen to indulge in my aunt's famous baking, I realized I knew just the way to do it.

———

"You need a dog."

Reese paused where he'd been pouring me a glass of water, the Brita pitcher still suspended mid-air and glass half full as he glanced at me from across his kitchen island. "What?"

"A dog. You know, the furry, four-legged things that wag their tails and lick your face? You need one."

He blinked, watching me a moment more before he turned his gaze back to the task at hand, filling my glass to the top. He filled his own next, stashing the pitcher back in the fridge before he acknowledged what I'd said.

"I don't need a dog."

"I firmly disagree."

He chuckled at that. "I haven't had a pet my entire life, Sarah."

"*What?*" I blanched, not bothering to hide the dramatic drop of my jaw. "You never had a pet? *Ever?*"

Reese shook his head.

"A dog? Cat? Rabbit? Hamster? Fish?"

He just kept shaking his head as I listed off all the possible pets he could have had in his lifetime.

"That's absurd," I finally said, still shocked. Then, I held my head higher, straightening my spine where I sat. "And all the more reason for you to get a dog."

Reese slid my glass of water toward me with an amused smile. "Dogs are a lot of work. I can barely keep myself alive, let alone another living, breathing thing."

"Right, because you're just *so busy* that you don't have time to pour dry food into a bowl or open that door to let a dog outside while you smoke your cigarette." I pointed at the sliding glass door between us and his backyard in example, but Reese just watched me, taking a sip of water.

I huffed, verbally confirming the frustration I felt inside. I had thought all night about the proposition, about what I could do to bring a little joy into his life. A dog was a great stepping stone. It was a step forward, a new relationship, a new beginning.

I had to make him see that, too.

"Look, it's been two years since everything went down between you and Charlie. You go to work every day with her, see her happiness, and sometimes even spend time with her family. Her *entire* family," I pointed out, and Reese's face sobered at that. "And then, you come home to this big, empty house that's entirely too large for a bachelor. It's sad, and as much as the *broody, broken sad boy image* might be great at getting you laid, it's time to make some moves forward. And a dog is step number one."

Reese's brows had slowly climbed the more I talked, and they shot all the way up into his hairline when I mentioned him getting laid — which, admittedly, had also made me blush fiercely once I'd realized what I said.

"Does *broody, broken and sad* really come off as appealing to the opposite sex?"

I rolled my eyes. "Like you don't know that that... that... *thing*," I finally said, hand flying up toward his face. "That you do with your eyebrows is ridiculously enchanting."

He smirked. "I do a *thing* with my eyebrows?"

"We're getting off topic."

"I think I like this topic better."

I shook my head, biting my lip against the smile that threatened to break. "*I* think we should go to the shelter and adopt a dog," I said firmly. I pulled my shoulders back, eyes meeting Reese's with confidence. "Today."

Reese's amused smile warped, concern etched in his features as one hand reached back for his neck. "Honestly, Sarah — I really don't know the first thing about taking care of a dog."

My heart picked up a notch when he said my name like that, like I was his closest friend in the world. It wasn't *Miss Henderson*, but *Sarah* — like we were friends.

Were we friends?

"I'll help you," I assured him. "And, it's not as hard as everyone makes it seem. I promise. You don't travel a lot, you have a great house and a big backyard. You're home plenty, especially in the summer, and you can hire a dog walker during the school year."

Reese's face screwed up like he still wasn't convinced.

"Come on," I begged, sliding off the barstool and rounding the counter until I stood in front of him. "Imagine having a fluffy, adorable, overeager dog greeting you at the front door every time you walked through it. And someone to cuddle with at night."

My neck warmed when that last sentence slipped out, but I didn't apologize, though it was the second slightly inappropriate comment I'd made that afternoon. Instead, I waited with my hands clasped together under my chin, hoping he'd say yes.

For a long moment, he just stared at me, eyes bouncing between mine as he tapped one finger on the counter like a drum. The longer he looked at me like that, the more I felt like a silly little girl. He didn't want a dog. He'd said as much, and his face was echoing the sentiment now. It occurred to me that my idea was kind of stupid, childish, and he was probably just trying to figure out how to say no without crushing me.

Like I was his child instead of his student.

My hope dwindled when his brows tugged inward, and my shoulders sagged, head following suit as I prepared to accept defeat. I was just about ready to climb into my shell of embarrassment and hide away for the rest of our lesson when he spoke.

"Okay."

My head popped up again at his response, eyes wide and hopeful. "Really?"

"Let's go get a dog."

I squealed, jumping up and down before I threw myself at him in a hug of joy. I didn't even think twice about it, about touching him, about *being* touched. All I could think in that moment was that I had won. He was going to get a dog, and it was going to make him happy whether he realized it yet or not.

I'd help him find joy, just the way he had for me.

He laughed when I launched at him, catching me with an *oomph* that faded into a heavy silence once we both realized I was in his arms, his hands at my waist, mine around his neck.

My traitorous eyes fell to his lips again, and my already hot neck nearly caught fire before I managed to slip out of his arms and put a few feet between us. I toyed with the crystal around my neck, heart beating in such an unfamiliar rhythm that I wondered if it was still my own.

"You want to go now?" Reese asked. "Before our lesson?"

I nodded, teeth bared in an unsure grimace. "Can we?"

A smile touched the creases of Reese's eyes as he watched me, like I was too adorable for him to say no to. If there was even a chance that was what he was *actually* thinking, I was going to hold that face for as long as it took to convince him.

"Alright, alright, stop looking at me like it's *you* who's getting the damn dog," he grumped, taking another long drink of water before conceding. "I'll drive."

"Yay!" I jumped in the air again, fist high before I skittered off to grab my bag, following Reese toward the front door. "This is going to be great. You'll see."

Reese shook his head with a smirk, but my smile only grew wider as I bounded out the door and into the passenger seat of his car.

He was going to get a dog. He was going to get a dog because *I* suggested it. He was going to get a dog, and all I'd really had to do to convince him was assure him I'd help him with it. And at the bottom of all that, I only saw one truth.

Reese Walker trusted me.

And I wouldn't take that for granted.

chapter nine

REESE

I needed a cigarette.

Every cell in my body ached for one as I stood rooted to the spot at the end of the first hallway of dogs, their barks ringing in my ears. Sarah must have sensed that I'd stopped, because she looked back over her shoulder once she was a few rows down. When she saw my face, she laughed, rolling her eyes and making her way back to me.

"Come on," she said, crossing her arms over her chest. The movement framed her beloved crystal in such a way that it was all I could stare at, like somehow it'd bring *me* peace the same way it did her. "They won't bite." Her face screwed up then. "Well, actually, I can't really promise that. Maybe don't go sticking your fingers in cages until we talk to someone."

That got a little laugh out of me, and I blew out a breath, scratching the back of my neck as my eyes wandered the hall behind her. "There are so many of them."

"I know," she said, voice softer this time. "Kind of sad, huh?"

I nodded.

Sarah watched me as I took in our scenery, the gray walls and black wire that made up the dog cages not doing anything to bring me comfort. It felt like we were in a prison, and being that I already felt that way by living in my fucked-up mind, I found I really didn't need a physical representation.

"Hey," she said after a moment, stepping toward me. She moved her head to the side until my eyes met hers, and then she smiled, the curl of her lips comforting and sure. "If you want to leave, we can go. I didn't mean to push you into anything. I just... I just thought this might be a good thing, to get a dog, to have a friend at home. And, you know, to get one lucky guy or girl out of here."

She looked around then, a shade of sadness passing over her.

My chest tightened as I watched the hope in her eyes slowly die at my refusal to move. There was something holding me back, and I hated that I couldn't place it. I wanted to let Sarah in, to tell her that I didn't mean to be the grumpy old man that I'd become — though saying I was *old* was a stretch at just thirty-seven.

Still, I was acting like an eighty-nine-year-old stuck in his ways.

The truth was I was scared.

But I didn't know how to tell her that, so instead, I blew out a long breath, shaking the doubts from my mind. I would have plenty of time to decipher them later. For now, the only mission I had was replacing that look of despondence on Sarah's face with one of excitement, like the one she'd wore when we'd left my house.

"So, we just walk through and..." I stopped, not knowing what else to say.

Sarah's smile returned at my words, and she nodded. "We just walk through, and if we want to bring any of them out to play, to get to know them a little more, we let a volunteer know."

I nodded, sliding my hands into my pockets. Then, without another word, I started walking.

The shelter had provided one-sheet facts about each dog, pinned to the wire that separated us from them, and I scanned those words as I passed each kennel. Some of them were born there, some were found on the streets, but the ones that really broke my heart were the ones who'd been surrendered by their owners. They were too wild, too energetic, too much trouble or, in some cases, simply too old for their owners to keep them any longer.

The more I thought about it, the more my blood boiled.

"How could anyone just give up their family pet," I said when we'd turned the corner down the second hallway of dogs. "How could they just... I mean, aren't pets sort of like family after a while? I can't speak from experience, but..."

Sarah nodded from where she walked beside me. "I could never have given up Molly."

"Molly?"

She smiled, but it was a sad smile, one that didn't reach her eyes. "My cat. Daddy got her for me when I was three, and I had her all the way up until my senior year of high school. I swear, that cat followed me everywhere. And don't get me wrong," she said, holding out her hands. "She was a little shit. But she was *my* little shit. And I loved her, up until the very day she left this Earth." She folded her arms around herself in what was almost a hug. "I really wished she would have stuck around longer than she did... her timing wasn't the best, given everything that..."

Her voice faded, eyes spacing out like she wasn't even in the shelter with me anymore. I wasn't sure she even realized what she'd said, but I knew it wasn't something she wanted to expand on. At least, not then. Not there.

I swallowed. "I'm sorry, Sarah."

She blinked, shaking her head with a forced smile. "Thank you. I miss her, and I think when I get all set up in New York, I'd like to get another cat. I think I'll be ready then."

And in that moment, I could picture it all — Sarah in a little apartment in New York, snow falling outside her window, her curled up in a chair with an orange tabby in her lap and a book in her hand. I didn't know why that vision came so easily to me, but I didn't wish it away.

"I think that will be the perfect time."

Sarah's eyes found mine, her smile growing a bit before she knelt down to pet one of the eager dogs through the holes of its cage. I watched for a moment, fighting back a laugh when the dog got smart enough to lick her face through the gaps in the wiring. Sarah squeezed her eyes shut in a fit of giggles, shaking her head and pinching her mouth shut, but she didn't move away.

I realized then that ever since I met her, Sarah had always seemed so grown up.

She was a girl, for all intents and purposes — twenty-one, wide-eyed and hopeful. But, whether she ever told me or not, she'd lived through more life than most people her age. She wore that fact like her crystal, a permanent accessory.

But there in that shelter, with that dog licking her face, I saw a girl when I looked at her instead of a woman.

It wasn't that she looked younger, that the mature way she carried herself slipped in that moment, but rather that for the first time since I'd met her, the ghosts in her eyes seemed to be subdued. She laughed without the edge of worry that always seemed to follow her around, and I let myself watch her play with that dog until my chest ached in a completely new way. It was that same tinge of warmth I'd felt when I watched her with Danny, one that seared me with the urge to protect her, to guard that innocence she'd let show in that moment, to somehow save it and nurture it and help it grow.

Before that urge could take over my entire body, I tore myself away, scanning the cages of dogs as I made my way down the new hallway. They were all adorable. They were all friendly, tails wagging and tongues lopping out of their mouths as they watched me pass. They all wanted a home.

I had no idea how to even begin to make the choice of which one I'd grant that wish to.

Being that I had approximately zero knowledge when it came to animals, I read the breeds and names with a sort of distant recognition.

Bulldog, terrier mix, shih tzu, german shepherd, labrador, beagle, boxer.

Anxiety crawled up my neck more and more with each step I took, each kennel I passed, each dog's eyes I made contact with. And for some reason, it wasn't that I felt bad for the ones that would stay behind when I'd left.

It was the one that would come home with me that I worried most for.

Even at thirty-seven, I still felt like a child in all ways. I let my laundry pile up to an impressive mountain before I finally broke down to do it. I'd hired a maid to come by and clean my house once every two weeks because I couldn't be trusted to dust and vacuum correctly. I still drank and smoked like I was in college, and I ate cereal for dinner more times than I would ever admit to anyone who asked.

How the hell was I ever going to take care of a dog?

I frowned as a softer truth settled in under all those excuses, and as I reached the end of the hallway, I was finally able to name that unfamiliar pressure in my chest. It wasn't that I was scared of being able to take care of a dog, or that I didn't think I'd be able to handle everything that went along with that care.

It was that I was scared of loving the damn thing.

Everyone I loved had left me in some way — whether by choice or by fate. Sometimes, I'd pushed them away. Sometimes, I'd missed my chance. And sometimes, I'd wasted the years I had with them, so sure I'd have forever, only to realize how much I'd missed out on once they were gone.

The truth was that I fucked up every relationship in my life. I was like Midas, except everything *I* touched turned to shit.

I was alone because I *should* have been alone.

That was the one lesson life had taught me and I'd learned well.

But all of that worry, all of that truth slipped away like a cloud on a breeze when I locked eyes on the dog in kennel forty-two.

Unlike the other dogs I'd passed, this one didn't wait for me at the gate, tail wagging and paws scratching at the metal to get to me. Instead, he stayed back in the corner, curled into a ball with his tail limp on the concrete floor.

I glanced at the sheet, where I learned *he* was actually a *she*.

She was a pit bull, and her name was Rojo — pronounced *ro-ho*, like the Spanish word for red. I decided it fit her well as I noted the deep burgundy and chocolate brindle stripes that lined her fur.

When I didn't move on from her kennel, she looked up at me from where she was resting, her tail flicking a few times before it was still again. I smiled, bending down to her level and placing two fingers through one of the gate holes. Rojo lifted her head at that, looking at me curiously as her tail began to come to life again.

It was like she couldn't believe I'd stopped at her gate, that I'd found any kind of interest in an old dog like her. At first, she didn't move at all, and I wondered if she thought I'd disappear just like all the other humans that wandered through here idly each day, picking and choosing who to rescue.

After a moment, Rojo heaved herself up, walking slowly toward me with her tail tentatively wagging. She sniffed my fingers, her snout cold and black, and I reached in farther so I could rub her chin.

"Would you like to meet her?" someone asked.

I glanced up at the smiling volunteer who had stopped at the kennel, a blond, twenty-something kid with braces. His smile was genuine, and without me even answering, he moved forward, unlocking the gate as I stepped back to let it swing open.

Sarah joined us as I knelt down again, this time without any metal barriers between Rojo and my hand. She sniffed it again, and just like before, I rubbed her chin. She closed her hazel eyes in what I swore was an appreciative grin, and then she moved in closer, letting my other hand come up to pet her back.

"Rojo has been with us a very long time," the volunteer said, and the way he said it made my stomach pinch.

"How long?" Sarah asked from where she stood above me.

The volunteer checked the sheet hanging on the gate, and his face softened as he read the number. "One-hundred-and-seventy-two days."

I did the math in my head as I turned back to Rojo, who was full on wagging her tail and leaning into me now. Nearly six months she'd been at that shelter, in that kennel.

Alone.

I scratched behind her ear, smiling a little as she let her tongue flop out.

"What's wrong with her eye?" I asked, noting the cloudy mist that covered the left one.

"It was like that when she came to us," the kid said. "Owner told us some story about her being born that way, blind in one eye as the runt of her litter, but, if I'm being honest, we've always suspected some foul play."

I swallowed, teeth clenching together at the thought of anyone hurting her.

We were all quiet for moment, me petting Rojo as Sarah and the volunteer watched from above. I noticed the curious way he took in Sarah, and then me, like he was trying to put the pieces together.

Clearly, we weren't related.

"She still has great vision through her other eye, though," he continued, seeming to shake off whatever questions he had about mine and Sarah's relation as he bent down to pet the dog with me. "And she had two healthy litters of puppies before she was brought in to us. We spayed her, of course, once she was in our care." He paused, smiling when Rojo tilted her head into his touch. "She loves chewing on bones and cuddling, and though she walks slow, she seems to really enjoy getting out and laying in the sunshine. Not much of a fetcher, but I imagine she probably enjoyed it when she was younger." He shrugged. "I guess what I'm saying is that she's seen a lot in her life, regardless of that eye."

"How old is she?"

He frowned. "She's nine, which is why she's been here so long, we think. Most people want a puppy, or at least a young dog." The kid stood, and Rojo turned her attention back to me, leaning into my hand as I rubbed under her collar. "She's at high risk."

"What does that mean?" Sarah asked.

When the kid didn't answer, his silence was the loudest response.

I swallowed, a rubber band snapping around my chest as Rojo put one paw on my leg. I smiled, bringing my other hand up to pet her, but she didn't stop. She pushed into me, nuzzling me with her head and climbing up until I had no choice but to fall back on my ass and let her into my lap. That dog was way too big to be a lap dog, but there she was, curled up in my lap like she'd been in the corner when I first passed her kennel, her eyes closed, tail still wagging softly as I pet her to the tune of Sarah and the volunteer's laughter above us.

And in that moment, we all knew that Rojo's days of being at risk were gone.

SARAH

"I think she fits right in," I said, sipping on the hot tea Reese made for us when we got home. We were both standing in the kitchen just like we had earlier that afternoon, only now the sun had set, and we were both watching Rojo chew on her brand-new bone. She was also curled up in her brand-new bed, placed near the front door just to the right of the couch, and she had a brand-new collar adorning her neck as she chewed, tail wagging, a content little grin on her face.

She might as well have been a brand-new dog for how happy she seemed.

Reese smiled, and it was in a way I'd never seen him smile before — not until that day at the shelter. Seeing him bent down and loving on an old dog was enough to make my heart swell up to the size of a balloon. And now, back in his home, Reese watched that dog with a sense of protection and care.

"I can't believe anyone would ever give her up," he mused after a long moment, sipping the hot Earl Grey from his own mug with his eyes still on Rojo. "Humans can really suck sometimes."

My stomach twisted, something about the way he said those words striking me in a way I didn't expect. A flash of my last night at Bramlock hit me like a branding iron to the face, and I closed my eyes, squeezing the images away before I opened them again.

I wondered if those flashes would ever stop, if they'd ever fade, or if that night would be on permanent replay in my mind.

"Trust me, I know," I whispered.

Reese turned to me, his eyebrows meeting at that beloved crease. He didn't say anything for the longest time, just scanned my face like he could peel apart the layers of that last sentence I'd spoken. I could feel the questions swirling in his head like they were cars racing around me as I stood still in a parking lot. But he didn't ask a single one of them. Instead, he took another sip of his tea, his eyes falling to where his hands rested on the counter.

"I wish you didn't."

My eyes snapped to him, but he didn't meet my gaze. He just took another tentative sip of his tea before looking across the kitchen and into the living room again. He smiled when he found Rojo, and I turned, smiling, too, when I saw her bone had been abandoned, her eyes closed, legs curled up under her as she rested.

"I bet she is worn out from today," I said.

"*Her?*" Reese asked incredulously. "I feel like I need to sleep for two days."

I laughed. "Oh, come on, it wasn't that bad."

"Tell that to my lethargic body."

"What was it that zapped your energy?"

Reese shrugged. "I don't know, seeing all those dogs just waiting to be picked, to be taken home, to not be in that shitty kennel anymore. What an awful existence." He paused, frowning. "Honestly, I think it exhausted me because I know exactly how that feels."

I didn't know what to say to that.

"I mean, none of them asked to be there. They were good dogs. They loved their owners, at least, those who had the chance to *have* owners." Reese tapped his thumb on the handle of his mug, still watching Rojo. "But, that's what makes it such a bitch. You can love someone, give them everything you have, and still not be enough."

My heart squeezed, and I willed Reese to look at me, to let him see himself through my eyes.

But I understood what he meant.

"That's kind of how I feel about piano," I said softly.

Reese finally turned his attention back to me. "What do you mean?"

"Well," I tried, eyes finding the ceiling as I searched for the right words. "Like I told you, I've never been in love with another *human*, but I've loved the piano ever since I first touched it, since it first touched *me*." I smiled, shaking my head as the feeling filled me from the heart out. "I mean, I have given everything to piano. I've sacrificed dating, friendships, nights out on the town in college." I swallowed then, finding Reese's gaze. "Time with family. And maybe even a little time I should have given to myself."

Reese nodded in understanding, his lips pressed together.

"But, I *wanted* to. I wanted to give myself to the piano, and I still do... I just realized when I left Bramlock that sometimes, no matter how much you love someone or some*thing*, and no matter how much you're willing to give up for it..." A shiver raced down my spine. "Sometimes, like you said, you're just not enough."

Reese's thumb stilled where it had been drumming away on his mug, and he dropped it altogether, crossing his arms over his chest as he shifted his body toward me. "Why *did* you leave Bramlock?"

A short, bitter laugh hit my throat. "You want the truth or the well-curated lie?"

"The truth."

I shook my head, gaze falling to the tea growing cold in my mug. My pulse quickened as the words formed in my mind, the ones I could bring to life with my voice, if only I were brave enough. All I had to do was speak.

I was raped by my professor.

I wondered if I'd feel relief if I told him, if even one person knew what had happened to me — other than Dr. Chores, the one who'd said it was better to keep it between us.

I swallowed, throat burning as the truth slid down.

It didn't matter if I told him, Reese Walker couldn't save me. He couldn't take away what had happened, and he couldn't make any of this any easier for me.

"I can't..." I finally said, voice just above a whisper. "I'm sorry."

I was still staring at my tea like it held all the answers when Reese reached over, his hand slowly crossing the space of counter between us until it reached my wrist. His fingertips stretched out first, barely touching me, and when I didn't jump or pull away, they wrapped around the dainty bone before sliding down. I released the cup with my heart pounding in my throat, my ears, anywhere but my chest where it should have been. All I could see was the contrast of his skin against mine. All I could feel was the warmth of his blood, pumping through his palm as it melted with mine, his fingers wrapping themselves around my own.

And with my hand in his, with our hearts racing together, trying to find the same rhythm, Reese said exactly what I needed to hear.

"You have nothing to be sorry for."

My eyes watered, and I knew it must have confused him, must have made him wonder if he'd said the wrong thing. How could he know that I blamed myself, that I looked back on that night and wondered if I'd done it to myself, if I was the reason I was raped. Maybe if I wouldn't have dressed the way I did, if I hadn't put on makeup and done my hair before every class. Maybe if I wouldn't have pushed so hard, if I wouldn't have become the injured deer at the mercy of a hungry wolf. Maybe if I would have spoken up when he requested to administer my final so late at night, if I'd told him it made me uncomfortable. Maybe if I hadn't trusted him so blindly, so naïvely. Maybe if I would have said no more forcefully, if I would have screamed louder, if I would have told someone else.

Maybe, maybe, maybe.

"You do not ever have to tell me your truth, your reason why you left," Reese said, thumb smoothing over my wrist. "But I am going to ask you to tell someone."

I looked at him then, eyes wide in horror. *Does he know? Is he going to make me go to the police?*

Reese simply pointed to the piano in the den, the one he'd been teaching me at, the one I'd been slowly opening myself up to.

"You don't have to tell me, or your family, or your friends," he continued, still pointing as his eyes leveled with mine. "But you do need to tell that piano. You need to let it feel your pain, your loss, and let it take all of that and transform it into music." He dropped the hand that had pointed to the piano, but the other still held mine. "That is your duty as a pianist. That is your cross to bear as a musician. And that is what will get you to Carnegie."

My eyes flicked to where the piano was in the other room, though I couldn't see it from where I sat. Then, I pulled my gaze back to Reese with an understanding nod.

The point made, our attention seemed to fall back to where we touched, both of our eyes casting downward at the contact before Reese cleared his throat and pulled away.

My hand was still warm where he'd held it, and instinctively, I pulled that hand into my lap, covering it with the other like I could save it from being tainted.

"Well, we kind of blew our lesson today," he said with a smile, trying to lighten the mood.

"It was worth it, though, right?" I pointed out, glancing over at Rojo.

Reese sighed, looking at his new family member with a prideful smile. "Very much so."

Rojo hauled herself up once Reese and I started moving about, me packing up my messenger bag as Reese went over my homework for the weekend. I wouldn't sit at his piano again until Sunday, and since we'd missed today, he wanted to make sure we didn't fall behind. I took notes of his instructions as we made a plan — occasionally bending to pet Rojo where she rubbed against my leg — and then before I was ready to be, I was standing on his front porch, the soft sound of crickets chirping the only sound between me and Reese.

"Don't forget to take her out before you go to bed," I said. "And feed her in the morning. Once in the morning, and once at night, if you do a whole cup of food. That's what the vet we spoke to recommended."

He smirked. "I was there, too, you know."

"I *know*," I said, elongating the word. "But you did also make it very clear to me that you were about as helpless as a fish without gills when it came to taking care of another living thing."

He raised his eyebrows at that in a conceding shrug. "Very true. Hopefully Rojo will still be alive when you come back Sunday."

I blanched.

"I'm kidding, Sarah," he said on a laugh, and again, my stomach filled with warmth at my first name rolling off his lips. That warmth spread like propane, igniting into a blue flame when Reese reached forward, hand wrapping around my wrist and tugging me forward until I was in his arms.

He wrapped me up in them like a blanket, my face nuzzling his chest as he rested his chin on my head. For a fleeting second, I felt self-conscious about the fact that he'd find no hair there, no feminine reminder of who he held in his arms. But it was gone as soon as it had come, especially when he sighed, the sound reverberating through my body as he wrapped me in closer.

"Thank you," he said on a breath. "For today. For Rojo."

I squeezed his middle where my arms had wrapped around him, inhaling the fresh scent of soap that mixed with tobacco on his shirt. It'd been so long since I'd been hugged like that by anyone other than my mom. I'd shied away from all human touch, so much so that I forgot how warm it could feel, how comforting, how safe.

"Thanks for trusting me."

He stiffened in my arms a little at that, as if he'd only just realized that he'd done what I'd accused. And with that tension came a stilling of the night around us, a quieting of the insects, a dimming of the porch light that shone down from above us. Reese pulled back a little, and I watched his Adam's apple bob in his throat. He still held me, his hands on my arms, mine pressed against his chest.

"And for the record," he said. "You *are* enough."

I glanced up, catching his eyes for the briefest moment before he leaned in, his scent invading my senses again. And as if I wasn't dizzy enough, the distance between us closed, and Reese pressed his lips tenderly to my forehead.

I closed my eyes, holding my last breath as heat spread from where his lips touched me. It expanded slowly, like a trickle of water, pooling together at my shoulders before spilling down like a waterfall, touching my navel, my thighs, my ankles and toes. I was swimming in the warm waters of that kiss long after he pulled away, and when I opened my eyes and looked up at him, I wondered if he was drowning with me.

He held me there a little too long, a little too close, but neither of us made to move. His eyes searched mine, and mine drank him in, and we said nothing at all at the same time we said everything we knew we couldn't.

It was all in that look.

It was all in that embrace.

And it was all lost as soon as Reese released me, stepping back more than necessary, his hands shoved forcefully into his pockets as he offered a tight smile.

"See you Sunday, Miss Henderson."

Miss Henderson.

The air around us snapped back to life, a car whizzing by on the road in front of his house as if to remind us what universe we were in, what rules existed here. Its headlights temporarily blinded me, and I blinked as my eyes adjusted to the night again with his goodbye ringing in my ears.

I swallowed, understanding the meaning that lay beneath the name he'd addressed me with. His eyes nailed that intention home, the wide circle of his pupils telling me to take a step back, to make the line clear again, to fall back into my role so he could stand firmly in his own.

Teacher, and student.

I nodded, both to his spoken confirmation of our next lesson and his unspoken request of remembering where we each stood. My feet carried me numbly off his porch and into my car, and the engine purred to life like it was happening in another dimension as I strapped my seatbelt on.

I pulled out of his driveway without looking back at him, willing my heartbeat to steady, my breathing to calm. I wondered if I'd imagined it, if Reese was just being nice, entertaining me by adopting a dog and then thanking me like any other person would.

But it was him who'd reached for my hand.

It was him who'd held me close.

And it was his lips that had touched my skin, the first time in my life that I'd wanted it, asked for it, even if I hadn't spoken the request out loud.

All of those facts scrambled in my brain like eggs in a frying pan, and the longer I analyzed them, the more they burned, the smell of it all so nauseating I had no choice but to shake the thoughts altogether.

It was just a hug, just an innocent kiss on the forehead.

That was the last thing I told myself before I chose not to think of it again.

chapter Ten

REESE

Another crack of lightning flashed, illuminating the entire house before it fell completely dark again. The low roll of thunder quickly followed, melding with the rain that hammered the roof in a chaotic symphony. Rojo whimpered a little, snuggling even closer to me on the couch, her chin resting on my chest.

Thunderstorms had rocked through Mount Lebanon all weekend, and for once it felt like the universe was on my side. I wanted to be miserable, to lie in a dark house with nothing to do but sulk and watch my candles burn. Another low rumble of thunder reverberated through the house, as if the weather was saying *you're welcome*.

The date had snuck up on me for the first time in my life.

June twenty-ninth usually started hovering over my head somewhere in the middle of May, and I'd watch that little square on my wall calendar get closer and closer, knowing that when it hit, it'd mark another year without my family. But this year, I'd been so caught up in my routine, in playing at The Kinky Starfish and working with Sarah that I hadn't noticed. Figuring out my new routine with Rojo added to it, and I'd spent the week taking her for walks and exploring nearby dog parks, completely wrapped up in the bliss that she brought, in the warm, long days of summer.

No, I hadn't felt that cloud hovering, not until the moment it let loose and a thousand rain drops descended on me like a bucket of ice water.

Today marked five years without my parents, without my little sister, Mallory.

Without my soul.

I wasn't sure if it was the shock of the date coming without me realizing it that had knocked me on my ass, or if the jolt of this particular hit rested in the fact that it had been five full years — a milestone that had come in what seemed like the blink of an eye. Whichever one it was, it had rendered me nearly dead, and I was thankful it was a Sunday, that it was storming — the weather outside just as miserable as I was inside.

I was also thankful for Rojo, who must have known something was off. From the moment I woke up, she was glued to my side, or — like now — to my chest, her body sprawled out over me in a protective blanket of heat. I rubbed the fur under her collar, dry eyes locked on the ceiling as the day slipped away.

Every year on this date, I'd think of their smiles, their voices, the little quirks that made them so uniquely them. I'd think of how old they would be, what they would be doing if they were still here. My sister would be married, I imagined — maybe pregnant, or maybe already with a kid or two. My parents would be retired, no doubt, and likely living out Mom's dream of owning a lake house out on Lake Mockamixon. I wondered if I'd still be in New York, if they'd fly to visit me for Christmas, if we'd all meet up for a week in the summer at the lake house. I could close my eyes and picture it, the four of us together. A family.

Except I couldn't see them as clearly, anymore.

Five years had passed, time slowly erasing their faces — their voices — from my memory. I could look at photographs, like the one that sat on my piano, but I couldn't close my eyes and just *see* them or *hear* them, anymore.

My chest ached with the realization that they might be leaving me, *for good* this time. Forever.

Rojo nuzzled me, licking my chin before curling herself into me more. Tears pooled in my eyes but they stayed there, no blinks to set them free as I swallowed past the tightness in my throat.

"Sorry your new owner is such a mess," I spoke softly to Rojo, running my hand over the smooth fur on her head.

She laid her head on my chest again, letting out an exaggerated breath through her nose. I imagined if she had a voice, she'd tell me to stop being such a baby and get up and do something with my day. But, even if she could tell me that, I'd just have to add her to the list of people I'd let down in my life.

There was nothing getting me off that couch.

It wasn't quite dusk yet, but the heavy storm made it feel like it was midnight, the sky black and ominous outside my window. The only light was the low flicker of the two candles I'd lit on the coffee table, and I tried to find comfort in their warm glow as I closed my eyes again.

I just wanted to see them, to hear Mallory's obnoxious laugh that I used to make fun of her for, to feel my parents' arms wrap around me in a hug the way they did when I was nine years old. It had only been five years, and already I felt them slipping away. Life had gone on without them, moving at the same steady pace it always had, and somehow, that offended me. It wasn't fair that the world kept spinning like that, when everything in *my* world had been taken.

A knock at the door caught me off guard, my eyes snapping open as Rojo scrambled off me in a fit of barks. Her nails skittered across the hardwood floor as she ran to the door, and I groaned, throwing the blanket off me and peeling myself out of the permanent home I'd made in the cushions that day.

As I suspected, there was a perfect indention of my body left behind.

"Alright, alright," I said to Rojo as I made my way to the door. She continued barking, not at all fazed by my acknowledgement that I, too, knew there was someone at the door.

Who was there was another story altogether.

I'd cancelled my lesson with Sarah, explaining that I was feeling under the weather and didn't want her to get sick, too. No one else was expected, and with it basically tornado-ing outside, every normal human being should have been inside.

Rojo was still barking when I opened the door, and on the other side of the screen door was the absolute last person I wanted to see.

Charlie stood on my porch, shielded by the overhang as she wrangled an oversized umbrella back to its folded state. The rain poured heavily behind her, a flash of lightning illuminating her silhouette like it wanted to brand it into my memory forever.

"Charlie?" I asked, swinging the screen door open and ushering her inside. Rojo was still barking, hopping around at my feet first before she moved to Charlie and circled back again. "What the hell are you doing here?"

Rain dripped off her floral print jacket and onto my floor, and she stood at the entryway with an almost apologetic smile, umbrella in one hand and her car keys in the other.

"I'm sorry," she said, almost too softly to be heard over the rain and Rojo's barking.

I closed the door behind her, helping her out of her wet coat and hanging it on the rack by the door along with her umbrella.

"I should have called," she said again, her voice more clear now that the door was closed, the storm muted outside. Rojo licked at the water on the floor before nudging Charlie's hand. She smiled, not even needing to bend over to reach Rojo's head with her small hand. "Who is this?"

Confusion still whirred inside me like the wind outside as I stared at her in my house. I hadn't seen her since school let out, and I hadn't planned to.

"Um, this is Rojo," I finally answered, shoving a hand back through my hair.

"You got a dog?" Charlie asked, smiling at me as she peeked up from where she was petting Rojo.

I nodded. "Had her a little over a week now."

Rojo licked at Charlie's hand before prancing back over to the couch. She neglected the bed I'd bought for her completely, hopping back up on the middle cushion and looking at me like she expected me to resume the position I was in before Charlie showed up.

"She's so cute," Charlie said, crossing her arms over her chest. We both watched Rojo for a long moment, Charlie smiling and me frowning before I turned to her again.

"Charlie, what are you doing here?"

Her smile fell, eyes softening as she looked up at me. "I just wanted to see you."

"Does your husband know you're here?" I asked flatly, not bothering with niceties. I wasn't in the mood to pretend.

Charlie narrowed her eyes then. "Of course he knows I'm here." She sighed, eyes falling to the floor before she lifted them to mine again. "I just... I know what today is, and... I don't know, I just wanted to check on you."

Her words might as well have been a fist around my ribcage, crushing the bones into my lungs with the weight of them. I didn't know what hurt worse — the reminder of what day it was, or the fact that she remembered, that she still cared about me enough to give a shit.

But not enough to be with me, I reminded myself.

"Thanks," I finally said, sniffing. "But I'm fine."

Charlie nodded, surveying my living room with a look that said she didn't believe my lie for even a second. There was an ashtray on the coffee table, evidence that I'd been smoking like a chimney inside all day, and with only a couple of candles lighting the entire house, it felt as dark and dreary inside those walls as it did inside my heart.

"You know you can still talk to me, Reese," Charlie whispered after a moment, her eyes on the low flickering flame of one of the candles. "I know things didn't... well, I know that we—"

"Charlie, please," I interrupted her, holding up one hand as my eyes squeezed shut against the possibility of what she was about to say. I shook my head, swallowing to steady my voice before I spoke again. "Don't."

I didn't want to open my eyes again, to see her standing there and giving me the same look of pity she'd given me since the moment she told me she was staying with Cameron. But I didn't have a choice.

Another knock at my door forced my hand.

Rojo jumped off the couch again, skittering into action just like she had before as I let out a frustrated growl. "Jesus fucking Christ, what now?"

I crossed behind Charlie, not bothering to apologize for my language before I ripped the front door open.

Sarah stood there just as Charlie had, except she had no umbrella, and no rain jacket. She was soaked from head to toe, a grocery bag slung over one shoulder and her oversized t-shirt hanging off the other, sticking to her skin as her eyes widened, brows tugging inward the more she searched my face. "Reese? Are you okay?"

The girl was soaked and standing in the rain, and she asked if *I* was okay.

I clenched my jaw, swinging the screen door open and ushering her inside before I shut it again. Rojo stopped barking once she saw it was Sarah, but she greeted her with a vigorously wagging tail as she licked at her soaked jeans. Sarah smiled at her, bending to scratch behind her ears with water still dripping off every inch of her.

And there we were, Charlie, Sarah and me, all standing in my now very-wet foyer.

Sarah's smile fell when she saw Charlie, and her eyes flicked to mine and back again, all color draining from her face. "Oh... I'm sorry, I didn't realize..."

"No, no," Charlie assured her, holding her hands out. "Please, don't be. I just stopped by unannounced. Don't tell me I'm crashing your lesson... again." She smiled at that, and Sarah tried to return it, though it looked a little more like a grimace.

"Well, actually—"

"Yes, we really should get started," I interrupted Sarah, who gave me a perplexed look as I turned my attention to Charlie. "Thank you for coming by, though. I appreciate it."

Charlie's little mouth popped open in an *o*, but she closed it promptly, nodding with a glance in Sarah's direction before she looked at me again. "Of course." Her eyes surveyed me then, as if she'd just realized I was in my sweat pants and an old t-shirt. I knew she was trying to put the pieces together, because *she* knew I wouldn't dress like this when I had a student expected. "I'll let you two get to it, then."

I avoided her questioning eyes, helping her into her coat and passing her the still-dripping umbrella when she was back on my porch. She said a goodbye to Sarah, wishing her luck with today's lesson, and then just as quickly as she had come, she was gone again.

I shut the front door, locking it behind me like it would prevent any other unwanted guests from showing up. Then, I leaned my back against the door with my eyes on my bare feet, letting out a long sigh before my head fell back with a thud. I stood there for a beat, not wanting to meet Sarah's heavy gaze for fear of what I might find there. And when I finally did, it was exactly what I expected.

She didn't look at me with pity, or with sorrow or empathy. No, there was only one expression she wore when my eyes found hers.

Disappointment.

And it was the worst one of all.

SARAH

"I brought soup," I said after a moment, holding up the reusable bag I'd had hanging from my shoulder.

Reese was still standing at the door, his back pressed against it, feet planted in the puddles of water my clothes had left on the hardwood floor and heavy breaths wracking his chest as he watched me like he knew everything I was thinking. I tried to smile, to at least level my expression, but I knew I was doing a terrible job of trying to hide the question I needed to ask.

"I'm not actually sick."

I cocked one brow. "No shit."

At that, Reese let out a loud breath, kicking off the door and crossing to the kitchen. "It's not what you think."

"How do you know what I think?" I probed, following him. He disappeared inside his refrigerator as I threw the grocery bag on his kitchen island, and when he returned, he held a beer in his hand.

"Maybe the fact that you're wearing your disappointment like a full face of makeup." He cracked the beer open, swigging half of it down in one gulp before he leveled with me again. "She just showed up, okay? I didn't invite her, and she was here for all of five minutes before you got here."

I crossed my arms, shifting my weight to one hip as I waited for more — not that he owed it to me. I was honestly surprised he even acknowledged Charlie's presence at all before I brought it up, and I wasn't even sure I *would* have.

It wasn't my place, even if I desperately wanted to know.

Reese sighed. "Look, I know it looks bad. I fake sick and cancel our lesson and then you show up, and *she's* here, and..." He stopped, shaking his head like it didn't matter before he took another drink from the can. "Why *are* you here, anyway?"

"I was trying to be nice," I said, and I couldn't place the annoyance that slipped through in my statement. "You said you were sick, and it's raining and gross outside, so I thought maybe you'd like some soup delivered."

"You're my student, Sarah. It's not your job to bring me soup when I'm sick."

My nose flared, chest hollowing at the way he threw that in my face. Like we weren't friends. Like everything I thought we'd shared together was all in my head.

And maybe it was.

"I didn't realize being your student meant I couldn't also be your friend, but thank you so much for reminding me."

With that, I turned on my heel, abandoning the bag I'd brought with me on his counter. I convinced myself I didn't care as I stormed across the living room to his foyer, Rojo trotting behind me all the way to the front door. I didn't care that he didn't want me there. I didn't care that he'd cancelled our lesson, faked that he was sick, and then I'd found him with Charlie.

So what, he was with the same married woman who'd broken his heart, the one he'd been pining after for two years.

So what, they were alone, doing God knows what before I showed up.

So what, I'd looked like a fool, bringing him soup to be nice only to find I had interrupted... *something.*

So what.

My neck was hot, teeth clenched together so tight I knew I'd give myself a headache if I didn't release the tension, but I couldn't find it in me to care. I had my hand on the front doorknob and a string of curse words ready to let loose in the safety of my car when Reese called from behind me.

"Sarah, wait," he said on a sigh, his footsteps heavy as he crossed the house.

I paused, hand still gripping that knob. I didn't turn at first, debating whether I should adhere to his request or rip that door open and get the hell out of his house.

But the way he said my name wouldn't let me leave.

I turned, hand still on the knob as I faced Reese. He stopped a few feet from me, running his hands back through his disheveled hair — which was down and flowing to his shoulders for the first time since I'd met him. He let his hands fall back to his sides with a *thwack*, his eyes searching mine, begging me for something — understanding, perhaps? Or maybe just for me not to go. Either way, that look pinned me to the spot, and I traced the pain that was etched into every inch of Reese's face. It twisted up the longer he looked at me, his hands reaching up again to fist in his hair, throat constricting with a heavy swallow.

"I'm sorry," he finally croaked out. "I've just had a really rough day and... please, stay."

My shoulders fell at his words, chest squeezing at the desperation underneath them.

"Please?" he asked again when I didn't respond, taking a few tentative steps toward me.

Rojo looked up at me, too, her eyes wide and pleading, and I chuckled when she nuzzled my leg.

"*Y tú*, Rojo?" I said, bending to rub behind her ears with both of my hands. I glanced up at Reese, who was smiling down at us now. "I kind of regret begging you to get a dog now."

Reese threw one fist in the air. "*With our powers combined, we—*"

The air went out of him in an *oof* as I yanked one of the throw pillows off his couch and chucked it at his stomach. He caught it easily, grinning when it was in his hands.

"You're making me soup," I said, standing and making my way past him back into the kitchen without another glance.

Reese chuckled, following behind me. "That's fair. But so is the warning that I am a terrible cook."

"You just have to pour the contents of the can into a pot, throw it on the stove, and take it off once it's hot," I deadpanned.

Reese held his hands up. "Don't say I didn't warn you."

I sighed, shoving him to the side when he went for the grocery bag. "Move. I'll make it."

He grinned. "Works every time."

We both fell silent as I dug out the ingredients, turning the knob on the stove to get it warm as he pulled a pot out from a bottom cabinet. He took a seat on one of the barstools, letting me work on the soup as he watched.

"I'm sorry I cancelled our lesson," he said.

I shrugged. "You're the teacher. You kind of make the rules here. If you didn't want to have a lesson, it's not a big deal."

Reese nodded, taking a sip of his beer before we both fell quiet.

"So, you going to tell me what happened?" I asked after a while, keeping my eyes on the can I was opening.

Reese was silent for so long, I glanced over to be sure he'd heard me. He stared at the beer can in his hands, fingers tapping away on the sides, his eyes tired, lips turned down.

He still didn't speak.

I poured the chicken noodle soup into the pot, putting it on the stove before I rounded the island to stand next to where Reese stood. He glanced up at me briefly, then returned his gaze to the beer can I was almost certain was empty by now.

"Can I ask you something," I said, leaning a hip against the counter.

Again, his eyes found mine for just a second before he nodded.

"Why don't you just tell her to leave you alone?"

Reese's fingers paused, bringing the drumming he'd been doing to a stop.

"I mean, just be honest with her. Tell her that while she might want to be friends, you can't do that. You've tried, you thought it was what you wanted, too — but it's hurting you."

I paused when he didn't respond, his brows tugging inward like what I was saying was absolutely outside of the realm of possibility.

"I mean... unless..." My cheeks flamed as it dawned on me that maybe that's not what she wanted... to just be friends. "If you guys are still..."

At that, Reese sighed, squeezing his eyes closed and pinching the bridge of his nose. "Jesus Christ, no. No," he said firmly, shaking his head with his eyes still closed. "This isn't about Charlie."

I swallowed.

"Oh... I just, she was here, and I thought—"

"Trust me, I know what you thought," he said, cutting me off. He opened his eyes then, finding my own. "And I know I'm not the easiest person to believe, but I wasn't lying when I said she just showed up here. Right before you."

"I didn't mean it like that."

"I know," he said, a heavy sigh leaving his chest. He wrapped his hands around the beer can again. "I'm sorry. I just don't really know how to talk about this." At that, he sort of laughed, more to himself than out loud. "Funny, what happened between Charlie and I slipped out so easily when I told you, up there on the Incline. But this..."

His face grew even more grim, like his stomach had soured with those last words. I wanted to reach for him, my hands nearly doing just that before I mentally stopped them, crossing the kitchen to stir the soup, instead.

"You don't have tell me, then," I said, stirring as the storm raged on outside. The wind picked up, so I spoke louder over the sound of it. "We can talk about something else. Like..." I thought for a minute, resting the heel of my left foot on the opposite calf. "The weather. Or that eccentric couple that keeps coming into The Kinky Starfish — you know the one, guy always has a feather in his hat and his wife laughs at everything you say to her, even if it's just *let me take you to your seat*? Or we could talk about the election coming up. Are you a Republican or a Democrat?"

Reese didn't respond, so I kept going.

"I'm a Democrat, though I really don't like siding with one or the other. To be honest, I think the whole system is flawed. Why can't we just have independent people running for what they believe in, whether it falls in red or blue or whatever. Like, is there no—"

"It's the anniversary of my family's death."

My hand stopped mid-stir, all the words I'd planned to say instantly gone, like they'd been zapped by a powerful laser into nothingness. I just stared at the soup, at my hand gripping the wooden ladle.

"They died five years ago."

I closed my eyes, a familiar ache in my chest spreading like a slow fire as I thought of my own father, of that loss. I abandoned the ladle on the paper towel next to the stove, crossing the kitchen to stand next to Reese again. He was still staring at the can in his hands, and I just stared at the floor in front of my feet.

"That's a long time," I said after a moment. Saying that I was sorry didn't feel right, and I knew it never made me feel better when people said it to me, when I told them about my dad.

He nodded. "Which is what knocked me on my ass, I think. Five years. Five years without them, with life moving on like they didn't matter." Reese gripped the beer can a little tighter, the sound of the aluminum folding breaking the silence.

I wanted to reach for him again, the urge so strong now that I shifted until my hands were behind me, tucked between me and the counter I leaned on. "What happened to them?" I asked.

He cracked his neck, heaving himself up from the barstool long enough to trade his empty beer can for a full one. When he was seated again, he cracked it open, taking a long swig before he spoke.

"Did you ever hear of the mass shooting in New York City?"

I swallowed. "Which one?"

At that, his face paled, his hands stilling before he shook his head. "God, that's so sad."

I didn't answer. I didn't have to.

Reese ran a hand back through his hair, and I traced the movement, marveling at how much hair he *had*. It was always tied back in a messy bun at the nape of his neck, but today, it flowed freely, the loose waves in it barreling down just past his shoulders.

"It was in Central Park, right behind the Met," he said after a moment. "There was a little concert."

Five years ago, I'd been about to go into my senior year of high school. It was a hard year for me, applying for college without my dad being there, hoping and praying I'd make it into my top choice — Bramlock. I hadn't really watched the news, but a distant memory of the shooting he was referring to came to mind. I remembered my mom staring at the TV, one hand over her mouth as she listened to the account of what had happened.

"I think I remember," I said softly, heart aching. "Were they... were they there?"

He swallowed. "Front row."

I tore myself from where I stood, forcing a breath to keep myself from crying as I crossed the kitchen and stirred the soup again. It was done, so I cut off the burner and moved the pot to one that wasn't on to let it cool.

I doubted either of us would want a bowl now.

Turning, I leaned against the counter, keeping distance like if I heard the rest of the story without standing next to him, I'd somehow be unaffected. "Were *you* there?"

Reese shook his head, frowning. "No." Then, he laughed to himself again, a sardonic sort of chuckle. "No, I was at their place, waiting for them to get home. Waiting to ask them for money." He laughed again, louder this time. "Like the absolute piece of shit I was."

My shoulders fell. "Reese..."

"No, Sarah, honestly, I was. I still *am*." He shook his head, staring at the beer can in his hands like it was responsible for all the pain in his life. "Everyone I love gets hurt in some way. I'm like a walking tornado, just fucking shit up and leaving destruction behind. I hurt my family, let them down, took my talent and their generosity for granted, and partied my way through life instead of making something of myself. Then, I broke a woman's heart who loved me, who cared for me in the worst time. My friend and roommate, Blake." He shook his head, tears glossing over his eyes.

The sight of that nearly sent me to my knees.

I covered my mouth, chest squeezing so tight my next breath was nearly impossible as I watched him.

"She loved me, and I didn't see it. Not until I was back here, when she told me," he said, still shaking his head. "And by then, it didn't matter. Because I loved Charlie." He laughed, a tear breaking loose and gliding down his cheek to his jaw. "And I hurt her, too. I hurt everyone. And now, everyone I love is gone. And I can't even be mad."

He was hysterical now, laughing with tears brimmed in his eyes.

"Because it's my own damn fault. Maybe I'm meant to be alone, you know? I mean, I was afraid to even get a *dog*, scared I might fuck up its life, too. And you know what?" He stopped, every part of him stilling, all laughter gone as he whispered his next words. "To this day, I still feel like it should have been me."

He lifted his head, his eyes locked on mine. Then, he repeated the worst thing I'd ever heard him say.

"It should have been me, Sarah."

I swallowed. "No, Reese."

"Yes. Yes, it should have been. I wish it was. I wish it was me who was gone, and they were still here. I wish I didn't have to know what it was like to live without them. I wish so many fucking things."

And then, the man who seemed to carry all his pain on his shoulders broke under the weight.

His head fell into his hands, shoulders shaking as he sobbed. I crossed the kitchen in three steps, wrapping my arms around him like I could shield him, like he was crying from being struck by bullets that I could somehow stop with my own flesh. As soon as I touched him, he sobbed harder.

I couldn't help but cry, too.

Maybe it was because of my own loss. Maybe it was because I understood everything he said, everything he felt about having to keep living now that his family was gone. Maybe it was seeing a full-grown man break like that, submitting to his emotions, letting me see him weak and vulnerable and not okay.

Maybe it was that my heart was tied to his, perhaps from the very start. And when he was in pain, so was I.

It was impossible to say how much time passed with my arms around him, his face in his hands, the soup growing cold on the stove. Eventually, he grew quiet, his sobs turning to sniffs before he shifted under my arms. I pulled away, letting him straighten, and my chest squeezed again at the sight of his red, puffy eyes.

"God, I'm sorry," he said, reaching for one of the napkins in the holder on his counter. He blew his nose, wiping away the tears from his eyes with an embarrassed glance in my direction. "This might actually be the most mortifying thing I've ever done."

I smiled, but it was weak, falling too soon as I took the seat next to him. "What, you're embarrassed that you have feelings, that you're hurting on the anniversary of your family's death?" I shook my head. "If you didn't feel like this, I'd be concerned you were a serial killer."

He smirked, letting out a long, low breath. "Yeah, well, I should have had this breakdown alone. Not with my student." He eyed me then, smirk climbing. "Not that I had a choice in the matter."

"I brought you *soup*," I defended. "Excuse me for being a nice human being."

He chuckled, silence falling over us as he wiped a hand over his now-dry face. Reese took a swig from his beer can as an uncomfortable wave rolled over me. I swallowed down the urge to vomit.

"My dad died, too."

Reese snapped his attention to me so fast I thought he'd broken his neck. He opened his mouth, let it hang there, and then closed it again, waiting a long moment before he spoke. "I thought... you talked about your parents a couple times, I just always assumed..."

"I know," I said on a sigh, folding my arms over my chest with my gaze on the floor. "I don't really talk about it much. I don't really talk about *anything*, mostly because I feel the same way you do." I wrinkled my nose. "Well, not *exactly* the same, but... I understand what you mean when you say that you feel alone. That maybe you're *meant* to be that way."

Reese grimaced. "You're too young to feel that way."

I laughed at that. "Yeah, well, I'm too young for a lot of the shit that's happened in my life. But, that's just how it is sometimes."

He was quiet at that, and just as that silence fell over us, a loud rumble of thunder rolled through the house.

"My dad was just in the wrong place at the wrong time, kind of like your family," I continued after a long pause. "He stopped at a convenience store when it was being robbed. The kid shot him without even a second thought." I shook my head, remembering the security footage my mother and I had to watch at the trial — like any punishment was suitable for what he'd taken from us. "It was like a nightmare, seeing how fast his life was taken from him. Just a flick of a boy's finger on a trigger — one not much older than I was at the time — and a bullet was sent straight through my father's head. And then, he was just... gone."

Reese's shoulders fell, and I knew without him saying a word that he completely understood that feeling.

"My life seemed so perfect up until that point," I whispered. "And I swear, ever since then, everything has gone downhill."

Reese chuffed. "Isn't that the wildest part? I felt the same way, like I lived in this bubble of oblivion where I felt invincible, like nothing could touch me or the people I loved. And then that bubble popped, and I woke up in an entirely new world."

"And this new world is a cruel sonofabitch."

He nodded, bringing his gaze to me, then. "How old were you?"

"Fifteen."

I glanced at him just in time to see him close his eyes, like how old I was when it happened wasn't fair. I guess, in a way, it wasn't. I was just so used to it, so used to the narrative of my life that I didn't even know how to feel sad about it anymore.

"I'm so sorry, Sarah," he said after a moment. "Not that that helps at all. But, I'm just... I hate that you had to go through that."

Every muscle was wound so tight in that moment that I was physically sore, and I reached back to rub one shoulder as I shrugged. "People have been through worse."

My eyes met Reese's then, and the way he looked at me was with a newfound respect, like everything about who I was as a person had changed now that he knew what I'd been through.

If he only knew that wasn't even the half of it.

A crack of lightning lit up the house, the thunder that followed waking me from my daze. I shook my head, forcing a smile as I stood straight. "So," I said. "Soup?"

Reese smiled, letting out a long breath like his chest had been wound up tight just like mine. "Soup. I'll grab the bowls."

The soup had grown cold, so I reheated it in the microwave once we'd split it between two bowls. Then, Reese and I curled up on opposite ends of the couch, Rojo between us as an old movie played on the TV, the rain still pouring down outside. I wasn't sure either one of us even watched the film, but the noise was comforting, the occasional reason to smile or laugh a nice relief.

Rojo laid her head in my lap once I'd finished eating, and I rubbed behind her ears absentmindedly, my thoughts drifting all over the place. I thought of my father, of how the anniversary of his death would come up soon. It had been almost six years now, which meant that really, Reese and I had been going through the same thing at the same time on two opposite sides of the country. I wondered how many other people were dealing with that grief right now, losing a parent or friend or — worse — a child.

Death never scared me, not after I lost my dad. Truthfully, it was easy to die, to have your life snuffed out and slip into nothingness. Maybe there was a heaven. Maybe a new life started all over again.

Regardless, it wasn't death that hurt.

It was *surviving* the death of others that was the real killer, the real pain we should all be afraid of.

And I hated that Reese knew that pain, too.

I was still lost in my thoughts when Rojo heaved herself up off the couch, lazily crossing to where her food was in the kitchen. When she came back, she climbed up on the opposite side of me, forcing her way between the arm of the couch and my body. I laughed, scooting over so she could actually fit, though her hind legs were still in my lap.

Reese snickered. "Just a little over a week here and she already runs this place."

"She certainly seems to feel right at home."

"Oh, just imagine that same attitude when we crawl into bed at night." Reese shook his head. "She takes up the whole thing. I have a tiny little sliver for myself."

As if she heard him, Rojo stretched out, feet digging into my sides. It didn't hurt, but it tickled, and I scooted away in a fit of laughter as Reese chuckled, too.

Both of us stopped when my leg hit his.

I sobered, face falling flat when I realized I was sitting right next to him, our thighs in line, the seam of my still slightly damp jeans touching his sweatpants. My eyes trailed up from where our knees touched, following the line of our bodies until I found the hem of his t-shirt, his muscular arm, his broad chest. I swallowed when my gaze trailed over his lips, and the ability to breathe left me completely when my eyes found his.

He watched me with that familiar crease between his brows, his emerald eyes flicking between mine.

"I never thanked you," he said, his stare more like physical hands holding me to that spot. "For coming over. For not leaving when I was a complete ass to you." The corner of his mouth flickered into a smile at that, but it fell quickly. "For not looking at me like you feel sorry for me."

"Trust me," I said, something between a laugh and a scoff springing from my throat. "*Sorry* is the last thing I feel for you."

Reese blinked, his gaze flicking to my lips so briefly I swore I imagined it. "What's the first?"

I didn't answer, didn't have *time* to answer before his gaze dropped again, and this time there was no second guessing it.

Reese Walker was staring at my lips.

He was staring at my lips like he wanted them for his own, like every muscle in his body ached for him to close the distance between us so he could taste them.

I opened my mouth to respond, but no words came. I just sat there, lips parted, breaths so shallow in my chest that I was dizzy from the lack of oxygen. Reese reached for me with his gaze still on my lips, his hand touching mine before he trailed it up to my wrist, my forearm, gripping me lightly behind my elbow and pulling me in closer.

My breath caught, Reese's eyes darting up to meet my gaze as his hand continued up my arm. I shuddered when the warmth of his hand slid over my cool neck, his fingers wrapping around the back of it, thumb and forefinger framing my ear. He swallowed, and I watched the way his throat tightened, the way those muscles ebbed and flowed as he pulled me in closer.

My heart thundered under my chest, the pouring rain outside doing nothing to cover it. It was all I heard, the beats of it erratic in my ears, my throat throbbing with the pulse. I hoped it had pushed enough blood to my organs to keep me alive, because it stopped beating altogether as soon as Reese tilted my chin, lowering his lips to mine.

I closed my eyes as soon as our lips touched, the kiss so light and gentle that I almost wondered if it were happening at all. He still cradled my face, our lips barely brushing, and then he tugged me in closer, pressing the full weight of his mouth on mine.

A breathy sigh left my nose, everything that had stopped kicking back to life in a whir — my heart, the rain, *time*. It all seemed to rush in like a flash flood, taking me down with it. Reese's breaths came just as hard as mine, like he was drowning too as our lips melded together, my hands threading around his neck, pulling him closer, needing more.

Everything about that man was so hard — the bend of his brows, the sharp edges of his jaw, the muscles under his white t-shirt. But his lips? His lips were the softest command, smooth like rose petals, yet powerful enough to bend me in a silent plea to submit. I opened my mouth on a gasp, and his tongue swept in, both of us letting out moans that sent chills racing down to my ankles.

I climbed into his lap like I'd done it before, like I wasn't home until every inch of me touched every inch of him, like the cells in his body called to those in mine. My legs spread, knees hitting the couch on either side of him as he kissed me harder. He groaned when our middles met, when the hot center of me brushed against the hardness of him, and he bit my lower lip like it was taking everything in him to restrain himself after that.

Who even was I?

The way I surrounded him, the way I touched him was the way I'd always imagined I would one day — when the right man came along, when I made it out of the house and away from my piano long enough to fall in love. I imagined being kissed just like this, being held just like this, being in *control* — just like this.

Only this was so much more than I even could have imagined.

Everything about him invaded my senses — the warmth of his lips, the hot pressure of his hands, the strong scent of him; fresh soap, tobacco, pine.

Man.

He was all man, all hard muscle and protective care. He held me reverently, lips moving with slow, calculated pressure as I succumbed to him. I'd wanted that kiss for so long, wanted to feel his hands on me, wanted to have my hands on *him*. It wasn't just a crush. It wasn't just a school girl lusting after my teacher.

I *saw* Reese, just as he saw me.

It didn't matter if it was wrong, if he was older, if I was his student.

I wanted him.

And the way he touched me, I knew he wanted me, too.

I moaned, hands weaving back into his hair to tug as he released my lip with a pop. And in that moment, I was lost. In that moment, I wasn't Sarah Henderson at all — I was the object of Reese's desire. I was the lips he kissed, the skin he touched, the woman he wanted.

Desire pooled between my legs as I rolled my hips against him, and he growled, hands moving from where they framed my face to grip my waist, instead. He squeezed tight, holding me in place so I couldn't roll my hips again.

And with that small motion, with that completely normal reaction — reality snapped back like a rubber band to my face.

Wolfgang's face flashed through my vision like a bolt of lightning as Reese released my lips, trailing hot kisses down my neck. I gasped, and he sucked the skin between his teeth, but it wasn't him I felt anymore. It wasn't him I saw.

Just relax. I'll get you where you want to be.

Reese's hands gripped me harder, his thumbs pressing into my hip bones as another cry left my lips, confusion rippling through me.

Shhh, don't cry. Don't scream.

"Fuck, Sarah," Reese growled against my throat before capturing my lips again. He sucked in a breath on that kiss, pulling me closer, like he could meld his body with mine entirely. "You taste so sweet."

You taste so sweet.

I pressed my hands into Reese's chest, and he let my lips go free again, bringing my fingertips to his lips before he moved in for my neck again.

You don't have to fight. It's okay, you know.

It's okay to like it.

"Stop."

The word croaked through me, but I had no voice. It wasn't even a whisper, just a dead, silent plea on my lips as my wolf's claws shredded me from the inside.

"Stop," I said again, and this time it was a whisper. "Stop, stop, STOP!"

I jumped off Reese in the next instant, body shaking uncontrollably from the loss of his heat, from the memory of my wolf. I fell to the floor as soon as I was out of his lap, and my feet peddled me backward until my back hit his entertainment center. I yelped at the shock of it, eyes wide, heart racing. I could only see Wolfgang, could only hear his voice.

I clamped my hands over my ears and screamed. "Stop!"

The shrill of my scream echoed through the house, Rojo frantically climbing on me like she could stop whatever it was that was hurting me. I creaked my eyes open again, letting my hands fall to her fur. And when I lifted my gaze, I nearly blacked out.

Reese sat on the couch, his hands up like he'd been caught stealing, eyes wide with panic. Heavy breaths wracked through his chest, his lips parted as he watched me.

"Sarah..."

"I have to go," I said, cutting him off. I peeled myself up off the floor, darting for the front door without another look in his direction.

He scrambled from the couch, hitting his foot on the coffee table in his hurried attempt to reach me. "Sarah, wait. Please."

But I didn't. I *couldn't*. I couldn't look at him after what I'd just done.

What I'd just ruined.

"Sarah," he called again as I ripped his door open.

He quickened his pace, reaching for me just as I bolted out into the rain, his hand barely catching my wrist before I yanked it free.

"Sarah!" he called again, the roar of his voice muted by the rain. I was soaked in an instant, lightning striking across the sky with a crack of thunder so loud I jumped, ducking into the safety of my car with my hands still shaking. They trembled still as I locked the door, struggling with the seatbelt before I shoved the key into the ignition.

Reese was already there at the window, beating on it as the rain soaked him, too. "Sarah, please. I'm sorry. I'm—"

The car roared to life, and I threw it in reverse, squealing out of his driveway without meeting his eyes. I couldn't even look at him once the car was in the street, once he was there, too — fading under the sheet of rain in my rearview as I sped away.

I gasped, sucking in what felt like my first breath, the oxygen burning my deprived lungs. My brain had turned on me, warping the past with reality, and I couldn't see past the illusion, couldn't slow my heart or overcome the confusion that paralyzed me. I shivered so violently I could barely drive, but I kept on, the image of Wolfgang on top of me still so fresh in my mind I would have sworn it was happening all over again if I couldn't feel that steering wheel under my hands. I shook my head against the visions, letting the tears mix with the rain on my face as the pain tore through me.

I'd always wondered, always feared, and now I had my answer.

I'd never be free of my wolf.

chapter eleven

SARAH

My eyes were dry as I stared up at the ceiling, counting the specks of glitter that freckled the popcorn ceiling in the guest room. I wondered if Aunt Betty had it sprayed with glitter or if it had been built that way. I also wondered if turning off the ceiling fan that spun above me would help with how dry my eyes were, but the thought of moving, of crawling out of the comforter I'd burrowed into for the last two days seemed nearly impossible. My knees would probably fail under the weight of my body, send me crashing to the floor.

It was my turn to fake sick, to call out of everything in life — including the last two days of lessons with Reese. I hadn't even been able to be the one to tell him I wasn't coming, pleading with my uncle to make the calls for me both Monday and Tuesday. I couldn't face him, not even through the safety of my cell phone screen.

I wasn't sure I'd ever be able to again.

Everything I'd worked for, everything I had planned out when I came to Pennsylvania was blown away in an instant Sunday night.

And it was my fault.

I groaned as the memory resurfaced again, just as it had over and over and over again since I left his house. Reese was my first *real* kiss — the first one I'd wanted, silently pleaded for, felt in every inch of my body once his lips were on mine. It was everything I'd ever wanted from a kiss, and it came from a man I knew could do better than me. He could kiss any woman he wanted, be with any woman in Mount Lebanon, and yet it'd been me he'd reached for.

And I ran away.

A gentle knock on my bedroom door made me blink, the memory fading away as Aunt Betty let herself in my room. Her face crumpled when she saw me, still buried under blankets and pillows, but she offered a soft smile as she carried the tray in her hand over.

"I brought more soup," she said, sitting on the edge of the bed. Her eyes trailed my bedside table, where the last bowl of soup she brought me still sat untouched — along with unopened boxes of cold medicine she'd purchased.

"Thank you," I whispered.

She watched me as silence fell over us, and I wished I could talk to her, open up to her, tell her something — *anything* — to make her feel at ease. I knew I was worrying her and my uncle both, that all they wanted was to help. But I was beyond their reach, beyond anyone's.

I just wanted to be alone.

Aunt Betty exchanged the bowls, placing the cold bowl of soup on her tray and the other on the table for me. Then, she folded her hands on the handles, staring at them a moment before she looked at me again.

"How do you feel about coming to the store with me?" she asked with a smile. "It won't be anything crazy, just need to pick up a few groceries. I thought maybe you could help me with this vegan recipe I want to try."

Every muscle in my body tensed at the thought, and I curled in on myself against the cramp, shaking my head almost imperceptibly. "I'd really like to rest, if that's okay."

"Of course," she said quickly. "I know you want to rest. I just..." She swallowed, eyes softening as she reached over and smoothed her hand over my arm. I didn't flinch away like I used to, maybe because I didn't have the energy. "Did something happen?"

I blinked, swallowing past the knot in my throat.

When I didn't answer, Aunt Betty squeezed my arm before pulling her hand away. "You know, it's okay. We don't have to talk. Just know I'm here if you need anything at all. Okay?"

I nodded. "I know. Thank you, Aunt Betty. And, I'm sorry."

She smiled, standing with the tray in her hands. "Don't be sorry for being sick, sweet girl."

Aunt Betty let herself out, a quiet *snick* of the door closing letting me know I was alone again.

The fan whirred on, providing the white noise I needed to let my thoughts run wild. They seemed to have more energy than my body ever would again. For a moment, I debated peeling myself out of bed to go to the store with my aunt, knowing it was already Wednesday and I'd have to face the world again sometime.

But the bigger part of me just wanted to live in the solace of my bedroom a while longer.

I sighed, blindly reaching over for where my phone was buried under a pillow. I swiped to my mom's name, putting her on speakerphone and resting my head again once it was ringing.

"*Mwen chouchou,* I was wondering when I'd hear from you."

I didn't speak, but my eyes watered at the sound of her voice, my bottom lip trembling before I bit down hard to stop it.

"What is it, sweetheart? What's wrong?"

I squeezed my eyes shut at that, setting the tears I'd managed to hold back free. They tumbled down my hot cheeks, dampening the pillow. "I messed up, *Manman.* I messed up so badly."

I cried harder, my mother soothing me from the other end of the phone. I imagined the comforter around me was her arms, that she was holding me and petting my hair — the hair I once had — telling me everything would be okay.

"Why don't we start from the beginning," she said once my sobs had quieted. "What happened?"

I sniffed, words stirring in my mind, but I couldn't bring a single one of them to my lips. I couldn't speak, couldn't tell my mom that I was kissed by my piano teacher, that I'd wanted him to kiss me, and that I'd run away from him because the man who raped me was haunting me like a permanent ghost I'd never be free of. I didn't know how to explain that I felt shame for something that had happened to me, for the way it had permanently scarred me, for the way I'd tarnished a moment that could have been one of the best of my life.

Ever since I could remember, I'd dreamed of being kissed like that, of having a man frame my face and look into my eyes and *see* me before his lips touched me. I'd read about romance, watched it on the television screen, but I'd never been sure it actually existed. I always wondered if it was only in fiction, if it only existed within the realms of our mind's fantasies and creations.

But it was real.

The butterflies I felt around Reese, the way my heart sped up when he was near, the way I *finally* wanted to be touched by someone — no, not by just anyone, but by *him* — it was all proof that it was out there. Love. Respect. Desire.

Hope.

Reese had given me my dream kiss, a kiss I'd dreamed about, one I wasn't sure could ever be reality.

And I'd run away from him.

All because I couldn't shake my wolf.

Mom sighed on the other end after a moment. "Ah," she said. "You can't tell me, can you?"

I sniffed again, wiping at my nose with the sleeve of my hoodie. "It's complicated."

"Most things in life are," she said.

She paused after that, and I wondered why I'd even called. How could I expect her to comfort me, to help me, if I couldn't even open up to her?

"Can you tell me anything?" she asked. "Doesn't have to be specifics. But, maybe we can just talk about how you're feeling."

I blew out a breath, nodding even though she couldn't see me. I wanted to try, but I didn't know where to start.

"I feel embarrassed," I said first. "And ashamed. I feel... damaged. And hardened. And just... sad. So, *so* sad, *Manman*."

"That breaks your mother's heart," she whispered, her voice breaking like she, too, was crying.

I squeezed my eyes closed, shaking my head against another flood of tears. I hated that I was hurting her, hurting my aunt and uncle, hurting *everyone* around me because I couldn't face the thing that had hurt *me*.

"Can I ask you something?" Mom said after a moment. When I didn't answer, she continued. "What you're feeling now, the embarrassment and hurt... does it have anything to do with what happened at Bramlock?"

My throat tightened. "Yes," I whispered.

Mom was quiet a moment, and I considered switching to video chat so I could see her, see what she was thinking through her big, soft brown eyes.

"And this thing that happened... is it what has been affecting your playing?"

My face twisted with the threat of another sob. "It's been affecting *everything*."

I bent in on myself again, curling my arms around my middle in a big hug. It was true, that what Wolfgang had done to me had seeped into every facet of my life. I even wondered if he was the reason I felt what I felt for Reese. Maybe it wasn't him at all, maybe it was a twisted version of Stockholm syndrome, gearing me toward an older man again, toward my piano teacher. Maybe I wanted love from him because I'd had nothing but hate from Wolfgang.

But none of that felt right.

Not when I thought it, not when I poured it out on the mapping table of my brain, staring at the contents and trying to make them all fit together. I knew without question there was something more there with Reese, something past the fact that he was forbidden, that he was off limits to me as my teacher, as a man older than me.

I wanted him, and yet I'd run from him.

Nothing made sense.

"Listen to me, Sarah," my mother said, pulling me back to her just as I'd begun to spiral again. "Some things — no matter how close we are — some things will be hard to talk to your mom about. And that's okay. It doesn't mean anything other than there are just some things we go through as young adults that parents won't understand." She paused for a long moment. "I think you should call Reneé."

"I can't," I squeaked.

"I know, I know you feel like you can't. You think she's mad at you for leaving the way you did. And maybe she is, but I can guarantee you, she misses you. She wants to hear from you. And I really think you need to hear from her, too."

I sighed, shaking my head like it wasn't possible, but my heart swelled a bit at the thought. Maybe I could call her, apologize, let her in on what happened.

My stomach twisted.

"Or," Mom said after a while. "Maybe, you could open up to Mr. Walker."

I stopped breathing at that.

"Hear me out," she said, as if she could see my freakout through the airwaves. "I know he's your teacher, and he's a man, and he's older. But, I also know he's earned a lot of your trust over the past couple of months. You've worked with him so much, and he's proved to you that he cares about your wellbeing and your music. Maybe, if you open up to him about what happened at Bramlock, it would help you tackle the vulnerability aspect in your playing. I know you said that's something he's been asking of you."

I blinked, processing her words as I propped myself up more in the pillows.

"Do you think he would listen, if you told him what happened?"

"Without a doubt," I said softly. "I just don't know if I could tell him. *Manman*, I'm not sure I can *ever* tell *anyone*."

"I know," she said on a sigh. "I know. And I wish I could crawl into that head of yours. I wish I could comfort you without you telling me a thing. I just... I think we might be past that, *mwen chouchou*. I think you might be at a very critical point in your journey of healing, where no matter how much it hurts, you have to talk to someone about what happened in order to keep moving forward."

I brought my hand to my mouth, closing my eyes at the touch as her words settled in. The thought of opening that mouth my fingers touched, of letting the words that held my truth tumble out of them nearly paralyzed me. I couldn't imagine being able to get through the whole thing, and I definitely couldn't fathom feeling better once the words were out.

Still, I felt it in my heart when my mother spoke those words that they were true. It was in the way that bruised, broken thing kicked to life at the prospect, at the thought of someone else knowing, someone else being able to understand.

At that someone being Reese.

"You don't need to answer me or make a decision today," Mom said. "Just... think about it. Okay?"

I nodded. "Okay." Then, a long, sigh of a breath left my chest. "I miss you so much it hurts sometimes."

"Oh, sweetie." Mom sniffed. "I miss you, too. But if you ever need me — *ever* — you just say the word and I'll be on the first flight up to Pennsylvania."

"I know. Thank you, *Manman*. I love you."

"And I love you, *mwen chouchou*."

REESE

Sweat dripped from my hairline, little drops splattering the concrete at my feet as I curled the weight, my bicep screaming. Rojo was sprawled out just a few feet away, a lazy smile on her face as she soaked up the afternoon sun. She didn't seem fazed at all by my grunting and panting, though I imagined she was probably used to it by now.

I gritted against the urge to stop, reveling in the feel of physical pain as opposed to the internal pain that had been gutting me since Sunday night. Four days had passed in a sort of daze, a numb transcendence of work and piano during the day, smoking and drinking at night.

It wasn't the routine I wanted, the one I'd found so much solace in over the summer. I longed for my lessons with Sarah, for the balance she'd brought into my life. But I hadn't seen her since that night, since she ran away from me like I'd burned her, like I'd hurt her.

My stomach twisted again at the thought that I truly had.

I dropped the weight with a grunt, stretching out the arm I'd been working before switching to the other. I was sore — probably too sore to work out the way I was — but I needed a release. I needed to do something, *anything*, to keep my mind off what I'd done.

I thought it was impossible to feel like a bigger piece of shit than I already did, but it turned out that, just like with everything else in my life, I'd been wrong.

I shook my head, guilt crawling its way back up my spine like a sticky acid as I curled the weight in my left hand now. I couldn't verbally abuse myself enough for what I'd done, for making a move on a student — a student who had trusted me, who I had taken under my wing. It was the absolute worst betrayal, to have Sarah open up to me as much as she had and take advantage of her.

It made me sick to think about — so physically ill that I'd actually forfeited my dinner into the toilet Sunday night. It'd been nearly impossible to stomach food since then. How could I? Sarah had been there for me on a night I thought I wanted no one around. She'd listened, all judgment gone as I broke down like a fucking child in her arms. And more than that — she shared the same pain. She didn't look at me with pity in her eyes, but with understanding.

I didn't realize how much I craved that connection until I had it.

And because I'm a stupid fucking man, I acted on it. I let those feelings, that vulnerability *rule* me, like all self control had been blasted out the fucking window. And in the process, I'd hurt the first person I'd felt close to since Charlie.

Fucked-Up Midas, turning everything to shit again.

The weight fell from my hand with a *clink* as I sighed, brain more exhausted than my muscles. I just wanted to stop thinking — even if just for a single minute. I couldn't escape what I'd done, not even when I was sleeping. Sarah's wide, terrified eyes haunted me even in my dreams.

All I wanted was to apologize to her, to look her in the eyes when I told her I truly was sorry, that I would never do anything to hurt her, and that I would swear on my life and hers to never do that again — even if I wanted to.

But I didn't have the chance.

She'd cancelled our lessons both Monday and Tuesday, Wednesday was our day off, and I hadn't heard from her yet today. I wasn't sure if I'd ever hear from her again. I wondered if her uncle was telling me she was sick to stave me off, if she was actually packing and getting ready to fly back to Georgia.

If she *was* leaving, she certainly hadn't told her uncle what happened between us. He didn't sound like anything other than his normal, joyful self when he'd called.

Still, it was *her* I wanted to talk to, her voice I wanted to hear.

It was her eyes I wanted to look into when I apologized.

Sweat rolled down my neck, my chest as I made my way back inside the house, Rojo trotting along behind me. She made her way to her favorite spot on the couch as I rounded into the kitchen, pouring a tall glass of cold water. I drained it all before refilling it again. Every muscle in my body screamed from the torture I'd put it through, the physical challenges I'd given myself to distract from the mental ones.

I needed a shower, and maybe some ibuprofen.

Although, a beer sounded better.

Abandoning my glass on the counter by the sink, I weaved through the kitchen, the piano room, stripping off my soaked t-shirt and tossing it in the pile of laundry that needed my attention before turning into my bathroom. I reached behind the shower curtain for the faucet, but before I could turn the handle, my doorbell rang.

Rojo sprang into action, barks echoing through the house as I stood frozen in place, my hand still hovering over the knob as my heart kicked into my throat. Somehow, I knew it was her. Maybe it was an energy, a subliminal buzzing that I couldn't fully comprehend. Whatever the reason, every nerve was alive with awareness of her as I crossed my house, breaths shallow and muted, like they were in someone else's body altogether. The apology I'd practiced a thousand times in my head stirred to life, too, like a carousel of *I'm sorry's*. I didn't know if she'd hear me out, if she'd even be able to look at me. And for the life of me, I couldn't figure out why when I opened my front door and saw her standing there, an unearned relief washed over me.

Sarah stood on my porch just as she had Sunday night, only now, the sun was shining, the sky clear and blue above her. She was staring at her feet when I opened the door, but slowly, her gaze climbed until her eyes connected with my own.

She didn't have to say a word for me to know she'd been through the same hell I had the past few days.

"I'm sorry I came by unannounced," she said, voice surprisingly steady and firm. "I know our lesson isn't until this evening, but I wanted to come by earlier to talk. If that's okay."

That guilt that had somehow washed away at the sight of her crawled its way back up, sticking to my throat and making my next swallow nearly impossible as I stepped back, holding the door open for her. "Of course. Please, come in."

Rojo had been impatiently waiting behind me, and as soon as I moved, she squeezed through, greeting Sarah with a wagging tail and wet, sloppy kisses to her hands.

Sarah smiled, bending a bit to pet Rojo as she made her way inside. When we were all in the foyer, I closed the door behind her, shoving my hands in the pockets of my gym shorts.

"Thanks for coming by," I said, snapping my fingers at Rojo to let her know it was time to calm down. She sauntered over to the couch, tail still wagging and eyes locked on Sarah, begging her to join. "I'm sorry the house is kind of a mess," I continued, running a hand back through my damp hair. "I've been... busy."

Sarah nodded. "Oh, it's okay. I understand." Her eyes washed over the living room — the empty cans of beer, blankets strewn everywhere, pillow on the couch where I'd tried to sleep since the bed was no reprieve, ashtray on the coffee table, evidence that I hadn't cared enough to even go outside to smoke.

Then, her gaze turned to me.

She swallowed, the constriction of her throat all I could watch as her eyes took in my naked, sweaty chest. They lingered on my navel, dropping briefly to where my abs met the band of my shorts before they popped back up to meet my eyes.

"Shit, I'm sorry." I scrambled over to the couch, plucking the sleep shirt I'd worn off it and tugging it on. "I was just about to get in the shower."

Crimson shaded her cheeks, but Sarah didn't otherwise acknowledge the fact that I'd been shirtless. "Can we sit?"

"Of course." I hurried into the kitchen, pulling out a barstool for her like a fucking idiot. I even held it there, like a waiter about to scoot her in and ask if she'd like sparkling or spring water.

Sarah's eyes softened a little, a smile touching the edges of her lips as she took a seat.

"Do you want a drink or anything? Water?"

"I'm okay," she answered.

Sarah wouldn't look at me now, her gaze solely focused on her hands, which were folded in her lap now. I slid onto the stool across from her, throat sticky and tight. Every apology I'd had seemed completely deficient now that I had her in my house. And the sickest thing was, in that moment, with her sad eyes cast down and unable to look at me, I wanted to kiss her just as badly as I had Sunday night.

I was the worst kind of fucking person.

"Sarah," I breathed, swallowing down what nerves I could. "I am so sorry about what happened."

She squeezed her eyes shut, shaking her head like my words had caused her pain, and it killed me when I realized I actually had. A sharp pang of guilt ripped through me, and I winced against it.

"I wish I had more to say, some sort of... I don't know," I said, words scrambled as I tried to find the right ones to say. "Reason, I guess. Or excuse. Something to make what I did—"

"Please, don't apologize, Reese," she said, eyes still squeezed shut.

I frowned, wishing she'd look at me. My hands reached forward, but I stopped myself before I could touch her, planting my palms on the granite, instead. "But, I am. I am so fucking sorry, Sarah. What I did was inexcusable. I betrayed your trust. I—"

"There's no one I trust more than you," she said, cutting me off again as her eyes flew open. Her breaths were labored, her cheeks flushed as she looked behind me at the fridge. "I'm sorry, I think I actually would like some water."

"Of course." I popped up, plucking a glass from the cabinet and filling it with water from the pitcher in my fridge. Sarah downed half the glass once it was in her hand, and she kept her fingers wrapped around it like a safety blanket once it was back on the counter.

"I don't want you to be sorry about what happened..." she said after a long moment. "It's *me* who's sorry."

I frowned. "*You?* Why on Earth would you be sorry, Sarah? You did nothing wrong."

A bawdy laugh left her throat, and she shook her head, eyes still on her hand that wrapped around the glass. "I jumped off you, screaming, and then bolted out your door like a crazy person."

My stomach twisted at the memory, guilt strangling me like actual hands around my throat. "Honestly, I don't feel like that reaction is out of place at all after what I did."

"Stop saying that, stop saying *what you did* like you punched me instead of kissed me."

We both quieted at that, at the verbal admittance of what had occurred. It was like skirting around the word somehow kept us in a safe ring, and now we were back in the wild, back where there were no lines or rules or designated areas where we were supposed to reside — me in one, her in the other, never to cross over.

Sarah sighed, her eyes flicking to mine before they fell to her hand again. "I *wanted* you to kiss me, Reese."

I closed my eyes, letting out a long, slow breath through my nose to calm the energy that sparked to life inside me at her words. I wanted to pull her into me, to kiss her again, to say *to hell with what anyone thinks*. But all of that was dangerous — for her, for me. And even if she'd wanted to kiss me, too, she'd been the one to say stop.

I was the older one, the teacher, the one who should have been in charge. And yet it was *her* who was strong enough to say no, to remind me where we stood.

I'd failed her.

"Sarah..."

"No, please, Reese." She gripped her glass tighter, pulling it toward her like it was the water she was pleading with, or like it was me she held in her hands. "I came here to explain something..." Sarah shook her head, biting her lip against the tears welling in her eyes. "But it is so, *so* hard for me to even consider telling you what I'm about to. And I don't know how this is going to come out, or what you'll think of me when it's all done. I just... I need you to just listen to me. Please. If you can."

"Of course, I can," I said, and this time I reached for her, wrapping my fingers around her forearm with a squeeze. I willed her to look at me, but she still wouldn't. "Whatever it is, I'll always listen to you."

I couldn't do anything right, couldn't comfort her the way I desperately wanted to. She pulled away from my grip like it had burned her, eyes squeezing shut again as she tucked her hands under her thighs. She stared at the ground, at the counter — at anything but me.

And I couldn't blame her.

I couldn't find any fault in that innocent, wide-eyed girl who sat across from me, who had trusted me, who I'd betrayed. Now, she was here to tell me something that was so hard for her that she was visibly shaking, and I had a feeling I already knew what she needed to say.

We can't do this, Reese.

You're my teacher, I'm your student.

I'm sixteen years younger than you.

You work for my uncle.

I'm leaving for New York, I have my whole life ahead of me. And you... well, you're nothing. You're not what I need.

You're not what would make me happy.

"I don't know where to start," she whispered after a long while.

I sighed, swallowing down any hopes that were still alive. "It's okay, Sarah. You don't have to say it. I know. I know what happened can't happen again, and I know—"

"I was raped."

Her hands clapped over her mouth as soon as the words were out, her eyes wide in horror as they lifted to meet my gaze. Tears welled over those golden irises so quickly she didn't have time to try to stop them before they broke the levy of her lower lashes, falling down her cheeks to meet where her hands still covered her lips without so much as a blink.

For a moment, she stared at me like she couldn't believe she'd said what she had, or like she was waiting for me to run, like somehow *I* would be tempted to bolt after what I'd just heard.

The only thing I was tempted to do was full on Hulk smash whoever the motherfucker was who put his hands on her without permission.

Everything slowed in that moment — my breathing, the strong beat of my heart in my chest, my thoughts. They almost came to me like zombies in a fog, slow and gruesome, disappearing again before I could latch onto them and digest them fully. I couldn't think, couldn't speak, couldn't do anything but try to breathe and loosen the menacing grip my fists had wound into.

I wanted to murder him, and I didn't even know who *him* was.

More than that, I wanted to pull Sarah into my arms, shelter her from the pain, from the memory, from the tears falling freely from her eyes. I'd never had an urge to protect someone more in my entire life.

But all I could do was sit there, breathing.

And even that took all my effort.

Sarah dropped her hands into her lap along with her gaze, tears still leaking out of her eyes. Every now and then, she'd sniff, reach a hand up to wipe the wetness from her cheeks — all the while staring at her lap while I stared at her.

Nothing that came to mind felt right to say in that moment. I wanted to ask her who it was, when it happened, what happened to him when she told someone — *did* she tell anyone? I wanted to know if that motherfucker was in jail or if I could get his address and kick his ass myself.

But none of that would help Sarah. None of that would take her pain away.

I wasn't sure anything ever could.

"It was my professor," she whispered after the longest time. Her face broke again with the admission, letting more tears run freely. "That's why I left Bramlock."

My entire body squeezed on the next exhale, hands shaking as I ran them back through my hair with my eyes still on her. "Wolfgang?" I asked. "Wolfgang Edison... he... he..."

"Raped me?" Sarah asked, like she knew I didn't even want to say the word. Her voice was stronger as she lifted her eyes to mine. "Yes. He did."

My nose flared, muscles tensing with the urge to fly to Florida and fuck him up. No wonder she'd freaked out at the end-of-the-year concert when I'd mentioned him. I'd brought up the biggest monster of all right before she was about to perform. He was her professor, her *teacher* — the one she had to spend the most time with, the one she trusted the most.

I sobered at the realization that I was the same.

And I'd betrayed her trust, too.

She seemed almost numb as she stared at the kitchen counter. "It sounds awful when I say it out loud. You know?" She shook her head. "You always hear about it happening to other people, see it on TV, on the news, in the movies... but when it actually happens to you?" Sarah swallowed. "There is no more shameful pain in this entire world."

I sucked in a breath that scorched my esophagus.

"Sarah," I breathed her name, shaking my head as I swallowed past the burning thickness in my throat. I felt sick. I felt responsible. "I am so sorry. I am so sorry this happened to you." I shook my head. "And you have nothing to feel ashamed of. Okay? Do you understand me? Nothing."

Her face twisted again, eyes welling as she nodded.

Silence fell over us, Sarah sipping her water as I stared at the granite counter between us. I'd never been in this position, never been the one a woman trusted to tell something like this to. I was at a loss for words, and the longer the silence stretched between us, the shittier I felt. I wanted to hold her, comfort her, tell her it would be okay.

I wanted to go back to Sunday night and take back what I'd done.

"Sometimes, I feel stupid for not seeing it coming," she confessed with a sniff. "There was this gut feeling, you know? Not at first. Not at any point in my first year working with him, if I'm being honest. But, sometime in my sophomore year, I started to feel his attention more. Sometimes, he would comment on my appearance, or touch me in a way that felt wrong. Like, once, after a rehearsal, he held his hand on the small of my back as he talked to the rest of the performers. It didn't feel *wrong,* since it was in front of everyone and all, but... it didn't feel *right*, either."

Sarah paused, her eyes lifeless as they stared at the granite counter.

"But I didn't question it. I trusted him, perhaps blindly. I just... I never thought..." She bit her lower lip, blinking several times. "Maybe if I wouldn't have dressed the way I used to, or if I had talked to someone when I first felt uncomfortable. I mean, maybe I led him on, by not outright rejecting him. Maybe—"

"Sarah," I interrupted, squeezing her hand in mine. I lowered my gaze until she looked at me. "It is not your fault. His actions are his responsibility, not yours. The way you dress, the way you look, the trust you gave him, the time you spent with him — *none* of that is permission to touch you. Okay?"

She looked down again, and the burn in my chest shifted, transforming in a need for her to understand.

"I don't want to talk about it more right now, if that's okay," she said, blinking away the tears that were beginning to form again. "I just... I wanted to tell you because that's why I ran. I wanted you to kiss me, Reese. And I wanted to do more than just kiss. But... I'm damaged goods. I'm fucked up." The words came from her lips in bursts between her cries. "He was the first to touch me... to ever have me. And when *you* were touching me, I felt amazing. It was perfect.

I wanted you. For the first time, I wanted to be kissed, to be touched... but then... I saw him. And felt him. And..." she choked, more tears falling. "*Remembered* him."

"Jesus Christ." I stood, rounding the counter until I was standing next to her. She turned in her stool just as I approached, standing when I reached her, and I pulled her into my arms and held her as tightly as I could. "I am so fucking sorry, Sarah. I am so sorry. But you're okay. You're safe. Okay? I promise."

I wished I could hold her so tight I could take away what had happened, take away the pain, the memory. She cried harder now that she was in my arms, her small hands fisting in my t-shirt. And I gritted against the urge to break everything in my apartment since I couldn't break Wolfgang's face. He'd taken something so precious from her, something so delicate.

My blood was boiling.

And under that anger was the true feeling — helplessness.

I was confused, and grappling for something — *anything* — to say or do to make it all better.

"I want you to know how thankful I am that you felt comfortable enough to tell me this," I said after a long moment, still holding her in my arms, hoping the physical comfort would help my words sink in more. "And I also want you to know that what he did to you, it does not define who you are. And it does not define who you *aren't*."

Sarah whimpered a little, fisting her hands in my shirt, and I tugged her in even tighter. I couldn't get her close enough, couldn't surround her with myself enough to feel like it was adequate protection.

"And I want *you* to know you didn't do anything wrong," she mumbled into my shirt, the one she was staining with her tears. She pulled away enough to look up at me with a sniff. "You didn't. Okay?" She rolled her lips together. "But we... we can't..."

"I know," I said, finishing for her. "I know. You don't have to say it." Then, I tilted her chin with my knuckles, searching her eyes — the eyes of the strongest woman I'd ever known. "I promise, Sarah, that I will never hurt you again. I will never betray your trust. I respect you, and the boundaries between us. And I'm so sorry I ever made you question that."

Her brows pulled together, eyes welling with tears again as she shook her head and buried it in my chest. I soothed her, holding her tight, one hand cradling her head to my chest as the other held her to me.

The pain she felt radiated through me, and I closed my eyes, chest aching as the unwanted imagery hit me. Had he held her down against her will, forced himself on her and not listened when she'd screamed for help? My stomach twisted, nausea washing over me at the thought. I knew he wasn't in jail, and that was perhaps what upset me most.

How was he still teaching? How was he free to do whatever he wanted, and Sarah had to live with what he'd done to her?

I squeezed her to me tighter, shaking my head as a resolve set deep into my bones. As Sarah sobbed, as she broke in my arms, I repeated the vow I'd made to her, over and over, until it was solid as steel.

The need I'd felt before to protect her expanded, taking over everything inside of me. I didn't know if I'd ever be able to forgive myself for adding to her pain, for showing her yet again the way the power of a teacher can be abused. But I knew one thing was certain.

I would do everything to keep her safe.
And I would never cross that line again.

chapter Twelve

SARAH

I learned very quickly after that day that if there was one, solid truth about Reese Walker, it was this: he was true to his word.

I asked him not to tell anyone what I'd told him — namely my uncle — and not to pressure me into telling anyone else, either. After all, I'd already tried to tell someone, and I saw how far that got me. It was over, what had happened between me and Wolfgang, and I wanted to leave it behind, to let it go.

Reese respected that.

I knew it couldn't have been easy for him to do, to not tell my family what happened or take me straight to the police station. I could see it in his eyes, in the crease between his brows when he'd agreed to keep it between us. He didn't like it, but he agreed because it was what I wanted.

True to his word.

And for the first time since it happened, someone else knew what I'd been through. It was the relief I never knew I needed, and it seemed to unleash what I'd been holding back at the piano.

After I'd dried my tears and blown my nose about eighty times that day, we had our first piano lesson since he'd kissed me. It was short, but it was our first step into normalcy — and after that, the rest came just as easy.

Within a few days, we were back into our lessons, picking up right where we left off. We were back to Reese instructing from the corner of the room, not touching me, not holding me, not looking at me like he wanted to devour me.

Within a week, we were moving on to new challenges — transposing, fighting the bad habits I'd developed from earlier teachers in my life, and, as always, vulnerability and tension at the piano. We discussed piano and nothing else, just like we should.

The Fourth of July passed with both of us working at The Kinky Starfish — Reese playing for the patrons while I bussed tables. On his break, we stood outside and watched the fireworks over the city, and it'd been the closest we'd stood since he hugged me in his kitchen when I'd told him about my wolf.

And now, a little more than two weeks after the night Reese pressed his lips to mine, we were completely back to normal — well, as close to *normal* as we could get. I saw him on lesson days and, sometimes, for brief breaks at work. He would assign me pieces and critique my execution of them, giving me new things to work on. I was getting stronger, feeling better — my wrists and fingers finally able to keep up with the demand I put on myself as a musician. I wondered if the strength came with my admission to Reese, or with our practicing, or perhaps a combination of the two.

Everything should have felt perfect.

But there was a stirring inside me, one that had come to life the night Reese had touched me. And though I knew it was the right thing to keep our distance, to put those walls back up between us, to move forward as student and teacher and nothing more — I couldn't deny that I missed him.

I missed talking, missed laughing, missed opening myself up to him and listening when he did the same. I missed that connection, though it was still there, under the surface, buzzing like the universal *om* of the universe. It was the strangest thing, that we were still together, yet Reese felt so distant now.

He said he would never cross that line again, that he would respect me and the role he played in my life.

And, again, he was true to his word.

"I have a new piece for you," he said to me at our Monday lesson, taking a seat on the bench next to me as he set up the sheet music in front of us.

He kept plenty of space between his leg and my own, and though it was what I'd said I wanted, what I said I thought was best, I wished in that moment that I could close the distance.

"It's not classical. In fact, it's quite modern. But... well, I think it will open you in a new way."

"Why do I feel like I should be scared right now?"

Reese chuckled. "Don't be scared." He paused, eyeing me for a moment before his hands found the keys. "Do you sing at all?"

"Sometimes," I said.

He nodded, fingers already moving over the keys as a slow, sad melody came to life at his will. "I want you to sing this as I play."

I balked. "Uh... no. I'm not singing in front of you."

"Come on," he said on a laugh. "It's just us. I'm not judging. I just want you to read these lyrics, sing them, feel them. They're as important as the music in this particular assignment."

I whined. "Reese, I'm terrible. I'll split your eardrums."

But he didn't acknowledge me, just kept playing, his body moving more with the notes as the opening stretched on. Then, he closed his eyes, that crease between his brows making itself known before he opened his mouth and sang.

And the voice that came out of that man nearly knocked me off the bench.

My jaw dropped dramatically, though Reese couldn't see with his eyes closed like that. Everything about that moment surprised me — the raspy, deep rumble of his voice echoing off the walls as he played, the way the lyrics melted with the music, the fact that Reese was *singing* in front of me. The lyrics spoke of no one knowing him like the piano in his mom's house, and he sang on, moving with the dramatic notes in the music as he did.

His hair was pulled back, fastened loosely at the nape of his neck with the dark strands falling out of place to frame his jaw. That jaw was thick with stubble, the skin under his eyes dark like he hadn't been sleeping. And as he bent and flowed with the music, singing each word like he felt it in his soul, I truly believed he did.

Reese Walker was only thirty-seven years old, but he'd lived a thousand lives. Of that, I was sure.

I was enraptured, pulled into that moment with him — like the music was a magic carpet that transported us to another world. And the longer I watched him, the more I wanted to reside in this world instead of the one we'd just been in before. In this world, I felt like I could hold Reese. In this world, I felt like he could kiss me.

225

In this world, we could lose ourselves between the strings of that piano forever.

When the song came to an end, he opened his eyes, bringing his hands to his lap as he turned to me.

"Reese... that was beautiful."

His eyes searched mine, and for the briefest moment, it was the way he looked at me before. *Before* he knew. Before I'd said no, and he'd listened.

Reese cleared his throat, standing and crossing the room to his corner like he had to put space between us or he'd kiss me again.

Part of me wished he would.

The bigger part of me knew he couldn't, that I wouldn't let him.

"Thank you," he said as he walked. When he was back in the corner, he turned, folding his arms over one another. "It's called *No One Knows Me* by Sampha. Relatively new song, but when I heard it..." He swallowed. "It just hit me in a soft spot. And I feel like it will do the same for you." He smirked. "Maybe help us get over this vulnerability mountain we've been climbing."

I returned his smile, nodding gently before my hands found the keys. I read the music on the sheet in front of me, feeling out the new song, piecing it all together.

"Take that home with you," he said as I played around with the music. "I want you to sing as you learn it, really listen to not just the music, but the lyrics. Okay?"

I pulled my hands away from the keys, reaching for the music to tuck into my messenger bag, instead. "Okay. But I'm going to tell Uncle Randall that it's you to blame for the windows breaking when I sing."

Reese chuckled.

Rojo lazily trotted into the room with us, drooling around a yellow tennis ball in her mouth. She dropped it at Reese's feet and sat, looking up at him with her tongue hanging out.

"I know, girl. I know. We'll go play soon," he said, rubbing her head.

"She fetches now?"

He nodded. "When I lift outside, she likes to go out with me and play. At first, she just laid there in the sun, but now, she'll bring me this ball and fetch it for a while. I was thinking about taking her to the dog park this weekend, get her out of the house a little."

The image of Reese without his shirt on the day I'd come to tell him about Wolfgang was one I was sure I'd never get out of my head, and it was easy to picture him out back, sitting on the bench I'd noticed a few times with weights lining the bottom of it. I wondered if he did calisthenics, if the neighbors watched the sweat rolling from his hairline the way I had that day, following it in a trance as it slid down his temple, his jaw, his neck, chest, abdomen.

I swallowed, shaking the thoughts away.

"Can I come?"

The words were out of my mouth before I realized I shouldn't have asked, shouldn't have invited myself to hang out with Reese outside of our lessons. That was what I'd asked him for — those boundaries.

Now, they sort of felt like prison bars.

Reese furrowed his brows, scratching at his jaw as he considered my request.

"I'm sorry," I said on a sigh, shoving my folder into my messenger bag along with my new assignment. "I just... I don't get out much on the weekends, other than our Sunday lesson. But that's not your problem. I shouldn't have asked you that. It's your weekend, I'm sure you'd like to spend it without the student you have to put up with all week."

I was trying to joke, aiming for lightness in my voice that I somehow missed.

"I don't mind if you join."

I glanced up at him from the bench. "Are you sure?"

It seemed like Reese was at war inside that head of his, like he was battling between what he should say and what he wanted to. "Yeah. I'm sure. Rojo would love it."

Would you love it, too?

I smiled, swallowing that question down. "Okay. As long as you're sure."

———

REESE

"Wait, wait, wait," I said, still laughing around a mouthful of pretzels. "You're serious? *You* used to fish?"

Sarah nodded, swallowing the last bite of her peanut butter and jelly sandwich. "Mm-hmm. It was one of my dad's favorite things to do on the weekends, and I was hell bent on being his fishing buddy. I'd help him pick out lures, hook worms, fix reels. The whole shebang."

"You stuck hooks in worms, and now you're vegan?"

She threw a pretzel at me. "I told you, I was young. I didn't know any better!"

I was still chuckling as she smoothed out her long skirt, crossing one ankle over the other. We were both seated on an old blanket of mine, the shade from the dogwood tree we'd parked under offering reprieve from the hot sun. A cool breeze whipped in from time to time, blowing back the light, creamsicle-colored orange scarf Sarah wore around her neck. It was the brightest color I'd seen her wear, and it matched the gem stones in the small earrings adorning her earlobes.

She looked happy and free, and it was my favorite way to see her.

Rojo had played in the park all afternoon, but now she was sprawled out on her side, half in the sun and half in the shade on the other side of Sarah. I'd considered cancelling, telling Sarah I changed my mind and wouldn't be able to take Rojo to the park like I'd planned. I knew being with her outside of our lessons was dangerous, a fire I shouldn't play with or even stand next to for warmth. But, the temptation to spend more time with her won out, along with the dejected look on her face when she'd thought I was going to say no when she originally asked.

The truth was, I missed her.

I missed talking to her, missed her laugh, her jokes, her incessant need to give me advice on my life even though I hadn't asked for it. If it weren't for her, I wouldn't have Rojo — and that dog had become my everything within a month.

Sarah had brought light into my life, and when we'd put those boundaries between us again, it was like a thick, gray cloud had returned.

I just wanted a little time in the sun again.

"When I was that age, I'd do just about anything to hang out with my dad," she said after a moment, her smile back as her eyes gazed off in the distance. "He was my hero. Then again, I suppose that's every little girl."

"Did he listen to you play?"

She nodded. "Oh, yes. He's the reason my dream is what it is."

I frowned, reaching for one of the bottles of water we'd packed and cracking it open. "What do you mean?"

"He took me to a performance at Carnegie Hall when I was eleven." She shook her head, eyes lighting up as she reached for her crystal. "It was when Daniel Barenboim played with the Staatskapelle Berlin string quartet."

"Wow."

She laughed. "Right? I remember sitting there in the audience, dressed up and holding my dad's hand, mouth hanging open pretty much the entire performance."

"I would have been catching flies, too."

Sarah chuckled. "It was so incredible, and so moving. One moment I'd be smiling and laughing, bouncing with the music. The next? I'd be quietly crying. And my dad squeezed my hand and never let go the entire time." She softened at that, picking at the grass near the edge of the blanket. "When the show was over and everyone got up to make their way out, he made me stay and sit. And when the theatre was nearly empty, he pointed up at the stage, and he said, 'You belong up there. That's going to be you one day.' And from that moment on, it was my dream to make his words come true."

The breeze picked up, blowing what was left of the spring blooms on the dogwood above us. Little puffs of white floated down and around us, surfing the wind until they landed on the grass or our blanket. I just watched Sarah pick at the grass until Rojo shifted, her head rolling over onto Sarah's leg. She smiled at that, rubbing behind Rojo's ear.

Suddenly, it all made sense — her passion, her drive, her optimism when it came to Carnegie, despite all the obstacles life had handed her. She could have quit after her father passed, or after her injury, or after her professor assaulted her. But instead, she'd taken that pain and used it as fuel. She'd made a promise to her father and to herself, and no matter how out of reach it seemed to get on that stage in New York, she was going to do it.

She believed it. I believed it.

It would happen. I knew that more than anything in my entire life.

I watched her petting my dog as all that sank in, as my heart swelled with respect and care. I'd never talked to anyone in my entire life the way I talked with Sarah, the way she talked with me. How was it that we'd only known each other a few months, and yet, she was so easy to open up to, to show my scars to?

And her scars didn't scare me. They looked just like mine. I understood them — the shiny skin, the curve of the mark, the deep branding of the cut. I knew it all too well.

This.

This was what I missed.

Her stories, her unique way of looking at life, her optimism, her unmovable belief that she would make her dreams come true. Sarah was unlike any woman I'd met before. She was positive despite the cards life had handed her. Where I broke under the tragedies of my life, she flourished under hers.

"Anyway," she said, shaking her head as she turned to me. "What about you? What are your dreams?"

I let my head fall back as a bark of a laugh left my chest. When I looked back at Sarah, her brows were drawn in. "Wait, are you serious?"

"Of course, I'm serious."

I laughed again. "Sarah, I'm thirty-seven years old."

"What does that have to do with anything?" She scrunched up her nose. "You can have dreams no matter how old you are. Surely, there must be *something* you want to achieve, somewhere you want to go, some place you want to see?"

The way she was looking at me, it was the first time in my life that I felt ashamed of my answer to that question. I'd always just embraced it, accepted that my life was never going to turn out the way I thought it would when I was twelve. My family was gone. The woman I wanted to marry married someone else. I pissed away my talent instead of putting myself to work in Manhattan. I was a mess in every sense of the word, and I'd always been okay with it.

Until I had to answer to Sarah.

"The only thing I want is to survive," I said, and then I sort of scoffed. "And honestly, even that comes in waves."

Sarah's face crumpled at that. "Reese..."

"I don't mean it like that," I said quickly, yanking the hair tie from where it was holding my hair at the nape of my neck. I ran my hands through it, situating it again before replacing the tie. "I just mean that my time for dreaming has come and gone. I just want to play piano and make enough money to pay my bills." I looked at Rojo, who was panting from laying in the sun, her eyes closed and little mouth turned up into what could be a smile. "And take care of that one, now, too."

Sarah rubbed Rojo's head, but her mouth was pulled to the side when she faced me again. The way the sun streamed through the tree above us, it highlighted her mocha skin in little streams of gold, the flecks in her eyes coming to life with each blow of the wind.

"You're not too old to dream, Reese," she said softly. "But if you're happy, that's all that matters."

I internally laughed at that. *Happy.* When was the last time I could say that word in a sentence that described how I felt? But, this was just another difference between us, Sarah and I. She was young, she had her whole life ahead of her. And I did not.

My time had passed, and whether I wanted to be in Mount Lebanon teaching piano to prep school kids or not didn't matter. I had a job, and a house that was my own. I had my health — for the most part, though I knew smoking wasn't going to help me keep that statement accurate for long.

I wasn't necessarily *happy*, but I was okay.

That was enough for me.

"Have you ever written a song?" I asked her, changing the subject away from me. "For piano? Have you ever composed?"

Sarah took a deep breath, eyes floating up to the tree branches above us. "Only once. After my dad died." She chuckled. "It was awful, but it meant something to me."

"You should play it for me sometime."

"That will never happen," she said quickly. "It's really hard for me to create music. I can play it, but asking me to figure out how to build a song, how to find a melody that conveys what I'm feeling? It's like asking me to design a website. I know nothing."

"That's not true," I said. "You just have to have the right inspiration. I didn't write my first song until after my family died, either. And the first *real* one I wrote that I was proud of came when I least expected it."

"Who was it for?"

Her question hit me hard in the chest, because she could have asked a number of other things — *when did you write it, where did you play it, what kind of song, have you ever played it for anyone* — but instead, she asked who it was for.

Because a song was always written with someone else in mind.

I didn't answer, and we both knew I didn't have to. She knew who the song was for. And I was so painfully aware of how pathetic I was in that moment that I wished I'd never admitted to writing a song at all.

Another gust of wind set the dogwood blooms flying, and one landed in a fold of Sarah's scarf. I leaned over, plucking it free before I even realized I was doing it.

Sarah's eyes met mine, the air between us sparking to life the way it always seemed to do.

I cleared my throat. "They have rollerblades for rent over there," I said, nodding toward a little stand near the trail that circled the park. "What do you say? Want to give it a try?"

"I've never skated before."

I smiled. "Well, then this should be fun."

"I'm going to crash, I'm going to crash, OHMYGOD I'M GOING TO CRASH."

Sarah's hands were out at her sides, arms stiff and knees locked as she skated ahead of me and Rojo — if you could even call what she was doing *skating*. It was more akin to standing as stiff as a board, slowly rolling along the concrete. She had knee pads under her skirt, elbow pads wrapped around her arms, wrist guards protecting the bones and muscles we'd worked so hard to heal, *and* a helmet — all of which made her look like she was roughly thirteen years old. Combined with the giant smile on her face and eyes the size of stars, it was impossible not to watch her.

It was impossible not to smile, too.

"You're not going to crash," I said on a laugh, letting Rojo trot at her own speed as I skated behind her with the leash in my hand. "But if you don't loosen up, you're just going to float around like a stiff board all afternoon."

"I'm trying not to fall."

"Why?" I asked, skating up beside her. She looked half excited, half terrified as she shuffled her feet in the blades. "What would be so wrong about falling?"

She glanced at me, eyes flicking back and forth between me and the sidewalk in front of her. "Well... I don't know. It would hurt."

"Maybe for a second. But you'll survive. Come on, ditch the fear and let's do this." I reached out the hand that wasn't holding Rojo's leash for hers. "Do you trust me?"

She swallowed, eyeing my hand like it was a rose disguising a bomb. "I do... but—"

"No buts," I said, folding her small hand in mine. "Just hold on."

I started to skate a little faster, letting Rojo adjust to my speed as well as Sarah. She gripped my hand like a lifeline, making little squeaks with each stride we made.

"We're going to crash," she said when we zoomed by a jogger.

I laughed. "We are not going to—"

But before I could finish the sentence, a dog off its leash ran across the trail right in front of us. I veered us left, but Rojo chased after the dog to the right, tangling me and Sarah both in her leash. I stumbled, still holding onto Sarah and trying to save us, but my wheels couldn't catch enough friction to combat gravity.

It was too late.

I pulled Sarah into me, shielding her as much as I could from the fall just as I lost my footing and we tumbled to the ground, rolling off into the grass with Rojo still barking.

"Shit," I said, pulling back from where I held Sarah to examine her. "Are you okay? I'm sorry, I didn't see that dog until it was too late."

Her honey eyes were wide, her hands shaking, and for a moment I thought she might cry as I searched her for blood or bruises. But instead, she tilted her head back and laughed.

She laughed like a woman set free, the noise bubbling out of her chest like a spring. The longer I watched her, the more the corner of my mouth lifted. She waved me off, like I was the reason she was laughing uncontrollably as she tried and failed to catch her breath. Tears were in the corners of her eyes when she was finally able to stop, and she swiped them away, still smiling as she looked up at me from the grass.

"God, that was so much fun."

I chuckled. "I told you. Falling isn't so bad."

We both grew quiet, and where my attention had been focused on her safety before, it was now acutely aware of how close we were. The way we'd landed, I was practically on top of her, one leg between hers with my arm under her neck, the other hand holding me up where I framed her.

Sarah's eyes flashed between mine, and when her gaze fell to my lips, I inhaled a stiff breath as every nerve below my belt kicked to life.

One of her hands was on my chest, the other on my bicep where I held myself up, and she wrapped that hand around the muscle, squeezing. I swallowed, allowing myself one, brief glance at her plump lips before I cleared my throat and rolled away.

I stood quickly, adjusting myself in my pants before reaching down a hand for hers. I forced a smile with the gesture. "Come on, let's try again."

For a moment, Sarah just stared at my hand, her cheeks a shade of pink. Once she took my hand and I helped her up, her gaze fell to something behind me.

"Well, it's about time I ran into you."

I whipped around, and I knew there was no use in trying to hide my surprise when I realized it was Jennifer Stinson that Sarah had been looking at. Her platinum blonde hair was pulled up into a high ponytail, and she sported a tight-fitting, matching athletic set that accentuated all of her well-developed curves, as well as her tan, toned stomach. She was *dressed* like she was there to work out, but she still wore a full face of makeup — complete with crimson red lips, as always.

At her feet was a tiny chihuahua, that Rojo was now inspecting.

I tugged her leash, snapping my fingers once for her to sit down. "Jennifer," I said, holding Rojo by the collar once she was seated so she wouldn't eat Jennifer's dog by accident. "Nice to see you. I didn't know you had a dog."

"I would have told you if you would have taken me on that date we discussed," she fired back, arching one manicured brow. The corner of her lips rose as her eyes flicked from me to Sarah. "I didn't know *you* had a daughter."

I frowned, because there was absolutely *no way* Jennifer honestly believed Sarah was my daughter. We obviously looked nothing alike. The more her gaze shifted as she appraised Sarah, the more I realized she just wanted to point out the fact that I was hanging out with someone much, much younger than me — and she wanted to know why.

"This is Sarah Henderson," I explained. "Randall's niece. She's taking piano lessons with me."

"In the park?" Jennifer asked.

The question was innocent at its base, but the way she said it, the tone of her voice and arch in her brow as she appraised me again let me know it wasn't a friendly question at all.

"It's sort of a lesson on fear, combating it both in life and at the piano in order to play the more emotional pieces," Sarah said from beside me, her voice surprisingly firm and confident. She held her chin high as a small smile graced her lips. "It's hard to understand if you're not a musician, I'm sure."

Jennifer's lip curled at that, but she smiled despite it, offering Sarah a little nod. "Well, I'm sure it's a great lesson." She turned to me again then. "After all, you've got the best teacher in town."

Rojo tugged away from me, eager to sniff the tiny dog at Jennifer's feet.

"Sarah, this is Jennifer Stinson. We met at a fundraiser a couple years ago."

"Oh, don't let him fool you," Jennifer said, wicked smile climbing. "I asked him to dance, and he turned me down.

He's been playing hard to get ever since. But, I'm a patient woman. And I know a catch when I see one."

Her boldness shouldn't have surprised me — that was exactly how she'd always been. But for some reason, it made me feel uncomfortable that it was all taking place in front of Sarah this time.

Because she's your student, I tried to convince myself.

I cleared my throat, forcing as much of a smile as I could manage. "We were actually just about to get going," I said. "But it was nice seeing you."

"Are you free this weekend?" Jennifer asked, ignoring my attempt to break free.

"Uh..."

"Come on," she said, stepping a little closer. Bold as ever, she reached up and pulled a few blades of grass from my shirt, all the while staring at my lips in no effort to hide the thoughts that underlined her next sentence. "I've waited long enough, don't you think?"

I stepped away from her, tight smile still in place. "You have. I'm sorry, I'm not avoiding you." *Lies.* "I've just been really busy with lessons and work. But, let me check my schedule and I'll give you a call."

"This week," she said.

It wasn't a request.

"Um... sure. This week."

"Great!" She seemed appeased, and she offered Sarah a big smile. "It was nice to meet you, sweetheart. Good luck with your *studies*."

Jennifer's eyes flicked to me quickly before she zeroed in on Sarah again, and without another word, she strutted off down the trail, her tiny dog following.

chapter thirteen

SARAH

The car ride back to Reese's place was absolutely silent. Reese hadn't reached forward to turn on the radio, and neither of us had said a word since we climbed inside the car. Even Rojo was sound asleep in the back, tuckered out from the day at the park.

It didn't matter that the car was completely quiet, because my thoughts were as loud as train whistles.

Jennifer Stinson had practically pissed on Reese in front of me, which shouldn't have upset me as much as it did. She was his age. She was *gorgeous*, and clearly fit, and, apparently, they ran in the same circle. She'd be a great girlfriend for him, a great woman to get him over Charlie and moving forward.

All of that might have been true, but I still hated it.

I hated it because I wanted it to be me. I wanted it to be *me* who was strikingly gorgeous, fit and bold and confident enough to march right up to Reese in the park and demand a date. I wanted it to be me — in another world, another time, another place where I wasn't his student and he wasn't my teacher, where I wasn't so fucked up from the first man who touched me that I couldn't even let Reese try.

"I'm sorry about that," Reese said once we were on the highway. "Jennifer can be... brash."

I swallowed, stomach flipping around at the sound of her name on his lips. I had no right to be jealous, to care, but I did. It was something about the casual tone, the friendly way he referred to her — like he knew her, like she knew him.

I only wanted to hear my name on his lips like that.

"I think she's refreshing," I said, folding my hands over my stomach like I could soothe it with a sort of hug as that lie slipped through. "She knows what she wants, and she's confident." I turned to him, then. "You should go on a date with her."

"*What*?" Reese's brows pulled in so fast I thought he'd give himself a headache. He shook his head, shifting one hand off the wheel and replacing it with the other before he glanced at me. "You're kidding, right?"

"Not at all."

Reese eyed me for the longest time before he pulled his gaze back to the road, cracking his neck without responding.

"I'm just saying, it's been two years since you quote, unquote, *dated* — and even that is a stretch, all things considered."

Reese's face fell flat at that.

"I'm not trying to dredge up old Charlie feelings or anything," I said quickly. "I'm just saying... even if Jennifer isn't the *right* one, she could be the right one to get you out of your funk. Maybe open you up to dating again. You know?"

Reese apparently *didn't* know, because he just stared forward, the muscle in his jaw flexing as he gripped the wheel so tight his knuckles were the color of my uncle's face. He shook his head, almost imperceptibly, before he finally responded.

"So, you want me to go on a date? That's what you're saying?"

No.

God, no.

Not even a little bit.

It's the absolute last thing I want.

"Yeah," I answered instead, swallowing down any other response my brain was screaming at me.

Or rather, my heart.

"I do. I think it'll be good for you."

Reese laughed, the sound so soft and laced with distaste that I wasn't sure it could even be classified as a true laugh. He shook his head, but didn't look at me again.

"Fine. Guess I'll go on a date, then."

I swallowed, forcing a smile like I'd won, like him agreeing to take Jennifer out was somehow a victory.

When we made it back to his place, Reese offered me a stiff hug goodbye before taking Rojo inside. I stood there in his driveway for the longest time, staring at his front door. I didn't know why I was rooted to that spot, why I felt so physically ill that throwing up was the only thing I wanted to do in that moment to find some sort of relief.

But I tore myself from the spot, climbing into my uncle's car and driving the ten minutes it took me to get home in complete silence.

This is the right thing, I told myself. *Reese will be happier with someone like her.*

Someone who isn't me.

I said those words in my mind, over and over and over again — even after I'd slipped inside the house and closed the door to the piano room, taking a seat at the bench. I immediately began working on the piece Reese had assigned me, but it felt flat, and my desire to sing was somewhere right around my desire to see Jennifer Stinson again.

My shoulders fell, hands collapsing on the keys as an ugly string of notes rang out.

If this was the right thing to do, if pushing Reese away was what was best... why did I feel so sick?

———

A week later, I stared at my former best friend's name on my phone like pressing the DIAL button would set off a nuclear bomb.

It'd been a rough seven days.

The piece Reese had assigned me was harder for me than I expected — mostly because I couldn't tap into the same emotion as the composer. I wanted to nail it, drive it home when I performed it tomorrow at our Sunday lesson, but I felt like I was miles away from grasping what I needed to in order to accomplish that.

Not only was I struggling with the assignment, but Reese had been distant and cold at our lessons that week. If it was even possible, he seemed to be back to the same grump he'd been the first time we'd met. I tried to convince myself he was just doing what I'd asked him to do. He was acting as my teacher, not my friend. And that's what I wanted. I didn't come to Pennsylvania to make friends.

The problem was that I had, anyway.

Whether I wanted to admit it or not, I loved hanging out with Reese. I wanted to be around him — not just when he was teaching me, but *all the time.*

Maybe that's why my stomach had lurched at our Thursday lesson when Jennifer had called him and he'd agreed to take her out Saturday night.

AKA tonight.

He hadn't so much as acknowledged the call when it was over, picking up our lesson right where he'd left it like I hadn't just heard him tell another woman that he'd pick her up at seven on Saturday night. And I knew it didn't matter, that he was doing *exactly* what I'd asked him to do — true to his word, just like I knew he would be.

But I still sat there on his piano bench with a thick, sticky tongue for the rest of our lesson.

Now, here it was five o'clock on Saturday evening. Reese was probably showering. He was probably shaving, laying out his clothes, spritzing himself with the cologne that I loved so much. He was probably combing his hair back into a nice, neat bun at the nape of his neck, probably lighting up a cigarette to ease his nerves.

And I was here, alone.

It was just as it should be. I *wanted* him to date, to move on from Charlie, to find a step forward. I wanted him to be happy.

I just hated that it couldn't be with me.

I needed to talk to someone before my thoughts drove me up the goddamn wall. But I couldn't tell my mom, *definitely* couldn't tell my aunt or uncle, and I'd pushed every other person in my life away when I'd left Bramlock.

Including Reneé.

Sighing, I shook my head and finally tapped the DIAL button, putting the call on speaker. As soon as the rings started filling my room, my stomach tightened, a knot forming in my throat that I had to swallow past when she answered.

"Hello? Sarah?"

I tried to swallow, but couldn't. I just sat there, tears welling in my eyes at the sound of her voice.

"Sarah, please tell me it's you."

"It's me," I croaked.

"Oh my God," she cried in response, and the tears in my eyes welled more, slipping over my cheeks as I covered my mouth with one hand. "It's really you? I thought you'd died. I thought... I don't even know. I thought I would never hear from you again."

"I'm so sorry," I said, choking on my own tears. "I'm so sorry I left you, that I didn't call or text. I don't have a valid excuse but I'm so sorry."

"It's okay," she assured me. "It's okay. Whatever your reasoning was, I understand." She sniffed. "Now, tell me everything to make up for the fact that you've given me premature gray hairs."

I laughed, swiping the tears from my face as I pictured my best friend — warm, brown skin, wide chocolate eyes, hair wild and curly, smile as wide as her face.

"Seriously, start talking. Why the hell didn't you come back last semester? Where have you been? What have you been doing? Are you sick?" She gasped. "Oh my God... are you dying? Sarah, if you are just now calling to tell me you have some sort of disease and only have a few days to live, I swear to science I'll fly to wherever you are and kill you myself."

I chuckled again, fluffing the pillows on my bed before leaning back against them with the phone on my chest. "I'm not dying. I'm perfectly healthy. And I'm in Pittsburgh... well, Mount Lebanon. I'm staying with my uncle and taking piano lessons with Reese Walker. Oh, also, I sha—"

"Wait, wait, wait," she said, cutting me off. "You're in *Pennsylvania?* And you're taking lessons with *the* Reese Walker? What the hell, Sarah? Why haven't you told me? Why have you ignored my calls and texts?"

I sighed. "It's... complicated."

"Break it down."

"I can't," I said on a swallow. That earned me a huff on the other end, and I sat up a little straighter, pinching the bend of my nose. "Look, I know it's frustrating. I left, I didn't come back, I ignored you and everyone else who reached out to me. And now, I call you out of the blue, and I still can't tell you everything. I know that is stupid and upsetting, but... I love you, Reneé. You're the closest thing I've ever had to a sister and I really, really need you right now. And I know it's not fair, but I'm asking you to understand that I can't tell you everything about why I left Bramlock, but that I am okay." I paused. "Well, for the most part, anyway."

She huffed again, a long pause lingering between us before she spoke. "That's really not fair."

"I know."

"And it's really selfish, too."

"I know."

Reneé paused. "But, I love you. And if you can't tell me yet... then, I guess that's okay."

I let out a long breath of relief. "Thank you. Thank you for understanding."

"Yeah, yeah," she mumbled. "Now, you said something about needing me. What's going on?"

"Well... it kind of has to do with Reese."

"*Reese?* You're on a first-name basis with a piano god?"

I blushed, fingering my necklace. "I may be on a lip to lip basis with a piano god."

"WHAT?! Okay, enough teasing. SPILL."

I laughed, launching into the story from the very beginning. I told her about the lessons, how I still wanted to go to Carnegie and play in New York City and Reese was my way to get there now that I had dipped out of school. I told her about our lessons, about the incredible way he played, the way he taught. I told her about Charlie, about Reese opening up to me, and me opening up to him about my dad — which she gasped at, since she was pretty much the only other person I'd ever told. Then, I told her about the kiss — and how I'd jumped off him and ran out.

We'd had to run over that quite a few times for her to understand.

Of course, I didn't tell her what I told him — about Wolfgang, about what had happened that December night at Bramlock. But, I tried my best to explain that it was clear we couldn't be together like that.

When all was said and done, Reneé blew out a long whistle, digesting everything I'd said.

"So, your hot ass, piano god of a teacher makes a move on you. You *reciprocate* that move, and then you run out because... you're too young for him?"

"*And* I'm his student. And he's my uncle's employee."

"Yeah..." she said on a long sigh. "I guess that all makes sense. But, you still like him. You still want more, even though you told him you don't."

I sighed, because she was right... but even with telling her all that, I was leaving out the biggest piece of the puzzle.

I'm scared. And damaged. And I don't know how to be intimate with anyone because all that desire was stolen from me.

"*And*, you told him he should go on a date with someone else," Reneé continued. "And he listened."

"Damn him for being true to his word."

She chuckled at that. "Well, bestie, as much as I hate to say this, I think you put yourself in this pickle."

I groaned, covering my face with a pillow before throwing it across the room. "I know, okay? I know. The question is, what do I do about it *now*?"

She let out another long sigh, the silence growing between us.

"Honestly? I think you should tell him how you feel."

I scoffed.

"No, seriously. Tell him you still like him, you don't want him to go on dates with other women, but you also don't know how to even begin to *be* with him yourself. Tell him everything that worries you — his relationship to you as your teacher, his job with your uncle, the age thing. Just give him a chance to talk to you about all your concerns, see if they concern him, too. If they do?" Reneé clucked with her tongue. "Well, then, there's your answer. You draw the line and stay on opposite sides of it. But, maybe he has answers for the questions. Maybe he doesn't care about the age or his job. Maybe he wants you, and that's all there is to it."

I made a face. "That's an awful dreamy way to look at things."

"My favorite way."

I smiled at that, because it was true. If there was a way to personify sunshine, it would be recreated in my best friend.

"I've really missed you," I whispered. "Thank you, Reneé. For listening. For being there for me when I was gone for so long. And for not judging."

"I've missed you, too. But you're never allowed to leave me like that again."

"Deal."

"Oh, and please, you know I'd never judge you. Honestly, I don't know how you thought I could with this situation. It's like every girl's fantasy." She snickered. "I wish *my* hot professor would kiss me."

My stomach dropped at that, bile rising in my throat when I realized she was talking about Wolfgang. I was still swallowing that bile down when Reneé spoke again.

"By the way, did you hear that he got the Roger H. Belanger Award today?" She laughed. "I'm surprised it took them so long. He's clearly the best professor our campus has ever seen. Anyway, they're doing this big award ceremony for him. It's next week." She gasped. "Oh, my God. You should come, Sarah! You can stay with me, we can go out, you can see everyone again. I know you're over our measly university now that you're studying with *the* Reese Walker, but you could slum it for a while, right?"

That bile I'd been able to swallow down quickly resurfaced, black invading my vision as I blindly felt my way through my bedroom to the bathroom attached.

"Come on, you have to come! I graduate at the end of the summer. This could be a last little send off."

I blindly felt the bathroom wall for the light switch, flicking it on without a single inch of light reaching me. The darkness creeping in was too strong, and I blinked against the black, trying to see. Trying to breathe.

"I have to go," I managed. "I'll text you."

"Sarah?"

But I didn't answer. I *couldn't* answer.

As soon as I ended the call, I hit my knees and forfeited my dinner into the toilet.

chapter fourteen

REESE

"So, that's when I said... *'just because these red bottom heels are hot doesn't mean I won't shove one straight up your ass if you talk to me like that again.'*"

Jennifer snapped her fingers, laughing at her own story as I turned the steering wheel, finally making it to the street her house was on. I forced a smile, trying to be polite, but I was about to crawl out of my skin if I didn't get her out of my car in the next five minutes. I couldn't wait to put this night in my past, to go home and drink as many beers as it took to forget every minute of it.

I'd known before I'd even agreed to the date that it would be a nightmare, and I was right.

And it was all Sarah's fault that I'd subjected myself to it.

I knew I shouldn't blame her, *couldn't* blame her — not when I was a grown-ass man capable of making my own decisions. But it had been her who had pushed me. It had been her who had said I should go on a date with someone who *wasn't* her.

She'd wanted to make a point, and I'd heard it loud and clear.

Again, I couldn't be mad at her for pointing at that line between us and reminding me of it. That day at the park, I'd proven to her that my word wasn't as good as I'd promised. I'd stared at her too long, stayed too close to her after our fall... and I'd clearly failed to hide the fact that I desperately wanted to kiss her again. I'd failed her in every way possible, and she'd nailed her intentions home when we were back in my car.

She literally begged me to go on a date with another woman. *That's* how badly Sarah wanted me to stay away from her.

And in all honesty, after that day? I thought maybe she was right. Maybe I should go on a date with a woman my own age, get my head right in all aspects — mind off Sarah, moving forward after Charlie. I got it. I understood how it could possibly be a good thing for me.

But in my gut, I knew it was a terrible decision.

And from the moment I picked Jennifer up, I'd been living in my own personal hell.

As if the mindless conversation and completely overpriced dinner hadn't been bad enough, she'd practically molested me under the table, making her intentions *very* clear. I didn't know what made me more uncomfortable — the stuffy suit I was in, the stuffy restaurant I'd had to endure for two hours, or the stuffy woman who couldn't keep her hands to herself.

When I pulled up to her house, I realized the worst was yet to come.

"Well, this is me," she breathed, glancing at her beautiful, luxurious home that was entirely too much for one woman before turning back to me. Her eyes were lazy from the wine, red lipstick smudged a little at the edges as her lips curled into a wicked smile. "Thank you for a wonderful evening, Reese."

I forced another smile. "It was my pleasure."

Her eyes slipped from mine to my lips before she leaned over the console, her mouth on track for mine. My heart thundered in my chest as I considered my next move. Whatever it was, it would be ugly — because I was not kissing that woman.

Thankfully, I didn't have to figure it out just yet, because she paused with her mouth just a few inches from mine. Her hand grazed my knee before she ran it up the inside of my thigh, and as much as the old me would have jumped for joy at the easy lay, the new me wasn't even capable of getting hard.

She wasn't what I wanted.

She wasn't *who* I wanted.

"Why don't you come inside," she whispered, licking her lips as her hand crawled higher. "I'll make us some drinks."

I'd always given Jennifer credit for her boldness, but in that moment, I wished she were a little more coy. I wished she wasn't so aggressive, just so I wouldn't have to have the very uncomfortable conversation that was about to take place.

I covered her hand with my own, clearing my throat as I stopped her before she could grab what she really wanted to. It only seemed to fuel her, that wicked smile climbing on her lips as she leaned in closer.

"I think we should call it a night, Jennifer."

She paused, just an inch between us, her eyes still on my lips like she wasn't sure she'd heard me right. Her salacious smile slipped just marginally before it was back, more drive than ever in her eyes as she closed the distance between us.

"Yeah, sure. Let's call it a night," she said just before her mouth met mine.

She inhaled at the contact, sucking in a breath on a sexy moan as she kissed me. And everything I'd tried to escape that night was no longer avoidable.

I pulled back on a grimace, placing my hands on her arms to hold her away from me. Jennifer panted, eyes flicking between mine as her chest heaved, confusion rolling over her.

"I really think I should go," I said, firmer this time.

At that, her little mouth fell open in a stretched *o* before she popped it shut again.

Her brows drew in, lips pursed as she yanked away from my grip. "What the hell is wrong with you?" she seethed, snatching her purse from the floorboard and strapping it over one shoulder before turning on me again. "Do you not see how incredibly out of your league I am? You should be so lucky to take me on a date, let alone get an invitation inside my house at the end of the night."

I fought the urge to roll my eyes. "If you're so out of my league, then it shouldn't bother you that I don't want to come inside."

Jennifer scoffed, poking me hard in the chest. "What is your deal? You want me, I know you do."

"Jennifer," I sighed her name, pinching the bridge of my nose as I shook my head. "Please, don't do this. It was a nice evening, but really, I—"

"She doesn't love you."

The words I was about to speak died on my lips, hanging there along with my jaw. "Excuse me?"

"Charlie," she clarified, spitting her name like a curse. "Charlie Pierce does not love you, Reese. She never did.

She never will. She's *married*," she spat. "In case you forgot again."

I gritted my teeth, the muscle in my jaw tight and tense. "I don't know what you're—"

"Oh, cut the bullshit, Reese. Everyone in this town knows that something happened between you two, even if we don't have all the details. She had an affair, got it out of her system — got *you* out of her system — and now she and Cameron are happier than they've ever been. And you?" She laughed. "You're walking around town like a sad, pathetic loser."

"You don't know what you're talking about."

"And here *I* am," she said louder, ignoring me. "Offering you something most men in this town *dream* about, and you can't even find your balls for one fucking night to—"

"THAT'S ENOUGH."

My voice was loud and firm, chest heaving as Jennifer sat there in my passenger seat, gaping at me like a fish.

"You don't know anything about me, Jennifer. *Nothing*. And I don't give a fuck what you or anyone else in this town thinks. There is only one person on my mind tonight, only one reason why I do not want to go inside that house with you, and it's not Charlie."

Her eyes narrowed. "You haven't dated anyone. Who else could you possibly be thinking about?"

"It's none of your goddamn business," I seethed, hitting the *unlock* button even though the doors were already unlocked before. "Goodnight."

Jennifer was still watching me through the slits of her eyelids, her mouth pursed as she tried to decipher what I'd just said. I was pissed that I'd said *that* much, but she'd pushed me, and bringing up Charlie was like shoving her long, manicured fingers into my most tender bruise.

"*Goodnight,* Jennifer," I said again, hands on the wheel and eyes on the road.

I didn't look at her again, not when she huffed, flinging her door open before slamming it behind her, and not when she stormed up her driveway to her house. Even though I wanted to peel out of there like a man on fire, I waited until she was safely inside, letting out a long breath of frustration as I finally threw the car in drive.

I sped the whole way home, mumbling curse words as steam rolled off me more and more with every turn. How *dare* she? How dare she presume to know anything about me, and then, take that "knowledge" and try to use it against me like that.

Jennifer Stinson was a bitch — that was just the only fucking word for her. Capital B-I-T-C-H. Still, her words had struck a chord.

She doesn't love you.

Only it wasn't Charlie I thought of when she'd said that.

I swallowed, trying to fight through the chaos of the night to digest the feelings I had beneath it all. It seemed impossible, to peel back the layers I'd sheltered myself under for years. I didn't want to figure it out, I decided, and I was in the process of locking up that cellar of shit when I turned onto my street.

I was within minutes of a beer, and it was all I could focus on.

Until I saw her.

Sarah was on my porch, sitting with her feet on the step and her arms wrapped around herself in a little ball. She rested her chin on her knees, barely lifting her gaze when my car swung into the drive.

I watched her from the safety of my car for as long as I could before dragging myself out of it, locking it behind me with two beeps that broke the silence of the night. Sarah sat up a little straighter as I approached, her wide eyes scanning the length of me before her gaze found mine.

Why did the entire world seem to stop when our eyes met?

Those honey pools sucked me in, pulling me under like a rip tide as she looked up at me. She seemed so small in that moment, so vulnerable and exposed with her sweater-covered arms wrapped around her long legs. It was unlike I'd ever seen her before. Even when she was telling me about her assaulter, she held her chin high, back straight, strength rolling off her like steam off a train.

She was unbreakable, it had always seemed — and yet, in that moment, she was a woman in pieces on my doorstep.

I slid my hands into the pockets of my dress slacks, glancing down each side of my street before I found her gaze again. I didn't know what to say.

Should I ask why she's here? Invite her inside? Ask if she's okay?

I wanted to reach out to her, but the petulant side of me that had been brought to life by Jennifer's comments refused to let me. It didn't matter that I knew I couldn't blame Sarah for putting me in that situation. I still did. And as much as I wanted to hold her, to make sure she was okay — I also wanted to tell her to leave me alone.

I wanted *everyone* to just leave me the fuck alone.

All those thoughts were stuck in my big, stupid head, and the only thing I could do was wait for her to speak first.

Time stretched between us, long and heavy as we watched each other. There were a million questions in those eyes of hers, and I knew she likely saw each and every one of them reflected in my own.

Slowly, after what felt like an eternity, Sarah unwrapped her arms from where they held her legs, bracing herself on the large column by the stairs before pushing herself to stand. Her brows drew together, and where she stood now under the porch light, I saw the remnants of dried tears on her cheeks.

"I think I'm ready to play the song."

SARAH

Reese wouldn't look at me.

Not as he unlocked his door, letting me into his foyer first before he came in behind me. Not as Rojo nearly knocked me over, barking and wagging her tail in joy at seeing us both. Not as he steered her through the house and out the back door, letting her outside. And not as he silently poured us each a glass of water, one hand unfastening the tie around his neck as the other handled the pitcher.

I watched him yank on the tie from where I sat at the kitchen counter, my palms damp, heart racing. My gaze bounced around, landing on him for only a brief moment before I'd look at the glasses he was pouring water into, or the paintings that hung on his wall, or at Rojo, who was roaming around the kitchen with a toy in her mouth, tail wagging.

I couldn't look at him very long, either. Not with him dressed like that.

Not with him looking so handsome I wanted to cry.

Jennifer had been with him all night looking like that. She'd been able to stare at his bright smile across what I imagined to be a candle-lit table. She'd been the reason his hair was styled and neat, his jaw freshly shaved, his hard, god-like body covered in a tailored, charcoal suit that brought an edge to him I'd never seen before.

And as he let that tie fall loose around his neck, popping open two buttons on his dress shirt with a sigh of relief, I found I had to tear my eyes away again.

"How was your date?" I asked, breaking the silence as he replaced the water pitcher inside his fridge.

A short, snuff of a laugh came from his nose. "It's nine-thirty and I'm already home." He paused, locking eyes on mine. "*Alone.* So, how do you think it went?"

He slid me one of the waters, staring at the one in his hand before shaking his head. He dipped back inside the fridge, this time pulling out a beer and leaving the glass of water behind. He cracked the can open, chugging half of it in one go.

I stared at the glass in my hand.

"Why are you here, Sarah?"

I lifted my gaze, and I wanted to die when I met his eyes. He watched me like me being in that house with him was the most painful thing, like he was trying to breathe clean oxygen and I was a roaring fire, causing him to inhale hot, black smoke, instead. And when my eyes fell to his lips, my stomach twisted painfully at the smudge of red that marred them.

He'd kissed her.

Of course he'd kissed her.

"I... I told you," I said, swallowing, hands still fastened around my full glass of water as I tore my eyes away from his lips. "I think I'm ready to play the song."

"Right." Reese's grip tightened on the can of beer in his hand. "But, our lesson is tomorrow. Why did you come tonight?"

Tears stung the corners of my eyes, and I ripped my gaze from his, taking a tentative sip of water before I pushed the glass away. I couldn't even drink that without my stomach churning in protest. I felt sick — from the day, the week, the news from Reneé, the sight of Reese dressed up for another woman.

But I couldn't *say* any of that.

There was only one way I could communicate in that moment.

"Please," I finally said, voice barely a whisper as I looked up at him once more. "Just... please, let me play. I think I have it. I think I can play it now."

Reese finally looked at me then — *really* looked at me — his eyes softening as he considered my plea. After a long moment, he sighed, running his hand over his face before taking another sip of his beer. Then, without a word or a nod or a confirmation of any kind, he turned, leaving me in the kitchen as he rounded the corner into the piano room.

He was just like the man I'd first met.

Gone was my warm, tender Reese who laughed and played, who skated in the park with me and rubbed his dog's belly in the sunshine. He'd been replaced by the cold, quiet Reese I'd first met.

And somehow, I felt like I was to blame.

I followed him into the room where his piano was, and he was already in his corner, arms folded over his chest where he waited in the shadows. He must have wiped his mouth, or perhaps it was the beer, but the traces of red lipstick he'd worn before were gone now. The room was dark, save for a candle I assumed he'd just lit, and the flame of it flickered around us as I took my seat at the bench.

I flipped the wood cover up, exposing the ivory keys as I tried to steady my breath. I didn't expect to be nervous, not when I'd played at that piano so many times for Reese, but I was shaking, too aware of the man in the corner of the room. My hands floated over the keys, touching each one softly as I warmed up, the pedal giving way to my foot under the bench. I took my time, loosening my wrists and relaxing my shoulders as I played.

Once I was warm, I pulled my hands away, stretching them up above the keys and rolling my wrists a few times. I cracked my neck next, blowing out a long, slow breath. I felt Reese there in the corner, watching me, waiting — but when I closed my eyes, he was gone. When I closed my eyes, I was exactly where the song said I should be.

At the piano in my mother's home.

I could see it — our old house, the octagon-shaped window with the crack in the veneer. I could feel the sun shining through it, touching that same spot it always did on my left forearm as I played. I smelled the vanilla and lavender, two of mom's favorite scents, and I felt the long, shaggy carpet under my toes as I played. I was no longer in Reese's home, but in ours. In the one we'd left behind. In the one I'd never forget.

There, in the corner, instead of Reese, it was her. It was Mom.

And Dad was there with her.

———

REESE

The minute Sarah opened her mouth and sang the first line of Sampha's song, every ounce of pent-up frustration I'd been carrying around with me all night melted away.

Her eyes were closed, body moving with her hands in a dramatic bend and flow as she poured her heart out at my piano. The strong, raspy voice that came from that girl nearly knocked me off my feet. It was the last thing I expected — the power, the strength — and yet once I heard her, I wondered how I could have ever imagined anything else.

How could I have ever assumed her voice would be soft, sweet, gentle and tentative when everything about her screamed the opposite?

Sarah was the embodiment of strength, of pain, of healing. And in that moment, in my dark little piano room, I watched the woman I'd always known was inside her all along bloom to life.

She emerged from the shadows like an angel, breaking through the shell of the girl who had imprisoned her. But unlike an angel, she didn't glow softly or sing lightly — she roared, like a wildfire or a lioness, and she belted out the lyrics of Sampha's song like she were the creator, herself.

Her fingers moved over that piano like I'd never seen before, her shoulders relaxed, face twisting up with emotion more and more as the song progressed. And when she sang the part of the piece I predicted would hit her hardest, when she sang of the time coming, of the loss of a loved one and how the piano held her close and never let her go, she broke.

Right there, at the same piano Charlie had once sat on top of while she listened to me play, the same piano I'd sat at as I mourned everyone who'd ever left me, and the same piano that had once sat in *my* mother's home... Sarah Henderson broke.

Her eyes squeezed shut even tighter, bottom lip trembling as she tripped over the lyrics, the emotion too strong. Her fingers stalled, an unscripted pause somehow making the song even stronger as she succumbed to the tears fighting their way through her closed eyelids. I watched those tears stain her face, running over the same dried treadmarks I'd noticed when she was on my front porch, and my next breath burned with the need to hold her and wipe those tears away.

Just like I knew she would, she felt the song.

She felt it the same way I did.

And though she sang about no one knowing her like the piano, I knew now that it wasn't true.

I knew her, too.

And she knew me.

Sarah was still crying as she sang the last few words, and I was already moving toward her, abandoning my spot in the corner of the room. Her eyes blinked open when I took the seat on the bench next to her, and my hands found the keys alongside hers. We finished the song together, playing the end with tears still streaming down Sarah's face, and when the last note floated between us, my hands hovered over the keys, but Sarah's flew to her face.

She buried her pain inside those beautiful hands — the hands that had just brought to life the most emotional piece of music I'd ever heard in my home — and softly, quietly, she sobbed. Her small shoulders shook, and every piece of me broke along with her.

I wished I could save her, wished I could go back in time and take away every single shred of impurity that had ever touched her. I wished I could undo the pain, the hurt, and see her as she once was — whole, untouched, unscathed.

But then again, I knew it was her pain that made her so beautiful.

It was her strength, her unyielding drive, her unwillingness to ever give up or give in that I admired most.

And it was everything she'd been through that allowed her to play with the emotion she just did.

Still, I wished it didn't have to be that way for her.

The silence stretched between us as I pulled my hands from the piano, my heart breaking for the woman crying next to me. And though I knew I shouldn't, though I tried to fight against the urge, I couldn't help but reach for her. It was like trying not to watch the stars that peppered a dark sky — absolutely impossible.

And when I surrendered the fight, when my arms surrounded her and pulled her into me, when Sarah sobbed even harder, burying her face in my chest and twisting her tiny fists in my dress shirt, I knew there was no other place in the world I would rather be.

For the longest time, I held her there against me, soothing her as best I could as she fell apart. It was like she was shedding her skin in the most painful way, fully embracing the raw, ragged being beneath the exterior that had been begging to be set free. Her pain was palpable, and it bled into me like ink on paper, spreading over me in a way that would permanently change me forever.

Eventually, her sobs grew softer, her grip on my shirt loosening as she sniffed, but still, I held her. And she held me.

Even though the room was completely silent, I still heard her voice. I could close my eyes and see her moving with the music, changing right before me like a butterfly emerging from its cocoon. And when her sobs had finally quieted altogether, her breathing steady once more, I pulled back, the tips of my fingers gently finding the smooth skin of her jaw. I lifted, reveling in the feel of her warmth against me as her eyes finally met mine.

"Sarah," I breathed, searching her honey eyes as they glistened in the soft flicker of the candlelight. "What you just did, it was more than anything I ever could have expected. It was otherworldly," I said, trying to explain, though words seemed to fail me in that moment. "It was more beautiful than I could ever say. And I know it hurt. I know it didn't come easy."

Her little face warped then, tears flooding her eyes again as she watched me.

"I'm so proud of you," I whispered.

That broke the levy, the tears that had washed over her eyes breaking free and streaming down her cheeks. But before they could fall far, my rough hands were there, wiping them away, my eyes still searching hers for some kind of understanding as I tried to erase her pain.

Sarah leaned into my palm, closing her eyes as a long, slow breath escaped her parted lips. Then, her eyes opened again, connecting with mine in what felt like a new universe. She wasn't the same girl who had walked through my door earlier that night. And when she looked at me, I felt her in a way I never had before.

In a way I'd never felt anyone.

"Reese?" she finally whispered.

"Yes?"

She sniffed, eyes flicking between mine as her fingers fisted in my shirt again. She pulled me closer, just a centimeter, and her gaze fell to my mouth before she spoke again.

"Will you kiss me again?"

I audibly groaned at her request, my next breath leaving my chest in a singeing burn. I couldn't take my eyes off her, couldn't pull away, couldn't tamp down that feeling in my heart that her words had spawned. It beat loud and steady in my chest, urging me to answer her plea, to pull her into me and kiss her breathless.

"This is dangerous," I said instead, the words croaking out of my dry throat. I still held her, and she held me, our eyes dancing across the short space between us. "I hurt you before, and I swore I never would again."

"Please," she spoke again, and this time, she broke with the word. Her eyes glossed, her bottom lip trembling before she sucked it between her teeth. "Please, Reese. Kiss me. Kiss me like I've never been kissed before, like I'm not damaged, like I'm new and whole and pure. Please," she pleaded on another cry, swallowing as she tried to keep her composure while she broke what was left of the wall I'd put between us. "Erase the memories I have. Take away what I've seen and felt and fill me with the memories of *this* kiss, of a man touching me because he cares about me." Sarah paused then, her hands twisting my shirt even more. "Of a man touching me who I *want* to touch me, and a man I want to to touch, too."

My own eyes watered, but I sniffed back the urge to give in to those emotions. The pain I felt for her was excruciating, but it was nothing compared to the admiration and care I felt for her, too. And in that moment, with that last request, there was only one thing I could do.

I kissed her.

My hands framed her face, pulling her into me with gentle care as my lips found hers, soft and surrendering, yet firm with desire. There was no one in the world I wanted more than Sarah, and I poured everything I had into that kiss to help her see it was true.

She bent under the weight of my lips, falling limp in my arms as I pulled her in closer. Her hands crawled up my chest, wrapping around my neck and into my hair as she tugged, asking for more. And I delivered, thumb brushing her jaw as I tilted my head to one side and slipped my tongue over her silk lips before she opened her mouth to let me inside. And when I tasted her — *truly* tasted her — a guttural groan erupted from my chest like a volcano.

Sarah gasped as I swept my tongue over hers, sliding my hands from her face to wrap around her small frame and pull her into me. The candlelight danced around us as we melted together, the kiss as alive as the hearts beating rapidly in our chests. Her hands explored me, mine held her, and when she finally broke for a breath, the energy between us crackled in an unbearable heat.

"Take me to bed," she breathed, her eyes searching mine.

One arm swept under her legs, the other cradling her back as I lifted her from that bench and carried her across the house to my dark bedroom. The only light that reached us was from the moon outside my window, and it cast Sarah in a soft, cool glow as I gently laid her in my sheets. My lips were on hers in the next instant, stealing her breath again, my body sheltering hers as I slid between her legs. Her core was warm against me, and she gasped when I rocked my hips against her, letting her feel how much I wanted her, how much I *needed* her.

But I wouldn't have her.

Not tonight.

Tonight, I wanted to make Sarah feel safe, and wanted, and cared for. I wanted to bring her pleasure, to let her slip away from reality for as long as she needed to. I didn't know everything about what happened with Wolfgang, didn't *want* to know how he violated her, how he stole something so precious from the most amazing woman I'd ever known. All I wanted was to erase those memories just like she asked me to, and replace them with those of a man reveling in the feel of her against him, in the absolute pleasure of being allowed to touch her.

I should have walked away. I knew it, distantly, like a voice screaming from some chamber in the depths of my mind. She was my student. She was too young. I was too old, too broken *myself* to have a prayer of fixing her. But it was all I wanted, all I could think of or desire as I pulled her to stand with me at the edge of my bed, my lips still fastened to hers.

"Sarah," I breathed, kissing her again as soon as her name rolled off my lips.

"Yes?"

My hands moved from her hips up to her neck, sliding just under the collar of the sweater she wore. "I'd like to undress you," I whispered, pulling back until her eyes met mine. Both of us panted, our chests heaving with each breath, and her eyes widened in fear at my request. "But, I won't — not if you don't want to. Not if it scares you or if you don't trust me." I paused, swallowing as I searched for my next words. "You're beautiful, Sarah. And I want to show you that. I want to make you *feel* it — the way I have since the moment I met you."

The corner of her lips curved into a soft smile, but instead of answering me, she pulled away from my hold, backing up until she was in the low beam of moonlight that streamed through my window.

And with her eyes locked on mine, she tugged the zipper that lined the front of her sweater down, down, slow as ever as it revealed the top of the dress she wore beneath it. Her lips parted as she peeled it off one shoulder, and then the next, letting it fall to the floor at her feet.

It was the most I'd ever seen of her.

Her shoulders were dotted with the same freckles as her cheeks, and I counted each one as her hands fell to the front of her thighs. She bunched them into fists, the fabric of her dress lifting with the motion, and she repeated it over and over, slowly inching the hem of the skirt up until it was in her hands, her thighs and knees exposed beneath it. Then, in one fluid motion, she tugged it up and over her head, letting it fall next to the sweater.

And it wasn't about her taking her clothes off. It wasn't about her showing me her skin. That action, undressing herself — it was her taking back the power Wolfgang had stolen from her.

I swallowed, stepping toward her as slowly as I could as my eyes drank every inch of her in. Those freckles dotted her from head to toe, like tiny stars in the dark night sky of her skin. Her hips were wide, her waist narrow, the swells of her breasts humble but absolutely perfect. It was more than I was prepared for, the image of her in nothing but a simple white bra and matching dainty panties. It was impossible to say what I imagined, what I though I'd find if I ever had the chance to see her this way.

She was more. She was always so, so much more.

The shadow of my hand broke the stream of moonlight on her stomach as I reached for her, the rough calentuses of my palm eliciting a shutter from her when I finally touched her ribs. My hands nearly encompassed the whole of her as I wrapped them around her, pulling her into me and dragging my gaze up until I found her eyes again. I held her close, trailing my fingertips up over her arm until I framed her cheek once more.

"You are a masterpiece, Sarah," I breathed. "An absolute deity."

She shook her head, trying to look down between us, but I held her chin, held her gaze, held her in every way I could as I spoke again.

"You are," I repeated. "And I won't stop worshiping you until you see it, too."

I kissed her to seal that promise, pulling my hands from her only long enough to strip off my suit jacket and unbutton my dress shirt before peeling it off, too. I dropped them both on the floor next to her clothes, and Sarah's hands slipped over my shoulders, my pecs, trailing down my abdomen and sparking a wave of chills in their wake. She pulled away from my kiss, breathing through parted lips as her eyes danced over where her hands touched me.

"And you say *I'm* the deity," she murmured.

I chuckled, pulling her back into the bed with me and covering us with the sheets before I slid between her legs again. I still wore my pants, much to Sarah's disdain, I found, as she tried to undo my belt under the covers. But I held her hands, pulled them back up until they were pressed into the pillow on either side of her head as I kissed her softly, slowly, with purpose.

"I want to kiss you," I whispered.

"You already are."

I shook my head, running my tongue along her bottom lip before I pulled back. "I want to kiss you *everywhere*."

I slid down her body, kissing a trail across her dainty collarbone, over the swells of her breasts exposed by her bra, along the length of her long, lean navel. She wriggled under each new touch of my lips, and when I settled between her thighs, moving until the backs of them were on my shoulders and my hands were braced on the top of them, she leaned up on her elbows and watched me with wide eyes.

"I want to kiss you here," I breathed, sucking the tender skin on the inside of each of her thighs before I hovered over the white cotton of her panties. "Is that okay, Sarah? Can I kiss you here?"

"Yes," she breathed, wiggling under my grip again. "*Please.*"

I kept my mouth on her, kissing along her thighs as I gently pulled her panties down. She lifted her hips, every muscle trembling as she did, and I slid her panties over her ass, down her thighs, pulling back long enough to free them of her ankles before I settled between her legs again. The sweet scent of her hit my nose as I trailed one hand up the inside of her thigh, brushing the crease of it before I tugged gently on the soft pubic hair covering her.

"I like this," I mused, smiling a little at the new chills that broke out over her legs.

My eyes found hers, and then I lowered my mouth, kissing her where I wanted to most.

Sarah gasped as I swept my tongue over her sensitive clit, arching her back off the bed as her fists twisted in the sheets. She let out a long, seductive moan as I swirled my tongue, the tip of it circling her clit before I sucked gently. Her hands flew from the sheets to my hair, tugging in a silent plea for more.

I groaned, running my tongue flat against her before sucking her bud between my teeth again. Her moans turned to whimpers, legs shaking on either side of me the more I tasted her, and every squirm fed my desire.

This.

This was what I wanted — to make her feel good, to make her fall apart with the pleasure she deserved to feel, the desire she deserved to elicit from the man who was lucky enough to touch her. I didn't know why that blessing was mine, why it was me who got the opportunity to erase what had happened to her before, to replace those memories with ones of ecstasy.

All I knew was that I wouldn't waste my chance.

Carefully, with as much patience as I could muster in that moment of all-consuming desire, I slipped one finger between her lips as my tongue worked her clit. She sighed at the sensation, and I ran the pad of my finger along her wet slit, teasing her, warming her up before I slipped just the tip of my finger inside her.

"Oh, God," she breathed, arching off the bed again. Her hands twisted in my hair, thighs spreading to allow me access.

She was so tight, so tender and sensitive as I slowly slid my finger in more, centimeter by centimeter, until she swallowed my first knuckle. I curled that finger inside her, working in rhythm with my mouth as she wriggled under me.

I'd had countless women in my lifetime, more than I cared to admit, but in that moment — with Sarah in my bed, her thighs on either side of my face, her hands in my hair, her body succumbing to the pleasure I brought her with my tongue — it was like being reborn again. It was my first time. It was her first time. It was the first and the only and the everything when I touched her.

I hoped she felt it, too.

She grew tighter the longer I worked, her muscles contracting as her breaths came shallower. She was close, and when I slipped another finger inside her, carefully — but with a firm command — she let out a moan that nearly made *me* come.

"Yes," she breathed, squirming under my touch. "Reese, yes. *Yes.*"

I worked my tongue faster, curling my fingers inside her, and when I knew she was close, I climbed my way up her body with my fingers still inside her. My mouth found hers, and I swallowed her next moan, letting her taste herself on my tongue as the palm of my hand rubbed her clit. I moved my hips with my hand, driving my fingers into her over and over again until she tightened around me.

Sarah broke our kiss in the next instant, moaning my name as she found her release. I kissed her neck, her breasts, driving her to the finish line as she shook around me. She raked her nails down my back, crying out as she rode the waves, her orgasm long and intense if I were judging by the way she trembled and moaned. And when she was done, she fell limp, every muscle in her body releasing at once as she softened beneath me.

I kissed her again, firm at first before I softened, sweeping my tongue over hers. Her hands found their way back into my hair, and she held me there as I kissed her like I had all night, like we'd only just begun. I gently pulled my fingers from inside her, and she shivered at the loss, pulling me closer like she was afraid I'd pull my mouth away next. But I only kissed her harder, rolling until we were both on our sides, our legs tangled together, arms wrapped around each other, breaths dancing between each kiss.

We stayed like that for a long while before our kisses slowed, our breath evening out as I kissed my way up to her nose, her forehead, holding my lips there before I pulled away and found her gaze with my own.

"Thank you," I breathed, running the tips of my fingers over her shoulder.

She blushed, shaking her head as she buried her face in the covers. "Thank *you*," she mumbled into them.

I laughed, rolling her until her back was against my chest, my arms wrapped around her, her legs tangling with mine as I spooned her. She lifted my hand to her lips, kissing each pad of my fingertips before she tucked that hand around her chest once more. A comfortable silence fell over us as I held her, and I prayed to a god I didn't believe in that the bubble that shielded us from reality wouldn't break.

I prayed that I'd made her feel wanted, that I'd erased what she'd asked me to. I prayed that she'd felt every moment like I had, that tonight was as special to her as it was to me. I prayed that I could hold her like that all night, that I could keep her, that I could somehow have her in a world where everything screamed I never could.

If there really was a god, if there was a chance I could choose my own fate, I prayed that she was it.

The morning would come.

I knew it would. I knew that with the daylight, we'd have to face every mountain between us.

But tonight, in the soft light of the moon, Sarah was mine.

And I held her like she always would be.

chapter fifteen

SARAH

I woke to the sound of Rojo's soft snores, her body sprawled out on the bed in front of me while Reese hugged me to his chest from behind. His legs tangled with mine, a light sheen of sweat sticking us to each other. He was still in his dress pants from the night before, and I was only in my bra, my panties forgotten along with the rest of my clothes somewhere on the floor.

It was hot.

The morning sun streaming through the window shed a light on everything the moon had hidden last night. I was naked in Reese's bed. I'd stayed the night. And we'd definitely crossed whatever line still existed between us.

I had no doubt that my phone was buzzing away in the other room, missed calls and texts from my uncle wondering where I was. I needed to come up with a story, but right now, all I wanted to do was hide from reality a little longer.

So, I twisted in Reese's hold, fighting against the covers and his dead weight until I was facing him. His arms lifted long enough to let me turn before they were wrapped around me again, pulling me to his broad, god-like chest as Rojo huffed from the other side of us. I giggled at that, and Reese slowly creaked one eye open, a lazy smile on his lips.

"Mornin'."

I snuggled into him more. "Good morning."

His smile grew, a long, sleepy breath coming from his chest as he stretched. I did the same, reveling in the sweet soreness between my legs. I'd never woken up in a man's bed before, never stayed the night with someone other than a girlfriend, and yet, somehow, I felt more comfortable than I ever had in a bed alone with Reese's arms around me like that.

I closed my eyes, blushing at the memory of him looking up at me the night before, the feel of his fingers curling inside me, his tongue tasting me. It had been more than I could have ever imagined intimacy could be. I thought I was broken. I thought I would never be able to feel like that, to enjoy being touched, to want to touch someone else.

I was wrong.

So, *so* wrong.

I squeezed my knees together, tightening around Reese's thigh that was between them now.

"What are you thinking about?" he asked when I opened my eyes again, but his smirk told me he already knew.

"How perfect last night was."

At that, he propped himself up on one elbow, looking down on me with a concerned crease between his brows. "Yeah?"

I nodded. "Yeah. Were you worried?"

"A little," he confessed. "I just... I hoped it was as special to you as it was to me."

My heart melted at his words, swishing around in my chest like sticky goo as I ran a hand up over his bare chest, sliding it over his shoulder and pulling him down toward me. I leaned up just enough to meet his lips with my own, both of us breathing out a sigh of relief at the contact, like that kiss was all we needed in life.

Maybe it was.

I never thought I'd be here — in Reese's bed, in Reese's arms. Everything seemed so impossible — not just with him, with the hurdles between us, but with *anyone*. I never imagined I could feel whole again, desired, wanted. I never imagined that I could ever *want* to do the things we did last night.

I thought the damage my wolf had inflicted was permanent, irreversible, detrimental.

But Reese kissed me and brought me back to life. He touched me and I took what felt like my first breath.

I didn't know how I could ever properly tell him everything that last night meant to me.

Reese groaned when I deepened the kiss, hands fisting in his hair and pulling until he was on top of me, his core between my legs. Just thinking about last night made me want him again, made me want even *more*. Now that I'd been awakened, I was thirsty, hungry — an absolute fiend.

He broke away when I thrust my hips, gasping at the feel of his hard-on against my middle. His pants were the only thing between us, and I wanted them gone.

"You're killing me, woman," he breathed, kissing my nose before he propped himself up on his elbows again.

"I want you," I whispered, trying to pull him back into me.

"And you have me," he said. He pulled my hand from where it was trailing down between us, kissing my fingertips and holding them to his lips as he watched me. The morning sun played on the emerald flecks in his irises, and his pupils danced as they flicked between my own. "What happened last night?"

"I mean... do you want me to give you a play by play, or should we just relive it..." I tried to roll my hips again, but Reese growled, kissing me hard before propping himself up again. He slid down, putting his abs at my middle instead of his erection, desperate to put space between us.

I pouted.

"I meant, what happened *before* I got home?" he clarified. "You came to play the song. And you'd been crying."

I sighed, the not-so-fond memories of last night making my chest ache. I stared at where Reese held my fingers to his lips, wishing we could focus on that part of the evening, instead.

"I called my old roommate," I said after awhile. "Remember, the one I was telling you about that I completely left behind when I walked out of Bramlock?"

Reese nodded.

I continued staring at his lips, feeling how soft they were under the pad of my fingers. "I called her and caught her up on everything... well, *almost* everything," I amended. "I talked to her about being here. About you. But I left out why I wasn't at Bramlock anymore."

Reese smirked. "What did you say about me?"

"I'm not telling you that," I said, cheeks heating. "It's girl talk. Very private."

"You told her how hot your teacher is, didn't you?"

I scoffed at that. "Please. She already knows what you look like. Like I said, there are videos of you online, mister."

He frowned. "I feel like there's some sort of invasion of privacy happening with that, voyeurism, even... but whatever."

"*Anyway*," I said, smiling as he kissed my fingertips again. "Everything was great at first. We caught up, she gave me some advice on how I was feeling about you being out on a date..."

His eyebrows shot up. "What kind of feelings were you having?"

"Again, not the point," I said, but the smile he'd elicited fell as I spoke the next words. "At the end of our call, she invited me back to Bramlock."

Reese was quiet, watching me, waiting.

I swallowed. "She invited me back because Wolfgang has been given a prestigious award, one that our university is very picky about bestowing on anyone. They're having a big ceremony for him... and I know it probably sounds stupid, but I just... I couldn't breathe when I heard that. I saw black. I hung up on Reneé, then I threw up, and then I was just crying, and I... I thought about the song... and about my dad... and then, I ended up here."

So many emotions passed over Reese's face as I spoke — anger, understanding, sorrow, empathy. But it went back to anger after a long moment, his jaw clenched tight and nostrils flaring before he spoke. "That motherfucker got an *award*? How is he even still allowed to fucking teach?"

My eyes fell to his chest. "Well... it's not like anyone knows what happened."

I didn't have to look at him again to know he was watching me with questions in his eyes, or maybe with murder. To him, I imagined, it probably seemed so easy. Get raped? Call the police.

But that just wasn't how it worked.

"I tried to tell someone," I clarified. "I just... the person I told said we should keep it between us. And it wasn't just a friend or something... it was the music director. She had power, she could have helped me... but... well, she didn't have to say the exact words for me to hear everything she wasn't saying." I shrugged. "He's Wolfgang Edison. It would have been my word against his, and who's going to believe a young, *black* female against an old, prestigious, award-winning, white, male piano legend?"

"Me," Reese said without pause. "I believe you. And I know I wouldn't be the only one."

My heart swelled, beating with an unfamiliar emotion at his certainty, his unyielding belief.

"What if we went to the police together," he offered. "We could—"

"No," I said, shaking my head firmly. "This isn't up for debate, Reese." I lifted my eyes to his again. "I'm sorry, but it's not. Okay? I don't want to tell anyone about it. And I trust that you never will, either."

At that, he lowered his lips to my fingers again, kissing them with promise. "I would never tell anyone. It's not my story to tell. And I respect you too much to ever do that."

I nodded. "Thank you."

The silence stretched between us, the sun warming the bed as much as Rojo did. She was still sprawled out beside us, snoring lightly, little hind legs twitching a bit.

"Reese?"

"Mm?" he answered, shifting his weight to the opposite elbow. He still seemed lost in thought from our last conversation.

I chewed the inside of my cheek, debating my next words. "Did you and Jennifer... have you ever... you know... with her?"

He smirked. "Have I ever what?"

"Please don't make me say it."

Reese chuckled as my cheeks burned. "No. We didn't. Do you really think I'd fool around with her and then come home and do what I did to you?"

I shrugged, picking at the blanket wrapped around us. "I don't know. When you first got home, there was lipstick on your mouth. I just assumed..."

"She kissed me when I dropped her off," he said bluntly. "But I didn't kiss her back. I stopped her, and asked her to get out of my car."

"Why?" I breathed. "She's beautiful. She's..."

"Not you," he said. My next breath stalled in my chest, and the corner of Reese's mouth quirked to one side as he pulled my fingertips to his lips again, kissing them lightly. "She's not you, Sarah. That's why I didn't kiss her back."

I wanted to trust it, the way my heart soared at his words. But it didn't seem possible. It didn't feel real, that he could want me, too. That a young, damaged girl like me could be anywhere near what he wanted or needed.

But the way he looked at me...

I swallowed, tapping his lips. "So... what do we do now?"

Reese sat up a little more, that familiar crease showing between his brows. "What do you mean?"

"I mean... I'm your student. Your boss is my uncle. And..."

"I'm an old man?"

I chuckled, running a hand back through his hair before I rested it at the nape of his neck. "Thirty-seven is not *old*."

"It's a hell of a lot older than twenty-one."

I frowned, twirling the strands of his hair between my fingers. "So... does that mean... can we not..." I couldn't figure out how to ask what I wanted to, what I *needed* to. My eyes fell to his chest, a thick, sticky knot in my throat as I tried to swallow past it. "Was last night it?"

Reese watched me for a long moment before he dipped down, forcing me to look him in the eye. "Do you *want* it to be?"

I shook my head immediately.

"What *do* you want?"

I almost laughed, like it was easy to say, to achieve. "I want you," I answered simply. "I want... *us*. But, I'm scared. I don't want you to get fired, and I don't know how my uncle will react. Or what people will say, how they'll see us. What about The Kinky Starfish? And the parents at Westchester, will they worry about their kids? And what about..." I sighed, biting my lower lip. "I don't know if I... I don't know if I'm *enough* for you. I'm young, and inexperienced, and—"

"Hey," Reese interrupted me, tilting my chin with his knuckles until my eyes met his once more. "Do you remember what I said to you that night we adopted Rojo?"

I loved the way he said *we,* like we were a unit, a team, a *thing*.

I nodded.

"What did I say?" he probed.

"You said I was enough," I whispered.

Reese's eyes danced between mine. "I did. And I meant it. Then, and now. You are enough, Sarah. And I want you, too."

My eyes widened. "You do?"

He chuckled at that, leaning in to press his lips tenderly to mine. "I love how you act so surprised, like you're anything less than the most beautiful, most incredible, *strongest* woman I've ever known."

I beamed, pressing up to kiss him again before my head fell back into the pillows. I shook it, staring up at the most beautiful, most incredible, strongest *man* I'd ever known — wondering how in the hell he saw the same in me.

But none of that mattered to anyone outside of these walls.

All *they* would see is a teacher abusing his power, a student feeling like she was in love when she was just enamored by an older man. They'd see perversion, not beauty.

"What do we do, then?" I asked him. "How do we..."

"We'll figure it out," he said, kissing my fingertips. "*I* will figure it out. Okay? But we don't have to have all the answers right now." With that, he rolled, rubbing Rojo's belly before popping up out of bed. His hair was a disheveled mess, but all I could stare at were the muscles that lined his rib cage, his abdomen, leading all the way down to the sharp V above his belt. "Right now," he said, reaching a hand back for me. "We both need a shower. And then you need to figure out a story for why you stayed out all night."

I laughed, letting him pull me up. "Yeah... that will be a fun conversation."

"Was it worth it, though?" Reese asked, pulling me flush against him. His lips found mine, hands splaying the small of my back and pulling me into him as he stole my breath.

And I didn't have to answer out loud for him to know my response.

It was worth it.

So, *so* worth it.

—

REESE

There was one day from my childhood that I had always remembered.

I wasn't sure why this particular day stuck in my mind, especially since nothing *truly* remarkable happened, but I'd never forgotten it. It was just a weekday over the summer, right before I went into my sophomore year of high school. Mallory and I were in our backyard with Charlie and her older brother, Graham. This was before I saw Charlie as anything other than my best friend's little sister, and before I lost my family, and before I realized that anything could ever come between me and my love for the piano. It was just a hot summer day in Pennsylvania, and we were in the back yard, flying down a homemade slip-n-slide we'd made.

It kept us entertained the entire day.

I remember listening to the new Pearl Jam album, spraying my little sister with the water and talking to Graham about the hot new freshmen we'd be fighting over when school started. Mom had been working on the house inside, but stopped to bring us lunch. She'd watched us play for a while, laughing every time I'd try to run all the way down the tarp without falling.

I never succeeded.

And when Dad got home, he came out back, still dressed in his suit and tie from the work day. Rather than just watching, he'd stripped down to his old man boxers and dove straight down the tarp on his stomach.

We'd all chased after him.

That memory was as brazen in my mind as it was the very day it all happened. Maybe it was because it was a time we were together as a family. Maybe it just reminded me of simpler days. Regardless, it had always stuck with me — and it wasn't necessarily what happened on that day as much as it was how I felt. I was alive, young, with limitless opportunities ahead of me. It was a lazy summer day, one where I had nowhere to be and nothing to do, one where everyone I loved was right where they were supposed to be.

It was the same feeling I'd had since Saturday night.

Only now, it was because of Sarah.

Just like that day, she made me feel alive. She made me feel young, and limitless, and wild and free. It'd only been a few days since we'd surrendered to each other, since the night we crossed every line that still stood between us. I wanted her, and she wanted me, and we had so much still to figure out but nothing else mattered outside of the fact that we were together.

She was the light I never thought I'd see again, the purpose I thought I'd lost forever.

The last few days had been a blur of piano lessons that didn't last long enough and kisses stolen between songs. After she stayed out all night that Saturday, she'd been trying to be more careful, returning home to her uncle's as soon as our lessons were over. For three whole days, she'd been all I could think about, and yet we hadn't had more than a few hours together each day.

But tonight, she was mine.

She told her uncle she was staying at a friend's after work, and for the first time since Saturday, I was going to have her all to myself again. It was enough to make me bounce in the shower as I scrubbed my hair, my body, wishing I could fast forward through the night to when we were coming home together.

I liked me better when I was with her.

Rojo was sprawled out on the bath mat when I got out of the shower, still dripping. She glanced lazily up at me, as if *I* were the inconvenience as I stepped around her for my towel.

"You actually going to share the bed tonight?" I asked her with a smirk, scrubbing the towel over my hair.

Rojo just huffed, flicking her tail a few times before she gave me an exaggerated yawn and spread out on the mat even more.

I chuckled. "Guess not."

I turned on the same Pearl Jam album from my favorite childhood memory as I got ready for work, singing along with Eddie Vedder to the best of my abilities. I felt like a high school kid again, bouncing around, singing and smiling and floating like a damn fool because of a girl. I wondered idly if Sarah and I had gone to high school together, if she would have been interested in me.

I knew without a doubt that answer was no.

I was a little shit, and I didn't know how to treat a woman back then. Hell, maybe I *never* learned that lesson. Judging by the way I'd done Blake, the way I'd tried to steal Charlie from Cameron — I didn't exactly have the best track record.

But I'd change that with Sarah.

It was a vow I'd made to her, to myself. I knew how the odds were stacked against us. I knew it wouldn't be easy. But, I also knew I'd make it work. I'd find a way.

I had to.

For the first time since my family died, everything felt right. I cared for Sarah, and she cared for me. It was reciprocated, which I found was entirely different than anything I'd ever experienced with any woman in my life before. She made me feel *right* — for the first time since I lost everything... maybe for the first time *ever*.

And tonight, after work, I'd get to see her again.

I'd get to hold her, kiss her, *be* with her outside of our lessons.

I just had to make it through one short shift.

Checking my watch, I snatched my wallet off the table and rubbed Rojo's head where she was now sprawled out on the couch. "Be good," I told her, plucking my keys from the table next. "I'm bringing your favorite person home later."

Rojo just stretched out farther, eyes lazily drifting closed. I smirked, swinging my front door open and wishing I was at the part of the night where I was walking back *inside* instead of out. I paused at the sight of a familiar car in my driveway, tilting my head to the side as hope fluttered through my chest.

Sarah?

Maybe she couldn't wait until after work, I thought. But it wasn't her who stepped out of the old Toyota.

It was her uncle.

I frowned, something tugging at my gut in warning as he watched me from under bent brows once he was out of the car. I swallowed, locking up behind me before I trotted down the stairs and across the drive.

"Evening, Mr. Henderson," I greeted, offering a warm smile. "How are you tonight?"

Randall returned my smile, though it was tight at the edges as he slipped his hands into the pockets of his slacks. "Good evening to you. I'm doing well, all things considered."

He didn't ask how I was.

I nodded, still smiling. "Glad to hear it. Uh... I'm actually about to head to The Kinky Starfish for the night," I explained, thumb pointing back over my shoulder toward downtown. "I wasn't expecting you."

"I know, sorry for showing up unannounced. I actually just dropped Sarah off there for her shift," he explained. "Seems she's staying the night with a friend, so I offered to drop her off and take her car in for an oil change in the morning."

The way he said the word *friend* put every nerve in my body on high alert.

His smile was gone, his gaze hard.

I didn't need a second guess to determine that he wasn't sold on Sarah's story.

"Oh," I answered, twirling my key ring around one finger before tucking it into my pocket. "Well, that's good. I'm glad she's making friends."

"Indeed." Randall watched me, eyes narrowing as he rolled his lips together. "You know, that's actually why I stopped by. Apparently, Sarah stayed with this friend on Saturday night, too."

Again, the way he said *friend* told me this conversation was anything but friendly.

"Oh?"

He nodded. "Yeah, except, she's never mentioned this friend before. And I've never heard of the young lady. Of course, I'm not insinuating that I know *everyone* in town. But, well... as you know, I'm familiar with most."

I didn't respond. At this point, I didn't feel like I was invited to.

Randall wouldn't be concerned if he believed Sarah truly *had* been at a girlfriend's house. He'd wanted her to make friends, to be welcomed by Mount Lebanon. And at twenty-one, Sarah was too old for him to be interfering in her life the way he would if she were in high school.

He didn't believe her story.

And the way Randall was looking at me told me I had more to worry about than her right now.

"I just want to make sure she's not getting mixed up in the wrong crowd," he said, taking a step toward me. "You and I both know how dangerous that can be for such a young, impressionable *girl*."

I swallowed, trying to smile past the guilt. "She's a smart *woman*," I said. "And she's picky about who she spends her time with. I don't think you need to be worried, Mr. Henderson."

Randall smiled, but it fell too quickly, and he took another step toward me with a menacing glare. "Listen to me, Reese Walker. I may not know everything going on in my niece's life, but I know enough to know she's been through enough shit to last a lifetime. She came here for a break, for a means to an end, and that is *it*." He lowered his voice. "I also know that you have a tendency of wanting what you can't have, and I just wanted to remind you of your role in her life. In case you had forgotten."

I swallowed, jaw tight from grinding my teeth together so I wouldn't pop off and tell Mr. Henderson *exactly* what I thought about his assessment of me, of what I wanted, what I'd done, and what *role* I played in Sarah's life.

But through the rage, I saw Sarah.

I made a promise to her, and if I wanted to live in a world where we could be together, I had to curate that.

Punching her uncle in the throat wouldn't help.

So, instead, I held my chin high, chest broad, and I pretended like I didn't have a fucking clue what he was insinuating.

"I'm not sure what all of that means, sir," I said as calmly as I could manage. "But, I assure you, I have nothing but the utmost respect for your niece and her dreams. I want her wellbeing just as much as you do."

Randall narrowed his eyes into slits, but not getting a rise out of me seemed to anger him more than appease him. It didn't make sense. We'd always been friends, and he'd been nothing but kind to me since I'd arrived back in town.

Then again, I supposed if he knew anything about what happened between me and Charlie, I couldn't blame him for being suspicious of me. He was right, I *did* have a bad habit of wanting what I couldn't have. And in all ways, Sarah fit into that category.

But I didn't believe in boxes, anymore.

Regardless of what Randall thought, of what *anyone* thought, Sarah and I were good together. She had saved me, and I hoped I could do the same for her, in time.

"Seems we're on the same page," Randall said after a long while, taking a small step back. "Let's touch base after this week's lessons to discuss next steps for Sarah. I know she's anxious to get to New York City, and you've got connections to get her there sooner rather than later."

What he was implying was crystal clear. He wanted Sarah out of here, away from me, and he wasn't going to take no for an answer.

That was fine.

I'd made a promise to Sarah that I'd find a way for us to be together, that I'd figure everything out. I knew in order to achieve that, I'd have to show her uncle — show *everyone* — that I cared for Sarah. She was important to me, I respected her, and I wanted her to succeed just as much as her family did — maybe even more.

Yes, I was older. Yes, she had been my student. But what we had was real, and I would prove it.

He was right, I *did* have connections in New York. If I could help her achieve her dream, help her get to the place she wanted to be, it would show not just *her* how much I cared, but everyone around her, too. And as Mr. Henderson offered me one last wave over his shoulder before climbing back into Sarah's car, I pulled out my phone, flipping through it until I found an old, familiar name.

I knew just who to call.

chapter sixteen

SARAH

I might as well have had roller blades strapped to my feet for the way I was gliding around The Kinky Starfish Wednesday night. Then again, judging by the way I'd fallen on my face in the park, maybe that was a bad analogy. Still, I felt like I was skating, floating, completely weightless as I bussed tables and helped the wait staff fill orders. We were busier than normal, every seat in the house taken, and while everyone else was wearing the stress on their sleeves, I couldn't stop smiling.

Maybe it was because I could still taste Reese on my lips from the day before, could still feel him pressing me into the piano when he'd had enough of our lesson and wanted to spend our last hour together very much *not* working. Maybe it was the memory of his fingers inside me Saturday night, the butterflies that flurried to life in my stomach when I thought of the possibility that we could have a round two tonight. Kissing between lessons had been nice, but ever since I'd had a taste of Reese, I'd wanted more.

Tonight, I hoped I'd get it.

I told my uncle I was staying the night with a friend, to not expect me home after work, and though he didn't seem entirely comfortable with the idea, he'd agreed. It wasn't that

I really needed his permission. I was certainly old enough not to have to ask. But, I was staying in his home, under his roof, and I wanted to respect him and all he'd done for me that summer. It was more of a courtesy, letting him know where I'd be.

Even if that courtesy was technically a lie.

But I couldn't find it in me to feel guilty, not with Reese stealing glances across the room at me all evening long. The way his eyes darkened when they found me, the way the left side of his mouth quirked up into that familiar smirk — it was enough to drive any woman mad.

And I was the one who had his attention.

He had just finished playing one of my favorite songs by Debussy when I slid behind the bar, collecting the dishes from the couple who had just left. We had a long line of people waiting to be seated, and as soon as I cleared those two spaces, someone else would occupy them. I glanced at Reese as the last note played, and when our eyes met, he winked, sending a wave of heat from my neck all the way down to my toes. I felt the flush shading my cheeks as I tore my eyes away, smiling and shaking my head as I continued clearing the bar.

"He's incredible to watch, isn't he?"

I smiled even wider, still collecting dishes. "He really is," I answered, but when I lifted my gaze to the woman who had spoken, every hint of a smile fell from my face in an instant.

Jennifer Stinson.

"Oh, hello," I breathed, trying to replace the smile. My lips twitched, but I couldn't manage anything more than that. "Jennifer, right?"

Her lips curved up wickedly at my attempt at nonchalance. "That's right. And you're Sarah Henderson,

294

Randall's niece." Her eyes narrowed, sizing me up from head to toe before she tilted her head to the side. "And the lucky little lady studying piano with tonight's main attraction."

My cheeks burned again, though this time it was much less pleasant. "Is there anything I can get you?" I asked, even though she already had a full glass of red wine clutched between her manicured fingers.

She tilted the glass in my direction, still smiling as she took a sip. When the glass was back on the bar, she tilted her head to the other side, not bothering to cover her blatant observation of me.

"It must be somewhat distracting," she said after a moment. "Learning from Reese. I mean, let's not be coy, dear. He's not exactly hard on the eyes, is he?"

I swallowed, tossing the last dish in the bin I'd carried over from the kitchen before whipping out a rag to wipe down the bar. "I don't really look at him like that," I said. "He's my teacher."

"Oh, right," she said, face twisting up conspicuously as she made an *ok* sign with her hand. "I'm sure your professional relationship with him makes it impossible to see how insanely hot he is."

All pretenses of fair play were gone with that sentence, with the way her eyes narrowed as she took another sip of wine.

"Well, enjoy your evening, Miss Stinson," I said, tossing the rag on top of the dirty dishes in the bin. I picked it up, balancing it on my hip as I turned for the kitchen, but I didn't make it a step before she spoke again.

"It really is too bad, you know," she said.

As much as I wanted to just keep walking, to deny her request for me to play whatever game she had in mind, I turned anyway, still balancing the bin against my hip as I waited for her to continue. "What's that?"

"Well... it's just that... as his student, I'm sure you know how well he works with his hands." Her eyes slipped over my shoulder, and I knew she was staring right at Reese. "Let's just say that talent isn't only reserved for the piano."

All the blood drained from my face, trickling down my spine like icy cold water. My feet were frozen, rooting me to the spot as I tried to blink, tried to breathe, tried to shake off what she'd just said.

She's just trying to get to you, I assured myself. *She doesn't know anything.*

But I could still see the lipstick on his mouth from Saturday night. I could still close my eyes and imagine his lips on hers, her hands on him, the two of them rolling in what I imagined to be red silk sheets on her bed.

He said she kissed him, and he didn't kiss her back.

He said he only wanted me.

He wouldn't lie to me... *would he?*

I internally shook my head, because I already knew the answer. He wouldn't. Reese cared about me. He wouldn't lie about something like that.

"Aw," Jennifer said, and I popped my eyes open, not realizing I'd squeezed them shut. She clucked her tongue, shaking her head at me as she sipped on her wine. "You really think what you two have is special, don't you? Let me guess, he fed you all his sad, *woe is Reese* stories about Charlie, right? He told you he felt different around you, that you're what he wants, that she broke him, but you make him feel whole?"

I tried to swallow, but it came up dry.

Jennifer chuckled. "Oh, sweetie. Reese is very good at saying what he needs to in order to get what he wants. But trust me when I say that Charlie is the only woman he's ever loved, the only woman he ever *will* love. And you're just a distraction."

A chill ran down my spine, and I shook my head against it, glancing at Reese over my shoulder as Jennifer spoke again.

"I know the truth hurts, but once he's had you, once he's gotten his fill?" She clucked her tongue again when I turned to face her. "He'll find a way to get you out of his hair. It's what he did with Blake, and with me, and I assure you, you're no different." She tilted her glass toward me, taking another sip off the top. "No matter how many times he tells you otherwise."

I still couldn't swallow as I watched her turn in her barstool. She was focused on Reese once again with a satisfied smirk on her face, like the dagger she'd just shoved in my heart brought her absolute joy.

I forced a breath, dragging my lead feet back into the kitchen and dumping the dishes into one of the giant sinks. My vision blurred as I ran the water as hot as I could, letting it burn my skin as I scrubbed the dishes that weren't even my job to wash. I needed to move, to keep my hands busy, to work and think about anything other than what Jennifer had just said to me.

In my heart, I wanted to believe there was no way she could be right.

Reese cared about me. He wouldn't hurt me. He wouldn't lie to me.

But even as I repeated those words, I felt the doubt in them.

Reese said Jennifer kissed *him*, that he'd pulled away, told her to get out of his car. But then how did she know about him and Charlie? If I was the only person he'd ever told? Did he lie about that, about me being the only one?

Did he lie about what happened with Jennifer, too?

He wouldn't lie to you, I tried again, but every muscle in my body was wound tight at the prospect.

Because as much as I hated it, what Jennifer said made sense.

Reese had told me about Blake, about how she loved him, gave him all of her and still he couldn't see past Charlie to give her what she wanted from him. And I'd been there when Charlie had shown up to his place — not once, but *twice*. He assured me nothing had happened, but how was I to know that for sure? Maybe that day she came to see him, she only left quickly because I was there. And during the storm? Charlie could have been there for hours before I showed up.

Maybe that's why he'd been in such a mood.

Maybe it was why he'd kissed me.

He wanted relief from the pain, from the loss of her, and he found it easily in me. I'd all but thrown myself on him that night.

I shook my head, squeezing my eyes shut to try to stop the thoughts. But they roared on, a blistering fire searing every other attempt at rationalizing the situation.

He wouldn't lie to you. He wouldn't use you. He doesn't want to get rid of you. What you have is real. Trust him, not her.

It was all I could do to keep breathing through the rest

of my shift, repeating those words over and over until they quieted everything else. After work, we'd be together. Reese would take me home, and we'd be alone, and I could ask him for myself. He'd hold me and kiss me and silence my anxiety for good.

He'd make it all better. I knew he would.

I just had to make it through the next three hours.

REESE

I made it.

It might have been the slowest night ever at The Kinky Starfish, which was sort of an oxymoron, since it was busy the entire time. But knowing I'd have Sarah in my home after, knowing the exciting news I had to tell her? It made every single second drag by like a year. By the time we finally made it into my car, all I could do was sigh with relief.

I made it.

I reached over the console when we were on the road, resting my hand on Sarah's thigh with a gentle squeeze. "Are you hungry?" I asked. "How do you feel about me whipping up some of my famous spaghetti when we get home."

When we get home.

I loved the sound of that.

Sarah glanced at me, a ghost of a smile touching her lips before she looked out the passenger side window again. "I'm not really hungry."

I frowned. "Alright. No spaghetti, then."

She didn't respond, and an uneasy silence fell over us as we hit the highway.

"How was your night?" I asked.

She shrugged. "Busy."

I nodded, shifting my hold on the steering wheel. When we'd climbed in my car after work, waiting until everyone was gone from the back lot, I thought I'd felt something off. Sarah wasn't smiling, or bouncing around the way she had been the first half of her shift. She was quiet, and reserved, and seemed to be lost in her own little universe.

I wondered if something happened, if she heard more about Wolfgang getting his award. The thought made me squeeze the wheel tighter, jaw aching as I reached forward to turn on the music. Kings of Leon filled the silence between us, and I hoped giving her some space on the way home would help her clear her mind.

I couldn't go back and undo what he did to her.

That was the hardest pill to swallow. If I could go back in time and change anything, it would be that — and I had plenty of things in my *own* life that I should have wanted to use my *go back in time card* for. Still, nothing mattered as much as she did.

But I didn't have a time machine.

All I could do was be here for her *now*, help her see how beautiful she was — inside and out. I could hold her, and kiss her, and talk to her, and listen to her. I could believe in her and her dreams. Randall had tried to remind me of my *role* in her life, and whether he agreed with it or not, *this* was my new role.

All I wanted was to help her feel whole again, the same way she'd done for me.

When we pulled up to the house, I threw the car in drive and jumped out, jogging over to open Sarah's door for her. She smiled, letting me help her out, but then her hands immediately slid into the pockets of her work vest. I held my hand at the small of her back, not quite touching her, just guiding her inside.

Rojo barked as I fiddled with the key, and when I finally got the door open, she bounded out, nearly knocking Sarah over in an attempt to lick her to death. Sarah finally smiled at that, bending to rub Rojo behind the ears before the dog sprinted off the porch and out to the grass to pee. As soon as she was done, she bolted back inside, and was already chewing on her favorite toy when Sarah and I made it into the foyer.

I chuckled, watching Rojo from the doorway. "You know, for how much I fought you on getting that damn dog, I can't imagine my life without her now."

Sarah's eyes sparkled, but her smile was weak. "I told you so."

I dropped my wallet and keys on the table, turning to pull Sarah into my arms as soon as my hands were free. She was stiff, arms at her side as mine wrapped around her waist.

"Hey," I whispered, dropping my forehead to hers. She closed her eyes at the contact, a heavy breath flowing through her chest. "Are you okay?"

She swallowed, a small nod her only response, eyes still closed.

"Sarah?" I asked, pulling back so I could see her.

She opened her eyes, and I hated the way she looked at me in that moment — like she was unsure, like she didn't want to be in my arms. I knew the look well. It had to be hard for her just as it was for me, to let someone in, to trust that someone could make the pain go away.

I didn't know why she was hurting, but I hoped my news would make her smile again.

"Can I kiss you?" I asked, voice soft and low.

She blew out a long breath, shaking her head before she finally smiled — *really* smiled. "Yes," she breathed, and her arms moved from her side to wrap around my neck. I tugged her closer, searching her eyes before I lowered my lips gently to hers.

I sucked in a breath at the contact, at the sweet connection of her lips on mine. They were so soft, giving, plump and perfect. I took my time, peppering her with soft, slow kisses until she submitted more, opening her mouth, tongue seeking mine. And when I'd kissed her thoroughly, I pulled back on a grin, and she shook her head, burying it in my chest.

"I'm sorry," she mumbled. "I just... I had a rough night. I'm all up in my head."

I kissed the head she referred to with a chuckle. "It's okay. You are not required to be happy all the time, and I'm here for both the good and the bad days. Okay?"

She nodded against my chest, pulling back on a smile. "I lied. I do want spaghetti."

I laughed at that, sliding my hand down until it wrapped around hers. "Come on," I said, tugging her toward the kitchen. "Let me feed my girl."

Sarah followed me into the kitchen, and once she was set up at the bar, I poured her a glass of water and handed her my phone to play her choice of music. She was still thumbing through my playlist as I started pulling ingredients out of the pantry.

"So, I have some exciting news."

"Oh?" she asked, eyes on my phone as she swiped. She landed on Debussy, and I smiled when *La Mer* floated through the kitchen.

I nodded, filling a large pot with water before placing it on the stove. I clicked the burner on, crossing the kitchen to stand at the island with her. "I do. Are you ready for it?"

She set my phone down, bracing her hands on the granite with a look of resolution and a confident nod. "Ready, sir."

I smiled, but the longer I looked at her — at this amazing, resilient woman — the more my gaze shifted to one of admiration. Not just for her unspeakable beauty, for her bold, unapologetic way she carried herself, but for every scar she wore proudly.

I reached forward, taking both her hands in mine as I leveled my eyes with hers.

"We've been working together all summer long," I said, smoothing my thumbs over her wrists. "I've watched you take not just steps, but leaps and bounds overcoming your injury. Your technique was good when I first met you, but now? It's spectacular. *You* are spectacular," I amended. "And strong. And vulnerable. And now, when you play, I am held captive from beginning to end. I don't even feel like an adequate teacher anymore," I confessed. "Because I can't find a single thing to critique. I am just completely enamored by you, by what you can accomplish, what you can bring to life when you sit at the piano." I shook my head. "I am so proud of you, Sarah."

Her brows tugged together, and she squeezed my hands. "Such a softie."

I laughed. "I know. I blame you."

Sarah chuckled at that, tilting her head to one side as her eyes searched mine. "So, what's the news, then?"

I bit my lip. "Well… I have this friend. James Conroy. He was a grad student when I was a freshman at Juilliard, and one of my greatest mentors. The man is a legend, an absolute anomaly when it comes to the piano. I've never seen anyone play like him before. He's played at Carnegie several times, is one of the most sought-after concert pianists in the city, and is, in my opinion, the best teacher and connection anyone could ever ask for in our industry." I paused, squeezing her hands as my grin doubled in size. I couldn't help it, the excitement was killing me. "I called him today and told him about you."

Sarah's face fell, dark lashes fluttering over her cheeks as she blinked several times.

"He wants to work with you, Sarah," I said, practically buzzing. "I told him about you and where you want to be and all the work we've done. He wants to help. He'll be your mentor. In New York City." I said every word slowly, making sure it was all sinking in. Judging by Sarah's stunned face, I knew she was just as excited as I was. "This is it. This is what you've worked for. And I truly believe that it won't take you long working with him before you'll be on that Ronald O. Perelman stage at Carnegie Hall." I squeezed her hands again, lifting them to my lips to press a kiss to her knuckles. "And I'll be in the front row, if you'll have me."

Sarah stared at me so long I thought she hadn't heard me.

"Sarah, did you hear what I said?"

She blinked, tugging her hands free from mine and sitting up straight. "I heard you."

"I know it's a lot," I said, smiling. "But, you earned this. You have worked so fucking hard — not just this summer, but before you even came here. Before I even knew you existed. And now, you're one step closer to making your dream come true."

Her nose flared, tears flooding her eyes before she brought her gaze to where her hands rested in her lap. She shook her head, silent for a long while before she lifted her head again. And when her eyes found mine, I found I couldn't breathe.

Those weren't tears of happiness.

"So, that's it, then?" she asked, little shoulders lifting in a shrug before they fell again. "You've had enough of me? You get me naked in your bed and then magically, you have this connection in New York?"

My face fell. "What? No, that's not it at all, Sarah," I said, reaching for her.

She yanked away from me, nearly falling off the stool before she stood to catch herself. She wrapped her arms around her like a shield, backing away even farther.

"*Hey, Sarah. Thanks for the fun. I got you this connection in the city. See ya,*" she mocked.

"That's not—"

"I can't believe this," she said, shaking her head as two tears slipped free. I ached to wipe them away, to pull her into me and quiet her anxiety. But she stepped farther and farther from me, like I was everything causing her pain in that moment.

Perhaps I was.

"This is exactly what I said I would never do," she choked, finally looking at me again. "This is what *he* wanted. It's what

I walked away from. And now here I am. I slept my way up the ladder, just like he said I would." She sniffed, shaking her head. "It has nothing to do with my talent."

"It has *everything* to do with your talent, Sarah," I argued, holding my hands out like she was a cornered, wild animal and I was the tamer. "And your drive. And your passion."

"Yeah?" she asked, gaze hardening. "Then why didn't you make the call *before* you had your hand inside me?"

I shook my head, mouth gaping like a fish as my head spun. This was the exact opposite reaction of what I'd expected, and I was so caught off guard, I couldn't keep my head above water to figure out what to say, how to explain what I thought was so obvious.

"You weren't ready then," I tried to explain.

"And I'm suddenly ready *now*?"

"Yes," I said, but then I shook my head, pinching my eyes shut. "No. No, that's not what I mean. It has nothing to do with us, Sarah. With what happened."

She scoffed, throwing her hands up before storming across the house to the foyer just as the water boiled over behind me. I cursed, running to cut the burner off and remove the pot before I chased after her, and when I caught up, she was already ordering an Uber ride on her phone.

"Wait," I said, beating her to the door and standing against it to block her from leaving. "Just, wait a fucking second. Please. Listen to me."

Her gaze was seething, and she crossed her arms over her chest like I was wasting my breath. Maybe I was. But I couldn't let her leave — not like that, not with those God-awful thoughts in her mind about me and what she meant to me.

"I didn't see it then, okay?" I tried to explain. "You were shut off, locked up. The technique was there, but you wouldn't break yourself down enough to show me what you could really do. You didn't show me your vulnerability until recently, and it was *then* that I saw it — all of it. You, your talent, your drive, your passion, your endurance, your *strength*."

"You saw me naked," she argued, spitting the words like venom. "*That's* why you made the call, Reese. You got what you wanted, you got your student in your bed, your nice little distraction from the woman who broke your heart. And now, you're done with me, aren't you?"

My face crumpled, heart squeezing up so tight it stopped beating for a pulse. "You don't honestly believe that," I whispered. "Sarah, please. Tell me you don't think any of that is true."

She didn't answer, just dropped her gaze to her feet on a shrug. "I had my eyes opened to a lot of things tonight," she said. "And I didn't want to believe it, but now... I can't see it any other way."

"What does that mean?" I tried, reaching for her. "Talk to me. Please."

Sarah pulled away, swapping places with me in a sort of dance until it was her back against the door. "Do you not still love her?" she asked. "Can you look me in the eyes right now and tell me that you feel nothing for her now?"

Everything was spiraling out of control, and the more she stared at me like the absolute last person in the world she could ever trust, the more my knees gave way. I felt it coming, the imminent crash to the floor if I didn't find a way to reach her.

But she reached for the door, instead.

"Sarah," I croaked, throat burning.

Her hand paused on the door handle, and she glanced back at me with tears in her eyes.

"This has nothing to do with Charlie. I care about you. I care about your *dreams*. I did this for you because I believe in you, not because I want anything from you, or because you gave yourself to me the way you did. I told you Saturday night and I'll tell you a million times over — I cherished that night with you. Every *moment* with you." Memories of Blake, of Charlie, of every relationship I'd ever fucked up flooded me like an icy cold bucket of water. "You *saved* me, Sarah. Please. Don't leave me now."

She sighed, bottom lip trembling as her head fell forward, eyes squeezing shut. She was trying to block me out. She didn't want to believe a word I was saying, and I guessed she didn't really owe it to me.

I hadn't proved to anyone that my word was worth a damn.

"God, I'm doing it again!" I screamed, beating my chest hard with one fist. "It's exactly what I told you. I always hurt the people who mean the most to me. See? Even you. And I don't mean to, I don't..." I ran my hands back through my hair, desperation stealing my next breath. "It's like my fucking curse. I burn everything I touch."

Sarah looked at me again, and for the briefest moment, I thought she saw me. The *real* me. But as fast as it had come, it was gone, and her face turned to stone once more.

"Well, you'll never touch me again," she said, a flash of headlights through the front window casting the house in a sickening glow. Her ride was here, and she had nothing more to say to me.

The door opened.

The door closed.

She was gone.

I was alone.

And with my chest on fire, with tears in my eyes and a fiery scream scorching my throat, my knees gave way to the final blow. I crashed to the floor, hitting rock bottom in the most literal sense.

It was right where I deserved to be.

chapter seventeen

REESE

S arah didn't show up for our lesson Thursday night.

I shouldn't have been surprised. I shouldn't have stared at my phone, counting the endless texts and calls I'd sent her way that had gone completely unanswered. I shouldn't have ever imagined a world where she and I would make it, where we would be together, where I was anything more than the absolute fuck up I'd always been.

But I was. And I did.

"Something a little cheerier, Reese?" the manager of The Kinky Starfish suggested, a tight smile on his face as he greeted a customer walking past us. He lowered his head again once she was gone. "It's Friday night, for God's sake. The people want to dance."

I nodded in response, cracking my neck before I launched into one of my favorites from Bach. Even though the music was joyful, I played the piece as if from a distant world. Everything was hollow. Everything was void.

And Sarah was avoiding me, working in the kitchen instead of out on the floor.

I knew she was there. I could feel her presence, a familiar buzz that warned my body she was near. It used to warn me to stay away, to keep my distance, to remember what I could and could not have.

I should have listened to it, then.

Now, it only served to punish me, to remind me what I'd lost, what was so close yet so out of reach.

It was the worst brand of torture.

The night passed in a sort of gray fog, my fingers flying over the keys, a forced smile on my lips, a voice that seemed to be someone else's greeting the patrons and talking between pieces. To everyone else in that room, I imagined I seemed the same. But inside, I was burning.

It wasn't until my first break that I felt a tiny flash of relief, and I told the patrons I was taking a half hour, even though that was twice what I usually took. I needed a moment. I needed space.

I needed Sarah.

And I was on my way to the kitchen to find her when I ran into Charlie, instead.

"Reese," she said, hand wrapping around my bicep and pulling me to a stop just before I hit the swinging door to the kitchen.

I let her turn me, heart squeezing at her proximity, at the voice that I knew so well, at the warm chocolate eyes that I could close my eyes and see perfectly. But it was different this time. I didn't want to reach for her, to hold her, to inhale her scent and imagine the days when she was mine.

I just wanted her to leave me alone so I could go find Sarah.

I hadn't seen her since she showed up at my house unannounced on the anniversary of my family's death. I'd dodged her calls, her mother's calls inviting me to dinner, her father's calls inviting me to have a drink and play a round of golf, her brother's calls saying he wanted to catch up. I loved them, and I knew in my heart they would always be a sort of family to me.

But I'd needed space. I'd wanted to heal. And Sarah was helping me do just that.

Until I ruined everything.

"Charlie," I greeted, scratching the back of my neck. "I was just about to head outside to smoke. Could we talk after my set?"

"No. We can't. This is important."

Her reaction surprised me, and it wasn't until then that I saw the bend in her brows, the concern etched on her little face. She pulled her hand from where it held my arm, crossing her own over her chest.

"Graham has been trying to reach out to you. So have I." She swallowed. "We *all* have, and you haven't answered any of our calls."

"I've been busy," I explained.

Charlie paused, like she was waiting for more — busy doing *what*, she seemed to ask me with her doe eyes. But I didn't feel the need to explain further, not when the only thought on my mind was getting inside that kitchen and talking to Sarah.

"Jennifer Stinson called my mother earlier today."

I didn't understand the correlation, but the heavier Charlie's gaze became, the more I was on alert. Why would Jennifer call her mom, and why would Charlie need to talk to me about it?

"Okay..."

"She wanted to talk to my mom because she's on the board at Winchester, and apparently, Jennifer wanted to voice some concerns about a particular teacher. She didn't want to go straight to Mr. Henderson, especially because, in her own words, *this teacher is a close family friend.*"

I gritted my teeth. "So, me?"

She nodded.

"What the hell did she say?"

Charlie looked around us, like the conversation wasn't safe to have in public. Then, she tugged me off to the side, to a back corner behind a booth that was vacant, looking around once more before she spoke in a hushed tone.

"She said you had taken high interest in a particular student, and she worried that it might not be a *professional* one." Charlie paused, eyeing me like she was looking for some sort of tell, some sort of reaction from me. "She said she ran into you and Sarah Henderson in the park one day... that you were both acting strange... and that she spoke with someone here, at the restaurant, and they confirmed her suspicions."

I scoffed, shaking my head. "That's bullshit. No one here knows a fucking thing."

Charlie's shoulders fell, brows folding inward as she covered her mouth with one hand. "Oh, Reese..."

And I realized then that I'd confirmed the story without even realizing it.

"It's true, isn't it?" Charlie's eyes widened as she shook her head. "I thought... I was so sure there had to be a mistake. I was so sure you could never do something like this."

"What do you mean *like this*?"

Charlie looked around again, lowering her voice even more. "She's a *girl*, Reese. She's twenty-one. You're her teacher, for Christ's sake. *And* she's the niece of the man who signs your paycheck. Do you not understand how grotesquely *wrong* this all is?"

Indignation rolled through me like a tidal wave, swallowing all rational thought as I stared at the woman I once loved. And I knew it then, in that moment, that it truly was past tense.

I *loved* her, but I didn't love her, anymore.

"How dare you, Charlie." The words came out in a whisper, like my voice wasn't caught up to my brain yet, like it didn't want to betray my heart that once beat for only that woman in front of me. "It's not wrong. It's not *grotesque*," I said, spitting her word back at her. "You don't know anything about Sarah, who is not a girl, by the way. She's more of a woman than anyone I've ever met." I stood taller, each word giving me more strength. "And you don't know anything about me anymore. Or what I have with Sarah."

The look of pity Charlie gave me in that moment made me want to smash my fist into the nearest wall.

"Reese..."

"No," I said, holding up one hand to stop her from saying anything else. "I know what you must think, what *all* of you must think, but you don't know anything about us. And honestly, it's none of your goddamn business."

"This isn't you," she said, reaching for me. "I know you're hurting, I know—"

"JUST STOP."

I tore away from her before she could touch me, and a few patrons glanced our way as Charlie offered a smile and a soft apology. She watched them until they turned around, pulling her gaze to mine again, then.

"You don't get to do this to me, Charlie," I said, keeping my voice as low as I could. "You don't get to say that you see me hurting, or look at me with pity, or feel like you have any fucking say in what I do or who I spend my time with. I'm healing. I am *finally* moving on."

"But—"

"You already broke my heart," I said, cutting her off as I took a step toward her. My nose stung, but I sniffed back the emotion, shaking my head. "Isn't that enough, Charlie? Haven't you had enough?"

The kitchen door swung open, and I turned just as Charlie's eyes shot over my shoulder at the person who was behind us now.

Sarah.

She glanced at me first, then Charlie, and when she looked at me again, her eyes were cold as ice. She didn't so much as nod as an acknowledgement of our existence before she balanced the bin in her hands on one hip, making her way toward the bar.

Shit.

"I have to go," I said to Charlie, already on my way after Sarah.

"Wait, Reese. Please." She tugged at my sleeve, holding me in place as she pleaded. "I never meant to hurt you. You know that. I never meant to... everything just got so..."

Tears flooded her eyes, and just like always, the sight of her hurting broke me.

But she wasn't mine to comfort, anymore.

And she wasn't the one I wanted, either.

"I know," I assured her, scrubbing a hand back through my hair on a sigh. "I know. Okay? I do. But whether you mean to or not, you *do* hurt me, Charlie. Every time you look at me like that, or ask me to come to dinner, or pretend like we can still be friends when you know good and well that it's impossible."

Her shoulders fell. "I didn't..."

"It's okay," I said, not letting her finish.

It was my turn to talk, to say what I'd needed to for two long years.

"It is. Truly. We loved each other, no matter how fucked up the circumstances were, and that will never change. But you have *got* to let me go, Charlie. Just like I have to let you go. And I can't do that with you inserting yourself in every aspect of my life." I shook my head. "So, please. *Please*, Charlie. Leave me alone, and let me finally stop loving you."

Her bottom lip trembled, her delicate fingers reaching for it as she nodded against the tears flooding her eyes. "I'm so sorry, Reese."

"Me, too," I whispered. "Me, too."

I reached forward, pulling her into me and kissing her forehead before I let her go — physically, mentally, literally, and figuratively. In every sense of the word, I let Charlie Pierce go in that moment.

And I ran to the woman I loved.

The realization flooded me as my feet carried me across the restaurant, chest swelling with the surprise of it while I shook my head, knowing I should have realized it long ago. How something could feel like such a revelation and also like something I'd known my entire life was beyond me, but there it was, pumping blood into every vein in my body.

I loved her.

I loved her.

And I couldn't lose her now.

Sarah glanced at me from where she was clearing dishes when I rounded the corner into the bar area, but her eyes fell quickly, back to her hands as they worked. I slid up beside her behind the bar without her acknowledgement, without a greeting, without a prayer in hell that she'd talk to me.

But I had to try, anyway.

"Sarah, please," I said, eyeing the patrons at the bar to make sure they couldn't hear us before I spoke again. "Can we go outside and talk?"

"I'm working," she said firmly, holding up the dish rag she was wiping the bar down with as proof.

"Take a break."

She sighed, shaking her head as she slapped the damp rag back on the bar and began scrubbing vigorously. "There's nothing more to say, Reese. I called your guy. I'm leaving for New York in two weeks."

Her words knocked the air from my chest, a tornado of mixed emotions set loose in a snap. I was so happy for her. This was what she wanted. This was what *I* wanted for her.

But I didn't want her to leave like this.

"Why do I feel like no matter what I say to that, there's no right way to respond?"

Sarah rolled her eyes. "Why don't you go talk it out with Charlie? I'm sure she can help you sort through your thoughts."

"She's not the one I want to talk to."

Sarah ignored me, slapping the wet rag into the bin before balancing it on her hip again and shoving past me toward the kitchen. "You know, I shouldn't have been shocked to see you with her when I came out here for the first time tonight," she said, stopping long enough to pin me with her gaze. "It was just *too* predictable, I didn't want to believe it. But it looks like nothing has changed."

"You don't mean that," I said quickly, before she could turn away. "You don't believe what your anxiety is trying to convince you is real."

"You don't know anything about my *anxiety*," she spat. "Or me."

"I know *everything* about you," I argued, stepping into her space.

Her breath stilled, eyes falling to my lips before she ripped them away, meeting my gaze once more.

"I know nothing makes you happier than a good peanut butter and jelly sandwich and a shady day in the park. I know you thought your love of reading had died, but it was only reading happy endings that you'd lost passion for. You finished *Fight Club* in three days, and you've had a new book in your bag every week since, because escaping into someone else's reality is easier than facing your own."

Sarah's lips parted, her eyes softening as they searched mine.

"I know you wrap your fingers around that crystal that hangs from your neck because it brings you peace, because it makes you think of your dad, of your mom, of everything that keeps you breathing. I know your favorite composer used to be Beethoven, but somewhere along the way, you started favoring Debussy. My bet is because his music makes you believe in love, however impossible it may seem to have faith that it exists."

She adjusted the bin on her hip, brows tugging together. She seemed torn between the choice to turn and walk away from me forever, or to jump into my arms.

So I kept talking, hoping I could steer her toward the latter.

"I know nothing in this world means more to you than the piano," I said, a long sigh leaving my chest. "But that you've felt lost over the past year because for the first time in your life, that relationship that came so easy turned complicated. You were injured. Then, you were taken advantage of. You were *hurt*, Sarah, and you got angry — just as you should have. You turned your back on the piano, on loving it, on letting it love *you* and started treating it like a means to an end, instead. You thought if you could accomplish all the checks on your list, that you'd feel better, you'd find success. And along the way, you only found more loneliness." I swallowed. "Until you met me."

She wasn't leaving, though I knew if I reached for her, if the spell I had her under was broken for even a moment — she'd be gone in an instant.

Still, I couldn't help it.

I had to be near her. I had to touch her, to let her feel me when I said the next words. My hand reached forward, and my pinky laced with hers under the shadows of the bar where no one could see.

"I know that you are the strongest, most resilient woman to ever walk the face of this Earth. I know that even though *you* don't see it or believe it, you will move mountains in the piano industry, and it will be *you* who future students look up to. I know that you will soar." I curled my pinky around hers tighter. "And I know you love me, Sarah. Just like I know I love you."

She gasped, eyes shooting from where they'd been staring at my chest to meet my gaze. Her pupils dilated, eyes flicking between mine as she opened her mouth, closed it, opened it again, closed it. She was utterly speechless, her wide eyes and trembling lip not betraying any of her thoughts.

I had lied.

Because I *didn't* know if she loved me, too.

But I hoped.

"I'll quit my job," I said, and I'd never meant anything more in my life. "I'll leave Westchester, I'll leave this *town*. I'll go to the city with you, and be whatever wind I can be beneath your outstretched wings if you'll let me. But you have to let me, Sarah. You have to choose me, too."

The moment stretched between us as I waited for her response, for her to say she *did* love me — for her to say anything at all. That energy that always buzzed to life around us was an entire universe in that moment, and it was just for us. I begged whatever god existed to help me, to let her feel my sincerity, my care, my love. I prayed for relief, for her to throw herself in my arms and assure me that what I felt wasn't one-sided. That it was real. That whatever or *who*ever tried to step between us would never win.

And for that long pause in time, I believed — in God, in His plan for me, for her, for *us*. I believed she would see it, too. I believed we would make it. I believed there was no other way, no other possible outcome.

Until the moment she pulled away.

Her eyes fell to the floor between us at the same time she withdrew her hand from mine, tucking it around the edge of the bin against her hip instead. "I have to go," she whispered.

And she disappeared back into the kitchen without another word.

SARAH

"Oh yes, you *have* to take that one. It's my favorite," Mom said from where she sat crosslegged on my bed. She was watching me pull clothes from one of the boxes she'd brought with her from Atlanta as I tried to figure out what to take with me to New York.

New York.

I was going to New York.

It was everything I'd wanted, everything I'd worked for, and I couldn't even find it in me to be twenty-percent happy.

"Keep in mind that I'm going to live in a shoe box," I reminded her, folding up the floral kamino dress she'd said couldn't stay behind. "You can't keep saying yes to every piece of clothing I've ever owned."

Mom twirled the straw in the smoothie she was drinking. "But you *need* that one. And all your winter clothes, it'll be cold there soon. And what if you want to go out with friends? You need nice clothes to go out in. And casual clothes to relax in. And if you perform at Carnegie, then—"

"I'll go shopping," I finished for her, chuckling. "No wonder you need a walk-in closet."

"Hey, I wore the same t-shirt and ratty pair of shorts most of my childhood," she reminded me. "So I like to indulge now. Sue me."

I smiled, pulling out the next shirt and holding it up for Mom to inspect. She nixed it, waving it off as she took another drink of her smoothie. She'd driven all the way from Atlanta just so she could haul about eight boxes of my clothes, wall décor, and random knick-knacks from my bedroom back home. Most of it would be shipped back to Georgia, but I loved that she brought it all, anyway.

Her baby girl was moving to the big city, and I could see it in her eyes that she was half proud, half terrified.

Having her in Uncle Randall's house was the comfort I needed — though nothing could take all the pain away. The last two weeks had dragged by like the longest decade of my life, especially the days when I had to work at The Kinky Starfish. I hadn't been to Reese's house since the night we fought, cancelling all our lessons since then, but I couldn't escape him at work.

Tomorrow would be my last night there… and therefore, my last night with Reese.

Somehow, that fact tore me up more than seeing him did.

I'd completely shut down after our fight, the same way I did after what happened to me at Bramlock. Maybe it was a defense mechanism, my brain and body doing whatever they needed to do to protect me and help me survive. It didn't matter, anyway — there was nothing more to say to Reese and nothing more he could say to me.

Because Jennifer had been right.

I swore to myself when she got in my head that it was wrong, that there was no way any of it could be true. But he'd proven me wrong not even ten minutes after we got to his place that night.

Just like Wolfgang said I would, I slept my way to the next stepping stone on the way to everything I wanted.

I wondered if there was any way *not* to do the same in New York.

It felt like the cruelest joke, to finally start trusting again, feeling again, *wanting* again — and then have the person at the center of all that betray me worse than the one who'd put up the walls in the first place. I was sick when I thought of it, hence my lack of appetite since that night. I trusted Reese. I thought he was different.

And yes, maybe he was right.

Maybe I loved him.

But it was a lie, a fake love, one that couldn't possibly be real — not when he loved Charlie still, and not when he would even consider that getting me a connection in New York was what I was after the night I undressed for him.

I clutched the next dress from the box between my hands, remembering the power I felt when I stood in his dark bedroom, peeling my jacket off first before I slipped my dress overhead. I'd felt so wanted, so desired, so *respected* — and now, I only felt naïve.

I was only good for one thing.

That's what Wolfgang had said, over and over again as he raped me. He'd wanted me to know it. He'd wanted me to remember it forever.

You're only good for one thing.

I thought I'd proved him wrong before. Now, I wasn't so sure.

"Sweetie," Mom said from the bed. I glanced at her through blurred eyes, and when two tears snuck loose, slipping over my cheeks, my mom frowned more.

I shook my head, swiping the wetness away. "Sorry. I guess I'm just emotional."

"Come here," Mom said, patting the spot on the bed next to her.

I dropped the dress in my hand, crawling on top of the puffy comforter with a sigh as I sat next to her. We both leaned our backs against the wall, and as soon as I kicked my feet out, Mom grabbed the crystal around her neck.

It was the same as mine.

She squeezed it, eyeing the one around my neck until I did the same, and as soon as my fingers folded around it, I felt the relief. It was like an instant release of anxiety, a flood of peace, and I inhaled a deep breath, trying to seal the feeling in.

"You're not sad about leaving for New York," she mused.

I shook my head.

"But, you're not happy about it, either, are you?"

At that, my bottom lip trembled so hard I had to bite down on it to keep from crying. I shook my head again, still holding the crystal around my neck.

"Talk to your mother," she pleaded, shifting until her shoulder was against the wall, the frame of her body facing me. She reached one hand out, resting it on my knee before giving it a light squeeze. "Even if it doesn't make sense, just start talking."

With that touch, with those simple words, I broke.

It was like the dam breaking, so much emotion rushing through me at once I couldn't place it, couldn't find a raft to safely float on top. Instead, I was drowned immediately, no air in sight. Everything just hit at once — the memory of Wolfgang, of what he did, of what he said, of how he permanently changed me forever. And Reese, how he'd opened me up again, helped me through my injuries — internally and externally — and how he'd shown me joy again when I swore I'd never find any.

I squeezed my eyes shut and folded in on myself as the waves took me under, and mom cried, too, wrapping her arms around me in a shield. "Oh, *mwen chouchou,*" she whispered, rocking me gently. "What happened to my sweet girl?"

That broke me even more, and I pressed the hand that was around my crystal to my chest, trying to soothe the ache. Every breath burned, like I really was inhaling water, like I was drowning right there in my aunt's guest bedroom.

And that's when I knew.

That's when it hit me, all of it — the pain, the hiding, the sense of worthlessness, the fight to be more, the failure, the hope, the love, the gut-wrenching heartbreak. And I knew I couldn't take another step forward until I faced my past, until I looked every ghost in the eye.

Starting with my wolf.

For the longest time, I just stayed there on the bed, curled up on myself as my mom rocked me and ran her hands over my bald head in an attempt to soothe me. I could feel her own heart breaking, and I knew I was about to break it more.

But I couldn't keep my secret any longer.

I lifted my head, sniffing and wiping the tears from my face as my eyes settled on hers. "*Manman,*" I whispered, and my lips trembled again, but I held my chin high despite the fear blooming in my chest. "I was raped."

The water receded as soon as the words were out, even though my heart broke at the sight of my mother's hands flying to her mouth, her head shaking, her eyes welling with tears as she watched me. It brought her pain just like I knew it would, but I'd told her the truth. I'd told her what I should have so long ago, but didn't have the courage to.

And just saying those three words, I felt like I was staring my ghost in the eyes, not backing down, not giving up.

"Oh, no," she whispered through her hands, still shaking her head as tears ran down her dark cheeks. She reached for me, pulling me into her chest. She readjusted her grip, over and over, like she couldn't shield me enough, like she couldn't have me close enough. "No. No, no, no. I thought that was what had happened. It was what my heart told me when you came home, when you changed everything about your appearance, when you flinched away from my touch. But I didn't want to be right... Oh, my child, I didn't want to be right."

"I'm so sorry," I whispered.

She ripped me away from her chest at that, her eyes a burning fire when they landed on me. "No. You do not apologize for this. Ever. *Ever*, do you hear me? It is not your fault, and you have nothing to be sorry for."

"I'm just sorry I didn't tell you before," I amended, holding back tears. "I'm sorry I was such a coward. And I'm sorry I have to hurt you by telling you."

"Oh, sweetheart," she said, framing my face with her cool hands. "You are the furthest thing from a coward that could ever exist."

I nodded past the tears blurring my vision again, and she brought my forehead to her lips, holding them there a long moment before she released me. When our eyes met again, she wiped my tears away with her palms before framing my face once more.

"I want you to tell me everything," she said. "If you're ready."

"I am," I said quickly. "I am. And I need your help, too. Because... there's a guy."

She quirked a brow. "There's a guy?"

I cringed a little, nodding. And recognition touched my mother's eyes as soon as she saw my reaction.

I didn't have to say a word for her to know who I was referring to.

"Alright, *mwen chouchou*," she said, grabbing her smoothie from the bedside table. "Start talking."

It was after midnight by the time I finished telling my mom everything that had happened, and we'd both experienced every emotion on the scale of human capacity. All the muscles in my body ached from the tension, the tears, the admissions, the revelations.

I walked her through every aching second of that last night at Bramlock, even though I knew I was adding a scar to her heart that would never heal.

No one wanted to imagine their baby girl getting raped.

But she held my hand through every painful detail, holding me when I was crying too hard to speak, giving me space when I needed to get up and pace just to finish a thought. And when I was done, when I'd caught her up on that night, I just kept right on, flowing into the depression of the months that followed, the hollowness, the lack of joy in my life even when I sat down at the piano.

And I told her about Reese.

I told her about our lessons, about the way he pushed me to dig deep, to face my demons, to take my pain and turn it into music. I told her about all that he'd been through, how he'd brought me hope in a time when I thought it would never exist for me again. I told her about the kiss, about how I ran away, and then how we somehow found our way back together.

Only so I could walk out again.

I was a mess, a complete disaster, and I'd just dumped all my shit on my mom's lap and asked her to help me sort through it.

Tissues littered the bed around us by the time I'd finished, and Mom sat back against the wall again with an exhausted sigh.

"This is a lot," she finally confessed, glancing at me with as much of a smile as she could muster.

"I know."

We were both silent a long moment.

"What do you think?"

She sighed again at that, reaching for one of the bottles of water Aunt Betty had brought us when we'd skipped out on dinner. "I think I wish I still drank alcohol right now."

I chuckled.

Mom watched me, her eyes skating over every part of me like she was seeing me for the first time. I guessed in that moment, she sort of was.

"We have to go after him, baby girl," she said. "We can't let Wolfgang get away with what he did to you, what he could still be doing to other girls at that university. We have to stand up, and we have to fight — even if we're destined to lose. Do you hear me?" She sat up straight, crossing her legs again. "I know the odds are against us, and that it will be a hard fight, a *long* fight, but we will suit up for battle, nonetheless."

I didn't have any tears left to cry, but my throat constricted with the weight of her words. She wanted me to take Wolfgang to court, to press charges, to tell the whole world my story and let them judge it for themselves.

And I knew she was right.

He could still be there, right now, at this very moment, torturing someone else.

I couldn't live with myself if I didn't at least try to stop it.

"I don't even know where to start," I confessed.

"I'll figure that out," she assured me, sitting back against the wall again. "But, we can talk about that later. Right now, I want to talk about the *first* person you felt comfortable telling all this to, the one who brought back your happiness. Because I think that's the most important thing to discuss in this moment."

I nodded.

"Now, I'd be lying if I said I was thrilled about all of this. Reese is much older than you, and even though I know the connection you have with him is real, it does bother me that he was your teacher and allowed you two to get this close."

I swallowed, tucking my knees up to my chest and wrapping my arms around them. I felt like I was ten years old again, being scolded and grounded for skipping homework to play piano.

Mom eyed me sternly before taking a breath. "But," she continued. "That being said, I also know that sometimes — *most* times — love doesn't play by the rules we have set for it in society. And if anyone knows what it's like to fight for a love with more than just mountains to climb, it's your *Manman*."

I smiled, reaching out for her hand to squeeze it, because I knew in that moment she was thinking about my dad, about their love, about their journey. Their interracial relationship in the deep south when my father had been in the political circuit had tested both of them. They'd had bricks thrown through the windows of their first home, had their shoes spit on by people passing them on the street, heard the most vicious threats from the mouths of absolute demons.

And still, they'd fought together — for their love, for their life.

I wished he were still here to live it with her.

"Let me ask you this," she said, placing her other hand over where mine held hers. "Do you really believe what that woman told you about Reese, what your head is trying to convince you of? Do you believe he wanted something from you before he called his friend in New York, that he would use you like that?"

I dropped my gaze to my lap. "I don't know how to *not* believe that... not after what happened."

"No," Mom said, squeezing my hand until I looked at her again. "I want you to really stop for a moment, listen to your heart, and tell me — do you believe Reese would ever do anything to hurt you?"

The tears I thought had dried up flooded my eyes instantly, because I'd known long before she'd asked, long before I told her everything, long before I'd even walked out his door that night we fought.

I knew Reese would never hurt me, but I still ran away.

"He would never hurt me," I whispered, sniffing against the urge to cry again. "Never. Well, *intentionally*, anyway. But, even though he didn't mean to, he still *did*, Mom. He still hurt me."

Mom patted my hand again. "I know he did. And sometimes, when you love someone, you can't see straight. Sometimes we hurt each other when we think we're doing what is best." She paused, considering her next words. "I think you're right, though — I don't think he would hurt you in any malicious way. Want to know what else I think?"

I nodded.

"I think you're scared to fully trust him, and to let him into your life, because of what happened to you. And that is okay, Sarah." She lowered her gaze, searching my eyes with her own. "Do you hear me? It. Is. Okay."

I didn't realize I felt it, that I was ashamed of my own feelings, of the way I reacted, of the way I pushed Reese away until my mom said those words. And when she did, I shook my head against them, face twisting with the emotion they left behind.

I had no one else to blame but myself for the position I was in with Reese.

And I couldn't even fully explain *why* I'd put myself here.

"It's okay that you ran away from him," she continued. "That perhaps your *reasons* in his eyes or mine or anyone else's don't seem to make sense. It's okay that your anxiety spoke louder than reality in that moment of time when he was trying to express his care and love, but it came out in a form that pushed all your soft spots. And it's okay that your emotions won against logic — trust me, it happens to the best of us." Mom pressed her lips together in a soft smile. "Honey, you do not have to always be okay. And if anyone will understand the war you had going on in your head, the war that may *always* go on for you, it's Reese. You just have to tell him. You have to trust him. And you have to let him in. And if you can't do that?" She shrugged. "Well, then he isn't the right one."

I shook my head immediately. "It's not him. It's me. This is all me. He got me this... this... *incredible* opportunity. In the city I want to be in, with one of the most amazing mentors I could ask for, aside from him. And he did it because he wants to see me happy." I choked on a sob. "I think it's what he's always wanted. And I can't figure out why I fight it, why I seem to be so much more comfortable in misery than in happiness."

"Well, I think a lot of that comes from what happened with Wolfgang. And that brings me to something else we need to discuss." She paused, chewing her bottom lip a moment as she considered her next words. "I think you need to see a therapist in New York, Sarah."

Mom watched me like she expected me to fight, to throw a fit, to say I was fine and I didn't need to talk to anyone.

But none of that was true.

I *wasn't* fine, and I knew it.

"I think you're right," I whispered in agreement. "Honestly, maybe if I would have sorted through all this *before* I got to Pennsylvania, before I worked with Reese, I could have been more open to him. I wouldn't have pushed him away, pushed *us* away."

"Ah, but see, that's the funny thing about life, isn't it?" Mom said, a genuine smile touching her lips. "It seems that way, but if you would have talked to someone immediately, you might not have even ended up in Pennsylvania. Or if you had, Reese might not have seen the same pain in you that has lived in him, and maybe, he wouldn't have connected with you on the same level. Everything happens for a reason, *mwen chouchou*. But now, it's up to you to decide what happens next."

I returned her smile, nodding as she squeezed my hand. And slowly, like a balloon being filled with each new breath I took, hope started to float back into my soul. My heart raced at the thought of running to Reese, of telling him everything, of pleading with him to come with me to New York like he said he would.

Only, I didn't know if that offer was still on the table.

"*Manman*," I said after a long moment. "What if he doesn't listen to me? I mean... I've been *awful* to him. I ran out of his house. I accused him of terrible things, of using me, of doing the absolute last thing I know he would ever do." I swallowed. "And, I threw one of his biggest scars in his face. When I saw him with Charlie, I just... I snapped. I wanted to hurt him the way he'd hurt me, but it wasn't even him who had hurt me at all." I sighed, pulling my hand from Mom's so I could bury my face in both of them. "Everything is such a mess, I can't even see my way out of it."

Mom clucked her tongue, reaching over to rub my back as I tried to sort through it all.

"He said he loved you," she reminded me. "Right? The last time you spoke?"

I nodded, resting my chin on my knees so I could look at her. "He said I saved him, too."

At that, Mom's smile bloomed, and she shook her head, running the back of her knuckles along the side of my face. She stopped at my chin, framing it with her thumb and forefinger as her eyes watered over. "Oh, *mwen chouchou*. Who saved who?"

I choked on a sob, throwing myself in her arms as the emotion took me under again. Only this time as she held me, it wasn't pain that wracked through me — it was hope.

"Thank you," I whispered, my head still against her chest where she held me. "I couldn't do this without you."

"Do what?"

"Life," I said on a laugh.

Mom laughed, too, pulling back to frame my face with her hands. "So, now what, my love?"

My heart squeezed, a completely different kind of anxiety causing my muscles to seize. This time, it was born of the fear of rejection, the fear of putting my heart on the line only to have it passed up, like a bowl of peas on a dinner table.

"Now, I tell him how I feel," I said, heart racing as an idea came to me. It was stupid. It was big. It was risky. But if I had a prayer of getting back the man I'd lost, it would all be worth it.

"And how do you do that?"

I smiled. "By using the only language he'll understand."

chapter eighteen

REESE

At least the weather was on my side.

Just like on the anniversary of my family's death, there was a torrential downpour soaking all of Pittsburgh to its bones the day before Sarah was destined to leave town. I drove through the gray, miserable rain on my way across town, taking in the foggy skyline as the sun dipped away somewhere above the dark gray clouds. It was just another Friday night at The Kinky Starfish, another day in my monotonous routine of surviving — and that's all it was, surviving.

I didn't live anymore.

It was the same state of being I'd been in before Sarah walked into my life, and it didn't surprise me that with the knowledge of her leaving, I was slipping right back into my comfort zone of nothingness. For the last two weeks, I'd done the same thing every day — wake up, take Rojo for a long walk, work out at the house, play piano, lose an afternoon watching movies, pop open a beer as soon as five o'clock hit — unless I was working at The Kinky Starfish — and to be honest, even sometimes then. I was doing whatever I could to get my ass out of bed and keep going, even when it felt like there was nothing to keep going for.

But tonight was different.

Tonight, my pulse beat hard and haphazardly right along with the windshield wipers on my old car trying to combat the rain. Because I knew I would see her.

And I also knew it would be the last time.

I'd made a promise to Charlie when she chose Cameron that I would let her go as gracefully as I could. Well, it turned out I had about as much grace as I did vegetables in my pantry. That is to say — absolutely none.

But with Sarah, I would follow through on my promise.

I'd tried to keep her, tried to get her to listen, to believe me, to believe in *us*. I couldn't make her choose me, and so I would choose to be happy for her, for her next journey — whether I was a part of it or not. This time, I would have grace in letting the one I love go.

Maybe because she was the one I'd loved more than any other in my life.

It seemed impossible, even as my heart beat the truth of it into my chest. How could I love her after only knowing her a few months? How could I feel this connection to a woman just barely over half my age?

None of it made sense, and I guessed that was the most intriguing thing about love. It didn't have to make sense.

It didn't have to be reciprocated, either.

The potholes in the back lot of The Kinky Starfish were full of water, and I sloshed through them as I parked my car, pulling my rain jacket on and popping open a large umbrella as soon as my door was open. My shoes were soaked in an instant, the rest of me barely saved from the coat and umbrella. It was the kind of rain that was nearly impossible to shield yourself from.

When I made it inside, I shivered at the air blasting from the air conditioner in the back of the kitchen. Shaking my umbrella off, I propped it by the door before peeling my jacket off and hanging it on the rack.

I was in such a daze that I didn't realize mine was the only jacket there.

Or that my car was one of only two in the parking lot.

Or that the kitchen was empty, the lights dimmed, even though our doors would open in less than half an hour.

None of it hit me, not until I walked through the swinging kitchen doors and out onto the floor to prep my setlist for the night and saw that my seat was already taken.

It *all* hit me then — the dark, empty restaurant, the candles flickering from where they sat on top of the piano, the fact that I was completely alone in a place that should have been buzzing to life right now in preparation for a busy night ahead.

Well, almost completely alone.

Sarah sat at the bench I usually occupied, a soft melody flowing through the space between us as she let her hands glide over the keys. Her eyes were soft, hopeful, and yet I saw the fear in them as she watched me from across the room.

I stepped closer, broaching the circle where the piano sat under the chandelier. It was funny, the way the room was set up, because I was in almost the exact same proximity to her as when we were together in my home — her at the piano, me off in the right-hand corner. As soon as I crossed that threshold, Sarah paused, letting silence fall over us. Her eyes met mine, and I saw goodbye written all over them as I waited for her to speak.

But she didn't.

Instead, she closed her eyes, blew out a long, steadying breath, and began playing a song I'd never heard before.

The song struck violently to a start, a crescendo of sharp, dramatic notes causing my heart to kick harder in my chest as I watched her play. There was violence in that music, and pain, and sorrow — and she moved with every beat of it. Her shoulders were rounded, relaxed, her fingers flying over the keys as she brought the unfamiliar song to life. Her face screwed up as the harmony shifted, the volume of her playing softening in a gradual decrescendo until she stopped playing altogether.

She took a long rest, eyes fluttering open and meeting mine. She held my gaze, and the softest, sweetest smile touched her lips as she started playing again.

The new melody was strong and hopeful, romantic and sweet, like what you would imagine if you were strolling along the river boardwalk with a lover's hand in yours, the moon full and bright above. It felt like home, and adventure, like something fresh and new and somehow familiar all at once. I wanted to pull her up from that bench and dance with her, that's how powerful the music was.

Instead, I leaned a hip back against the low wall that circled the piano, watching as the shadows from the candlelight danced over her face, instead. She pulled her gaze back to her hands, moving with them as the song progressed, and the longer she played, the more dramatic it became.

Her fingers pounded the keys in a crescendo, the brazen forte making me suddenly feel uncomfortable, like I was in danger or on the brink of a discovery I didn't want to make. I felt every flex of her body as it moved with the beat, every tap of her foot on the pedal, every dramatic scale she took me on.

And it was then that I realized there was a reason the song was an unfamiliar one, one I'd never heard before.

It was because she'd written it.

I didn't know what it meant — her being here, the song she was playing — but I couldn't fight against the hope that bloomed in my chest. I tried to tamp it down, to quiet it and hold onto the moment for whatever it was worth. *She's leaving*, I reminded myself. But still, hope bloomed.

When she played the last note, long and soft and bittersweet, it felt like the music you'd hear at the end of the saddest movie you'd ever watched in your life. It was laced with goodbyes, with regrets and sorrows.

And still, somehow, hope bloomed.

Silence fell over us like a sheet being spread out over a bed, the fabric slowly descending, surrounding us in a bubble of the last note before it deflated altogether. And when the quiet blanketed us completely, Sarah stood, the fear back in her eyes as she took a careful step away from the piano and toward me.

"Did you write that?" I asked.

Sarah nodded.

"Did you write it for me?"

Her face broke at that, tears welling in her eyes as she rolled her lips together and nodded again. And that hope that had bloomed slowly in my chest exploded like a comet, searing a path across my heart.

"I'm so sorry, Reese," she finally said, eyes brimmed with unshed tears, the candlelight making them glisten like diamonds. "I'm sorry I left you that night, that I believed you would ever hurt me, that I took something so personal and shoved it in your face the first chance I got. I wanted to hurt you, Reese. I did. And I'm so sorry."

I frowned, torn between the urge to reach for her, to pull her into me and soothe her and the urge to run from her all at once. There was the proof, her admittance that she wanted to hurt me.

And she had.

I didn't know what to do with that.

"I don't have any excuse for the way I've behaved," Sarah spoke after a long pause, inhaling a deep gulp of oxygen before blowing it out again. "None that matter or make up for anything. But, I want to explain, if you'll listen. God knows I didn't listen to you, so I can't blame you if you walk out of here right now without letting me say another word."

She paused, like she was waiting to see if I'd bolt. When I didn't, she continued.

"Reese, from the very first time I met you, I couldn't fathom a world where you could ever be interested in me. The way I see myself, the damage I feel like a floor-length gown that I permanently wear, it stops me from ever even considering a life where I could be happy with someone else. So when things escalated between us, I ran away. I ran because all I could see was him. All I could picture when someone touched me was Wolfgang."

I swallowed hard, jaw clenching tight at the acid laced in her truth. I wanted to murder him, to torture him until his last breath to make him pay for what he did to Sarah.

But more than that, I wanted to hold her until she realized that what he did had nothing to do with who she was.

"And then, we set boundaries again. We fell back into our roles." Her lip quivered. "But I couldn't let you go. No matter how I insisted that you should go on a date with Jennifer, that you should move on with a woman your own age. I hated it. And when I showed up at your door that night, when I broke in your arms, I realized that even if it didn't make sense and even if you were completely out of my league, I wanted you, anyway."

I had to fight back a laugh when she said I was out of her league, like I was even on the same playing field as someone as beautiful, smart, and strong as she was.

"But it was still there, Reese," she said, taking a tentative step toward me. "That voice in my head that said I wasn't good enough, that said I was only good for *one* thing — my body. I'd quieted it, I'd tried to silence it, even. I was trying to listen to you, to my heart, to anything other than that voice. But all it took was one conversation with Jennifer Stinson to unleash its power again."

I frowned. "Jennifer?"

Sarah nodded. "She was here that night, before our fight. At the bar. And she told me you'd slept with her, that your hands had touched her, that just like every other woman, you had used her as a distraction from Charlie before tossing her away."

I fumed at that, taking a step toward Sarah as my neck heated. "I *never* touched her. Ever."

"I know," she said quickly. "I know that now. Hell, I think I even knew it then. But I couldn't see it, couldn't hear the truth past the voice in my head. Jennifer told me you'd do the same to me," she said, eyes tearing up again. "And then we went home, and you told me about Jason, and that voice inside my head just... it took over. It screamed that everything Wolfgang had said about me was right."

"Sarah..." I crumpled, shoulders folding forward at the absolute sorrow I felt that she could ever consider that true. I hadn't even thought of it that way, that she could see it as me trying to get rid of her instead of helping her on her path to what she'd always wanted.

I'd been naïve.

"I know," she said again, shaking her head as her gaze fell to the floor. "It's pathetic, but it's true. I self-sabotaged because it was the only thing that felt right. I didn't want to listen to you, or have hope that I was different, that what we had was special, that it was real. I couldn't even *consider* that when you told me you loved me, you meant it. Because I didn't even love myself."

"Come here," I said, reaching out my arms for her, but she immediately shook her head.

"No," she said firmly against the tears still flooding her eyes. A single blink would send them cascading down her cheeks. "No, I need to say this. I need to get this out."

My heart swelled with the need to hold her, to soothe her pain, but I respected her wish to stay a few feet away. I slid my hands into the pockets of my slacks to keep my promise.

"Reese, from the moment I met you, I knew you would change my life," she said, the left side of her lips curling up before they fell again. "At first, I thought it would just be musically. I was going to learn from one of the greats, hone my skills, make my dreams come true. But, it became so much more than that. Somewhere along the way, I started to feel beautiful when you looked at me. I started to feel valued when I'd speak and you'd listen, like I was the most interesting woman you'd ever met. And you saw me as that — a *woman*, not a girl. I think you were the first person to see me that way."

She crossed the space between us, hands reaching out to touch the buttons of my shirt. She watched her hands as they pressed against my chest, and just as I predicted, a single blink sent two parallel tears falling down her soft brown cheeks.

"I know you would never hurt me. And I have never felt more safe or more wanted with anyone in my entire life. You make me feel worthy again, like I'm not damaged, like I'm cherished and revered and cared for. That night in your bed was the most amazing night of my life, and not just because of the amazing way you touched my skin," she breathed, lifting her eyes to mine. "But because of the incredible way you have touched my soul, since the very moment you came into my life."

I couldn't fight it any longer, and my hands slipped from my pockets to frame her face, to wipe her tears away as I searched her eyes. She leaned into the touch, closing her eyes as more tears slipped free as soon as I'd wiped the first ones away.

"What are you saying, Sarah?"

She blew out a shaky breath, opening her eyes again with an unsure smile. "I'm saying... you were right. I do love you. And I want you to come with me to New York."

That hope that had bloomed in my chest, that had soared across my soul, it flooded my entire body in that moment. With Sarah's face in my hands, her eyes watching mine, her heart on her sleeve and mine firmly in her hands — I came to life.

"Do you really mean that?"

She nodded, smiling even with the tears in her eyes.

"Say it again."

"Come with me to New York?"

"No," I said, shaking my head as I smoothed my thumbs over the line of her jaw. "The other part."

At that, she folded, shaking her head before threading her arms around my neck. She lifted onto her toes, eyes searching mine for the longest moment before she whispered, "You were right. I do love you."

The words were barely out of her mouth before my lips were on hers, pressing, seeking, claiming. She melted into me, body bending forward as my arms swooped her into me. I held her close, held her tight, kissing her like it was the first and last time all at once.

And in that moment, I had everything.

Everything I'd ever wanted, everything I'd ever needed, everything I'd never thought I'd have for as long as I walked the Earth. All the pain, all the loss — it led me to this moment, to this girl, to this future.

I knew I didn't deserve it, didn't deserve *her* — but I held on tight, anyway.

"Wait," I said suddenly, pulling back on a breath. "What about your uncle, your aunt, your *mom*." My chest tightened. "We need to sit down and talk to them. *I* need to talk to them, to try to help them see that I'm not just some perverted old guy trying to steal their little girl away to the big city."

Sarah chuckled, crossing her wrists behind my neck. "I already told them."

I blanched. "What?"

"My mom, my uncle, my aunt. I told them everything, and they were weary at first," she admitted. "But... I think they can see it, what we feel. And they support it." Sarah kissed my lips quickly before adding, "Not that they really had a say, anyway. I would have still come here and said every word I said, with their blessing or not."

I chuckled, kissing her nose. "So, you're telling me my boss knows I've kissed his niece who's sixteen years younger than I am..."

Sarah cringed. "Yeah... and don't get me wrong, he was probably the least understanding. He was upset at first, and walked out of the room, even threatened to drive straight to your house."

"He *did* come to my house. Before work that night we fought. He basically threatened me. I think he knew even then."

Sarah nodded. "Maybe. But, regardless, he respects me. And you, Reese. He knows your character just like I do." She paused, swallowing hard before she met my eyes again. "And he told me to tell you that you still have a job. If you decide to stay in Pennsylvania."

I shook my head, smiling at the worry in her eyes as she spoke those words. "You actually think I would stay behind?"

She shrugged. "I would understand if you did, especially after all I've put you through."

My hands slid to frame her face again, and I kissed her softly, slowly, hoping she could feel all the words I couldn't find to convey what she meant to me. "I'd go through it all again and more if it meant I got to have you in the end."

Sarah shook her head, like she would never believe that I wanted her, that I was hers entirely. And I didn't know how long it would take to make her believe it, but I fully intended to find out.

She melted into me again when I lowered my lips to hers, wrapping my arms all the way around her and lifting her off the ground in a slow, movie-like twirl, which made her burst into laughter as soon as her toes were on the ground again.

"That was cheesy," she said.

"You think *that* was cheesy? Just wait. You're in for a whole lot of cheese."

"I'm vegan."

"Have you ever been kissed in the rain, Sarah Henderson?" I asked, ignoring her comment.

She cocked a brow. "No…"

"Well, come with me, then. Because you are the kind of girl who deserves to be kissed in the rain."

She tried to fight me at first when I laced my fingers with hers and tugged her toward the kitchen doors, but I kept pulling, kissing her at every stopping point along the way until we were outside. The rain soaked us both as soon as the back door kicked open, and she gasped at the cold sensation, eyes blinking rapidly as she adjusted.

"It's freezing!" she said on a laugh, but I pulled her into me, stopping the shivering of her teeth when I captured her mouth with mine. I kissed her with the rain pouring down around us, a bolt of lightning lighting the sky above. And I knew in that moment that she was the missing puzzle piece I'd been looking for all along.

I'd just had to walk the busted up, broken down road to get to her.

I picked her up again, twirling us in the rain before bending her back in a dramatic dip with my lips pressed to hers. Time seemed to stop with my arms around her, my lips pressed to hers, her hands fisted in the wet sleeves of my dress shirt. And when I pulled her back to stand upright, our chests heaving, the rain still pouring around us, I couldn't help but smile at the woman who'd saved me, who'd chosen me, too.

"You know," I said after a long moment, pulling her closer to warm her from the cold rain. "I've been writing a song for you, too."

Her brows shot up. "You have?"

I laughed, nodding. "I started writing it after that first night I met you. But... it's changed. It's changed so many times since then that it doesn't even sound cohesive now."

"Well," she said, running her hands up my chest, up over my jaw, back into my hair. "Maybe you'll figure it out one day, and you can play it for me then."

"It might take me a lifetime," I warned, tightening my hold around her waist.

Sarah smiled, lifting on her toes and touching the tip of her nose to mine.

"That's just fine by me."

SARAH

Later that night, after my last shift at the restaurant, Reese held me with one hand while the other unlocked his door. Rojo bounded out as soon as it was open, licking my leg as she ran past me and into the yard. I chuckled, and while I watched Rojo, Reese watched me.

I felt his eyes on me like all the wonder of the universe was streamlined in a single gaze. He watched me with reverence, with care, with absolute awe. And I blushed, a smile creeping up on my face as Rojo ran past us back into the house. I finally met his gaze, and he pulled where he held me by the hand until I was in his arms.

"You should have taken a picture," I whispered against his lips. "Would've lasted longer."

He smirked. "I just can't believe you're here, that tonight happened, that you... that we..."

"Are moving to New York together?"

Reese chuckled. "Yeah. That."

"You don't have to come with me," I said, eyes falling to my fingers as I trailed them down the buttons of his dress shirt. I stopped at the one right over the middle of his chest, tucking my fingertips under the fabric. "I know it's a lot... you'd be uprooting your entire life here, and we haven't known each other long, and—"

Reese's knuckles traced up my arm, my neck, until they tenderly tilted my chin up so I'd look at him again.

"You've rendered time useless in my life, Sarah. One moment with you, and I question how I ever lived before I knew you existed. One month with you, and I lived more than I had in years. One summer with you, and there's no going back to the man I was before. Not that I would ever choose to." He shook his head, the corner of his mouth quirking up. "There is no life to uproot here. *You* are my life now."

He lowered his lips to mine before I could even sigh, or smile, or blush, or insist I wasn't all that he thought I was. And when he kissed me, that thought disappeared. I believed him — I believed in his care, in our love, in what we had survived before we knew each other and even more in what we would accomplish together.

There wasn't a single question in my mind that Reese wasn't just my first love, but that he would be my only.

And every part of me hummed with the desperation to keep him forever.

My hands fisted where they held his shirt, and I pulled him into me, deepening our kiss as I pressed up on my tiptoes. Reese's arms surrounded me, warmth and comfort and care encompassing every inch until I was completely wrapped up in him. He pulled back, pressing a kiss to my forehead before holding me with a content sigh, and my heart kicked to life, beating hard and haphazardly against my rib cage.

"Reese," I whispered, my cheek pressed against his chest there on his front porch. The night air was warm now that the rain had subsided, but I curled into him as chills raced down my arms.

"Mmm?"

I swallowed. "Take me inside," I whispered, even quieter than before. Then, I lifted my head, capturing his eyes with my own. "Take me to your room."

His hands slipped up over my arms, brushing my neck before they framed my face. And when he looked at me, his emerald irises thinned, pupils dilating as he searched my gaze.

"I want you to be my first, Reese," I said, and my heart tripled its pace, the reality of the words I'd spoken hitting me in a mix of excitement and nerves. "My *real* first."

Reese shook his head, pulling me into him in the next instant, his lips fastening over mine as he wrapped me in his arms once more. That kiss was so different from any we'd shared before. It was filled with thankfulness, with care, with *love* — and I found myself wishing to be kissed like that all my life.

He stepped backward over the threshold of the house, and I followed, our feet moving slowly as we kissed, and touched, and felt. His hands slipped between the buttons of my work vest, loosening each one with a new step, and I tried and failed to school my breathing as my heart raced under my chest. I couldn't wait for him to touch me — *really* touch me — to erase every memory before him and brand me for his own.

My vest was undone by the time we made it to his bedroom, and he slipped it over my shoulders, letting it fall to the floor and kissing me for a long, sincere moment before he broke away long enough to put on music. The soft, familiar notes of *Claire De Lune* floated between us as he set his phone on the bedside table, and he smirked, reaching for me as soon as his hands were free.

"Debussy," I mused, running my hands up and over his dress shirt to wrap around his neck. "My favorite."

Reese smiled, kissing my nose before he pulled back, searching my eyes. "This is what you deserved your first time, Sarah. The first man to touch you should have cherished it, he should have realized in the moment you gave him permission to touch you that he was the luckiest son of a bitch in the entire world, he should have been so nervous that he couldn't keep his hands steady when he reached for you," he said, and as if to illustrate, his trembling hands tugged at the hem of my long-sleeve shirt that was tucked into my dress pants. He pulled it free, pressing his cool, shaking fingertips against the tender skin below my navel. "I can't go back in time and change what happened, but I promise, I will spend tonight, and every night you let me, worshiping your body until every memory of that night is gone."

My eyes watered, and I shook my head against the urge to let those tears loose. "Don't make me cry, Reese Walker."

He smiled, pulling me closer as his lips hovered over mine. His tongue snaked out, touching mine only briefly before he bit down on my lip and sucked it between his teeth. That sent a jolt between my legs, and I moaned, melting into him.

"How about I make you come, instead?"

I groaned again, and he snickered, trailing his hands down until they bunched at the hem of my untucked shirt.

"Arms up," he commanded, and I obeyed, breaking our kiss long enough for him to strip me free of the fabric before I fastened my lips to his again. Chills cascaded down every inch of my body like a hot waterfall, and my own hands mirrored his as I reached for the buttons of his dress shirt, trembling as I unfastened each one.

It was a slow dance — our lips tasting as our hands stumbled over the steps. He led, and I followed, trusting him to guide me on that dance floor of his bedroom. With each article of clothing we discarded, my heart raced more, and I grew more and more lightheaded with each new sliver of skin exposed.

When he was in his boxer briefs and I in nothing but my panties and matching bra, Reese broke away from our kiss, his hands skating up to my shoulders. He swallowed, gaze following his touch as he slipped his fingers under the straps of my bra. I closed my eyes at the sensation of his fingertips skating the sensitive skin, and when he unhooked the prongs at the back, slipping the fabric forward until there was nothing between my chest and his, I couldn't open my eyes.

"Sarah," Reese breathed. "Are you okay?"

I nodded. "Mm-hmm."

He pulled me into him, his warm chest pressing against mine, and I gasped at the feel of his skin against my hardened nipples. It sent another sharp wave of energy right between my legs, and every inch of me swarmed with want, with need.

"You are so beautiful," he whispered.

I creaked one eye open before the other, casting my gaze up at him. But his eyes were closed, his head bent, chest rising and falling rapidly with each breath. He was nervous just like I was, and just as he promised, I knew he was cherishing every moment.

My hands slipped between us, settling on his hips — which were somehow just as hard as every other muscle that lined his god-like body. The tips of my fingers curled under the band of his briefs, and he sucked in a breath, chills breaking at my touch. I stepped backward, slowly, kissing his neck and chest with each step before the backs of my knees hit his bed. I paused, bringing my gaze to meet his as my hands slipped between the fabric of his briefs and his hard, muscular ass.

Reese rolled his lips together at the feel of me touching him, and when I kept sliding my hands down, down, taking his briefs with me, his Adam's apple bobbed hard in his throat. He didn't move to help me, to strip himself free of the briefs, but instead, watched me as I slowly undressed him, like he couldn't believe it was actually happening.

Like he couldn't believe I was his.

His briefs fell to the floor once I slid them over his thighs, and his impressive erection sprang forward, making my heart stop altogether as I took in the size of him.

I swallowed.

"Reese," I whispered, trailing my fingertips over his lower abdomen. He shivered under the touch, hands framing my arms in lieu of an answer. "Can I taste you?"

He growled, head falling back before he met my eyes again. "You don't have to."

"I want to," I said, and I edged myself off the bed, pushing him back just far enough for me to lower to my knees.

When I did, another longing breath left his chest, and his hands reached for me, touching my chin, my cheeks, my ears. I waited, wondering if he would stop me. But when he didn't, when my hand wrapped around him tentatively, feeling the smooth, velvet-like skin of his member, I took it as the permission I wanted.

I lowered my lips, pressing them to his wet tip before slowly opening them, pulling him in, tasting him with my tongue. I glanced up at him when the tip of him was in my mouth, and our eyes met only for a brief moment before he groaned, closing his eyes and letting his head fall back.

I had no idea what to do, how to touch him, how to take him inside my throat. But I felt my way through it, sliding the base of my tongue over the strained muscle, tracing each vein before I swallowed him whole. He was too big to fit all the way in, but he moaned at the sensation, anyway — encouraging me to press on, to take in more, to lick and taste and feel.

This man, so strong and hard and scarred, had made me feel pleasure I never knew existed.

I wanted to do the same for him.

I brought one hand up under my mouth, closing it around the lower part of his shaft that my mouth couldn't reach. I sucked, fastening my mouth to the edge of my hand, and when I moved them in sync, Reese growled, legs trembling before his hands reached for my elbows and tugged me back up to my feet.

I released him with a pop, mouth still hanging open once I was on my feet and his lips fastened over mine again. He inhaled that kiss, pulling me into him like I was going to be the death of him if he let me stay on my knees even one moment longer.

This was what I loved most about Reese, about us together — that indescribable, undeniable energy that existed since the very first moment his eyes found mine across a dark and crowded restaurant. It was too powerful to resist, too intense to deny.

We were tied together before we even knew the other one existed, and all this time, we were just walking, searching, looking for something we couldn't place or name or identify. It was a feeling, a hope that should have died in both of us long ago, but was reborn the minute we found each other.

Nothing about us made sense, and yet, there was no other possibility.

It was me and him and *us*. It just was. And it always would be.

Reese must have felt it, too — that energy — because he lowered his forehead to mine, stealing a breath between our kisses as his arms trembled under my hands. He blinked his eyes opening, finding mine before he gently walked me back to the bed, his hand catching my head before it hit the pillow. And when he settled between my legs, the heat of him pressed against the heat of me, only the thin fabric of my panties separating us, we both let out a shaky sigh.

His lips were slow and purposeful, peppering me with long, tender, sweet kisses as he trailed himself down the length of my body. He paused to suck each of my nipples, making me writhe beneath him as the shocking sensation shot through me with each bite. He smiled, trailing his lips down lower, lower, a kiss to my navel, my left hip, my right hip, each inner thigh, and then, softly, right at the center of my panties.

I gasped, arching off the bed, and Reese took the opportunity to fold his fingers over the lace straps. I lifted my hips as he pulled, sliding my panties over my ass, my thighs, my knees. He freed them of one ankle and then the other, letting them fall somewhere behind him before he settled between my legs. His emerald eyes cast up at me, and he kissed each thigh again, working slowly toward where I wanted his lips the most.

With each kiss, I writhed and squirmed. With each touch of his hot breath against my skin, I sighed and moaned. And when his tongue snaked out, touching my clit with a feather-like pressure before it was gone again, my hands shot up against the headboard, desperate for the friction he denied me.

Reese chuckled, licking the inside of my thigh. "So impatient."

I didn't respond. Words were lost to me, along with the rest of the world, and when he finally lowered his mouth to my clit again, I surrendered to the pull into the vast, endless universe.

The nerves that bundled at that sensitive peak sparked to life with each sweep of his tongue, and the silence I'd fallen under was broken by unabashed moans. Reese slipped his hands beneath me, grabbing my ass and pulling me into him as he devoured me. He tasted me with the flat of his tongue, groaning as if it was *him* getting closer and closer to climax. But when he tensed his tongue, teasing my clit with the tip of it as he circled and jagged, I fisted my hands in the sheets and pulled. I needed something to hold, something to fasten myself to so I wouldn't float away.

Reese pulled one hand from beneath me, trailing his fingertips up my thigh until they settled under his mouth.

And slowly, *achingly* slowly, he slipped one thick finger inside me.

It was too much then — the flick of his tongue, the pressure of his hand grabbing my ass, the curl of his finger inside me. I felt my orgasm starting to burn from the center of my belly, but before it could catch, I reached for Reese's hair, tugging until his mouth was off me as I panted.

I didn't have to say a word.

Reese met my gaze with confusion at first, but it faded quickly, and he nodded, kissing my thighs before he crawled his way back up. He knew what I wanted, what I needed.

It was my first time. And I wanted to come apart with him inside me.

All the confidence he'd had with his face buried between my legs faded as his mouth captured mine once more, his elbows framing each side of me, balancing his weight. My hands framed his biceps, and I felt him shaking, felt *myself* shaking, each of us riddled with the sweetest anxiety as he lined up at my center. The smooth skin of him slipped between my lips, and we both inhaled a stiff breath, Reese breaking our kiss as he hovered over me.

In that moment, time slipped away like a silk sheet falling off the edge of a bed. We were floating, suspended, his eyes bouncing between mine as my hands gripped his biceps more, holding on, bracing for impact. One of Reese's hands swept over my cheek, folding behind my ear as if I had hair to sweep away as he watched me with tender care.

"I love you, Sarah Henderson," he whispered, searching my gaze. That crease between his brow begged me to believe him, urged me to understand what this moment meant to him.

To grasp what it meant to *me*.

I framed his face, searching his eyes with just as much earnest. "And I love you, Reese Walker."

He smirked at that. "Say it again."

"I love you," I breathed on a small laugh of my own, but that laughter faded when he pressed his lips to mine once more. This kiss was slower, softer, with a hint of timid hesitation. But in the next moment, he deepened the kiss, his rose petal lips bending mine into submission until I opened my mouth for him, letting him taste me.

His hand left me long enough to slip into the drawer of the bedside table, and I focused on his lips on mine, on the taste of his tongue as his hands met behind the pillow my head rested on. I heard the tear of the package, and then his hand slipped between us, rolling the condom on before he was lined up with me again.

I inhaled a breath when the tip of him found my entrance, and he kissed me harder, holding his lips to mine as he flexed his hips forward. It was just an inch, just the tip, but I gasped, arching off the bed at the sensation. I wrapped my arms around his neck, pulling him into me, arms shaking as I nodded against his lips.

"More," I whispered.

And he delivered, flexing his hips once more, slowly. And inch by blissful inch, I opened for him.

He promised to erase my memories of that fateful night in December, but when Reese kissed me, when he filled me, there wasn't a single other vision in my mind. There *were* no memories left of my wolf, of my stolen innocence, of the hateful man who touched me before the one who loved me could find me.

I was finally free of my wolf.

And it was all thanks to my prince.

Reese sighed when he withdrew, sliding inside me again just a little deeper, his arms trembling where they balanced his weight. His forehead fell to mine, and each shaky breath he took met my lips in hot waves. My hands gripped and pulled, desperate to have him closer, to have *more*.

"You are so incredible," he whispered, kissing my jaw, my cheek, before capturing my lips again. He flexed his hips again, and we both groaned, breathing into that kiss like it was the only oxygen we had.

The time that had slipped away in the moments before Reese was inside me snapped back like a rubber band, and I felt every minute, every second of him between my legs. I felt his hard back muscles under my hands, his muscular hips between my thighs, his stiff, pulsing member stretching me more, more, and with every thrust, he hit a tender spot inside me that I never knew existed.

"Reese," I breathed, feeling my orgasm build. It was a sweet, torturous cycle — each thrust of his hips touched that spot, each glide of his pelvis against my clit gave the friction I craved. My legs shook violently around him, my breaths quickening until they stopped all together, and in a moment suspended in time, the fire caught.

Every muscle tensed, an almost painful tension gripping me before it all released at once, the blood rushing between my legs in a fury of pleasure as I came undone. I gasped, surrendering to the moans that ripped through me, rolling my hips as I chased the friction. And Reese delivered, pumping harder, flexing his hips with calculated intensity as he swallowed my moans with hot, passionate kisses.

When I groaned his name, Reese quickened his pace until he stiffened all together, and even through the condom, I felt his hot release. I raked my nails down his back, reveling in the feel of him coming inside me as I rode down from my own climax. It was the hottest moment of my life, and the power I felt in that moment was indescribable.

I'd brought the infamous Reese Walker to the highest pleasure, and as soon as it was over, I found myself desperate to do it again.

"Mmm," Reese growled, still inside me as we both floated down, coming back to Earth, back to his bed. He let his head fall into the crevice of my neck, and I chuckled, wrapping my arms around him to savor the moment. I closed my eyes, memorizing the feel of his weight between my legs, of him softening inside me, of his hands holding me close, his lips tasting my skin.

I never wanted to forget this night, not for as long as I lived.

Reese rolled until we were both on our sides, him slipping out of me with a longing sigh of loss from both of us. He carefully pulled the condom off, reaching over to drop it in the small waste basket by his bedside table before his arms reached for me again, pulling me into him, his legs tangling with mine, bodies fitting together like the perfect puzzle pieces.

Our breaths evened out as the soreness between my legs made itself known, but I smiled at it this time, at the memory of how it came to be. We'd only just finished, and I already felt that energy sparking to life again, my hips rolling of their own accord, clit rubbing against the heat of Reese's thigh. I moaned, pulling him into me, and something between a growl and a laugh left his throat.

"Woman," he murmured against my neck.

I chuckled, kissing his forehead. "Mm?"

"Don't give me that innocent '*mm*'," he said, wrapping his arms around me tighter to hold me still. "Recovery. I need ten minutes. You forget, I'm an old man."

"Fine, but I'm setting a mental alarm."

Reese laughed, shaking his head before he rolled on a groan, balancing his head on one hand so he could look down at me. His smile slipped, that crease I loved so much making its presence known. I reached up to trace it, tapping his nose before I let my hand fall again.

We watched each other for the longest time — fingertips tracing, hearts beating steady, bodies finding warmth and comfort under those sheets. Reese's eyes skated over every inch of my face, like he was memorizing where each freckle was, and he shook his head.

"What?" I asked on a whisper.

He shook his head again. "I just can't wrap my head around the fact that you're mine, that we're here, that this is happening."

"Are we crazy to do this?"

"Do what?"

I reached up to brush his hair back, swallowing. "This. Moving to New York. Without a plan. Without anything but each other."

Reese smiled, leaning down to press his lips to mine before he propped his head up again. "Maybe. But if the one thing we do have is each other, I think the odds of us making it are pretty high."

"Yeah?" I asked, smile mirroring his own.

Reese nodded, framing my chin as his eyes searched mine. "I'd bet everything I own on us."

"Me and you against the world, huh?"

His smile doubled at that. "I like the sound of that. What do you think?"

I threaded my arms around his neck, pulling him down into me for a long, tender kiss. And in that moment, I knew without a doubt that I would do the same. If anyone could make it, if anyone could defy all the odds and somehow emerge even stronger on the other side, it was us.

It was him, the broken man too bruised to feel, too scared to love, who somehow found a home in me.

It was me, the scarred woman too afraid to trust, too busted up to believe, who somehow found music again in him.

And it was us, the unlikely couple, the man too old and the girl too young, the teacher and the student who weren't afraid of what others would say, what they would think, what they would assume.

If it really was us against the world, one thing was certain.

I couldn't ask for a better man to have on my team.

"I think nothing can stop us now," I answered on a breath.

And I knew nothing ever would.

epilogue

SARAH

Three years later

It must have been a fun house mirror.

That's the only thought I had in my mind as I stared at my reflection in the crisp white room, the bright lights that surrounded the mirror casting my skin in a golden glow. I traced every edge of the reflection that stared back at me, half with wonder and half with disbelief.

It couldn't be me.

It couldn't be me, standing there, confident and strong and collected. It couldn't be my eyes that glistened in the light, couldn't be my lips that parted, letting out a long, steady breath. It couldn't be my face that was framed by those short, tight, bouncy curls — each one hairsprayed to perfection. I reached one hand up, the reflection mirroring the movement, and touched one curl — just to be sure. I felt the rough tendrils of it, plucked it down before letting it bounce back into place.

Still, it couldn't be me.

It couldn't be me, standing backstage at Carnegie Hall, less than an hour from playing for nearly three-thousand people.

It couldn't be my hands — those cold, clammy things at my side — that would play the piano tonight.

It wasn't possible, and yet, it was true.

I was here. It was me. This was my literal dream come true.

Nerves fluttered to life in my belly like a hurricane of butterflies, and I pressed my hands against it with a smile, smoothing my palms over the silky fabric of my black dress. My eyes fell to where my hands framed my stomach in the mirror just as a knock sounded on my dressing room door.

"Come in," I said, still marveling at my reflection. When the door opened behind me, my eyes shot to the tall, dark figure who entered, and my smile slipped from my face like sand through an hourglass.

I turned, letting my eyes drink him in from head to toe as Reese let the door close softly behind him. He was doing the same as I was, his eyes trailing from my face, following every smooth inch of fabric that covered me all the way down to my crystal high heels before they climbed their way back up. And I took in every inch of him — his long, chestnut hair, neatly styled and flowing down just past his shoulders, his broad shoulders stretching the charcoal tuxedo he wore, the slacks hanging off his hips in a way that made my stomach spring to life with a completely different set of nerves.

And in his hands, he held a bouquet of lilies — my favorite flower.

Our eyes met at the same time, and we both smiled. Reese crossed the room to me, holding out the flowers as an offering between us.

"You look..." He swallowed, eyes trailing down again before they met mine once more. "You look like a dark queen, here to seduce us with your magic and eat us all alive."

I laughed. "Thank you?"

"It's a compliment. Trust me," he said as I took the flowers from his hands.

I inhaled their scent with a smile, careful not to get any of the pollen on my hands or dress as I turned back toward the mirror, placing them carefully in one of the empty vases provided by the hall. I was still facing the mirror when Reese slid up behind me, wrapping his arms around my waist and pulling me into his chest. One hand skated up, thumb brushing my bottom lip, which was painted a glossy, candy apple red.

"I like this," he murmured, but it turned into a growl when he removed his thumb and saw it was still painted red. "Fuck, I *really* like this."

I smirked. "You can take it off me tonight."

"Woman," he growled, pulling me into him more as he shook his head. I giggled, leaning into him, and our eyes found each other in the mirror as we both released a content sigh.

Three years.

Three years I'd been in New York City with that man holding me in the mirror.

Three years of living together, of learning together, of loving. There had been struggles from the very beginning — starting with Reese finding work after being removed from the city for so long. While I studied with James, working on my technique and networking my ass off to get the right connections to play at Carnegie, Reese had been looking for *any* place that would pay him to do what he loved. He'd started off as a tutor for private students, eventually landing a gig at a restaurant much like The Kinky Starfish. But it wasn't until last year, until one of his old colleagues reached out to him that everything changed.

They'd invited him to teach at Juilliard.

It was part time for now, but ever since he started teaching, I'd watched him bloom into a brand-new man. His purpose had been refilled, re*fueled* by these students.

"Their passion reminds me of you sometimes," he'd said one night at dinner. *"And I finally feel like I'm using my talent to make a difference in this world."*

Reese wasn't the only one who had to struggle when we got to the city, either. On top of feeling the pressure of studying with James, of networking, and playing whatever gigs I could find to make ends meet, I was also dealing with the trial.

After I told my mother what happened with Wolfgang, she went with me to press charges. And in a long, grueling process, we tried to fight against what happened to me — what could possibly have still been happening to others.

Unfortunately for us, no one else spoke out against him.

It was my word against his, no rape kit or witnesses to provide testimonies. The one and only person I told, Dr. Chores, testified against me, saying she had no recollection of my confession of what happened, nor would she have ever have brushed it off as I implied.

For the longest time, I felt crazy. Reese would hold me in our bed in our small apartment, rocking me as I sobbed and wondered if I'd made it all up. Did it really happen? Was I crazy? Did I invent the injury, the rape, all of it? Did I black out, thinking I'd told someone when I hadn't really?

But Reese was there, holding me through it all and assuring me to trust myself, my gut, my voice. He believed me. Mom believed me. Even Reneé believed me when I came clean, and she assembled the other female students still at Bramlock to petition for Wolfgang's suspension until the trial was over.

They won.

We, however, did not.

The trial had wrapped up over the following summer, and though it could have been a sad, painful day of loss, I didn't see it that way. When the jury declared that Wolfgang wasn't guilty, it didn't change the fact that he was. It didn't change the fact that he had assaulted me, and that against all odds, I'd fought back.

I didn't just let him go free.

And even though he was acquitted of the charges, the university still fired him — and revoked the award they'd bestowed upon him after I'd left. As far as I knew, he was still without a job, without tenure, without a prayer in hell of working with students again. Our trial had been televised, it had made national news, and there wasn't a pianist in this country who wouldn't forever remember his name — only now, *I* was in control of the narrative.

It may not have been jail time, but it was justice.

And I was set free.

Therapy helped more than I ever thought it could after the trial wrapped up. Mom had a peer she had studied with who lived in the city — Doctor Erramouspe — and after even our first meeting, I knew she would be instrumental in my recovery. She had all the right words to say to help me see I wasn't crazy, that my feelings were valid, that what happened to me did not define me, but it was still a part of my journey, and it was important to recognize that.

I still see her once every two weeks, and I know that with her help and the amazing team behind me, I wouldn't be standing backstage at Carnegie Hall right now.

"What's going on in that beautiful head of yours," Reese asked, swaying me gently in his arms.

I smiled, leaning into him with a sigh. "Just thinking of all we've been through, all we've done in the past three years."

"I know. *So* much sex. In *so* many places."

I laughed, smacking his arm playfully as he held me tighter, still swaying.

"I was referring to how hard we've been working, how much we've accomplished."

"So was I."

I laughed again, and my heart warmed with the same familiar comfort Reese always brought me. He was my person, in ever sense of the word — my protector, my warrior, my best friend, and my lover all rolled into one.

"Hey," he said, turning my waist in his hands until I faced him. My hands slipped over his tuxedo jacket, folding together behind his neck as he stared down at me. "How are you feeling? Are you ready?"

I blew out a shaky breath. "My hands are cold and clammy, and my stomach feels like someone is dancing inside it, but otherwise, yeah. I'm good."

Reese chuckled. "Well, if you were one of my students, I'd offer you some Propranolol to help with the hands situation. But, unfortunately, you actually *do* have someone dancing around in your stomach. So, no beta blockers for you."

His hands slipped from my waist to my stomach, framing it in a sort of heart as both of our gazes fell to the spot where he held me. My heart swelled at the sight — my little stomach, rounded just enough to show there was life growing inside it, and my husband's hands, holding our baby girl just as he always held me — with reverence and care. His wedding band glistened under the dressing room light, and I traced it with my thumb, noting how the diamond on my own finger seemed to glisten and dance in time with his ring.

"Bet you never thought that when this day came, you'd be playing with someone *else* on that stage with you," Reese mused, rubbing the silk fabric stretched over my belly.

"Never," I agreed on a laugh. "But, I'm kind of glad she'll be with me. It's a little less scary than going at it alone."

Reese smiled, his eyes capturing mine before his hands slid up, framing my face. His thumb traced the edge of my jaw, and he shook his head, staring at me like he couldn't fully comprehend the moment.

"I know tonight is going to be crazy," he said, voice soft and low. "I know it's going to fly by, probably in a blur, and you might black out as you play out there. But I want you to take this moment — this one right here — and celebrate. Because you did it, Sarah." He laughed once, an expression of awe and wonder as he dropped his forehead to mine. "Against all odds, with more mountains to climb than line the ones that line the Rockies... You. Did. It."

I squeezed my eyes shut, giggling as our daughter squirmed in my stomach. She seemed to be celebrating with us, dancing away, and I let one hand fall over my belly as the other touched Reese's cheek.

"*We* did it," I corrected him.

He shook his head, but I didn't let him argue before I pressed my lips to his. Tears pricked my eyes, and as much as I wanted to blame the pregnancy hormones, I knew in that moment it had nothing to do with science.

It was that man, that beautiful, broken, passionate man who had brought me back to life. And it was our daughter, growing inside me, thrusting us toward a new world where our family of two would be one of three. It was being there, backstage at Carnegie Hall, knowing thousands of people would start filling the seats that stretched out from the stage I would play on later that night.

It was the rough road we traveled to get to this spot.

And it was knowing that though this had been my dream for so long, it was never the end game.

It was only the beginning.

Reese groaned when I deepened our kiss, pulling back with a shake of his head. "I'm ruining your lipstick."

"That's your duty as my hot husband," I reminded him. And then, I wrapped both arms around his neck, pulling him closer. "And, my duty as wife of the birthday boy."

"Ugh," he groaned. "Don't remind me."

"Forty years old," I mused, fingertips wrapping gently in the tendrils of his hair as I marveled at every feature of the man who held me.

"Old man status."

"Hottest old man I've ever seen," I argued, pressing my lips to his. "And thank God you're *my* old man."

He shook his head, but kissed me anyway, not bothering to argue — which was smart of him, since we both knew who would win.

"Alright, I need to warm up," I said, breaking our kiss but holding him still in my arms. "Is Mom here yet?"

Reese nodded. "She is. And Randall and Betty, too. I just wanted to come back to wish you luck before we grab our seats."

"Is it weird that I'm more nervous to play for you four than I am for anyone else?"

He chuckled. "You could stand up there and just wave the whole time and we'd still give you a standing ovation."

A flutter of butterflies took flight in my stomach, and suddenly, though I knew I needed to warm up, I didn't want Reese to leave.

"And Rojo?" I asked, trying to make the conversation last.

He smirked. "I took her on a long nice walk in the park before we left, and the walker is going to check on her in a few hours so we can go out after."

"I wish dogs were allowed at Carnegie."

"She'd probably run up on stage so she could curl up near your feet the way she does at home."

I smiled, heart bursting as I looked at him — my husband. We had a family. We had a past, and a present, and a future.

We had each other.

"See you out there?" I asked, pressing up onto my toes to kiss him one last time.

"I'll be the loud one in the front row."

And I knew it to be true, without a single doubt in my mind. He wouldn't just be loud, he'd be the loud*est*. He would be there after the show, whether I crushed it or completely bombed. Forever my number-one fan.

Forever my number one. Period.

And I still didn't understand it, how we had somehow found each other in a world with billions of people, billions of lost, searching souls, trying to find the missing piece. Somehow, against all odds, we had come together. We had fought the demons of our past, and faced the challenges of our future — together. We had a million reasons why we shouldn't have worked, and yet, we *did*. We just did.

Maybe I would never understand it fully, I realized, as my husband smiled at me over his shoulder, closing the door behind him and leaving me alone in my dressing room. Maybe I would never see the full map, the roads that had led us to each other, the one road we traveled together now — as a team, as a unit.

But that was okay.

I didn't need to see the plan, didn't need insurance of any kind to know that this was it. Reese wasn't just my for now. He wasn't just a lesson, or a role played in my life when I needed someone to help me walk through the darkness.

He was my forever.

And what a beautiful forever it was.

I couldn't stop smiling as I warmed up my wrists, my hands, my fingers, playing a little of the songs I knew and loved on the piano set up in my dressing room. When the twenty-minute warning was given, my hands started playing the song I'd written for Reese, and I smiled when the little eggplant-sized human in my belly danced with joy at the sound.

"You like that one, huh?" I asked, smiling as I finished the melody. Then, I stood, smoothing my hands over my dress as I faced the mirror one last time.

And for the first time that night, I saw it.

It really *was* me — the hair, the skin, the wide eyes, the long, silky black dress, the dazzling crystal shoes. It was me, standing backstage at Carnegie Hall. It was me, reaching up to hold the crystal that hung around my neck.

"I feel you here," I whispered. "I hope you're as proud as I am."

My daughter danced again, as if she was speaking on behalf of her grandfather, and I laughed, placing the hand not on my crystal over my belly, instead.

"Alright, Mallory," I said, testing out the name. I hadn't told Reese yet, that I wanted to name our daughter after his sister. But when I said her name in that moment, a smile split my face.

Because everything about it felt right.

"Let's go knock 'em dead, shall we?" I said, squeezing my crystal and patting my belly one last time.

My eyes found the woman's eyes who stared back at me, and my heart kicked to life in my chest.

This is it.

This is what you've worked for.

And seemingly before I even did, that reflection smiled back at me, pointing her finger directly at my chest. She and I, we were survivors — warriors who had fought one hell of a battle. Despite the losses that had broken us. Despite the injuries that had hindered us. Despite the enemies who had tried to take us out.

We were still here. We were still fighting.

And this was our victory dance.

As I turned out the lights, making my way through the hallway and down the stairs that led to the stage, I couldn't help but count the biggest blessing of all: that I had the best dance partner in the world to celebrate with.

When the lights went out, when I stepped onto that stage to the tune of a thunderous applause, it was his eyes I found.

It was his smile that made my heart stop.

It was him I had in my heart as I played.

And it was him I would have in my heart always.

the end

author's note

I find myself struggling to find the right words for this note, so much so that I'm actually pulling a little of it from a book I previously wrote — the second season of *Palm South University: Anchor*. In that book, and in this one, I tackled writing about something that is a trigger for many women (and men) and that, I think, should be a topic of conversation.

The sexual assault of Sarah was not easy to write about, and my stomach hurts just thinking about putting myself in her shoes. Unfortunately, I know many women in my life who have been through what Sarah endured. And, even I, myself, have battled various levels of sexual abuse in my life. Sadly, I believe it's a part of life when you are a woman, and whether it affects you in the same way it affected Sarah or not, it's still something that changes you in some way.

While it was important for THIS particular character and story, for Sarah, to go down the path she did, I want you to understand as my reader that if you ever do or ever *have* found yourself in this terrifying situation or one similar to it, you have options.

If you become a victim of sexual assault, call 911 or RAINN at 1-800-656-HOPE immediately. Just like in Sarah's situation, four out of five rapes are committed by someone known by the victim. Similarly, 68% of rapes are not reported to the police, and 98% of rapists never spend a day in jail or prison.

This was a big reason why I chose to tackle Sarah's situation the way I did. I wanted to be real, to be raw, to steer away from the easy, happy ever ending and touch on the horrible reality that sometimes, even when you do everything right, justice is not served. It breaks my heart that we see this happen so often — to strangers in the news, to our friends, to our family — but even so, we must still fight against sexual assaulters and the injustices in our system.

If you're like Sarah, you may feel that it's useless to tell anyone — especially if the first person you trust to tell doesn't handle it appropriately. It may feel embarrassing, or you may worry no one will believe you, or, even if they do, that the abuser will end up winning in the end, anyway. But, no matter what, what I hope you will understand is that **it is not your fault and there is help available.**

Maybe it won't all turn out perfectly. Maybe it won't be the justice you want. But, it will be a fight, it will be a spotlight on that person who hurt you, and it will be you *not* sitting back and letting it all go. You are a human, a person, a living, breathing being — and you deserve to be treated like one. Fight for justice. Fight for yourself.

I hope you never find yourself in this situation and that you never have in the past, but if you're reading this and you feel isolated and alone, please, reach out to someone. Reach out to a friend, a family member — hell, reach out to *me*. You can email me at authorkandisteiner@yahoo.com. I am always here, and I care about you — every single one of you.

Take care of your mind, your body, and your soul. You're the only one who can.

For more information and resources, please visit www.rainn.org.

playlist

Music was an instrumental part of creating this story.
As you may have noticed in the eBook edition of this book,
I linked to several songs along the way to give the readers
the same experience I had while writing. For me, music has
always been tied to every facet of my life, and I believe it has
the power to move us as much as words do. Below is a link to
the *What He Never Knew* playlist on Spotify, as well as a list
of song titles and artists who I played on repeat while writing
this book. I hope you enjoy it.

Playlist
Debussy — Footprints in the Snow
Beethoven — Moonlight
Sjors Mans — Without You
Yiruma — River Flows in You
Benny Andersson — Embassy Lament
Mozart — Sonata 17
Robert Gafforelli — Sentiment
Franz Liszt — Hungarian Rhapsody
François Couperin, Alexandre Tharuad: Les Barricades
Mistérieuses
Gene Kelly — You Were Meant For Me
Sampha — No One Knows Me Like the Piano
Debussy — La Plus Que Lente
Bach — Prelude and Fugue
Debussy — Claire De Lune

acknowledgments

Just when I thought the writing and editing process couldn't get more challenging, I tackled Reese and Sarah's story. To say this one put me through the ringer would be a gross understatement. These were the most complex characters I've ever written, and I know I wouldn't have made it out alive if I didn't have an amazing team.

First of all, I have to thank Drew Pace, an old friend who came through in the most amazing way for this project. Drew, your knowledge of piano — not just the instrument, but the career, the *journey* of being someone tied to classical — it was absolutely invaluable. Hearing your stories helped shape *this* story, and without you, I wouldn't have been able to tap into the emotions, to the lessons, to the challenges. I really am at a loss for words, and I don't know that I can ever truly thank you enough to feel like it's adequate for all you did to contribute to this book's success. Thank you for being so open and honest with me, and for taking time out of YOUR busy schedule to help me create art. You are truly a gem in this world and I'm so happy to know you!

Staci Brillhart. In every book I've ever written since the day we first met, you have been on my team. You've been cheering me on, helping me work through the tough spots, celebrating when I achieved what I set out to do. But, with this book more so than any other, you provided tough, RELEVANT feedback that truly helped shape this into the final product it was always meant to be. And, more than anything, you believed in me when even I didn't. You knew I could survive the edits when I was looking at the notes and wanting to cry. I felt like I'd failed, like these characters would never come to life the way I wanted to, and you helped me pinpoint the biggest challenges and you helped me find solutions. I can never thank you enough for always being in my corner, and please know that even when it hurts, your feedback means more to me than I could ever say. I love you. More than tacos, babe!

Momma, as always, I could never do this without you. You raised me to be strong, to be independent, to chase my dreams and never, EVER let the setbacks make me quit. I don't know how you do all that you do, but I am thankful every day that I got the resilient gene from you. I love you.

To the lovely Karla Sorensen and Kathryn Andrews, you two babes helped me SO MUCH in these edits. Thank you for taking the time and the care to help me really bring these characters to life. Your insight is always so valuable, and I could not do this without you. More than your help on this book, thank you both for being such amazing friends to me. I love our trips, sleepovers, laughs and late nights. I never want to do this without you. Let's stick together — always!

Patricia Leibowitz — AKA QUEEN MINTNESS — I have to give you a huge, HUGE shout out for your help in this book. Not only were you instrumental in some of the big changes, but you are the ONLY beta reader who also read through the entire thing AGAIN after I made all the edits. You love this story and these characters just as much as I do, and your emotion while reading gave me life. I seriously cannot imagine doing this without you. I appreciate you more than you'll ever know.

To my amazing team of beta readers: Kellee Fabre, Sarah Green, Danielle Lagasse, Ashlei Davison, Jess Vogel, and Sahar Bagheri — YOU ARE THE BEST TEAM TO EVER EXIST. Seriously. Some of you read as I wrote, others read at the end, but ALL of you provided the best feedback that helped transform this book into the final product. I am so thankful for all of your time, care, and feedback.

To the most amazing, patient, hard working and bad ass assistant to ever exist — Christina Stokes — I don't even have the right words for you. Between hunting for stock photos for our teasers and finding copy to share on various social outlets to reading the story and petting my hair in times of need, you do it all. You do it ALL. Even before I ask, even before I KNOW that I need something, you do it. I cannot tell you how much stress you take away from my life, how much comfort and joy you bring me, and more than anything, how happy my heart is when I am around you. I am so lucky to not only have you on my work team, but to be able to call you my friend. Let's travel the world together. I love you!

Shout out to Sasha Erramouspe and Gabby Waltz for charlie reading this one. You both brought me so much relief that I had done what I'd set out to do, and your final feedback was like the little bow on top of this story. SORRY FOR MAKING YOU CRY, SASHA, but just know I love you more than whiskey — and we both know that means a LOT.

I have the absolute best editor in the entire world in Elaine York from Allusion Graphics. Thank you, my friend, for always working with my changing timelines, for sending me love notes as you read, and for helping me polish this to a high shine. You are an instrumental part of my team now and for always.

To the most wonderful PR crew: Nina Grinstead, Hilary Suppes, Chanpreet Singh, and the rest of the team at Social Butterfly PR — thank you for always helping me promote the fuck out of my books. Your fresh ideas and constant attention to detail are just some of the reasons I'm happy to have you on my team.

Flavia Viotti is my incredible agent, and I could never thank her enough for all the work she does for me — especially on the foreign and audio market. Thank you for hustling just as hard as I do to make our dreams come true, Flavia. I love you!

A huge shout out to Lauren Perry of Perrywinkle Photography and to Dale, the model on the cover of What He Never Knew. You both made my vision come to life and I am so thankful!

I always have to thank Angie Doyle McKeon for just... well, for just loving me. I always look forward to our conversations about life, love, family, the book industry and more. And I LOVE how passionate you are about reading my books and spreading the word so others read them, too. My little bumble bee forever and ever. I adore you.

Thank you to everyone in my special corner of the Facebook world — Kandiland. Your constant posts of love and motivation keep me going. I love that we have such a safe place to talk about books we love, and I hope we just continue to grow and grow. Don't ever leave me. I love y'all!

Lastly, but NEVER least, I want to thank you — the reader. If you've made it all the way to the bottom of my acknowledgements, you're seriously a rare gem that I am so thankful has stumbled upon my words. Writing is personal. Reading is personal. And I'm honored that you chose my book, trusted me to take you on this adventure, and I hope you loved it as much as I did. Thank you for reading, reviewing, sharing your love of my books with your friends, tagging me on social media so I can geek out with you LOL. I just... I love all of you so much and I could not do this without you. Truly. Without you, my life would lack purpose and passion. Thank you for being on this incredible journey with me.

other books

The Red Zone Rivals Series
Fair Catch

As if being the only girl on the college football team wasn't hard enough, Coach had to go and assign my brother's best friend — and *my* number one enemy — as my roommate.

Blind Side

The hottest college football safety in the nation just asked me to be his fake girlfriend.

And I just asked him to take my virginity.

Quarterback Sneak

Quarterback Holden Moore can have any girl he wants.

Except me: the coach's daughter.

Hail Mary

(AN AMAZON #1 BESTSELLER)

I used to love Leo Hernandez, but that was before I hated him. And now, I have no choice but to move in with him.

The Becker Brothers Series

On the Rocks (book 1)

Neat (book 2)

Manhattan (book 3)

Old Fashioned (book 4)

Four brothers finding love in a small Tennessee town that revolves around a whiskey distillery with a dark past — including the mysterious death of their father.

The Best Kept Secrets Series
(AN AMAZON TOP 10 BESTSELLER)
What He Doesn't Know (book 1)
What He Always Knew (book 2)
What He Never Knew (book 3)
Charlie's marriage is dying. She's perfectly content to go down in the flames, until her first love shows back up and reminds her the other way love can burn.

Close Quarters
A summer yachting the Mediterranean sounded like heaven to Jasmine after finishing her undergrad degree. But her boyfriend's billionaire boss always gets what he wants. And this time, he wants her.

Make Me Hate You
Jasmine has been avoiding her best friend's brother for years, but when they're both in the same house for a wedding, she can't resist him — no matter how she tries.

The Wrong Game
(AN AMAZON TOP 5 BESTSELLER)
Gemma's plan is simple: invite a new guy to each home game using her season tickets for the Chicago Bears. It's the perfect way to avoid getting emotionally attached and also get some action. But after Zach gets his chance to be her practice round, he decides one game just isn't enough. A sexy, fun sports romance.

The Right Player
She's avoiding love at all costs. He wants nothing more than to lock her down. Sexy, hilarious and swoon-worthy, The Right Player is the perfect read for sports romance lovers.

On the Way to You
It was only supposed to be a road trip, but when Cooper discovers the journal of the boy driving the getaway car, everything changes. An emotional, angsty road trip romance.

A Love Letter to Whiskey
(AN AMAZON TOP 10 BESTSELLER)
An angsty, emotional romance between two lovers fighting the curse of bad timing.
Read Love, Whiskey – Jamie's side of the story and an extended epilogue – in the new Fifth Anniversary Edition! (https://amzn.to/3FB1B7E)

Weightless
Young Natalie finds self-love and romance with her personal trainer, along with a slew of secrets that tie them together in ways she never thought possible.

Revelry
Recently divorced, Wren searches for clarity in a summer cabin outside of Seattle, where she makes an unforgettable connection with the broody, small town recluse next door.

Say Yes
Harley is studying art abroad in Florence, Italy. Trying to break free of her perfectionism, she steps outside one night determined to Say Yes to anything that comes her way. Of course, she didn't expect to run into Liam Benson...

Washed Up
Gregory Weston, the boy I once knew as my son's best friend, now a man I don't know at all. No, not just a man. A doctor. And he wants me...

The Christmas Blanket
Stuck in a cabin with my ex-husband waiting out a blizzard? Not exactly what I had pictured when I planned a surprise visit home for the holidays...

Black Number Four
A college, Greek-life romance of a hot young poker star and the boy sent to take her down.

The Palm South University Series
Rush (book 1) FREE if you sign up for my newsletter!
Anchor, PSU #2
Pledge, PSU #3
Legacy, PSU #4
Ritual, PSU #5
Hazed, PSU #6
Greek, PSU #7
#1 NYT Bestselling Author Rachel Van Dyken says, "If Gossip Girl and Riverdale had a love child, it would be PSU." This angsty college series will be your next guilty addiction.

Tag Chaser
She made a bet that she could stop chasing military men, which seemed easy — until her knight in shining armor and latest client at work showed up in Army ACUs.

Song Chaser
Tanner and Kellee are perfect for each other. They frequent the same bars, love the same music, and have the same desire to rip each other's clothes off. Only problem? Tanner is still in love with his best friend.

about the author

KANDI STEINER is #1 Amazon Bestseller and whiskey connoisseur living in Tampa, FL. Best known for writing "emotional rollercoaster" stories, she loves bringing flawed characters to life and writing about real, raw romance — in all its forms. No two Kandi Steiner books are the same, and if you're a lover of angsty, emotional, and inspirational reads, she's your gal.

An alumna of the University of Central Florida, Kandi graduated with a double major in Creative Writing and Advertising/PR with a minor in Women's Studies. She started writing back in the 4th grade after reading the first Harry Potter installment. In 6th grade, she wrote and edited her own newspaper and distributed to her classmates. Eventually, the principal caught on and the newspaper was quickly halted, though Kandi tried fighting for her "freedom of press."

She took particular interest in writing romance after college, as she has always been a die hard hopeless romantic, and likes to highlight all the challenges of love as well as the triumphs.

When Kandi isn't writing, you can find her reading books of all kinds, planning her next adventure, or pole dancing (yes, you read that right). She enjoys live music, traveling, playing with her fur babies and soaking up the sweetness of life.

CONNECT WITH KANDI:
NEWSLETTER: kandisteiner.com/newsletter
FACEBOOK: facebook.com/kandisteiner
FACEBOOK READER GROUP (Kandiland):
facebook.com/groups/kandilandks
INSTAGRAM: Instagram.com/kandisteiner
TIKTOK: tiktok.com/@authorkandisteiner
TWITTER: twitter.com/kandisteiner
PINTEREST: pinterest.com/authorkandisteiner
WEBSITE: www.kandisteiner.com

Kandi Steiner may be coming to a city near you!
Check out her "events" tab to see all the
signings she's attending in the near future:
www.kandisteiner.com/events

Made in United States
Troutdale, OR
04/28/2024